Across The Dark River

The Odyssey of the 56th N. C. Infantry in the American Civil War

by

Clyde H. Ray

1996

Parkway Publishers, Inc.

Library of Congress Cataloging-in-Publication Data

Ray, Clyde.

    Across the dark river : the odyssey of the 56th N.C.
Infantry in the American Civil War / by Clyde H. Ray.
      p.   cm.
    ISBN 1-887905-04-9
    1. Confederate States of America. Army. North Carolina
Infantry Regiment, 56th—Fiction. 2. North Carolina—History—Civil War, 1861-
1865—Fiction. 3. United States—History—Civil War, 1861-1865—Fiction. I. Title.
PS3568.A88P76 1996
813'.54—DC20
                                           96-30104
                                               CIP
                                             Rev.

To My Wife, Doris
and Son, Clyde IV

THE BATTLEFIELD

All day, the sun courses throughout heaven, its light sweeping steadily over the parked cars, the drifting lines of tourists, the kites floating high in the mid-summer sky. They do not last, they do not endure, such travelers as these. They do not really belong there. It is the pines that belong there; the shadows in the forest belong there; the dead belong there; silence belongs there.

The pines stand close together in dense brooding thickets. Beneath them, in the tangled undergrowth, random trails made by fox and rabbit silently weave through the tall grass and broomsage. The plaintive call of a single bird, the metallic buzz of a wandering bee, the only sound; the slow shift of light and shadow, the only movement. The ridge above the creek stands in silence, waiting.

There is no wind in mid-afternoon. There is only heat, heat that seems to pulse from the earth as much as from the blazing sky. Heat that curls grass stem and powders clay; heat that thickens air and takes the strength; heat that lies in a suffocating cloak among the silent pines. It is a timeless world, lost to itself, alone in itself.

Toward sundown, the first dark clouds begin to gather in the west. There is the mutter of distant thunder. An even greater stillness settles on the ridge. Shadows darken in the thickets, between the hummocks of broomsage, in the barely discernible trench following the false crest of the ridge.

Night comes stealthily into the forest and with it, at long last, the rain. A distant murmur at first, the rain slowly increases to a steady fall, with only a distant flash of lightning illuminating the dark columns of the pines. Water droplets course quickly, one after the other, down the trunks of trees, gather tremblingly on pine stem and needle only to fall invisibly into the darkness below; tiny rivulets run down the gentle slopes of the sunken trench to gather in minuscule pools. The rain is not hard, but it is steady. It only ceases toward dawn.

And it is in the silence of that darkest hour that the mist begins to rise from the creek below the ridge. In that darkness, the mist is invisible and silent. There is, among the pines, falling temperature, a rising humidity, a slight movement of the air through them, but that is all.

With first light, the mist can be seen at last beneath the ridge rising and silently enveloping the trees on the crest. Then the pines slowly, but relentlessly emerge from the night, thinly draped in soft gauze, in the close embrace of visible moisture. Nothing stirs, nothing whispers under this white shroud. Rabbit and blacksnake, fox and weasel lie close to the earth. The forest, lost in time and space, waits. In this long silence, there is only formless mist, chaos.

On the ridge itself, all is lost in the white silence except for a single pine, its highest branches just clearing the mist. One branch hangs lower than the rest, its needles heavy with moisture. It stirs once with a slight touch of the pre-dawn air, but then comes to rest again. Day will come, but not yet, not just yet. For a time, there will be only this - the faint light and the mist stealing past the branch. Nothing more.

There is silence here as well. Somewhere far below, the ridge waits. The mist is now motionless in the topmost branches of the pine. Three faint stars still burn in the pale dawn.

It is there, where my black companion and I meet forever in the night; it is always there where we find them at last, just before dawn, at the edge of a deserted field, in America, in the rain, in the mist.

....

Out of the mist, out of the deep night, out of the long silence, the men of the 56th North Carolina Infantry, Confederate States Army now once more step forward. There is a vague shuffling of feet as they slowly come to parade rest, and then stand there quietly, almost expectantly before us. At this distance, their ranks seem orderly enough, with the field officers front and center before the color guard. Through the eddying mist and falling rain, the enlisted men in line seem to be only country boys, mere rustics in non-descript clothing, with a variety of caps and hats, and the inevitable blanket roll crossing the left shoulder. The officers are somewhat more distinctive, with high stocked collars and grey frock coats, swords at the side. The regiment stands there utterly alone, utterly silent, utterly still, mysterious and foreboding.

We hesitantly step forward toward them through the mist, out of our own life and time and into theirs, to again pause after only a few paces. They make no further sound, no further motion. They could almost be statues, effigies. There is no movement, no response to our presence. They stare impassively forward, almost as if in some vague anticipation of some further impossible event, some further impossible visitor. There is no sound, only the steady sweep and fall of rain in the growing light.

We stand there for a moment longer, some distance before F and G companies, and then turn to look back in the direction from which we came, to face what they face so deliberately, to meet what they meet so intently. And we only see there an abandoned corn field slowly filling up with rain and death, a solitary crow sadly sitting on a faded split rail fence in the mist and onrushing day.   But there is something more than just this, for this field and this fence must surely become our one shared memory of the war, so that when we think of it in our great old age, it will never be of the flags and drums, or even of that last brief shock of final realization at the end, but only of this field and the rain falling everywhere.

....

And yet, it was not anything so mundane as that one field, its low furrows forever slowly dissolving back into the primeval mud under the rain that I remember. That wasn't it in the least. You see, fields like that, with their staggered rows of split rail fences in the rain were common enough in that part of the state, in that time of our service. No, it was nothing so simple and common as that which can bear memory now, even into these last years of the century. Rather, it is of the two of them, one white and one black, who came there in the night, on that long march north to Franklin. Yes, it is the two of them, there in the field, in the rain, in the dream who are the memory now. That falling rain and empty field were only the dark setting, the grey background to those shadows, those memorials to what we once were, to what we once did.

Even now I remember how it happened the night we found them as we were on our way north to the Blackwater in Virginia in 1862. We had a hard, five day march from the gutted ruins of the village of Hamilton in North Carolina to Franklin in Virginia. The men were all showing exhaustion by the third day, and we constantly had to tell them to Close Up, Close Up. And when we at last went into bivouac, fires were lighted, provisions cooked or (more often) eaten as they were, and then we rolled into our blankets for the all too brief night.

I had held up as well as most of them, as dirty, disheveled, and discouraged as any of them. I had thought being an infantry lieutenant would have benefits, but I was just as tired - Lord Jesus, but my sleep was as the Sleep of the Just. But toward dawn of the fourth day, I dreamed. And as I dreamed, it seemed the whole regiment was once again marching, as I knew we would be, but now moving forward on parade into an early morning light, into a rising mist in which a fine rain was falling. But there were no voices, no voices at all - only the ordinary sounds of accoutrements sounding, the tired shuffle of innumerable feet, the old sound of the regiment on the move to anywhere, to nowhere.

Then we suddenly halted for some unknown reason. No one spoke. No orders were given. We just stood there momentarily in the fine rain, looking across a mist shrouded field broken only by a split rail fence at the limits of vision.

A lone crow flew past silently in the rain only to disappear into the mist and then we saw them, standing there in a corner of the rail fence. They were some distance away and we could discern nothing but the two figures themselves, watching us speculatively, even intently through the rain. They made no sound, no movement, only continuing to stand there ghostlike, wraiths off at the edge of time and space, spirit visitors of whom we had already our full share - from home, of death, from the past, of the future.

And then the rain began to fall harder, a prolonged deluge that darkened the uniforms on our backs and our blanket rolls, darkened the little light remaining, until all that vast roar faded off at last into the rising, acrid smoke of innumerable campfires; the slow stir of the regiment coming wonderingly awake; the long pale light of dawn; The Long Reveille sounding; and the dull realization that we still had thirty miles to go before we would reach Franklin.

....
JAMES C. ELLIOTT, CLEVELAND COUNTY, N.C.

Rain, night, mist - all these were the trappings of death in that century, that nation. But what then of life and remembrance? What then of youth or love? For even after it has all ended at Appomattox, even forty years afterward, in the eventful year of 1905, Orville Wright keeps his uncertain aircraft aloft for over thirty-three minutes; the Russian Revolution begins in St. Petersburg; Albert Einstein proposes a new theory on relativity; time and space become all interchangeable at last; and I, James C. Elliott, return to Petersburg, Virginia after an absence of forty years.

I am sixty years old now, but I've looked forward to this journey with all the excitement of the young buck I once was. Oh, I still remember the great war - remember it well - but I'm not returning to Petersburg for that reason. No, sir-ee, Bob! I'm going back because something else happened to me there forty years ago.

You see, during the long winter of 1864-1865, while I was a lowly private soldier in the Confederate States Army, my regiment - that's the 56th North Carolina Infantry - was stationed in Petersburg. And part of my duty during that last winter of the war included transporting firewood for the army through a small canal right in the city itself. It was while I was hauling firewood to the barges that I made the acquaintance of a family living nearby. I had figured by that time that the war had taught me all I needed to know, but I hadn't counted on what a woman could teach me.

The family was a small one. First, there was "Mrs. Dean", a right smart widder lady in her forties, I guess; then there was 'Miss Jennie", a pretty girl still in her teens; a still younger sister I don't clearly remember; and a ten-year-old boy, who was the only man about the house. The whole family lived in a small cottage near the canal; they were still in mourning for an older son killed at Globe Tavern last August. They were lonely people - you could see that - just frightened civilians trying their best to survive in a town now in its sixth long month of siege.

I was only twenty and a God-send to them all. I'd bring them firewood and go to market for them; they'd give me home cooked meals in return. Their world was falling all to pieces around them and even then I knew that they saw me as some kind of pillar or rock to hold on to. So, when it happened, it happened naturally; when it came, it came quietly; during such a time and such a place, maybe the hardship and all made it all likely; however it might have happened, the day came when Miss Jennie and I fell in love.

It was an early, but bitter spring - that spring of 1865. She was only nineteen and she had "blue eyes, dark hair, most lovely form and features, of an honest, sincere expression..." The only problem was that there was no privacy and we hadn't gone beyond holding hands, maybe not even that. And the war interrupted whatever courtship that could take place under those circumstances. Finally, marching orders for the regiment arrived and this loving couple (if I could call it that) found that those guns off to the south and east were a stronger force than whatever it was that brought them together.

So, as in all wars and all partings, Jennie sadly prepared some sorghum molasses cakes to take with me and we parted with many promises and assurances that we would meet again and until then, we would faithfully write to one another. Then, the regiment left for the front at Hatcher's Run. Eleven days later, we marched back through the city in the dead of night. I was lost somewhere in the column passing the Dean house, lost - for all my thoughts were of that house, now so dark and still, and of the young woman asleep on the second floor.

A few days later, we went into battle at Fort Stedman, and there I met still another Armageddon (the Confederate Army those days had more of those than you could shake a stick at) and I was captured by other equally young Union soldiers who "came up with flashing eyes and the loveliest smiles on their countenances and shook hands with us in the most enthusiastic manner". Two days later, I found myself surveying the compound of the great Union prisoner of war camp at Point Lookout, on the Maryland East Shore. I was to stay there three long months.

After finally taking the oath of allegiance, I made my way home to Cleveland County, North Carolina. Of course, I remembered my promise to Jennie and a year later, when the mail service had been fully restored, I wrote to tell her that I had survived the war, that I was well and hearty, and that I would be more than gratified to hear from her again at her earliest convenience. Her response was hardly what I expected.

In a long and chatty letter, she casually informed me that she had married a young Confederate soldier by the name of Ned Jones and so she took pleasure in extending to me a most cordial invitation to visit them in the event that I ever returned to Petersburg.

So, I guess the war taught me a thing or two about life, as it already had about death. I never wrote to her again.

Eight years later, I married a North Carolina girl and we were very happy together. The great war continued to recede on into the past like some vanishing thunderstorm and Petersburg seemed very far away indeed. We lived in a small cottage in Cleveland County and we had children who grew up and then had children of their own. As the years wore on, a night fever finally took my wife and by the turn of the century, here I am—a widower, a grandfather, and already on the threshold of old age with all these memories.

Well, it is these memories that are going to be a problem. Maybe it is just simple nostalgia for vanished youth. Or maybe it is the reminder of the war, by this time transformed in the nation's memory into some great, glorious arena where gallant and epic deeds were performed and lauded on every Memorial Day. Or maybe it is just the sentimentality and romanticism of the day. And I at last have to admit it, perhaps I really did love Jennie Dean after all, and that simple fact of my youth will survive in spite of anything time or mortal man can do to destroy it.

Whatever the reason, the memories now seem to me to be more real than anything else. And I simply cannot forget Jennie, or as I sometimes humorously refer to her in my mind, "Mrs. Jones".

Oh, it is a problem, I tell you. Finally, I take the bull by the horns; I confront the issue head on; I determine to return once more to Petersburg and find her. After all, I am a widower, and by this time, might she not be a widow, as well? In that probable event, I think that "there might be a little bit of new romance in the Old Dominion". She really haunts me, that girl. The fact that almost a half century has passed since we last parted makes less and less difference the more I think about it. "I could think of her only as the lovely girl of nineteen", I write in my notes, "but I had to reflect that she, too, might now be a withered grandmother".

So, I decide 1905 will be the year in which I return to

Petersburg for one last time for what in actuality is a final desperate attempt to somehow reach back into time and retrieve the opportunity I lost when I was only twenty years of age. And it seems not so impossible. The new city so brashly bursting forth from its own ruins on the Appomattox; the old battlefields now visited by other, newer young men and women in loving indifference to what had once meant life and death to so many; even the war itself, now so swiftly fading into the past as the New America enters the New Century - all of these accepted realities now seem secondary, inconsequential, really, when compared to what is now promised. For there is something that had been lost, but which now against every odd and chance might now be regained and even preserved forever. And was not this the experience of the nation, too? After all, the Union has been preserved at fearful cost. The frontier has been settled. Spain has been defeated and the nation is a fledgling world power. So, in my own unheralded battle against fate and time, I, too will be victorious.

Oh, I have ample time to dream, to think, to dwell on all this during the long train ride through the flat, low lying coastal plain of North Carolina and Virginia. And with every hour spent on the rails, the wild possibility of actually reversing not only the hands of the clock, but even the past course of human life itself seems ever more certain of realization. With every mile, the nagging doubt that I might after all be following some ridiculous and absurd quest, some quixotic dream incapable of realization, seems ever more remote. For she will remember me. That is certain. I am the same man. I have successfully cheated the grim reaper, not only in the war itself, but in the peace afterward. What more can time do that the war and reconstruction in all their awful strength and terror have failed to do?

So I sit quietly in the coach and watch the passing fields, the lowing cattle, river and stream under the darkening clouds in the west, the upraised hand of a farm boy on a mule with ever growing anticipation. The hardwood cane resting between my folded hands seems somehow less appropriate and necessary with every passing mile. When the Seaboard Line locomotive draws at last into Petersburg Station, I am once again the young man of twenty with all the world before me. Forty years fall away as I pick up my satchel and quickly walk down the steps.

Pushing my way through the crowd at the station, I find myself once more on the streets of Petersburg. Climbing the steep hill from the railroad station, I walk over to the inevitable cluster of aged veterans sitting on the courthouse steps, whittling in the warm sunlight and chewing tobacco.

After an exchange of the usual pleasantries, I ask them if they know anything of the family of Mrs. Dean.

Yes, they know of her - and of her daughter, Jennie, as well.

Jennie had married some feller by the name of Ned Jones, but Jones - well now, he's been dead these two years...

I remain calm, they can not tell, I am sure they can not tell. "And how is Mrs. Jones now?"

"Oh, her", I am told by an old man with tobacco stains in his beard, "She is an invalid - not able to get out. Has a son and daughter living with her".

"Where does she live?"

"She lives second block - third house on the right."

I leave them then, as quickly as I can, to their quiet whittling, their memories, their age.

On my way to the house, I step into a small tavern to savor the moment and to compose my thoughts. Sitting at a small table over my beer, I rehearse over and over in my mind every detail of what I will say, how I will act. Falling into a friendly conversation with the proprietor, a Mr. Quarles, I all but ask the man if what is happening to me is really true.

Did he not know that I too was here in Petersburg during the great war? Did he not know that I met many fine and wonderful people in this very city during that terrible time? Did he too know of the family of Mrs. Dean, and especially of her lovely daughter, Jennie? Did she not still live just a few doors down the street from this very place?

The proprietor leans on the bar and gazes into the roar of the street. Yes, he knows of Mrs. Dean. He knows the whole family well. She had a son killed towards the end of the war - he himself had gone very near to going into that same battle at Globe Tavern with the Dean boy.

And yes, he knows of Miss Jennie. After her husband Ned died, she married his brother, Lewellyn Jones. They didn't stay in Petersburg, though. They moved to Crews, Virginia. Yes, he knows all the family well.

Mr. Quarles looks at me with the amused, all knowing wisdom of time itself. It is only with some difficulty that I am able to ask, "Where is she now?" " Dead." Quarles says the word with neither unconcern nor cruelty, but with the simple finality of the thing itself. "Dead these thirty years. Her husband remarried - has a family of grown children. Her little brother is still in Petersburg though. He's the last of the family living."

So, I become an old man again at that very moment when I had reached the end of the quest. The entire earth seems to shift under my feet as I step out into the crowds on Sycamore Street. The sight of the boarded up and rotting house a few doors down the street only sets the final seal to everything I have been told.

I stand on a street corner and see what I have not seen before. It is the Twentieth Century. It is, after all, 1905.   The streets are crowded with shoppers in crinoline and straw hat; Model- T's sputter past, their drivers hiding behind wide flaring goggles; a local theater marquee advertises the latest nickelodeon feature, "The Palace Of The Arabian Nights"; every one of the crowded three story buildings along Sycamore Street are made of brick and stone, not of wood; telegraph and trolley lines sweep the length of the avenues; street cars rumble down the center of all the main streets. The Twentieth Century - it is everywhere. And so it takes me, as it did her, leaving behind only the memory, the ghost, the reality.

The magnificent oak grove on the old camp ground is gone - in its place are crowded streets and hundreds of buildings. I cannot find the site of the old shed or even the street it was on; Thomas is long dead by now. And the old canal, long drained and filled, is now a sunken road and I can recognize only a single brick building in the whole neighborhood. Searching for some sign of linkage with the city, the people, indeed the whole past life and world I had known, I find nothing truly familiar.

Surely the battlefield will still be there unchanged. So much destruction of the earth as well as life must have left some unremovable mark upon the face of the land. Surely, anything at all so closely associated with those terrible events will be still inviolable, familiar, and secure. But when I ask where I might find a carriage or horse to take me there, I am told that the only way of conveyance is the new street car that now makes regular runs there.

So, by the time I arrive on the battlefield just outside the city, I am prepared for change even here. And so it proves. A clean, white clapboard building near the street car line houses a museum of war relics. A pine tree large enough for a saw log is growing peacefully in the crater from which over a thousand skeletons have been long removed. And those torturous trenches I helped to build in 1864 are just shallow ditches now, soft in pine needles. I sadly stir the needles with my boot—yes, the sandy soil, the earth itself I had once burrowed in so well—at least, it is still here.

And Blantford Church and its cemetery are still here. The ravine up which I climbed to safety on the dark morning of June 19, 1864 is still here. The gentle contours of the trenches and even one covered way are still visible, if only barely, under the waving grain. And when I wander on out into the fields, I see once again the same open sweep of countryside under the same sky, hear once again the same cadences, the same tramping of feet in the same dust, the same shouts and cries of the men, hear once again the same surly mutter of artillery.

Everywhere I look here, I see a haunted land. And these ghosts seem to come forth to me now in more flesh and blood than any man or woman of this newer century.

It is then that I know I really have to do nothing at all to recapture the vanished past. The war, after all, is the only true and lasting reality; it is really the only thing that matters to all of them, men and women alike, forty years ago; that terrible war and all the lost men of that forgotten regiment possess the only enduring truth in this swiftly changing world. And while this brave youth, or that virginal girl must be lost to Time's savagery, nonetheless that war and regiment will somehow live on in their own reality in the nation's heart. And if this is so, then all the young men and women of that generation gain not only immortality of a kind, but all might be ever young and alive as well. For all of them, who will and need it so, it will always be the spring of 1865.

....

I look to the west. It is wonderful to think so. But, shaking my head, I know better. It is 1905. It is all gone, vanished, lost. It is over now except for the rain now beginning to fall over the battlefield and the city it once defended.

In the early evening, in the approaching darkness and the rain now only a fine mist, I find myself standing in the middle of an open field that the regiment had once held against repeated Union assaults. While gently leaning on my cane and resting there, listening to all the host of innumerable voices all around me, I become gradually aware of a persistent and growing pressure under the sole of my boot, some silent, but imperceptibly relentless being moving there, something that seems to be some elemental force rising irresistibly there out of the primeval earth, toward me, lifting me.

I slowly move my foot and for a moment stare down into the sheared stubble of grass beneath me. Then I carefully bend over and my searching fingers at last find it in the fading light. It is covered with dirt and rust and it is a long moment before I recognize it.

It is a single flattened minie ball.

CHAPTER ONE

JAMES M. DAVIS, LIEUTENANT, COMPANY G

You think it quaint and strange, as they do, that now, in my great old age, I sometimes speak to the fire, ascribing it no doubt to an old man's wandering. But the fire is a good listener, a good companion, full of life, warm and robust, its bright glow with me through it all, here at the end and at the beginning. This fire knows me better than the woman, the grown children that surround me now. These two hands, held spread before it even as we speak, answer to its warmth, answer to its message. These leaping flames, faithful companions, to you as to me, tell all, for they know all. Then why should I, the Lieutenant James Davis of Company G in the old 56th so long ago, now speak of those years, for only in the Future is there hope to be found.

Leaning across the firelight, listening to the night wind rage out of all Texas, you, from the Future, ask me now if I remember Private Elliott - the tall, thin, gangling boy with a shock of blond hair and vacant eyes, over in Company F. I remember them all - even those who came at the last. But he wasn't there at the beginning. I was.

At the beginning, no one could have known what the war would hold for us. Elliott in all his youth could not have known. I, being older, should have at least suspected. But how could we, even as children, our young faces looking out into the early morning mist in '48 or '54 or '56, have seen its first coming. We were only children then, don't you see, our young eyes looking past window curtain and pane into the dooryard. We saw nothing of that dark shroud, that deep silence there. And what was there for children to see but that stillness, that heavy cloak of the ground mist over the beaten path, the gate post, the hollyhock, the sunflower already heavy with seed?

There was nothing else there, no motion clearly to be seen there, only in the faces themselves waiting behind the glass, in the eyes there, watching.

Still later, in the late summer of 1862, on the parade ground at Camp Magnum in the same pre-dawn light, there is no hollyhock or sunflower, no gate post or fence paling - only the same cold mist moving deliberately over the hard packed earth. There are no children here now. The past has them; they are locked away forever there; even now, they are part of the nation's history. No mist or vapor now (it's all burnt clean away); the only reality for these same faces now is the sun. Under the noonday sun, the earth is an anvil under that other fire, crossed furtively from time to time by random dust devils to the accompaniment of the harsh barking of officer or file sergeant. It is the sun that dominates everything now. This, and the dust passing in slow, deliberate waves across the field to where a thin, tired line of pines on the perimeter stand sentry. It is the second year of the war. And the only timeless reality that matters now is the hard earth itself beneath these same feet, standing and steadily moving in unison.

We come from all over the state, but I and my young brother come from the green heaven of Henderson County. We had grown up at Oakland, as all boys should, with all the pretension of plantation life in the Blue Ridge mountains. It was real enough to us - with slave quarters as lasting as the Big House, vast fields of tobacco (not cotton) under the sun, many horses, all the silver and cut glass on the mahogany table at night. Our father was "The Colonel" to folks round-a-bout, although he had only been a sergeant in the Creek Indian War. And although I was so young then, it was that distant war that was the shadow on the sunlit world of Oakland.

I had grown up with his stories of the one battle he was in - how Old Hickory had fought the Redsticks at Horseshoe Bend in the spring of 1814 and won a great victory over them. I thought it glorious, wonderful, and as all boys must and will, I relived it time and time again. But when I grew older, I learned that it had been less a victory than a massacre, for my father told me how the fleeing Indians, many women and children among the braves, had been indiscriminately shot down, their villages burned, their very presence erased from the land. Father said that it was the proper thing to do, for these were barbarians, savages. But living in these mountains, I had known of Indians from my own childhood, loved these mountains so replete with their place names, felt their spirit in these forests. I never really looked into the eyes of one until, as a young man, I once saw a young Indian girl, with her family, all in one rattletrap wagon on the crowded streets of Hendersonville. She had the face, the lowered eyelashes, the raven black hair falling all about her shoulders that a man will remember, even twenty-five years later. There is no savagery there, only the beauty of Woman, and something in her eyes which is of a higher order, deeper profundity, more lasting mystery than I will ever see in any woman. But when I rein in my horse and smile down at her, the only expression in those lovely eyes that lift to meet mine is fear and hate.

Therefore, as I told Lieutenant McNeely that night forty years ago, her face and the Horseshoe are indelibly printed in my mind both together, dual opposites and yet wedded together. They continually haunt me, for there was a lasting sin there, committed by my own blood and the nation against another, but never any atonement for that look she gave me on the Square.

I am more fortunate than my poor father, for I can assure that this war will not lead to such hard decisions, for it is over property, not race; over independence, not abolition. It is over simple things to be settled between civilized peoples; nothing indiscriminate, but all controlled and judicious, between gentlemen even (We can assure that; I will assure that). At the still relatively young and mature age of thirty-five, I will assure that this one ghost, albeit a beautiful one, will be enough for any man's memory; there will be no new ones to stand with the old.

When the war started, I was happily married to Mary Henry, with children, and had a good government job as postmaster at Horseshoe, North Carolina. I was commissioned as second lieutenant in the Henderson Blues, North Carolina Troops in April and my brother Charles was a lowly private in the same company. Part of it was patriotic fervor; part of it, desire to go in as volunteers rather than conscripts under the new law. In any case, within a month, we are on our way to Camp Magnum.

We are just beginning to settle down to what looks like a long, hard war. At the end of July 1862, it has been going on, start and stop, for fifteen months. We have successfully weathered the Peninsula Campaign that threatened Richmond; McClellan and the Army of the Potomac are still encamped at Harrison's Landing on the James. Another Union Army, under the command of General John Pope, is located near Manassas Junction north of Richmond. In the west, a similar period of calm comes as both sides prepare for what the papers call "a renewal of the conflict". But in most of North Carolina, a garrison atmosphere prevails - the war is something still far beyond the borders of the consciousness of most men, still far beyond the life experience of most of the inhabitants, soldiers included.

It is during this time that the 56th North Carolina Infantry is officially organized, trained, and mustered into active service, and then I suppose it just disappears into the war like all the rest. I say, disappears, for as with all of us of this generation, there is little clarity and less control during these first years. No high dramatics at Camp Magnum - the founding of the regiment is heralded by no call of trumpet, no tap of drum. We are announced, not celebrated. We quietly come into existence by the simple enough combination of ten companies at Magnum, a crowded training base just four miles west of the State Capitol at Raleigh. These ten companies have been in training at the camp on the North Carolina Railroad line for two months; now they are formally organized as a regiment. On the last day of July, the men elect their field officers, who impress one young private looking them over as "all fine looking men". The fine looking men of the new regiment's field and staff have high credentials, History will grant them that. Many of them were members of respected professions in civilian life before the war; many had military training and experience prior to their assignment to the 56th Infantry. For the most part, they are young men for whom the future is an open door.

Homer in the Iliad gives a Catalogue of the Captains; I shall give a Catalogue of the 56th Regiment. Paul F. Faison, for example, is our most illustrious commander. From Northampton County, he is elected Colonel of the new regiment. You can see him in the old photographs still - a tall man, very erect, straight out of West Point, with dark eyes that glare with the cold dignity, the remote stance of the Tsar himself. And it is not all appearance alone. Paul F. Faison comes to his first field command with a good background. Admitted to West Point in 1857, he built a distinguished record during the next three and a half years. Ranking in the upper third of his class, he received a good foundation in foreign languages, mathematics, English, military history, even chemistry and mechanics. He excelled in all the fuss and feathers of that time - military drill, company parade, the tinsel of military society. A sergeant of cadets in his last year at the Point, his classmates included two unknowns named George A. Custer and John Pelham. But in spite of all, he never graduated. History prevented that. Only a few months before graduation, he handed in his resignation due to the impending secession of North Carolina.

That letter of resignation had been signed in April of 1861. Now, two countries and fifteen months later, it would seem to have been a proper choice. He has been chosen by the officers and men of the unit as much for his character as for his military credentials. His dark heavy moustache makes him look far older than his years. He is only twenty-four years old. His future is assured. All of us feel that. But I fear he has some of the arrogance of any young man in authority and with power to command, the same arrogance and power that led to the Horseshoe. I do fear it, for I must. You understand why I fear it.

And yet no one person can denote a civilization, a society, a family, or a military unit. There are always other faces, other names. G. Gratiott Luke of Camden County, for example, is elected Lieutenant-Colonel. Only twenty-seven years old, he had been a teacher before the war. He is young, maybe too young like the rest of them, hiding youth behind a heavy beard. With that beard, he can comfortably project an air of supreme confidence. That is what all of us need. If the field officers believe, then we believe.

Or Henry F. Schenck, elected Major on the same day. Major Schenck impresses many of us as an affable gentleman of the highest type of citizen, a fine example of physical manhood who will beyond doubt outlast all of us. As with all young men, he takes such accolades as his rightful due. Prior to the war, he was an enterprising merchant in Rutherford County located in the foothills of the Blue Ridge. He never loses the shopkeeper manner, always smiling, always affable in this new trade.

Or Cader G. Cox of Onslow and also only twenty-five years old. He is the medical officer until we can acquire a duly commissioned regimental surgeon; hopefully that will be before the first battle. The list could go on. Suffice it to say that the rest of the regimental field and staff include an adjutant, quartermaster and commissary officers, a color sergeant, even two drum majors. None of them are over the age of thirty.

Yet even these men can not be said to represent the regiment. This is the story not of one man, but of many. Oh, I can say that the regiment is composed of ten companies from all over the state, each one commanded by a captain and from two to three lieutenants. I can say that the average company strength is roughly forty to sixty men, giving the regiment the mean average of five hundred men. I can say that most of the enlisted men are from small farms, while the company officers for the most part represent professional backgrounds.

There is Company A, from Camden County, in the eastern part of the state. Camden is a dirt poor county, despite a high yield in corn, oats, and cotton; almost a third of its people can't read or write. Almost two thirds are black and slave.

Despite all this, maybe because of it, Camden is bitterly divided when the state secedes. But these men in Company A have already demonstrated their patriotism. As twelve month volunteers, they had been captured at Hatteras in August, 1861 and only just recently have been exchanged before arriving at Camp Magnum. Their first choice for Captain had been the popular G. Gratiott Luke. After Luke's election to Lieutenant-Colonel, the company is led by Noah H. Hughes.

Company B is one of the more promising units to be added to the new regiment. These men, for the most part farmers, as most of us are, come from Cumberland County. People there make their livelihood from the trade on the Cape Fear River, but now the coming of the railroad severely limits the river traffic there. Two-thirds of the population are black, with the remainder busily engaged in marketing oats, corn, cotton, and wool. Only sixty miles from the state capital, the residents of the county seat of Fayetteville have easy access to North Carolina's largest city by road and rail; at least once during the season, entire families flock to the State Capitol to see the sights and bask in the aura of southern politics.

The company proudly styles itself The Cape Fear Guards. The Captain, Frank B. Roberts, and his men look over the newer companies of the regiment with a critical and experienced eye. A good part of Company B received training before the war in a local militia unit,"The Lafayette Light Infantry". When the war began, Frank, a well-to-do Fayetteville merchant, and other members of the "Light Infantry" enlisted in the 1st North Carolina Infantry and fought in the first engagement of the war at Bethel, Virginia. With the end of their six months term, Frank, now a captain, reorganized his company and with many of his men came to Camp Magnum to be mustered in as Company B of the 56th. Only thirty-two years old, Frank and his men are a seasoned addition to the new regiment. He has an easy smile, perhaps due to his certainty that the north can be defeated, as at Bethel. There is irony here, for Frank had been a native of Middletown, Connecticut before the war. New England is very far away now and his loyalty to the Confederacy is complete. Among us all, he knows the North, understands its weaknesses. He is supremely confident. We all are. The men say, "Cap'n Roberts knows the yanks better than any one, he's been one hisself." Even his beard is just like Abe Lincoln's.

Company C, under the command of Captain A. P. White, proudly style themselves "The Pasquotank Boys". Many of these young men are bitterly aware of the Union occupation of their county, located in the northeastern part of the state. Pasquotank County is low country, rural, like all that part of the State. Corn, oats, and wheat are the staples; black slaves in a number almost as many as the whites, provide the labor to grow those staples. And like the men from Camden and Cumberland counties, the men of Company C have seen prior service in the war. Most of the company, under earlier enlistments in other units, had been among the earliest volunteers and were captured at Hatteras along with Company A last August.

Company D, The Graham Rifles, is another unique company. Led by Captain John W. Graham, it stands out simply because of this officer. Organized in Orange County, the men come from a rich and beautiful part of the piedmont. Just forty miles from the state capital, Orange County is noted for its beautiful rolling countryside, its healthy climate, and its high yield in corn and wheat. The men of Company D have little previous military training or experience, but it is in their captain, as I have said, that they are unique, for Captain John W. Graham is not one of your average men.

Born into one of the most distinguished families in the state, John's father had been in turn governor, a United States senator, a secretary of the Navy, and a nominee for the vice-presidency of the nation. John, before the war, had been a tutor in Latin and mathematics at the University of North Carolina and only recently has opened a law practice in his home town. The twenty-three-year-old captain comes to Camp Magnum with high recommendations. He has seen service at Fort Macon on the coast with a commendation from General Richard Gatling, as an "efficient officer who always does his duty". Appointed to captain by the governor himself, there is every indication that his future will be remarkable. His nineteen-year-old brother, Robert, is elected a lieutenant in the same company.

The rest of us are lesser lights. Company E, The Moore Guards, was recruited in the central piedmont of the state. Captain Joseph G. Lockhart, a young farmer from Northampton County, leads a company of untried men. Most of them come from isolated farms, with no idea of the war; for them, a confused metropolis such as Camp Magnum is disturbing, disquieting.

Company F, The Cleveland Rifles, was organized in the county of that name. Again, the accolades: healthy climate, fertile soil, industrious citizens. It is led by Captain B. F. Grigg, a veteran who had served with Frank Roberts in the 1st North Carolina at Bethel. To these raw recruits on the parade field, his cold eye reminds them that he has seen a part of the war they have not. They do have one old soldier among them, a kind of religious visionary for want of a better term, complete with Bible and flowing Old Testament beard. I don't remember his name, but everyone called him The Parson. So, a visionary after Glory, like all the rest of us, like me, yet the Glory I seek is different from his.

Company G, The Henderson Blues, was organized in Henderson County in the mountainous western part of the state. In a regiment dominated by young men, it is led by older, untried officers, like me. A fifty-six-year-old farmer, Captain Henry F. Lane is little adapted to the rigors of active campaigning. It is charity to say no more. I am the thirty-five-year-old second lieutenant. It is honesty to say even less.

Company H, The Pettigrew Guards, was organized in the strong secessionist county of Caswell. There, with blacks outnumbering the whites, politics are conservative, dominated by prominent planters making their wealth in tobacco and freely giving their sons to The Cause. The men of Company H are led by Captain William G. Graves. He, too, is only twenty-two years old, but he has seen prior service in the 1st North Carolina.

Company I, The Rutherfordton Rifles, was also raised in the mountains to the west. Rutherfordton is a leading city there, with an unusually high number of lawyers, doctors, and merchants. While divided on the issue of secession, the county gave not a single vote to Lincoln in the 1860 presidential election. When the war comes, it gives instead a high number of its young men to the Confederacy - fourteen companies totaling over 1700 men to various military units. The company coming into the 56th North Carolina Infantry are veterans all, having seen hard service in Virginia while in the 16th North Carolina. These men had fought at Seven Pines during the Peninsula Campaign in Virginia.

The Captain of Company I, Lawson Harrill, a physician in more settled days, is less than twenty-five years of age and stands almost six feet tall. Harrill, well educated and a good writer, sees no conflict in taking life instead of preserving it. Working his way up to his commission from a private in the 16th North Carolina, Harrill is well respected by both officers and enlisted men.

And Company K, The Confederate Boys, was recruited in a depressed area of the state over a hundred miles from Raleigh. Alexander County, plagued by illiteracy and poverty, is fiercely loyal to the Confederacy, contributing over a thousand men to the service, almost a fifth of its total population. Company K was led by Frank B. Alexander, only twenty-one years of age and who had been a student at Davidson College when he enlisted. One of his second lieutenants is John F. McNeely of Iredell County. And I find that despite the difference in our ages, young McNeely and I can talk, maybe because at Mangum it sometimes seems neither one of us are really suited for the 56th. I am a thirty-five-year-old lieutenant among a field and staff still in their twenties. But John somehow just doesn't seem to fit in either. We sometimes sit together for hours over a flickering candle, trying to make some sense out of Hardee's Manual of Arms. Neither one of us can imagine what history and the regiment can hold for men like ourselves, who refuse to fit into the mold, who will not be led where we will not go.

So, of the ten companies of the regiment during this summer of 1862, only four have seen any kind of service. The remaining six have no prior military experience whatsoever. This lack of seasoning of most of the men is somewhat compensated for by the experience of company officers, most of whom were in prior service and are highly educated men. It will be their hard task to turn these largely rural youth into somewhat presentable soldiers. The war, of course, will be the final test.

Such is our Host, such our commanders, such the men they command. Our young Agamemnon, Faison of course, but who will be the Achilles, the Hector? Not I, but then who? And who the Priam and the Helen, if not those distant aged parents and young wives standing on the battlements all across this South, watching from every distant village and farm in the land we defend? And now we go forth to take that other Ilium on the Potomac, with its unfinished Capitol.

Homer gives a Catalogue of Captains, of Ships. No ships here, but men, wagons, horses, uniforms, medical supplies, goods, forage, ambulances, tents. In the summer of '62, we are well supplied at Camp Magnum. The paymaster regularly comes to camp to pay the men: field officers receiving more than $150 a month; captains, $139; lieutenants, $90; privates in the ranks, $11. And we are well clothed, for the war is still young. Officers of the regiment wear the regulation Confederate grey; full uniform includes double-breasted frock coats. Headware for officers and men: the visored kepi or forage cap, with the curved bugle over the brim. Officers can purchase their own swords for the high price of $33.50; most officers, including lieutenants also have the regulation Navy Colt revolver. The field officers, mounted on their own riding horses, obtain forage for their horses from the Army, with riding equipment all the way down to spurs and straps available from the quartermaster.

Most men in the regiment carry a rifled musket, a saber bayonet, a cartridge box and belt, a waist belt, pouches for holding percussion caps, a bayonet scabbard, and a gun sling - all of government issue. Haversacks, knapsacks, clothing account books, axe handles, trace chains, shoes, canteens, and overcoats are provided by the quartermaster. Some enlisted men sport non-regulation feathers in broad-brimmed hats worn at a jaunty angle. Morale is high, supplies are adequate, company enrollment is almost full strength during this first summer, ranging from fifty-one men in Company B to sixty men in Company I.

Medical supplies are ample and varied for us at this early date in the war. Supplies for the regimental surgeon include drams of morphine worth $28, four ounces of quinine for reducing fever (at $4 an ounce), twelve ounces of opium for pain. We use ichthyal ointment for carbuncles; soda bicarbonate for internal gas; tincture of ferrichloride for iron deficiency; magnesium sulfate as a laxative; calomel for jaundice, upset stomach, cleansing wounds; wine as a stimulant. There are assorted bandages, lint, vials, bottles, paper, corks, sulfuric acid, even penis syringes to irrigate the male genital tract in the certain event of venereal disease.

Our training and organization continue on through the long, hot days of July. Most of the men are untested, but for the rest, military life comes as no surprise. Some of the veteran companies that arrive at the camp show the wear and tear of active campaigning. Colonel H. B. Watson, commander of the Camp of Instruction, finds Company I's military discipline, appearance, and accoutrements good; the arms mixed, but serviceable; the clothing, knapsacks, and instruction, poor to worthless. The men of Company I hold a somewhat higher opinion of themselves as soldiers. To a man, they are convinced that they are the best skirmishers in the regiment.

Life at the Camp of Instruction is hard, with an unending succession of drill, maneuver, inspection, and field practice. Drill is conducted every day; soon even the newer recruits begin to acquire a more military appearance. Morale continues to be high and the men are confident. As the month passes on, we anxiously await active service. Sometimes elaborate pranks are developed by the enlisted men, and none are more successful than those in which these proud field officers find themselves victim.

A very naive and gullible recruit is told by his messmates that if he salutes the colonel by grasping his hat with one hand and strikes out in the air with the other, he will be given a bag of brightly colored marbles by the commanding officer himself. The boy promptly marches past the sentry, enters into the icy presence of young Colonel Paul F. Faison, salutes as told, and then announces, "Colonel, I've just come in here: I've drawed my outfit and I'm a-calling in to get my marbles." After a moment of silence, Faison roars - "The hell you say! Report to your quarters at once or I'll have you put in the guardhouse!" That poor young man then wanders off across the vast parade ground telling friend or stranger that he has been "cussed" by the Colonel for no good reason. Ever after, he is doomed to being asked, in the line of battle and in the dead of night, whether he has yet received his marbles. He is nameless and unknown, but remembered.

The long mornings of drill and the long afternoons of practice all take place in open country, and the encircling forests seem to be a protecting barrier against the intrusion of the outside world. At night, we sit for long hours over our fires; the sky overhead holds a thousand stars of which we take no notice now. Even in Virginia and Mississippi, the fronts are now quieter and the war seems to be some other reality, one that can little disturb so many of us away from home for the first time. All in all, it is a great and unforgettable adventure. There is no thought of ending, loss, redemption.

But there are times when strange winds, strange visitations come to us from the outside world. It is on a peaceful Sunday afternoon in the latter part of July. The trains passing slowly south by Camp Magnum that day carry wounded men from the battlefields around Richmond. Brother Charles is a private in Company G. I have to look after him (so Mother and his wife Hattie told me) to protect him as much as I can from the war. Probably Commissary will be a good place for him. In any case, he is a good boy, seeing all this as one great lark, supremely and confidently brave. He has only one fear because of an accident in childhood, a fear of horses. But one train brings something else to fear to all of us. My poor naive younger brother, now taking his pen in hand as clerk for Company G in this last summer of peace for the regiment, sees aghast the wood-burning train slowly working its way past the camp. Charles has never seen the fever in so many men's eyes; he has never seen so much dried blood. None of us ever have. "The trains are crowded with wounded soldiers. Our loss was great in the Richmond battles", he now writes to his young wife, "The Yankees must be tremendous".

The next day, July 31, the 56th North Carolina Infantry, its training at last completed, its field officers elected, is formally paraded and then listed as being in active service for the State of North Carolina. We are close to six hundred men strong, the drummers beating the call, the flag and color guard at the center of the line, the Post Band playing away at "The Old North State", and we glory in the glory of it all.

During the following week, additional supplies are drawn for the regiment; new muskets and accoutrements are issued; and the paymaster pays off the men. On August 8, we are formally transferred to the service of the Confederate States Government. Later on that same day, we leave Camp Magnum forever, bound for Goldsboro, some fifty miles to the southeast. All of us know the war will now begin for each of us in truth.

We remain encamped at Goldsboro until August 23, drawing additional supplies. Shortly after, we are transported by troop train and foot through the small villages of Warsaw and Magnolia to the large seaport of Wilmington, North Carolina. Going into camp at Fort Badger at the end the month, we find ourselves only a short distance from Fort Fisher on the coast.

There is time to rest now and to think over what the future might bring. When off duty, a leisurely walk across the sand flats to the edge of the surf gives most of us not only our first view of the sea, but also our first look at the enemy. We have spoken, and heard, and thought of them so much over the past few months, and now here they are at last. There, standing far out to sea, sometimes veiled in the rain and spray of a late summer storm, sometimes etched against the startling blue August sky with every spar and rigging visible, we can see the blockading squadrons of the United States Navy in the distance.

The announcement on August 31 at the final muster of the day that the 56th North Carolina Infantry is now officially a part of the Confederate States Army comes almost as an anti-climax. We have been on active service for the better part of a month and there is still only concern that the war might end before we can see action. After all, General John Pope has just been decisively defeated at Second Manassas. McClellan has withdrawn from the Peninsula. The Yankee gunboats have withdrawn from Vicksburg. Confederate armies under Braxton Bragg and Kirby Smith are invading Tennessee and Kentucky, and there are rumors now that Lee will soon cross the Potomac.

We are confident. And those silent, spectral ships waiting off there on the eastern horizon are far away, and perhaps they are not even quite real, so intangible do they seem out there.

That night, after a final visit to commissary, I uncertainly light a cigar and then carefully walk out through the camp of the 56th. The men are in rare good spirit. Most of them are standing or sitting around their camp fires, with great fountains of sparks rising when a new log is put on. One, with a driftwood log, is burning with blue and green flames. Talking, laughing, and singing can be heard everywhere. A five-string banjo is playing off in the distance. I nod my head to the sentry, casually returning his salute, and then walk on out on the beach.

I walk far enough until I can no longer hear the noise of the camp. Only the vast roar of wind and surf and the Old Atlantic is suddenly there before me. It's a beautiful night with the moon almost full. The off-shore wind is strong: even at this late hour, the terns are coursing the breakers. I stand at the edge of the surf, thinking I will never tire of this, for I have never seen the sea before. I look on out into the sounding darkness, but can see no sign of the U. S. Navy. They will be blacked out anyway, except for one lantern on the senior officer's ship. But I know that one lantern is there and it puts you in mind of the ones overhead, here and there awash in the moonlight, like distant campfires in heaven to match the ones below. Fire below, fire above. It is somehow fitting, somehow reassuring to know that this one element of fire can so bind men and suns together in a common experience. It is comforting to know that our own beginning, as a regiment in this glorious War of Independence, is on such a cosmic stage, before such a cosmic audience as this. Even as I watch, one faint meteor slowly passes through, I think, Cyngus, before fading in the east and then Sea and Night are as they were before, a million years ago.

What of Man? What can poor misplaced forked creatures like McNeely and I now attest before all these seething suns, before all this endless darkness? A sign from Man perhaps? Perhaps, a gesture from Humanity? Yes, Man can make a statement to all this. So I give the cigar to them, to all of them, one long rising arc of light lifting to meet all the rest, fire uniting with fire, its flowing trail passing them all in one long falling curve, making its own sublime statement to this night. But even as it vanishes, I know it is inadequate, perhaps foolish, perhaps only a child's gesture in the end. This is not it. There is something more that must be done, something that only men can do.

The moon breaks free of the clouds in the west and the sea, dark and deep, fills with iridescence now, new light coming now from the depths, smoothing over and over the sand at my feet, whispering sibilantly, like weeping or tears too deep for thought. I stand there motionless, listening to that soothing leveling of sand, ssshhh, waiting, listening to that weeping, ssshh, but no words at all do I hear or understand.

CHAPTER TWO

FESS SMITH, SERGEANT, COMPANY F

We stand at the campfire and watch him walkin' on out into the night. The wind is up; you can hear the surf; and ten to one he's already been into the likker like the rest of 'em. One of the men sittin' there laughs, "Well, Sergeant Smith, I never seed the like" and then spits his terbaccer juice into the fire. But we don't pay that much attention to that old man wanderin' off to practically spend the night on the beach, while all the other chicken-guts are still playin' cards and drinkin' their bust-head. Most of the damn officers are crazy anyhow and this one is just one more to the lot. It's a pure wonder the Parson didn't follow him out there and then there would have been the two of them howlin' at the moon.

We know pretty much most of what the officers know - we know our time is a-coming, just not exactly when or where. We can tell from the papers that these two months, September and October, are important ones for the Confederacy. Lee's invasion of the north is halted at Sharpsburg. The big invasion of Kentucky by Bragg and Smith is ended in a withdrawal. Old Abe issues his dam Emancipation. Grant's up to no good down at Vicksburg. We know all that.

But here in North Carolina, these are really peaceful months, with the blaze of Indian Summer comin' on back home. The war is still just a distant rumblin' off to the north and east and the men are restless for some action. They keep us busy, but it's mostly just guard and reconnaissance duty between Wilmington and Tarboro, all up and down the east coast of the state. We know them all - sleepy, one horse villages, hamlets, lonely railroad crossings in the middle of scrub pine forests: places like Warsaw, Magnolia,

Goldsboro (the one big city), other places almost without a name, sure not worth rememberin'. One gloomy day, we board flatcars pulled by an old wheezing locomotive and ride for hours through the flat low country while it rains on us the whole way. Smoke from that pine wood stokin' the engine rolls over us and when we get off, only the roll call can tell who we are under all that soot and grime. The dam officers hadn't prepared us for this back at Camp Magnum.

The fall is pretty mild, October is warm, but all the marching and outdoor life begins to have a tellin' effect on the boys. On October 22, we go into camp at Camp Clingman, near Goldsboro. Three of our company commanders are sick; fool lieutenants are commanding their companies. Most of us need some rest and medical treatment. I'm a sergeant and I can see our equipment all goin' down and in real poor condition. We are down at heart, just not much purpose to it. Times I would like a woman, but not much chance of that either.

At least, we do get a real medical officer, Columbus A. Thomas. Cox has done alright as assistant surgeon, but it's more than he can do. Thomas is another youngster in his twenties, but he passed what served for a medical examination board at Goldsboro. He knows more than Cox does, but he don't last as long. Thomas is gone in six months.

We're hopin' we'll go into winter quarters at Clingman, but on the first day of November, we get orders to march fifty miles north to Tarboro, where we're to report to General James G. Martin, commander of the district. When we get there, supplies are drawn right away for the regiment, right down to forage for the horses of the field officers and supply train. You can tell by the corn and fodder being issued that somethin' is up. Major Schenck is issued 700 pounds of corn and 800 pounds of fodder for his two horses. Since them officers on horseback usually get no more than 14 pounds a day, it's clear as mud somethin's in the works. But when we ask what it is, we're just told we'll find out soon enough. That's just the way they do the pore enlisted men.

Now, if sergeants learn one thing, it's how to listen and some of the biggest talkers are these young lieutenants. So, by listening here or hanging around there; by standing respectful like to ask a question next to some quietly talking officers, you pick up quite a bit.

And the one word, picked up again and again, is "Washington". That does it! It's Washington! We're goin' to Washington!

****

AN UNKNOWN PRIVATE SOLDIER SOMEWHERE IN GENERAL PALMER'S EXPEDITION

At the small village of Washington, North Carolina, I am in the large Union force being mobilized only thirty miles from Tarboro. Preparations have been completed for a special operation of this strike force; its departure, under the command of General John G. Foster, is expected at any hour. The general, a West Point classmate of Paul Faison in happier days, had been present in the Federal garrison at Fort Sumter in 1861 and a hardened veteran of the Roanoke and New Bern campaigns a year later. Able, aggressive, and experienced, he is committed to campaigning that will effectively end resistance. We are all fortunate to have a commander who will fight.

The most obvious objective of this expedition is the reb base and railroad junction at Tarboro itself and we hope the johnnies will think that, but we are really hoping that our advance will entice rebel units into the area. The destruction of all enemy troops operating between Washington and Tarboro is the primary objective of the expedition. We are heavy enough to perform the task. Our force includes three full brigades of infantry (totaling some 5,000 men) and twenty-one pieces of light artillery. Although some of our fifteen regiments are untried units, others are seasoned veterans and have seen combat. The 44th Massachusetts Infantry even includes some veterans of Burnside's expedition to the Outer Banks earlier in the year. This is significant, for there they had captured some men who we found later were presently standing in the ranks of the 56th North Carolina Infantry in Tarboro.

With five days rations distributed to the men, we finally march out of Washington on the morning of November 2. In close order and in high spirits, we move on to the west in a dense column. The first objective is the small village of Williamston, some fifteen miles away.

The day is hot, the roads bad, and the infantrymen push themselves to the limit. A Boston reporter with the expedition sees men falling from the ranks in exhaustion. The supply column bringing up the rear fares no better. One New Englander is inspired to pen a nonclassic verse or two of doggerel:

Then the mules strove and tugged
Up the hillsides steep and rugged,
Into which the mules, rot 'em,
Got so very far deluded
Nothing but their ears protruded
Picturing in a situation
Well Abe's administration.

But by dusk, our advance drives away the small picket force at Rawls Mill. On the following morning, we march into the totally undefended and deserted village of Williamston.

It is here where General John G. Foster first finds that his own worst enemy in this campaign is not going to be the rebs, but rather his own men. We are hungry and tired and it is at Williamston that the enlisted men first get badly out of hand. The town is deserted and, as far as the men are concerned, ripe for the taking. All unoccupied residences and stores are systematically looted. Pigs, fowl, potatoes, honey, apples - it all vanishes as if by a miracle. "It was a new business for us", one veteran confessed later with a smile, " but we soon got used to it". The night is one long festivity in which everything that can not be carried away is destroyed. Our soldiers wolf down contraband food, smoke contraband cigars, and dance in the empty streets with contraband hoop skirts and contraband parasols.

On November 4, the expedition, its baggage train loaded down with the first fruits, slowly marches out of Williamston and continues west toward Tarboro. The systematic wasting and destruction continues unabated along the line of march. One soldier observes that "every stray or deserted vehicle along our route, from a carry all to a hand cart, and every horse and mule ... was pressed into our service". The fact that we are already running low on the rations issued in Washington (for some lost reason, either of mismanagement or of unauthorized consumption on the route) does not help matters as we march on toward the next immediate objective.

This is the small village of Hamilton, some eight or nine miles away. The countryside lies supine before the Flag of the Union and it seems evident now that no rebel soldier will dare to show his head. Spirits soar in the ranks. All of us are now confident, in strength, loose in the countryside, and out for blood.

*****
FESS SMITH, SERGEANT, COMPANY F

Well, we marched into Tarboro and went into camp on November 3. That's where we first get word that the Yanks are in Williamston, but the evidence is all around us that it is so. Tarboro is just like some scene out of one of them comic operas; excitement is about as hysterical as it can get everywhere you look. Confederate troops are marchin' in all directions, frantic refugees from Williamston and Hamilton fill the streets with all they can carry on their backs, and big work crews of slaves trudge through the dust with pick-axes on their shoulders. We hear there has been a battle at Rawl's Mill where thousands of men have been killed. We immediately get ready for action, putting the baggage, supplies, and payroll under guard in Tarboro. Then we're ready to move out, all in light marchin' order.

That Commissary Charles Davis writes his wife "Our regiment has gone to the field of bloody strife and I am left here "(with the supplies)" Then he adds, "There is quite a great deal of talk here about peace, that England and France propose an armistice and mediation. I hope this may be and this cruel war ended". But that's just his own ignorance and foolishness talkin'. Most of us know better than that. The cruel war is only twenty miles away and we're going to get a chance at it at last.

The next day, we're formally reviewed before goin' into action by General Martin, the new commander of the forces now packin' into Tarboro, and by no less than the newly elected Governor of the State, Zebulon B. Vance! I reckon they were there to put backbone in us to drive the invaders from the sacred soil of The Old North State. Old Vance had on a high silk hat for the occasion. He probably was expectin' cheers, but got cat-calls instead and shouts of "Come out of that thar hat! We know you's in thar, 'cause we kin see yore feet a-stickin' out!" Speaking of feet, though, it ain't no laughing matter. Some of the men are already barefoot.

****
AN UNKNOWN UNION PRIVATE

We arrive at Hamilton, some fifteen miles away. The town is deserted and it is occupied with no resistance. It is now the turn of Hamilton to suffer the fate of Williamston.

All of the five thousand troops with us are not allowed to enter the town, possibly because of the depredations at Williamston. But, if so, then the precaution is made in vain. Those soldiers who do enter the town soon begin plundering and burning the finer homes; the streets soon resound with the cries of screaming pigs and poultry; military discipline rapidly disintegrates as other enlisted men, lured by the prospect of loot, steal into town as darkness falls. Officers do their best to restrain the men, but it is hopeless. The streets soon fill with staggering crowds of soldiers, drunk on applejack brandy, who boldly enter deserted homes and take whatever is not nailed down in the way of furniture and goods. The long night becomes progressively illuminated with houses and stores wantonly set on fire until at last a considerable part of the town is engulfed in flames. The troops are finally rounded up and march out of the village by the light of at least fifteen burning houses and stores.

Reactions to the burning of Hamilton are mixed. While some of our soldiers condemn the burning as unnecessary and outrageous, others complain that our only difficulty is the shortness of the stop. Be that as it may, the town is destroyed.

With the light of the still burning village on the horizon, the three brigades go into camp on a large plantation three miles out on the road to Tarboro. There, the troops regale themselves on the accumulated fruits of the expedition. Pork, grain, sweet potatoes, poultry - all are so plentiful and accessible. The war is already becoming a colossal picnic.

The next morning, November 5, we begin the planned advance on Tarboro. But, within a few miles of the town, reports are received of heavy rebel troop concentrations there. Light skirmishing is heard up the road from the advance column. Foster, aware of the growing fatigue and lack of control over his enlisted men, deliberates and then decides on a gradual withdrawal back to his base at Washington.

****

FESS SMITH, SERGEANT, COMPANY F

The sun comes up on November 5 in a clear, blue sky and the temperature is warm today. We don't pay much attention to the low cloud cover in the west and south as we muster that morning. General Martin has five regiments to drive the Yankees out: the

17th, 26th, 42th, 61st, and the 56th infantry regiments; a troop of cavalry; two or three batteries of light field artillery. After a last inspection, we bravely set out for Hamilton to drive back the foul invader. We meet them for the first time on the cloudy night of the 5th in a brief skirmish between cavalry scouts and pickets some ten miles east of Tarboro. The Yank pickets are driven back to their main line with not much loss to us. Then, under cover of darkness, we move on up to the sound of musket fire and sleep as well as we can through a long rainy night in line of battle. We're expectin' a general assault come first daybreak.

But morning just brings more of the long rain. Temperatures are falling now and the rain's freezing. Our patrols bring back word that the main Yankee force has abandoned its try to take Tarboro and are even now skee-daddling back to Hamilton. The 44th comes up during the night; we're now six regiments strong and we set out in pursuit.

****

AN UNKNOWN UNION PRIVATE

The weather is bad and is getting worse, but it is on our side now. It is hard, there is no gain-saying that. It rains on all through the long day; the roads are in terrible condition; and we are not pressed by the enemy. The rebs probably know we can still turn and fight like a wolf at bay. We still outnumber them three to one at best odds. Still, it is hard. Making sure the stragglers keep up in the rain and mud is bad enough, but what are we to do with these crowds of runaway slaves? There must be hundreds, thousands of them. Finally, we make it back into the gutted and smoldering ruins of Hamilton. We are exhausted and can only think of getting back to the base at Washington for a much needed rest.

We sleep in the streets and the rain falls hard in a driving wind long into the night. But then it gradually hushes and then fades away into the muffled and growing silence of a heavy snow fall. At daybreak on the 7th, we awake to find the world covered in a "silence deep and white". It is all a stillness of drifting snow which we will probably remember as long as any roar of the guns. And not just here - the snow is three to four inches deep in New York, Boston, Cleveland, Richmond; 30-40 lives are lost on the Great Lakes. But, we don't know anything about that until we read it in the papers back in Washington.

Mike Skerry, a private in the 5th Massachusetts, gambols through the snow, calling out in his rich Irish brogue: "And this is the Sunny South, is it now? The land of cotton, pineapples, and oranges? Here we be, knee deep in snow; Devil a bit have I seen of their Sunny South! By my soul, 'tis Greenland, I believe it is"! Another soldier from Massachusetts smiles at Skerry and returns to his own private reverie; it reminds him so much of home, "the flakes falling as thick and merrily as on a Christmas Day in New England".

With first light, we are on the road again, leaving Hamilton for Williamston. The snow continues falling all day long. There is no picking one's way, only forging straight ahead. It is terribly bad marching and the men are in a foul mood.

****

FESS SMITH. SERGEANT, COMPANY F

We of the 56th won't ever forget that day. The pursuit of the retreatin' Yankee column is slow; the men are worn out; and Captain Harrill of I Company has a hard time gettin' a wagon for the half dozen barefoot men stumbling along in his detail. For the rest of the day, we toil on through the deepening snow and mud until we at last go into camp after goin' only a few miles. Here, General Martin reorganizes the command into three brigades of two regiments each. Our own Colonel Faison is put in command of the brigade composed of the 17th and 56th regiments; our Lieutenant-Colonel Luke takes over temporary command of the 56th in the colonel's absence. The next morning, we force ourselves back into column and resume the pursuit. But by that time, the Yanks are back in Williamston.

****

AN UNKNOWN UNION PRIVATE

Williamston had not been badly damaged when we passed through it first only four days before. We hadn't handled it like we did Hamilton. Now this oversight is going to be corrected. You can see the enlisted men leaving the ranks in squads even as we march through the deserted streets. Great numbers of the runaway slaves are ransacking deserted houses for the second time around.

But you can see our men also chasing down frantic pigs and chickens; some are even over-turning bee hives for the honeycomb. And others I am afraid have already found applejack brandy in the cellars of these deserted houses. It is neither good for man, beast, ignition, or sanitation; it is "a sort of a cross between camphene and Fire-and-Brimstone". It sets "a soldier's brain on fire, with the fearfullest frenzy of drunkenness known to man". Such has it been described; such it is. The brandy spreads like wildfire through the ranks. The local jail and whipping post are reduced to kindling and burned; public documents in the court house are taken as souvenirs or scattered in the streets; drunken soldiers stagger from house to house in a wild spree of pillaging. It takes the provost guard a full hour to pull the men back into line and by that time, the orders are to bed down in the streets, as much as to sleep it off as anything.

At daybreak, on November 10, we march out of Williamston and return to Plymouth with no incident. The weather moderates; the sun comes out; soon the men smile a little more; their step quickens; their spirit rises. Then, a new marching song comes drifting down the column and it seems to sum up the fruits of the expedition:

> Here's to good old applejack,
>> Drink her down;
> Here's to good old applejack,
>> Drink her down;
> Here's to good old applejack,
>> It will lay you on your back;
>>> Drink her down,
>>> Drink her DOWN!

> ***************

FESS SMITH, SERGEANT, COMPANY F

On the following day, we march at last into the ruined streets of Hamilton. It's clear as day to us that the campaign is now over and we go into camp that evening to await further orders. Now, the men of the 56th are a lot more like those of the old days of Bony Part than they are of today; they live in a military world of sword and feather, of massed cavalry charges and the square, and all that. But this is different, this that they see all around them. This is maybe the twentieth century a-comin' on, a foretaste of what the rest of the world might come to know one day. But if that's so, they're not supposed to see it, no - not in these days.

So we see the effects of this total war, the total destruction all around us in shock and disbelief. Some boy in Company B turns over a pile of dried turds with his brogan and says, "Wal, look at this. Yankee shit in the Old North State. You shore kain't say they took everything with them when they left".

It ain't just the burned and gutted ruins; the litter blowin' across the streets; the stink of shit and vomit. The stealin' away of over 3,000 slaves along the Yankee line of march was proof enough that this war was goin' to be an attack on capital and property, just like the fire-eaters said it would be. Even though the Yanks failed in destroyin' us, they sure succeeded in tearin' up the civilians and their way of makin' a livin'. The Parson wasn't makin' things any better by goin' around sayin' the wages of sin is death; one of the officers had to call him down.

Although not a shot had been fired over the past week by the 56th North Carolina Infantry, this raid has given us our first taste of what the real war is like. And we learn some valuable lessons in this campaign, no gain-saying that, but it also shows up some danger points.

We got new experience in movin' men and supplies through all kinds of weather in a real combat operation; company officers got new experience in tellin' us what to do, or so-called "performance of their duty"; the field officers got valuable experience in commandin' high level stuff. The morale of enlisted men and officers both goes way up by seein' a big enemy force high-tail it at our advance. And many of the men see all that wreckin' and robbin' of the Yankees as a bad sign of their ability to fight.

Probably most of the company commanders, even maybe most of the enlisted men at Hamilton, can point to one or another area where we are now more experienced and more seasoned, more veteran after the operation. But hardly no one sees, even suspects the more quiet danger, the comin' danger that first looms over us in this first campaign.

It's the simple fact that all that staff work of those officers had put the regiment in a dangerous position, with no one at all knowin' of it. We knew the Yanks were out to wreak destruction on any and all Confederate military units in the theater of operation. They had only been frustrated in doin' that by bad weather, breakdown in discipline, and lyin' reports of our big reinforcements at Tarboro. We, unbeknownst to ourselves, followed Foster right into the jaws of a trap which only failed to spring due to their own stupid mistakes. During the long months to come, I bet you a bottom dollar we'll find ourselves followed by a dark cloud that dooms us to marchin' again and again, like total blindness, into more of them traps cooked up by the Yanks. Sooner or later, those teeth of the trap will snap shut, hold fast unless the lesson is timely learned by our officers. It warn't learned at Hamilton in the late autumn of 1862. I know it and some of the boys know it, but nary an officer there has the sense of a cat to see it. They take us right in and right out of a trap and never knowed the difference, any more than in that old fairy tale about them pore lost babies crawlin' around in the woods. An old cat would have had more sense.

I tell you what, Boy; you can go trippin' through the woods and step in all the traps you want, but sooner or later its goin' to snap. And that's what's goin' to happen to us if these officers don't get crackin'. Just look at them - Go to some college, talk big words in deep voices, but Ole Farmer Jim still comes a-shinin' through. Self-Made Man, Self-Made Shit, I say. Playin' cards and struttin' around like they're Lords or somethin'; standin' out in the ocean up to their necks lookin' at the moon instead of studyin' them charts and maps and things. They need to be figurin' the Yank's next move instead of up to foolishness like that.

It's just a week after that when we run into another runnin' event in our life. Virginia's not just a state, - it's somethin' more than that in the war. And maybe there's somethin' more than the generals plannin' that'll bring the regiment there time and time again. Who can ever say for sure?

But there seems to be somethin' else - somethin' that seems to show that the regiment, like the Old South we defend, maybe has a curse on it; it is doomed, and there ain't nothing field officer or enlisted man can do about it. But I know who I will look after.

Of course, this is all hidden away from us. We don't feel or see it; if we did, we wouldn't believe it. The orders for Virginia come and to most of us, it's an opportunity, not a threat. After all, we're goin' to Virginia and it's there where the war is goin' to be won at last. And Richmond Town's a big place; there orter be a woman or two there before the Peace is all signed and we go on home. Yes sir, boys, we're goin' to Ole Virginny.

CHAPTER THREE

JOHN F. MCNEELY, LIEUTENANT, COMPANY K

All our thoughts are of Virginia and the future. At first a rumor sweeping through the ranks, it is confirmed by no less than the Adjutant himself. We are all excited - I had never been there before. Lee is back from Sharpsburg and obviously we will be assigned to the Army of Northern Virginia. And Lee is invincible on his own ground: the Peninsula and Manassas Campaigns proves that. The fact that we will have a role to play there is immensely gratifying. Nothing seems impossible.

Captain Frank Roberts comes over smiling and says "Well, Lieutenant McNeely, this will be your first trip north, won't it?" I answer that it will not be as far north as Connecticut. He laughs and claps me on the shoulder, but there is a shadow in his eyes and I instantly regret saying it. I am very young, only beginning to learn that these older men have their own past.

We leave on November 15, a Saturday. The regiment is directed to proceed 75 miles north on foot to Franklin, Virginia. There it is to be temporarily attached to Pettigrew's Brigade, guarding the Blackwater River in Southside Virginia. It is first necessary to draw supplies for the long march and this is done in the shell of Hamilton on the morning of departure. Firewood and new shoes are distributed to each company. Officers pick up needed articles for the campaign: Captain Lawson Harrill over in Company I has the great good fortune to obtain a new officer's tent. Later that same morning, the regiment marches out of Hamilton for Franklin.

It takes four days. The marching is continuous and pushed to the limits of endurance. We finally arrive at Franklin on the morning of the 19th badly in need of rest.

The men are exhausted, disheveled, and without food. Attempts to secure supplies from the commissary are unavailing and the greater part of the regiment goes to sleep that night without rations. Captain Harrill receives an invitation to dine with Colonel Faison and other field officers that evening; the Captain chooses to share the hunger of his men. The invitation isn't extended to us - generally, lieutenants are little better than sergeants and a considerable step below captains. Lieutenant Davis and I share what meager rations we have. But at least we are now in Virginia and after all, this is where the war is supposed to be decided.

We have time to look over this new country of southeast Virginia. Vast level tracts of forest stretch to the horizon in every direction and the land is sparsely inhabited by old men, women, children, and blacks. Poverty is a common affliction for most of them and many Northerners no doubt feel that the entire area would be no great loss to the Union. But it is of vital military importance to the Confederates who control most of the crossings on the Blackwater River that runs roughly north to south through the desolate countryside. Major rail lines linking the capital at Richmond to the rest of the south extend through the area. The entire region can serve as an ideal invasion route for any enterprising Union force that seeks to cut the railroads and advance on Richmond from the south. The Federals are as aware of this as anyone: only fifteen miles east of Franklin is Suffolk, a major Union base complete with permanent log housing and comfortable canvas roofs for even the lowliest private.

Following its arrival at Franklin, the 56th, as ordered, is temporarily attached to Pettigrew's Brigade. During the following week, we are assigned to the construction of heavy entrenchments along the line of defense south of Franklin. The hard labor with pick axe and shovel is finally completed on November 26 under a cold, heavy rain. The next day is Thanksgiving.

Although not yet a national holiday, Thanksgiving is celebrated, but in different fashion on each side of the Blackwater. We found from prisoners taken later that the Union soldiers at Suffolk celebrate the day with two tons of roasted poultry confiscated from the surrounding countryside. Pretty ladies from the North come down from Norfolk to visit and amusements involving the contrabands that fill the town are organized for the day. One Union soldier writes that "all sorts of games were indulged in, the most mirthful of which was the sack racing by our colored servants. Tied up in a bag, each one did his best to out strip the others and the results were side-splitting in the extreme. Now Clem, now Tom, now Lam was ahead; and the spectators were convulsed with laughter ... Thanksgiving in camp will long be remembered". But in our positions across the Blackwater, conditions are austere and bleak and the day is observed accordingly.

November ends uneventfully, but during the first days of December, a Union expedition marches out of Suffolk to probe the Confederate defenses along the Blackwater. The expedition, composed of over 3,000 men and supported by artillery, sets out for Franklin that morning, followed by a long train of supply wagons, ambulances, and at least a score of pontoon boats for a possible crossing of the river. The Federal expedition arrives on the Blackwater in good order, driving Confederate vendettes across the river on December 2nd and even capturing a Confederate rocket battery. The 56th is not in the engagement, being located further upstream.

The following day, as a "cold, disagreeable rain" falls, our cavalry pickets are driven across the river at Franklin itself, but the Federals make no further attempt to cross with their main force. So the war along the Blackwater settles into a long period of watchful waiting. It is becoming more and more evident that we will be no part of the Army of Northern Virginia. Here we will rest - locked on the Blackwater with winter coming on, as stationary as if we are encased in ice, shrouded in frost, frozen in place.

And the winter comes in with a vengeance. Freezing rain falls from the heavy overcast; the sun is invisible from dawn to dusk; across the river, we are aware that Federal morale is beginning to suffer in spite of hot food and regular mail delivery. For many Union soldiers, the land and climate are the strongest depressants - "most dismal days" follow one another over "a desolate realm" of low-lying forests intersected by tiny cross roads. One Union soldier stated that on one twelve-mile patrol, only one "ancient darkey" was seen in all the land. It is unsafe for Federals to leave their camps; on the night of December 4, two pickets are shot by guerrillas on the

South Quay Road only two miles from their tents. There are even some desertions of Union soldiers to our side.

An occasional incident breaks the long succession of grey after-noons. A portion of the 56th is quietly rebuilding a destroyed bridge at Joyner's Store, some three miles north of Franklin. The line had been relatively quiet in this sector, but on December 8th a Federal gunboat comes steaming slowly north up the Blackwater. Lieutenant H. A. L. Sweezy of Company I sees an opportunity and quickly leads a small detachment of riflemen to the summit of a bluff over-looking the river and scatters several volleys of rifle fire across the deck of the vessel. The gunboat halts and then just as slowly retires down river. Naturally, the engagement is greeted as a great victory back in the Confederate camp.

The next day, the weather turns still colder. The detachment of the regiment which had been working on the bridge at Joyner's Store rejoins the unit in winter quarters at Franklin on December 9. Sharing the regimental camp site is the 52th North Carolina Infantry which had been stationed with the 56th at Wilmington the previous summer. As night falls, friendly visiting between the two units takes place around the camp fires and even though the war is still so new, the men so young, reminiscences and recollections are exchanged far into the night.

I am on picket that night and so do not share in the festivities. It is cold out on the river. The sun sets in a chill glow and the tempera-ture falls with alarming swiftness. Ice forms along the Blackwater thick enough to bear a horse. Toward midnight, the camp sleeps in a silence deep, grim, ice-locked under the stars, with random meteors the only movement and the only sound coming after twelve from the distant complaint of Union artillery shelling the camps down river at South Quay. But in time, even that ceases and the night is left to its own frozen silence, still and dark, ice-fanged, a silence and a still-ness broken only by the long passing of the blazing winter stars high overhead.

The next day, December 10, we are placed on alert, having received word of a possible Union advance; perhaps our comman-ders were a bit edgy after the previous night's shelling. Lieutenant Matthew Fatherley and a few men from Company C decide to imi-tate the brave exploit of Lieutenant Sweezy. Taking only a single rifle with them, they steal down to the junction of the Blackwater and Nottoway Rivers. A Union gunboat is quietly anchored there on patrol duty, and Fatherley and his men take turns with the rifle firing a number of rounds at the oblivious vessel before returning happily to camp.

The threatened Union advance never comes. The Federals are having their own problems with poor roads, Confederate reinforcements, and cold weather. But largely it is the work of the 56th and other Confederate units on the Blackwater during those bleak December days and nights that prevents a Union crossing of the river. Besides firing at prowling gunboats and repairing bridges, the regiment is busily engaged in blocking river crossings with fallen trees and constructing long lines of rifle pits along the western bank. As additional Confederate reinforcements continue to arrive at Franklin, it becomes more and more evident that the Federals will not attempt a crossing of the river this winter. Soon all action along the front dies away, except for the occasional cough of Union artillery dropping a random shell across the river.

On December 11, while men bleed and die at Fredericksburg 150 miles away, a portion of the regiment is detached for special duty. Lieutenant-Colonel Luke with four companies is left to guard the crossing at New South Quay while Colonel Faison with the remaining six companies march three miles north to report to General Pryor at Franklin. There they are attached to a foraging expedition that is operating near Carrsville and Windsor for two weeks. They return to Franklin on the 28th with no loss, one prisoner, and a number of wagons loaded with provisions.

Christmas 1862 arrives on the Blackwater. While the Federals across the river are celebrating the day with decorated Christmas trees and "handsome entertainment", the 56th North Carolina Infantry is quietly spending its first Christmas in the field. On the 28th, the six companies detached under Colonel Faison are reunited with the four companies still stationed on the Blackwater in newly constructed rifle pits set along the banks of the river. The rest of the regiment remains in permanent winter quarters three miles down river at South Quay.

Vague rumors spread through the regiment at this time that a Yankee deserter had said the Federals are going to advance on

Kinston or Goldsboro in North Carolina and that the regiment might soon be sent south. The morale of the men brightens considerably at the prospect of going home. Although there is "tolerable plenty to eat", the enlisted men find paper and stamps for their letters in short supply. Many are homesick and are beginning to feel that the campaign has lasted long enough.

The first day of 1863 dawns fair and tranquil. Across the Blackwater, Union soldiers are still celebrating the New Year with over 700 boxes of food and cigars just received from the North. But three miles downstream, at the Regimental Headquarters of the 56th, Private Charles Davis of Company G writes a letter to his wife Harriet in which he says:

> This beautiful New Year morn I take
> the pleasure of writing to you. You would
> laugh were you to see me today. I have on
> a pair of the captain's pants and they are
> about four or five inches too short for me.
> I hadn't but one pair of pants and they lost
> the seat; so had to get a woman to reseat
> them. Thousands here are ten times worse than
> I in the clothing line.

But even if Private Davis is poor in dress, newspapers are available and avidly read. Young Davis goes on to write (not knowing of the battle still raging undecided in Tennessee at that very hour):

> I see from the papers a fight has probably
> been ere this at or near Murfreesboro. I
> suppose both of your brothers will be in it.
> I hope they will come out safe ... That fight
> is looked to with a great deal of concern as
> tending to end the war.

The long days of guard duty give us time to reflect and the end of the year 1862 provides an opportunity for silent introspection, reassessment, and summation. During this winter campaign, both officers and men have learned much and acquitted themselves well. Although combat has been limited to sporadic clashes with pickets and gunboats, we have become skilled in other areas of defensive warfare. These include holding natural lines of defense, repairing bridges, blocking rivers, building earthworks, undergoing random shelling, and living in winter quarters during a particularly severe winter. New experience has also been gained in reconnaissance and foraging. General Pryor says of our service that "Colonel Faison was always on time with his regiment" and it is generally agreed that the 56th is the best unit on the Blackwater in tactics, military discipline, and appearance.

The general health of the regiment is also much improved. By the end of the year, the only sick field officer is Major Schenck and even he is present for duty. Despite the harsh weather, sickness in the ranks is not prevalent, perhaps due to the able presence of Surgeon Thomas and Assistant Surgeon Cox. Both men are always present for duty with well stocked medical supplies.

Within three days, the 56th North Carolina Infantry receives new orders. For us, the campaign is over at last. We are ordered to withdraw from the Blackwater lines and return south. The makeshift tents are dismantled, inventory is taken, what farewells that need to be said are said. Then the regiment begins the long march to Petersburg. There we will take the troop trains that will return us to North Carolina.

I often think that no matter what season of the year it is, it will always be January of 1863. The snow has begun to slowly fall once more, and we are leaving Virginia on the trains. We board them at Petersburg at dusk and all through the long night the men huddle together for warmth in the freezing cattle cars, rolled in their blankets on the floor or leaning haphazardly all about, one against the other against the walls, fitfully lit by the one solitary kerosene lantern burning there.

I had told them earlier that when we reach Tarboro, perhaps some of the good women of the town will be there at the station with cups of hot tea and steaming coffee. They greet this with the usual chorus of ribald and skeptical reservations, but it has been quiet for some time now. And I have at last the leisure and the time now to watch the lantern there, the only seemingly independent moving force in all this long night, making its own slow deliberate revolution in exact time to the train's own precise motion.

Most of the men are asleep now. And that boy with the musket at his side almost twice his length, he shouldn't be here at all. There is a soft rustling of the straw as he edges nearer.

"I'm fine, Sir. I'll make it alright, Lieutenant. D'Ye reakon we 'll ever git back to Virginny agin? "

I put my hand on his shoulder and look again at the lantern slowly swinging there in the night.

"Perhaps some day, Billy. The war is only a year old for us and a lot can still happen."

CHAPTER FOUR

LAWSON HARRILL, CAPTAIN, COMPANY I

It's "Cap'n. Harrill" this and "Cap'n. Harrill" that, out on the drill field, on the march, in the orders from Regiment. But in camp, when they come up to me with an ailment, the quickstep, or just a misery, it's just "Doc". I will never understand how a medical doctor from Rutherford became a company commander. But the boys in Company I wanted it; the fates determined it; and Faison got himself another regimental surgeon at Magnum to take my place - a whole procession of them as it turned out. Actually, Regiment benefits - they get two surgeons for the price of one, and a company commander to boot. If Regiment's more intelligent than I give them credit for, I wouldn't be surprised if it was designed that way. And that is how Doctor Lawson Harrill, M.D. became Captain Lawson Harrill, Company I, 56th North Carolina.

As a doctor, I had brought my own share of infants into the world - two legged and four legged - and I was always impressed by that miracle, even if it was some dumb animal that would pull a plow for the rest of its days. A new beginning, you see, for something. The calendar is that way too - Sunday, a special day; May Day in the spring; January first, marking a new year as well as a new month. We are in the doldrums a bit after returning to North Carolina, but I know things change and there is 1863 just "a-busting to be born", like some of the boys in the ranks would say.

However, the new month of January 1863 is a quiet one on all fronts. The Union army remains on the bleak hills overlooking Fredericksburg resting after its heavy losses of the month before. Following the bloody battle of Murfreesboro, Bragg's Army of Tennessee withdraws toward Tullahoma. Both armies are in trauma and need recuperation after all the blood-letting. Harsh weather and the usual reluctance to mount a winter offensive brings something of a truce to hostilities all over. With the exception of the "Mud March" of the Federal Army on the Rapidan, both sides drill, build winter shelters, write letters home, and wait for spring.

On the evening of January 4, we finally march into camp at Rocky Mount, North Carolina. The regiment spends an uneventful two weeks at this station resting from its ordeal of a winter campaign in Virginia. On the 17th, we leave Rocky Mount for Magnolia to meet an expected Union advance from the coast. Three days later, the regiment stacks arms near Pettigrew's Brigade, two miles east of Magnolia Station.

However, it is only another false alarm and new orders come on January 21 to proceed to Kenansville. Arriving there later on the same day, the regiment is formally attached to Ransom's Brigade, with which we will remain until the end. Ever since its inception, we had drifted from one post to another, switching assignments in mid-course, practically adrift on the Sea of War. But now at last we have found a home.

Ransom's Brigade is already making a name for itself. It is composed of five North Carolina regiments: the 24th, the 25th, the 35th, the 49th, and now the 56th. Its commanding officer is Brigadier General Robert Ransom. Ransom is an experienced field officer, who has seen service as a brigade commander during the Peninsula Campaign the year before. We are all impressed by him and some of our staff officers make a big thing about going up to Brigade and hob-knobbing with the gold braid. I am a little more reticent. Brigades are like any organism. They are born, grow, age, and die, along with the men in them. Time will tell. I can afford to wait on the prognosis.

An uneventful month follows in camp at Kenansville. On February 22, orders arrive for the brigade to proceed to Wilmington on the coast. On our arrival at the state's largest sea port, we bivouac at Camp Lamb. The 56th is then detached from the brigade and ordered to proceed to Old Topsail Sound just north of the city. On arrival, we report for temporary duty to General William Whiting, commander of the Confederate defenses at Wilmington. The General had been favorably impressed by the regiment last summer and has been requesting the assignment of the unit to his command for some time. The request has at last been approved by the War Department.

So it is that two days later, on February 24, the 56th marches alone out of Camp Lamb and proceeds by easy stages to Topsail Sound. The long sandy road, bordered by stands of long leaf pine, leads us back to the blue waters of the Atlantic later in the day. The men are in good spirits in this warmer climate. The long beaches and the surf are still the same; the sea is a well remembered pleasure; even the ghostly ships of the United States Navy off shore have a certain reassuring quality. The regiment occupies Harrison's lines at Sunbury and settles down to two weeks of easy garrison duty.

On the coast, the weather is moderating and spring is in the air. On March 9, we are joined by the remaining four units of Ransom's Brigade. The reunited command spends another week or so in camp by the sea at Topsail Inlet. There are the usual inspections, drills, parades, of course. The blockading ships of the U. S. Navy appear as regularly on the horizon as the sunrise. The papers confirm the news that New Bern, Washington, Plymouth, and Edenton are still firmly held by Union forces. Everyone knows that spring will bring a further Union drive into the interior of the state. The men are confident, but it is easier to put all rumor aside and think of other things than the war. The sound of the unceasing surf on these sandy beaches and the long, warm days certainly promise no immediate change.

While the enlisted men remain in camp or occupy themselves with routine guard duty at Topsail Inlet, a number of the field and company officers take advantage of the calm and engage in other duties. In early March, a general court martial is appointed to meet in Wilmington only a few miles away. Lieutenant Edward J. Hale, adjutant to the regiment, is appointed to serve as one of the judge advocates for the court, to be followed in the same capacity by Captain John W. Graham of Company D. At the same time, Lieutenant Colonel G. Gratiott Luke and Captain Joseph G. Lockhart of Company E are absent on detached service with still another court martial meeting in session in Goldsboro. To these men, reports, depositions, and the military justice system are becoming more familiar than the parade ground. The war is far away now.

In spite of the mild weather on the coast and the relaxed atmosphere in camp, a certain amount of sickness begins to appear in the regiment in the early spring of 1863. Colonel Faison and Major Schenck are both absent on sick leave for the greater part of March. But by and large, the general health of the regiment is so good that Surgeon Thomas leaves the command for a two week furlough and a trip home during this period. After all, they have me to deal with the toe-itch, bloody piles, greybacks - a doctor's running stock-in-trade.

In 1863, there are few portions of the South that can expect to remain completely untouched for long by the war. The location of the brigade and regiment by the sea isolates us from the gathering forces in Virginia and Mississippi. But the officers and men are confident in their ability to meet any Federal advance into the central piedmont of the state. After all, they had served in Virginia during the preceding winter; they felt they had served well. They are also beginning to make a favorable impression on other observers in North Carolina. By late spring, the regiment is described by THE FAYETTEVILLE OBSERVER as "excellent troops". The brigade is professional enough to impress General Whiting as "disciplined and effective".

Such reputation cannot long go unnoticed or unused. A Confederate counter-offensive under the commands of General James Longstreet and D. H. Hill is in operation against the Union bases at New Bern and Washington, North Carolina. On March 23, we are ordered to proceed to Kinston to help support this Confederate spring offensive on the coast. General Whiting protests to the War Department to no avail as the brigade marches from Old Topsail and proceeds to the Wilmington and Weldon Railroad to board the cars. We are then transported by rail through Goldsboro and then southeast to Kinston. But by the time the brigade disembarks from the cars just a few miles west of New Bern on April 1, we receive word that the Confederate offensive has ended in yet another failure and our services are no longer needed.

Despite the end of the operation against New Bern, the brigade, much to its disappointment, does not return to Wilmington, but is ordered instead to remain at Kinston. On April 17, we march out of camp and cross the Neuse River to the east. The original orders called for the brigade to proceed some eighteen miles east to reinforce the 59th North Carolina Infantry on picket duty at Sandy

Ridge. But on hearing that unit had been withdrawn toward Kinston, the brigade has no choice but to stack arms on the banks of the river and wait for further orders. It all seems to serve no logical purpose.

Two days later, on April 19, the 56th is ordered to march on down the Dover Road and occupy Wise's Cross roads near Dover Station. A strong Union force had been reported in the vicinity and we leisurely form into line of battle with only the faintest expectation by now that we will ever see action.

The afternoon wears on without sound or movement to disturb the stillness. The crossroads seem to be absolutely in the middle of nowhere. Houses and farms are few and scattered; there are only a few large clearings among the dense stands of pines that close out the horizon. Off there to the left, there seems to be a swamp. The men loll in the sun and impassively gaze out at the shimmering pine forests to the east. One of the men, looking out into the brooding stillness, says "Well, Doc, sun come out and dried the Blackwater all up, but other than that, nuthin's changed". Everything about us seems to indicate that nothing had ever happened here; nothing ever will.

Later in the day, with the sun already in the west, the expected and inevitable word comes that the Union force, if it ever existed at all, has withdrawn to its base at New Bern. That evening, we leave the crossroads for what we sincerely hope is the last time and return back to camp at Kinston. There, some of the men remember the Blackwater, as harsh as it was, with something akin to nostalgia. At least, they had heard the sound of artillery there from time to time. And there was a clearly defined river on the opposite shore where there were equally clearly defined Federal pickets. And of course they tell the story of the gunboats again and again and again.

On its return to Kinston, the 56th has a day or two of rest from the extended and apparently meaningless maneuvering. For once, many of the officers and men take pleasure in busily taking inventory. Major Schenck has returned to duty from sick leave, but still suffers attacks of bronchitis. Captain Henry F. Lane of Company G is arrested on unspecified charges of negligence in the performance of duty. That leaves Lieutenant Davis, a Welsh mystic if there ever was one, practically in charge of a crowd of wild mountaineers. Behind his back, we call him "The Prophet". Some companies in the camp at Kinston are without tents and begin improvising makeshift brush arbors covered with blankets or sod. Ammunition is plentiful - forty rounds are issued to each man but there apparently will be no practical use for it other than target practice. It doesn't make it any easier to find that rations are scarcer than ammunition. Each soldier receives a daily portion of a fourth of a pound of bacon and a pound of corn meal. Private Charles Davis writes to his wife that "Could you see us some night sitting around a campfire with a piece of fat meat broiling it and a hard cracker in our hands, you would say 'poor fellows'".

The officers of the regiment fare a little better than the enlisted men. Some of us, even down to the grade of lieutenant, have their personal black body servants in the camp. The uniforms of all the officers are kept brushed and clean. Of course, such luxuries and amenities among the enlisted men are rare to non-existent; many of their clothes are ragged and their personal appearance, rough and haggard. However, despite my most careful observation, there are few signs of discontent among them. During the day, the men faithfully drill and go about the performance of their duty with only the average complaining. At night, they lounge about in their makeshift tents and discuss rumors of Confederate victories and Union atrocities on the coast. Some of the Federals on the other side of the crossroads at Dover are even accused of driving frightened crowds of civilians before them when they went into battle.

Talk over the campfires about the action or inaction of the Federals does have a little more relevancy here than it had at Old Topsail. After all, a major Union base is located only fifteen miles due east of Kinston. Between the two towns is the small village of Dover. Surrounding the small Confederate picket station occupying this post is Gum Swamp.

During the final week of April 1863, I am placed in command of three companies of the 56th and sent back out from Kinston to perform picket duty at Dover. When the 180 men of Companies E, G, and I arrive at the crossroads there, we find the small makeshift earthwork still lost in the empty countryside. We had been here only a little over a week before and absolutely nothing has changed. The railroad tracks at the earthwork wander off into the silent pine forest to the east. Surrounding them on all sides is the dense, brooding stillness of the swamp.

There is indeed something primeval about Gum Swamp. Most of it is covered with several inches of water the year round and it is thickly overgrown with scrub pine, reeds, and tall grass. Few farms or clearings break the monotony. The Yankee clerks and storekeepers in their army somewhere off on the other side of it are horrified by nature in the raw. A Union soldier with the 5th Massachusetts Infantry who saw it at the time painted a dismal picture of it: "Miles of mud knee and waist deep ... Miles of thick underbrush, of tangled wildwood, of brambles, of thorny copses, of water courses and stagnant pools ...". A captain with the 25th Massachusetts Infantry flatly stated that "not even the hellish draught compounded by the witches in Macbeth could have been more repulsive" than the water there. I myself smell malaria in the early morning mist coming out of the swamp and caution the men against breathing it.

Even we, whose land this is, find in it a different place and time. During the day, it teems with sandflies, rattlesnakes, butterflies, water moccasins, and great flocks of redwing blackbirds that rise only to settle once again in the marsh grass. At such times, it has its own wild beauty and timeless sorrow. But it is at night that it shows its true nature.

During the night, the men gather around their campfires in the small earthwork to listen to a deafening cacophony of frogs, toads, insects, and owls in the darkness all around them, a chorus of raw nature that only quiets down in the early morning hours. At night, we keep our distance from it, for it is then, as one of the boys describes it, "a profusion of owls, snakes, frogs, lightening bugs (and) mustqitoes". There is something disquieting about it at these times, something even faintly menacing and portentous.

CHAPTER FIVE

M. CROWDER, PRIVATE, COMPANY F

Lieutenant McNeely over in Company K is going around telling his boys Future Years Will Wonder At Us, so I am now taking my seat in hand to tell those years what happened that day in the spring of the year on that morning - April 28, 1863, it was. Then the name of M. Crowder, Private, Company F will live forever more, to the glory of the 56th and the honor of Crowder kin wherever they may be. The day come up fair and clear. Companies H and K, under the command of Cap'n. Frank Alexander, are holding down the Neuse River Road. And Companies A, B, D, and F under Major Schenck are over on the Upper Trent Road. One company stays in reserve - and I don't remember who's in charge of that one. But the center of the regimental line is held by Companies E, G, and I under the command of Doc Harrill. And them are the three companies at Dover.

The 180 men of them three companies under Harrill are in a just recent made breastwork or earthwork with four holes cut in it covering the railroad track. The walls are five to seven foot high and the whole thing has a seven foot deep trench or ditch in front. The whole earthwork is about 600 foot long. Seventy-five foot out in front is a line of rifle pits for the skirmishers. There ain't no artillery here, but it's figured it's strong enough for any three infantry companies to hold against anything short of a full scale attack.

****

AN UNKNOWN CORPORAL IN THE UNION FORCE AT NEW BERN

On this lovely Sunday morning, I take my pen in hand to record our recent operation against the Chivalry. It may be that future generations and our posterity may find some value and benefit in perusing these words and so reach a better understanding of our war for Liberty and Union. And it may be that in that restored nation, the humble offering of this corporal in the 37th Massachusetts Infantry, United States Army, will provide some insight into what was won at so great a cost.

In this glorious conflict, the generals made the plans; we carried them out. We were all in a hurry to stamp out the rebellion. That explains First Manassas, probably Second Manassas, certainly Fredericksburg, and for that matter the entire operation in Eastern North Carolina since last year. Stamp it out! Both General Foster and Colonel Palmer were of this sentiment, in which they were joined by every boy in blue.

The rebs thought they had the station covered against anything short of a full scale attack. But that was what was coming. Unfortunately for them and absolutely without warning, that was precisely what we had planned for them on the 28th day of April, 1863. The day before, three full regiments - the 17th, 45th, and 37th Massachusetts Volunteer Infantry, with a mounted escort from the 3rd New York Cavalry, three days rations, and a hundred rounds of cartridges to a man - marched through the sleepy streets of New Bern to board a train. Our commander was Brigadier General Innis N. Palmer; our objective, the total annihilation of the three isolated rebel companies at Dover Station.

The train halted at Bachelor's Creek only long enough to take aboard the 58th Pennsylvania Infantry. Then, our combined force, composed of over four regiments and over 1600 men strong, steamed toward Dover. As darkness fell last night, we went into camp beside the railroad and spent the night in a large cornfield. We knew that an easy march on the following day would bring us to Dover.

At first day dawn on the 28th, the weather cleared beautifully for us, but the ground was still wet and muddy. We first deployed three companies of the 45th Massachusetts as skirmishers and then began the general advance on Dover. At 11:30 a.m., the main column, with beating drums and waving colors, followed the skirmishers due west. Although a farmer picked up by the skirmish line assured our boys that there was a "right smart heap" of rebels on up the road, we were confident.

Our plan of attack was as simple as it could be. It called for a direct assault on two sides of the rebel position. The 58th Pennsylvania, the 27th Massachusetts, and the 3rd New York Cavalry would advance straight down the road to the junction. At the same time, the 17th and 45th Massachusetts would advance down the rail road. Both forces would meet at the under-manned rebel breastwork. The Lieutenant told us all about envelopment and flanking and coordinated assaults, but it was the end result of the plan that mattered to us. Victory would be sudden, decisive, certain.

****

M. CROWDER, PRIVATE, COMPANY F

Well, we're not totally unprepared for them. About a mile and a half down the railroad, Cap'n. Harrill had put an advanced picket post held by Lieutenant Jim Davis and twenty men out of Company G. Davis' first warning that they are a-coming is a woman in a nearby farm house who starts hanging out her warshing from an upstairs bedroom. The picket station is abandoned as Davis falls back on Dover Crossing, his men firing steadily as they retire. This small handful of men try to delay the Yankee advance by firing from log barricades, but they are flanked out from each one. This running fight goes on down the railroad all the way to the breastwork. For an hour, the firing is continuous and we can hear it coming closer and closer. We know they are in combat now and getting what we had all talked about for so long. Lieutenant Davis had the habit of mooning around camp in a brown study; I bet he's hopping pretty lively now. Yes sir, they're seeing the Elephant and it'll be our turn next.

****

(Colonel Cobham, 45th Massachusetts: "the column ... proceeded, driving in the enemy's vedettes and pickets. This duty performed by Company B ... the pickets being uniformly posted behind log barricades and uniformly driven out by flanking parties of Company B". Brigadier General Palmer: "the column arrived within 100 yards of the crossing, when (they were) suddenly saluted with a volley of musketry ... and found the enemy posted in rifle-pits ... and entirely concealed in the thick brush. Some seventy-five yards in rear was found ... heavy earthworks of some 500 or 600 feet front. (The Union forces) opened fire on the enemy's works, gradually advancing ..." Herbert Cooley, Private, 3rd New York Cavalry: "Their manner of drawing us up to their breastworks was quite novel indeed and one worthier of a nobler cause (for) after the pickets had been driven in not a man was to be seen until after the battle ...").

****

M. CROWDER, PRIVATE, COMPANY F

By the time Davis and his men come scrambling back into the rifle pits seventy-five yards out front, Cap'n. Harrill has deployed the three companies inside the breastwork to meet the oncoming attack. Company E holds the center, while Companies G and I are put on each flank. The swamp gives some protection on the sides. Orders are given not to open fire until the Yanks have advanced to 150 yards of the earthwork. There is nothing to do now, but wait for what will surely come. We are in line just like our great-grandfathers were in the First War for Independence and like them, we are going to fight or die game, just like we did when we beat the British at Bunker Hill.

****

THE UNKNOWN UNION CORPORAL

The 17th and 45th Massachusetts, advancing up the railroad, now deployed into line of battle and halted, calmly waiting for the arrival of the column on the Dover Road. It was only a few minutes before we saw them coming: first the skirmishers and the cavalry escort, then the long serried ranks of the 58th Pennsylvania and the 27th Massachusetts. We slowly began the advance with both forces then and the firing became general on both sides.

****

M. CROWDER, PRIVATE, COMPANY F

It's all so confusing in the earthwork. Smoke is everywhere and everyone is shouting. Looking over the wall, we can see long lines of the Yankees running out to the right and left. I count seven national and state flags along their line. Their fire, at first high, soon gets the range and you can see the minie balls walking up and down the wall. At this point, Colonel Faison makes a big entrance, like some knight out of the old romances. Galloping up, he jumps off his horse, sends an aide pounding back to Kinston for reinforcements, takes command, grabs a musket, stops just long enough to scratch at a grey-back or chigger a-gnawin' on his hind end, and then starts firing like a wildcat into the oncoming Yanks. It all makes a big impression on us then, but I wonder if anyone will remember Gum Swamp. It won't be long before it'll be forgotten and practically unknown, but it's real enough now.

****

THE UNKNOWN UNION CORPORAL

Gradually and moving cautiously, our main line of battle advanced, driving in their skirmishers until we were within fifty yards of the breastwork. They were pouring in a heavy fire, but it was all too high and we were all right. But, they in turn were not faring so well as we. We were putting in a converging cross fire into them and it was about this time, as we found out later, that one of their lieutenants fell with a minie ball in his lungs. We were knocking them off and we could clearly see the Rebs dragging their killed and wounded to the rear of the breastwork. They were game, firing away most of their ammunition, but their marksmanship wasn't equal to their dedication. One of the boys wrote home that "the breastwork was full of them and they were pouring in a vigorous though ineffectual fire. If the Rebel fire had not been most miserably poor, we must have lost ten times as many as we did".

****

ALBERT MCDOUGALD, PRIVATE, COMPANY E

I have had my chance to Try my hand at the
yankees Fighting is the Hardest work I ever
done ... john I saw not the enemy balls like
anything but like a hale storm ... in a windy
day and that the thickest ... I may be in 40
fights I never expect to be in any hotter place
than I was on the Evening of the 28th of April ...
I fired 20 rounds and took sight like as if
I was shooting a beef ...

****

THE UNKNOWN UNION CORPORAL

Colonel Cobham of the 45th Massachusetts at last gave the command that would decide the issue. The regiment was ordered to fix bayonets and to charge the breastwork. We moved out in double quick time and, with every man shouting, simply followed the Massachusetts State Flag down into the ditch and then up again and across the parapet. At almost the same moment, the 27th Massachusetts poured over the wall on its side of the breastwork.

But the Rebs didn't have the courtesy to wait for our visit. They grabbed their knapsacks and blanket rolls, fired a parting volley, and then retreated rapidly down the railroad toward Kinston. Most of their casualties were left behind and it was a complete rout.

We crowded then into the breastwork, loudly cheering and firing our muskets off into the air in jubilation. But we were almost immediately silenced by the sight of the handful of dead Johnnies left behind. For many of our boys from Boston and Dedham and Worchester, this was our first close look at the enemy. One curious young recruit, pushing his way through the crowds of silent men, saw three dead Rebs and noted in a letter home that their "miserable clothing, their haggard faces, long tangled hair, and neglected beards gave them a wild, hardly human appearance". We all thought that such is the nature of traitors; such is the reward for rebellion.

We didn't stay long. Soon we were reformed back into column and began the pursuit. It was late evening now and we came up on a second makeshift barricade that the Rebs abandoned with no resistance. They didn't even return our fire as we advanced, firing volleys on command, but rapidly disappeared on down the railroad toward Kinston in the gathering gloom.

General Palmer looked into the darkening forests to the west and decided that further pursuit was out of the question. Orders were given for a final withdrawal and that was fine with us, for every man was ecstatic over the easy victory. We went back to where the battle had been fought and did as much destruction as we could to the parapet and ditch in the fading light. We were already on our way back to New Bern by 7 P.M., arriving there at midnight in a pouring rain.

✻✻✻✻✻✻✻✻✻✻✻✻✻✻✻

M. CROWDER, PRIVATE, COMPANY F

It's a hard pressed retreat and it don't help none to know that's exactly what it is. We are plumb worn out when Faison halts us on the other side of the swamp. Then, the Colonel, pretty well played out himself, starts marching us back and forth across the railroad track in order to give any Yankee scouts the idea that we are heavily reinforced. It must work, for we see nothing more of the main force.

At 9 p.m., Company C of the 56th and two cavalry companies join us. The Colonel then orders the retreat to continue on through the night to Wise's Crossroads. Here we feel a little safer, for the 24th is there waiting for us. More ammunition and rations are distributed to the men and we don't roll into our blankets until the early hours of the next day.

Casualties are not as bad as they could have been with all the gunfire. The 56th lost three enlisted men killed and one lieutenant mortally wounded. Another wounded enlisted man was left behind in the breastwork and was captured. The Yanks said they lost only two dead and two wounded, but there were Yankees who told us during the truce they counted as many as fifteen casualties on their side. On the day after the battle, we went out under that flag of truce to get the bodies of the three enlisted men killed at Dover. The burials take place on April 30 in the soldier's graveyard at Kinston.

Lieutenant Jarvis B. Lutterloh, with a minie ball through his lung, was carried out of the earthwork by his men during the retreat. He was brought back to Kinston that night in great pain. Word by telegraph is sent to his mother and father in Fayetteville who leave immediately to see him, but they don't get here in time. Lutterloh spends a long, long night, drowning in his own blood, his hand held by his faithful black body servant, Bob. Before the battle, Lutterloh had told Bob that if he should fall, Bob was to return home with the personal possessions, but Bob refuses to leave the bedside. At dawn on the 29th, Lt. Jarvis Lutterloh says "Open the shutters, that I may see the glorious sun once more" and then expires. His mother, father, and the grieving Bob bring the body back to Fayetteville for burial. This ought to be remembered too, for this one family, black and white, will remember it until the hour of their own taking away.

I guess you could say we had been whipped good in our first battle, but we feel we performed well against the enemy. Any way you count it, we were outnumbered pretty bad, but we had defended the crossing with spirit and determination. Colonel Faison praised the officers and men for their gallant conduct under fire. Captain Lawson Harrill was commended for his coolness and said that "our officers and men behaved most admirably, not one leaving his post or straggling in any way".

Next day, the 25th goes back up and occupies the demolished breastwork at Gum Swamp, so we regain the lost ground after all. But the 56th itself remains encamped just outside Kinston. It is peaceful here, but we are all a bit worried that First Gum Swamp might be just a foretaste of what we could expect. And then we lose the services of our surgeon, who is ordered to report to the General Hospital at Farmville, Virginia. His replacement, Charles Ladd, isn't due to arrive until mid May. Even then, some days pass before he can assume duty because he is sick himself.

On May 1, we march out of Kinston at daybreak and head back up to Wise's Crossroads to support the 25th just beyond at Dover Station. There are now two full regiments at Gum Swamp and we feel the area is now secure. Days pass and nothing happens. Private Davis writes to his wife that "We have a heavy force now waiting for them, expecting a general engagement daily ... They never can drive us away from here". And then on May 16, Cooke's North Carolina Brigade steams into Kinston from Charleston, South Carolina to join us. We are ready for them now if they come again.

On May 17, the 56th marches through Gum Swamp and on the 19th, we are once again back in the repaired breastwork at Dover Station. The 25th withdraws several hundred yards to the rear and remains there in support. They had worked hard on restoring and extending the breastwork, which now even includes a piece of light field artillery. We are safe now against anything short of a full scale attack.

We keep hearing rumors. The men talk about Colonel Faison's scare at this very place and it's told around that he is still skittish. He's telling his staff it's a dangerous place to occupy; that only a cavalry picket should be here; that the Yanks can come roaring out of the swamp at any point; that we can't cover the whole front from Kinston to New Bern without weakening the picket post at Dover itself; that, in short, any Confederate force at Dover Station is a blood sacrifice, a lamb for the slaughter, thanks to the stupidity of brigade and division. And (we could hear him adding as he got really wound up) sacrificed not as any part of any brilliant plan with glorious victory as the outcome, but sacrificed needlessly, uselessly, with nothing to show for it but the missing face in the ranks.

But for us, there seems no more blood sacrifice, no more death in the air at Dover Station this May. The spring has come in strong now, with pleasantly cool damp mornings and just a touch of mid-summer heat at the noon day hour. The earth is a riot of small flowers and green leaves all bursting forth at its peak. At the ugly gash across the railroad tracks at Dover Station, there is only quiet and order now. The swamp is still enough outside the perimeter too, except on these hot afternoons when a thunderstorm will come crackling overhead, and then the thunder and the wind come out of all that tangled wild wood just a-boomin'.

CHAPTER SIX

FRANK ALEXANDER, CAPTAIN, COMPANY B

May, 1863. When I was a child, I was accidentally burned by a hot iron. I was very young, so I don't remember it, but oh, how it fried my hand, crisped my fingers, blackened my nails. That small hand of little Frank Alexander was branded for life. I'll carry these scars to my grave. But, it's not like the scar this month and year gave me. May, 1863.

Before it all happens, some of the officers - company commanders and junior officers, mostly - are talking about what might happen. And one of them says, "Well, Captain Alexander, what do you make of it all?" And I say that not a man in the nation is in doubt of an impending crisis looming over us. In Virginia, the Army of the Potomac, under its new commander Joe Hooker, has met a resounding defeat at Chancellorsville, but Old Blue-Light Jackson is seriously wounded in the same battle. In Mississippi, Vicksburg is cut off from support and the city is under siege by the Yankees led by U. S. Grant. Everything seems to me to be building up to the flash point.

In North Carolina, we know the Union staff officers in New Bern are planning something more for us. We can almost see them doing it, just as we do, poring over their maps by candlelight in the wind-stirred tents. We know they are less concerned with Chancellorsville and Vicksburg than with that lonely crossing by the swamp at Dover.

Since everything else is tending toward decision and crisis, we figure that our counterparts on the other side will be a part of it too, even if it will be action lost in the smoke of the greater war sweeping on to its nemesis far off to the north and west. Since they had demonstrated the same fell tendency to do so at Hamilton, Williamston, and Dover, we anticipate another good, hard stomp of the heavy boot on us. We just don't know when or where it will fall.

Later it becomes clear enough. The Union expedition, organized in New Bern in May 1863, has as its objective nothing less than the total annihilation of the strong Confederate force stationed at Dover. There is always a lot of irony in war, but this conflict seems to have exceptional ironies. The Federal commander is General John G. Foster, who had commanded the Union forces in the raid on Williamston and Hamilton the previous November.

Union Intelligence correctly reveals that there are two of our regiments at the Dover Crossroads and so the Union expedition is built up to deal with them - five infantry regiments, four companies of cavalry, and a battery of light field artillery. Their plan is both daring and ambitious, requiring hours of staff work in camp and sharp timing in the field. The 5th, 25th, and 46th Massachusetts Infantry regiments, supported by the cavalry, will attack the Dover Crossing from the east; this assault will be commanded by a Colonel George Pierson. At the same time, the 27th Massachusetts and 58th Pennsylvania Infantry, under the command of a Colonel J. Ritcher Jones, after a forced all night march, will fall on the rear of our position. The main assault will envelop the trapped Confederate force, front and rear, in overwhelming force. There will be no chance for us to resist, nor will there be any escape. The end for us will come with finality, with no delay or reprieve. And it will come with the combined assault set for the morning of May 22. So it is planned.

At dusk on May 21, the flanking column of the two Union regiments that will infiltrate to the rear of our position marches first out of New Bern; they have the longer distance to cover before dawn. Their march is an all night, fourteen-mile struggle through the morass of Gum Swamp. A civilian traitor leads them through the maze of clinging vines and water courses until at first light on May 22, Jones' command, wet and tired but fully ready, arrives in line of battle at a position one mile to the rear of the unsuspecting Confederates. The most difficult part of their plan is now completed and with surprising ease.

The morning comes up quiet and fair and we think we are ready for anything they might spring on us. The 56th is at the Dover Crossing, with the 25th stationed some distance to the rear in reserve. Reports had come in late yesterday afternoon that pickets some five miles out front had been driven in by a large Yankee force slowly advancing behind a screen of cavalry up the Dover Road.

Measures are promptly taken by the 56th to be ready for whatever morning might bring. Colonel Faison gives orders to double the guard and Companies D and K are sent into the improved breastwork to make sure everything is ready there for a final stand if it comes to that. We know something is coming, but we aren't sure just what it is, or when it will come, or where it will fall.

At 4:30 A.M., the first advance skirmishers of the main Union column finally arrive at the Dover Crossing. The firing of the pickets in the pre-dawn darkness is the first warning we have of an impending attack. The Colonel immediately orders the entire regiment into the breastwork and to prepare for action. Then we wait under arms for further orders.

At daybreak, the main Union column of three infantry regiments, artillery, and cavalry slowly hove into view and halt a mile from the earthwork. We can see them deploying out to each side in a heavily reinforced line of battle, with the cavalry waiting in reserve. They don't advance right away, only shaking out a line of skirmishers that cautiously approach to open a scattering fire on our fortification. Their main line of battle finally begins a cautious advance to probe our position, but it falls back whenever our fire becomes too heavy.

We stay low, only firing just enough to make them keep their distance. The Colonel and his staff patrol the length of our position, occasionally dodging a stray shot from Yankee sharpshooters hidden somewhere off to the front. The Yankees first probe our left wing, then our center, and then the right wing before they withdraw. An ominous silence settles down along the line - a silence broken only by an occasional, random shot by a picket. The Union drive has completely halted for some unknown reason we cannot fathom.

Two hours have now passed since daylight and the opening of the engagement. The Union line in front of our position finally settles down into an uncanny silence. The Colonel, becoming more concerned with every passing minute, sends a request to the Colonel of the 25th to move his regiment up to cover the exposed right wing of the 56th. But, the 25th has their own doubts and apprehensions about the silence and prefer to remain in reserve some two or three hundred yards to the rear where they can reach the road back to Kinston.

So, Colonel Faison immediately sends three companies outside the earthwork to guard an opening in the swamp a mile off to our right and hopes for the best. The three companies soon disappear in the tall grass and the remaining seven companies remain on guard in the breastwork. Everything in our front remains still and quiet. In the far distance, the Union line stands motionless. A random gust of wind stirring the flags and the occasional courier's horse passing behind their line are the only signs of movement.

The morning passes on in silence. The Colonel becomes increasingly uneasy and the unguarded right wing of the regiment continues to prey on his mind. So, shortly before 10:00 A.M., Captain Robert Graham and a small detail from Company D leave the parapet to reconnoiter the dense underbrush in that direction.

It comes with no warning, with no warning at all. Graham's detail has been gone only a few minutes when suddenly a heavy roll of gunfire breaks out in the immediate rear of our position. Behind a cloud of steadily firing skirmishers, the battle lines of two full Yankee regiments emerge from the woods behind us. At the same moment, the main Union line to our front raise their cheer and begin a rapid charge on our immediate front. A Yankee officer, who later said that the only task was "to gather up the fruits of the victory", was not far wrong.

Every one of the Colonel's imagined fears now comes true with a vengeance. He immediately gives orders for the 56th to abandon the breastwork and fall back upon the 25th. However, this maneuver right out of the textbook at The Point is impossible. The Yankees are already in our rear and, in any case, the 25th has already about faced and is marching hard for Kinston.

We are out of the breastwork in a matter of seconds and in the open, but the road to Kinston is effectively blocked by the two on-coming Union regiments. Colonel Faison then gives orders for the 56th to march on the double up the railroad toward Kinston. This maneuver had saved the three companies on April 28th, but now even this escape route is effectively closed. The Union lines move steadily in on three sides, firing into us from distances as near as forty yards. We doggedly move on up the railroad tracks with the swamp on the right. In spite of our desperate situation, the seven companies keep their formation and return the gunfire as we withdraw from the breastwork and seek the safety of the railroad.

But there is no hope there or anywhere. A railroad cut directly in our path of escape is almost immediately occupied by Yankee infantry who poured a galling, scathing fire into our front. We halt in growing confusion. The Union lines, still firing, now close in from three sides to within a few score yards of our column. The dense smoke of the musket firing drifts across and among us, a white cloud punctured by occasional yellow flashes. No doubt, the poor visibility saves more than one life, but we are taking casualties. One sergeant clutches me by the sleeve, but can only whisper "Cap'n ... Cap'n": other men are looking wildly about and shouting, "We're all goin' to die. We're goin' to die right here". The Parson is tuning up good when a lieutenant falls mortally wounded in front of him; that quiets the Parson down. The fallen officer is left behind.

Adjutant William Hale is wounded in the arm at the same time. Other enlisted men topple forward and sprawl across the railroad ties. We fight hard as the officers shout themselves hoarse with encouragement, but any man here can see we are being enveloped by two full brigades with no hope of escape.

Our discipline and formation has remained intact up to this point. But as the Yankees charge in upon us with fixed bayonets, the 56th suddenly disintegrates as a military unit. Panic sweeps through the ranks. The Colonel maybe has a second to shout a single order to fall back into the swamp, but by then he no longer has a regiment to command. Companies dissolve into squads; squads into individual men concerned with saving their own skin. Some men turn for an instant when they reach the tall marsh grass and trees, pause only long enough to fire at the pursuing Yanks, and then resume their frantic flight through the brambles, briars, and honeysuckle that abound there.

What the brave Union troops drive into the swamp this May morning is a crowd of shoving, shouting, frightened men who run through the clinging vines and reeds, and splash through the knee deep water in absolute and total panic. Years later, I came across General Foster's report on this morning - "(The Confederates) broke and fled in great confusion, taking to the swamps and escaping by paths known only to themselves". One of my men came to me afterward to say, "O, the shame and disgrace of it, Cap'n. Alexander! I grieved deep, hard for them all, I wept bitter tears for every one of them with every briar I tore from my tattered hide after it was all over".

Hundreds of wildly cheering Yankee infantrymen push on into the swamp in happy pursuit to find scores of our boys cowering in the reeds, hiding beneath logs, peering out from behind trees. Many prisoners are taken in the first few minutes of the debacle. The Yanks find no resistance; Confederates are scarcely encountered before they throw down their weapons and throw up their hands in supplication; and any who want to escape capture simply continue their own wild flight on into the deeper recesses of the swamp.

Once safe from that immediate capture, those who have escaped so far pause to catch their wind, to look on silent, brooding fields of cat tail and arrow weed, and listen to the distant shouting and cheering back at the railroad track. Then, most men look to their officers or sergeants for further direction. It is due only to their presence of mind that as many men escape as they do. Hearing demands for surrender from a few feet away in the dense underbrush, Captain Graham and Adjutant Hale order a few of their men to surrender while they quietly lead a larger number off in the opposite direction. I myself lead another group of 110 men to safety. But others are not so fortunate.

One Yankee squad, led by a sergeant, discovers a group of our boys with one officer resting at the foot of a large tree. According to the account of the Yankees themselves, the officer (dressed in an impeccable grey uniform, polished boots, a plume in his hat, proud as any peacock and surrounded by worse ragamuffins than you could find in any stew or dive in New York) says he isn't about to surrender to a sergeant; he will only surrender to another commissioned officer. "Do you then give your word you'll stay here 'til I come back with one?", the Federal sergeant asks in his nasal twang. "My word, even to a Yankee Hirling, is good" comes the lofty reply. So, the sergeant has to go all the way back to the railroad, bring a lieutenant to the tree, where the officer, still true to his word, freely hands over his sword. Such things occur all through the brush, up to a mile into the wilderness, before the Yanks give up the hunt. Many of the boys who do escape the Yanks also escape the Confederacy, for many become lost in the swamp as evening draws in, "spent the night with the mosquitoes", and only find their way into our lines to the west the next morning. The three companies detached to a position a mile away are not engaged at all in the action and provide a center of a sort around which the survivors can gather the day after the battle.

The Union force returns triumphantly to New Bern the following day, driving a large crowd of dejected Confederate prisoners before them at the head of the column.

The 56th has received an almost fatal blow. Almost half of the men have been taken prisoner. In addition to 165 prisoners, the Federals have captured the regimental ordinance wagon, twenty ambulances, eighty muskets, the twelve pounder howitzer in the breastwork, twenty-eight horses, and 11,000 rounds of cartridges. While none of the field officers have been killed or captured, all of them have lost their personal horses. All seven companies suffer casualties, but hardest hit is Company B, with twenty-one enlisted men and two lieutenants still missing two days later. In comparison, the Union force in this Second Battle of Gum Swamp has only eight casualties.

The usual storm of recrimination and blame for the defeat now bursts forth on all levels and in all directions. Most of the enlisted men blame the untimely withdrawal of the 25th for the defeat, but the press bear in on Colonel Faison with blood in their eye. Our officers and men are firmly confident that our brigade commander, General Robert Ransom, will surely exonerate the Colonel and indeed salvage the reputation of the 56th. This delusion is rudely shattered a few days later when the 56th learns that the blame for the disaster is not going to be excused, shared, or explained by anyone. Morale plummets to the depths. One of our officers says that "Ransom in a day has lost the popularity that he has been making for months ... he is not willing to make any sacrifice at all to save us from ignomy".

Those men who remain rally around Colonel Faison, who angrily demands a formal court martial to examine the true cause of the defeat. We are confident that any board of inquiry or investigation will surely find that we had done our duty under impossible circumstances. Driven into ourselves, we slowly and painfully begin the long process of restoring our own self confidence and unit pride with no support or encouragement.

But the defeat rankles, and the 56th is subject now to the ridicule and the scorn of other regiments. For we failed the final test, the ultimate reckoning for any military unit and we feel that it is the end of the Great Adventure for us.

That is the real fear we have in the days that follow, the fear that surfaces in heated discussion or in quiet reflection. We find that the war holds a grimmer fate than death on some honored field of glory. We find that it can bring failure, as well as success, cowardice as well as courage, shame as well as gallantry. To many of the men, the war is not developing quite in the manner they expected. Doubt begins to work its insidious way into minds that before had boasted of unquestioning loyalty to The Cause. The North no longer is seen as some distant threat lurking off on the horizon that can be readily dealt with by a multitude of Bull Runs and Chancellorsvilles.

The North coming to us at Gum Swamp is rather some raw, elemental force that relentlessly sweeps over us, leaving nothing in its wake but a flotsam of broken bodies and spirits. But there is something else too - some secret play of the cards that we know nothing of, some silent weaving of the loom over which we have no control. It is almost as if we, among all the regiments in both armies, are fated to a never ending succession of long marches, dismal camp grounds, enforced idleness. And when the violence of war does come to us at last, it is to deal with us casually, bluntly, blindly, even with a hint of impatient finality. Even our ending will come as an afterthought, an almost invisible footnote to the great saga of the war itself. This is the burden every man carries after that May.

As we turn our backs on Dover Crossing and Gum Swamp, we know we will be forever haunted by those hours of near annihilation in a coastal marsh at a lonely railroad crossing. For some of us, heads down in the driving rain or huddled close over our campfires in the dead of night, there will be other things to discuss, other things to look forward, or behind to.

But always for some of us, with the passing of every winter, we look with apprehension for it all to come once again down upon us, but this time for the final time, out of the laughing forests, in the spring time of the year.

***

We are back in Kinston a few days later, trying to rest, to pull back together and sort it all out. One night, a group of the officers are talking and arguing it over again, just as we did before, back and forth, when we notice The Prophet, leaning against a tree, not saying a word. "So, Lieutenant Davis, what do you make of it all?"

And he says "Military operations change, politics change, men change, but the earth remains here forever. So, long after this battle and these men are forgotten, Gum Swamp and Dover Crossroads will be here. America will be here.

"Ten years, fifty years, even a century or more from now, some traveler will pass through Kinston. It will be a new age and the town will be much changed - newer gas lights; newer wagons and carriages; certainly newer fashions - all as far different from us as we are from our grandsires of the Revolution. Streets will be crowded on market day; men will be as vain with commercial concerns as we once were; women as beautiful and as distant as they are now; and those few enlisted men of the 56th buried here will be sleeping still, both by night and day. It will be quieter come Sunday mornings; then Main Street will be a little more like it is now.

"Our traveler will ride on down to Dover in just an hour or two. He will have no expectation of encountering any ghosts at all along the busy new plank road until, without warning, he will suddenly cross the railroad bridge and then he will know that he is near them. Just off the plank road, he will find them. The older road, still crossed by the tracks, is where he will stop. Perhaps there will be a few ramshackle buildings and advertising signs; perhaps one or two drives; perhaps one tired old black man leaning against the wall of a locked store, smoking a pipe and desperately looking for his own future in the earth. The traveler will still hear the horse's hooves, the wagons rattling on the turnpike just a few hundred feet away, but he will not notice any of these."

"What he will notice will be what we remember so well - the tremendous blue sky rearing and vaulting high overhead, the long horizon reaching out to infinity, the soft sandy soil underfoot giving way, the railroad tracks lying gravely supine under the beating sun. And then he will know that he is here, in the right place at last. Off in the distance, a faint line of trees shimmer in the heat waves; that is what will be left of Gum Swamp.

"The swamp will be still silent and deep, undisturbed save by the redwing blackbirds flocking there in the spring, the gentle nodding of the reeds in the light breeze, the minuscule movement of water among the rushes. No one will go there but a few hunters, who with their rifles and shotguns carried at Right Port Arms, advancing with cautious step on the quaking earth, will maintain an old tradition here, whether they know or not, whether America remembers or not. And with these men too, the swamp will remain faithful, and secret, and remember."

"Then it will be time for our traveler to ride on to New Bern and shop perhaps for an hour in the new market in the grand new city, to purchase a new saddle and bridle perhaps, before having a steak dinner and coffee at the tavern. And perhaps after that, he will rest and read his newspaper, play with his child, make love to his wife, safe enough now in her soft arms, in his own time, with all those spirit memories left back in the night swamp; they, safe as well in their own hard and lasting reality. The darkness will protect each from the other."

"I don't believe in no ghosts, Lieutenant."

"I am speaking only of us, of the few of us left, standing now in silence over these reaching flames, tonight."

He says no more and we stare into the fire, dreaming our own dreams, but we do not understand, we do not understand at all.

CHAPTER SEVEN

N. B. COMBS, PRIVATE, COMPANY H

It's about a week after the battle, and we're still not much more than two or three company strength, I guess, when we get new orders. I get the word first confidential-like from the orderly, who said, "Now, privates ain't supposed to know this, but I guess it's all right to tell one of them". Shoot, he had done told half the camp getting here to Private N. B. Combs, but I was the first one in Company H to know it.

And what orders they are! The whole brigade is to leave at once for Richmond! And we are to be attached to the Army of Northern Virginia! That shakes us out of the old doldrums, all right. All kinds of rumors are going around that Lee is building up the Army for a march across the Potomac that will end the war for once and all - maybe even a campaign up north that will end in the capture of Baltimore or New York or maybe even puttin' the chain on the neck-bone of the Original Gorilla hisself. There are no limits to our imagination. Three days' rations are given to the men and special rail passage to Richmond is arranged by the government. On May 28, all the wagon trains leave for Richmond as we board the freight cars in Kinston. Cap'n. Graham writes home, "I am rather glad of the exchange as I had looked with horror on spending the hot summer months in these barren sand hills though I expect privations that I have not been used to in North Carolina". But most of us never think of no privations. It is relief enough to get out of here and away from that God-awful swamp. We had never heard of Gettysburg.

The trip on the train lasts all through the long, hot, dusty day and it is only late that night when we steam slowly at last into Petersburg, Virginia. The city is silent and still at this hour, without a light burning in ary winder, and we don't have much chance to see what looks to be just another sleepy Virginia town on the banks of a river with the outlandish name of Appomattox.

Next day, we march on up to Richmond and stack arms at Camp Lee. We figure on maybe a day's rest before we'll head on up to Fredericksburg to join up with Lee's Army. But then we get more orders and this is the second shock of the week, though as many of us are relieved as are downcast over it.

Old Jeff Davis's fearful of leaving Richmond all undefended during a summer of invasion of the North - no telling what Hooker would do with the Army of the Potomac. Marse Robert might protest and he does so, but the War Department goes right ahead and orders us not to go north with the rest of the army, but just sit tight near Richmond to protect the capital for the duration of the campaign.

So, on June 2, back we go to Petersburg to wait for our assignment. While the War Department tries to figure out what we'll be good for, we go on east to a one horse place called Ivor and then, on June 13, march cross-country to Drewry's Bluff on the James River. We camp there for several days in the permanent quarters built by troops stationed there last winter. Most of us have never seen permanent quarters like these before: log cabins, fireplaces, tables and chairs, clay chimneys. It's fine, almost like being back at the house.

On the 13th, too, the brigade gets a new commanding officer. General Robert Ransom is promoted to major general and transferred out; his replacement is his brother, General Matthew Ransom. Bob Ransom hadn't been popular with none of us, not after he backed down from taking up for us after Gum Swamp. Now this new commander, Matt Ransom, he had been a distinguished U.S. senator before the war and we like him a lot better. He's strict on discipline, but other than that, he's fair, and kind, and treats us with some decency. Never did two such dissimilar chicks hatch from the same hen.

We stay at Drewry's Bluff about a week. There are a few gripes, of course. Although we are only five miles out of Richmond, we still don't have no quartermaster. Firewood is rationed and a lot of us have to go a-foraging. But the paymaster is able to make his rounds and many of the men are paid off.

On the 17th, we return to Petersburg on new orders. There's a note of urgency as we head north on the Petersburg-Richmond Turnpike to Halfway House. Arriving there on the 21st, we occupy some more vacant winter quarters and wait for the next blow to fall. Less than a week later, the word comes. Reports had been received at Richmond of a Yankee advance from the east, of Spoons Butler's Army of the James. Ben Butler was called "Spoons" ever since he descrecrated the fair women of New Orleans and stole their silver. The government has a price on his head and the unit that captures it will have all the glory it can stand from them fair women.

On the 26th, we march through the night to the old battlefield of Seven Pines to ready defenses against this threat. But the threat never comes and on the 29th, we're put to work taking down Yankee breastworks McClellan had built there back in '62. The only Yankees we see here are skulls, leg bones, arm bones, such as that. We arrange them on the side of the trench in patterns and displays, and they keep us company as we take down their work. Don't have too much to say to us, though.

But we spoke too soon. Them old skulls knew more than we did; they didn't set there a-grinnin' in the sun for nuthin'. Turned out there is a threat, after all. In fact, there's a big Union force in the area and it's headin' for Richmond as fast as it can go, though at Old Spoons Butler's rate, my old granny could have beat it there. But it wasn't nothin' to laugh at. Under the command of General John Dix, it's made up of over three full brigades of infantry, reinforced with artillery and cavalry. We can muster up only three under-strength infantry brigades to counter that. On the other hand, we have D. H. Hill, who knows Spoons is a timid fighter on the field of honor. Hill knows he don't have the men to spread up and down the line between Petersburg and Richmond, so he puts us all into one mail fist and decides to hit the head of the approaching Yankee column as they come up on us. The time for the attack is set for July 2 and the place is Bottom's Bridge on the Chickahominey. But Ransom's Brigade and the pitiful remnant of the 56th will be carefully kept in reserve, out of harm's way. I don't think it's compassion or anything like that; they just don't feel we're front line troops after Gum.

Anyway, about sunset on July 2, Hills' mail fist hits the Yankee column at Crump's Farm, not far from the bridge. The Yankee infantry, never expecting what hits them, are routed at the first attack. After about an hour of shelling to cover their retreat, the Yank artillery withdraws too. We follow up on them hard and that's not hard to do, for they leave a trail of spanking new uniforms, brand new shoes and boots, canned sardines and lobsters - you never saw the like. I saw one of our fellers load up on a heapin' armload of boxes of cigars and then drop them for a load of mayonnaise and then throw down that load for a load of handkerchiefs. I don't know who's the craziest - the Yanks or us. We chase them all the way to the James where they're safe with their gunboats.

This ain't too bad, we all agree; being in reserve has its advantages. Ransom's Brigade only had two casualties and the 56th didn't have a single man hurt. The Yanks ran so fast they lost only fifteen prisoners and six men killed. After it's all over, we return that night to the Chickahominey and stack arms on the river bank. It's there we first hear that there is a big fight going on up in Pennsylvania. And there is no news at all from Vicksburg.

On July 11, we return to Petersburg and occupy what one officer called "a pleasant rustic encampment" just outside the city; in other words, a wooded grove, with plenty of fresh running water, good shade trees, soft grass to cuddle up to. And you could get you a woman or a drink if you had a mind to. Smith keeps talking about it, but I stay away from that 'un. Over in Rutherford County before the war, they say he popped a man's eye-ball out and grinned while he was doing it.

So for the next few weeks, we stay there, the only reminder of the war being the distant mutter of Yankee gunboats shelling the James River defenses. Gradually, we build back up the strength of the old 56th. New recruits are sent up to us from North Carolina and most of the men captured in the swamp are exchanged and return to the regiment. We are purty soon near about what we were, except for the memories and the bad dreams.

The daily round of camp life drifts on. Private Charles Davis in the commissary turns down an offered lieutenancy because he don't want the hard marching of infantry service that goes along with it; we understand, but don't respect his point of view. Cap'n. Henry F. Lane of Company G is still under arrest and confinement; he sure must've crossed the Colonel something awful. Major Henry

Schenck's absent again on sick leave. But, we're doing all right. Health's pretty good and we get supplies as we need them. We even get new blue-grey jackets issued that resemble Yankee uniforms at a distance.

And on July 25, the court martial requested by Colonel Faison at last reaches its decision about his responsibility for the disaster at Gum Swamp. The Colonel's found not guilty of any charge of neglect of duty in the presence of the enemy. That lifts everybody's spirits considerable.

On July 28, with Lee's Army safe back in Virginia, the brigade's ordered to return to Weldon, North Carolina. There was a chance it wasn't going to be just a peaceful homecoming. We are supposed to reinforce the 49th and 24th N.C. regiments that had briefly sparred with a Yankee force just east of Weldon. As soon as we get to the station, we form up into line of battle in case they want to push it. But they had just been probing along the defenses there and had already withdrawn.

For the next three weeks, we travel all across the coast and piedmont of the state and have a lot to do, though none of it's very important. On August 12, after spending eleven days in the small village of Garysburg, we go by easy stages to Halifax Court House and next day board steamboats there for a leisurely 73-mile passage down the Roanoke. After this pleasant journey, we go ashore at still ravaged Hamilton late on the afternoon of August 13. We spend two days repairing breastworks there in case Foster comes back with his raiders, though there wouldn't have been much left for him to take.

Then, on the morning of the 16th, we march back across country to Halifax. All that leisure hurt. It's hot and dry; it takes us two full days with frequent halts just to get our breath. Once in Halifax, we pick up some new recruits - one in my company, Charles Elliott, is just a stripling fresh off a fence-post at the farm. Elliott had been lounging around army posts and the like, hankerin' to git in by hook or crook, and finally makes it into the old 56th. Said while he was in "Hi Point", Longstreet's Corps come through on their way to reinforce Bragg and they told him, We`ll put the Yanks in a trot like we've been chasing them out of Virginia. On the 19th, we board the trains agin but head the other way from north Georgia, riding the rails instead to Weldon, then marching again for Garysburg.

Arriving there on the 20th, we at last stop all our migrating about and set up tents in a nearby oak forest.

During all this time of marching, boating, and riding from any-where to everywhere, Major Schenck at last resigned his commis-sion; he had tried hard, but all his wheezing and gasping with old bronchitis finally got to him and Surgeon Cox said he could no longer take it. Schenck's place is replaced by Major John W. Graham out of Company B.

On the same day Graham gets promoted to major, the paymaster visits the 56th. It appears there's a growing scarcity of printed paper, those printed vouchers. So a number of the men, offi-cers at that, have to write out their own vouchers by hand on what-ever scraps of paper they can find on the side of the road, out of bird's nests, even torn off strips from letters from home. On the other hand, supplies become more plentiful during the next four weeks. On September 25, the quartermaster issues several compa-nies new clothing. And the following week, we receive new paper, stationery, and envelopes. So we figure things aren't as bad as they seem. And we're doing all right, any one can see that. It looks like it's going to be a good year, a good fall, and we're back home in the Old North State where we belong. Yes sir, wherever kin-folks are, that's home.

All through that late summer of 1863, we continue to regain our strength, even the confidence we had lost in the spring. On September 6, with the regiment once again at Weldon, Charlie Davis writes to his wife:

> I cannot agree with you in your belief that the
> decisive blow will soon be struck and that to our
> ruin. The yanks may overrun every state but we will
> conquer our independence some day and then ho! for home
> and the humble life for mine - to settle down on a
> little farm with my dear little wife in a vine wreathed
> cottage; to see the sportive lambs gamboling on the
> green; to have sleek cattle and horses and to be
> independent and happy the rest of my life.

Some of the officers are hopeful at this time, too. Captain Robert Graham of Company B, writing of William W. Holden's anti-war editorials in THE RALEIGH STANDARD states, "I think his editorials are rather gloomy at times, as a great many call the present. I don't think we are in such a desperate condition after all, hardly as bad off as when New Orleans fell".

In September of 1863, the South, in spite of Gettysburg, is more than holding its own in the east; despite Vicksburg, the Army of Tennessee is still together and a force worth reckoning with. Cap'n Alexander, who has been to college, tells us that nowhere had the South been beaten as bad as the Revolutionary armies were against the British in the South less than a hundred years ago. And while we had learned what defeat is like, our campaign in Virginia and the verdict of the court martial investigating the Colonel's conduct gives us all renewed confidence in ourselves and what we can do when properly led.

We begin to feel that maybe we will triumph in the end - over the enemy, over ourselves if need be, over fate, if it has to be. And through it all, we will remain Gentlemen. Yes, we will remain Southern Gentlemen through the entire ordeal, for this is the code of our generation. We have no idea of total war, or the animal beast in the heart of every man.

Of course, there are animal beasts among us - like Smith and some others. There are those in any army. The 56th has more than several, no doubt about that, rougher than a cob. But it wearn't just them; it was the times and places that are to blame for what happened.

Like Hamilton or Williamston. We had been back through those little towns a time or two since getting back from Virginia. Lord, it was a sorrowful sight - chimneys standing all forlorn; big old piles of brick; women and children all gaunt and hollow-eyed begging for anything to eat. Those towns had been cleaned out good by Old Foster. Our hearts went out to them, for we knowed what it's like to go without.

But it was something else about those civilians. It wasn't just their tattered clothes and blankets; their starving faces; their wasted village. It was the hopelessness in those eyes, like it didn't make any difference any longer what anybody did, that the only thing that mattered was something to fill your belly and keep warm at night. Nothing else really mattered. Maybe we picked up on some of that attitude.

And then Spoons Butler, up in Virginia, showed us on his retreat how good the Good Life could really be. There it was for the taking - all them tins of sardines and lobster and mayonnaise. You took while the getting was good and that carried you on one more day, at least. We had scroungers, slackers, and scavengers that had a field day, but we were all a bit of it too. Hamilton and Williamston showed us what to avoid; the scroungers and scavengers showed us how to avoid it. I guess that was where and how the pattern was set firm in our minds. I guess that was what was to blame for what come next. You can explain it; you can excuse it; you can even understand how it happened. Then why did we lose our soul in doing it? How could we look at those two villages and then do the very same? How could we derile the Yanks and then become worse than them? The scavenger, the slacker, with his mouth full of ham and new boots on, he knows the answer better than us, but were we any better? Oh, that old animal beast that we just couldn't do without, or God Almighty help us, keep from becoming...

CHAPTER EIGHT

FESS SMITH, SERGEANT, COMPANY F

That sun-of-a-bitch Combs has no call to go around saying we're scroungers, scavengers. Who in the hell does he think he is? Didn't he take his share too? Where was he when it was a-goin' on? I'll tell you where - in there with the rest of us, in on the same take, he was. I'd bust his lip quick as I would look at him. Shit!

During the last of August, 1863, new orders come down. Companies H and E are sent off from the rest of the regiment and ordered off to Halifax. There, they have to guard the building of the Confederate Ram, the ALBEMARLE, at Edward's Ferry. The rest of us are ordered to report to various stations in the central part of the state. There, we're told to enforce the conscript law for the next several months.

We dread it at first. Arresting deserters and enforcing the law, well, it might be necessary, but it's still distasteful. But we soon find out there's benefits to it that we hadn't looked for.

The 56th works over a big area - nine counties in the piedmont and mountains on a regular basis. What we miss the first time, we get the second and third. You can read in the reports how well we did: 2,000 men arrested and sent to the front in just four months. That's about the same as a brigade or more in fresh soldiers, though I won't answer for the quality. Thirty-five more are killed or wounded while resisting arrest or ... well, I'll tell you what's truth.

Over in Randolph County, for one, there's a band of outlaws or deserters, though they call themselves patriots. Any how, we bust them up, catch their leader, take him, try him at a drum-head and have him shot just as we're leaving the area. We all have no questions about it. They're just deserters, renegades, trash. But sometimes the look they give us...well, I think it gets to our officers and to some of the enlisted men. Pure hate, it is. Don't stop us none - off they go to the war or the jail, hands trussed behind if need be; hog-tied in the back of a supply wagon, if has to be. But that look in the eyes. One company commander of the 56th writes home: "It cannot be denied that among the deserters are some of the bravest men of our Army - men that have been tried under fire. Our leaders do not seem to think that the morale is as great a portion of the army as Napoleon thought". But what would Old Bony have done with them?

Oh, maybe after a while, it hardens us just a bit. You see, we're army, disciplined, armed. These are just civilians, most of them. As a rule, they dasn't dare resist. That makes it easy - maybe too easy. After a while, we don't ask too many questions; just do and take. Then, it gets easier. By the time we leave the piedmont and head into the mountains, the die is cast. There are a lot of Yankee sympathizers we call "Buffaloes" in the mountains and that is even less call to ask questions - we just go and take. The goverment itself has a name for it - impressing. Well, we impress the hell out of them.

It's easy enough. Old man sittin' on the porch, his woman out behind the house with the warsh pot with her hand on her face; but we don't bother much with them. Look in the house; under the house; in the barn loft; down by the creek. You can generally find the boy and if he was 12 and over, he'll serve. Sometimes the danged fool will be standing right out in the porch yard where he can be taken up easy. Any how, off Little Billy Boy will go to the war with nothin' but the clothes he was wearing. Makes no difference any old how, for he's a liar and a traitor or he wouldn't be there. Ma and Pa a-cryin' and a-cussing until they see us not just taking their young blood, but getting the government's ten per cent too, although it is, to tell the truth, near about all they have - apple brandy, beef, milk, honey. Sometimes they'll say they's loyal, have a son with Bragg or Lee, but it makes no difference. We take it anyhow. When we go back to the piedmont, we're experienced and fall like the plague of locusts on the a-rabs. We take particular pains with Unionist counties like Wilkes, but we don't make no exceptions. So many horses, mules, jack asses, cows are impressed and used in the 56th that one soldier says he reckons he's serving in a Critter Company now.

It gets pretty bad, I'll admit that much. Governor Zeb Vance even writes to Old Jeff about us, says we robbed whole districts and reduced the civilians to the verge of starvation. Said cattle and horses have been taken from loyal men, carried to the next county over, sold, and the cash divided up among us. It's a good business - officers and men make a right good heap of money out of it. And them officers are in it too, thick as thieves. Faison, Luke, Graham - company officers too. They turn the blind eye at first, then they start a-grabbin'. The Prophet looks on it all with his calf eyes, but then he takes his fare cut too, just like the rest of us.

And this is what it was about, isn't it? We send their boys off to the army, then whut's in it for us? I'll tell you whut. Whut we desarve, whut they desarve, that's whut. Up in that hayloaf in the barn, where we prick the bastard out on his bare ass with the old bayonet, Draggin' him out the door, here comes his sister, a-screamin', and a-clawin', and a-carryin' on about her brother. Meybe I shouldn't do it, but I grab the little bitch and slap her lopper-jaw for her sassin', her gettin' up, wiping the blood off her mouth and one hand tryin' to cover her knobby little boobies with her tore shurt. Hell, I drag her into the stall, throw her down in all that horse shit, suck her little titties raw, then give her what her Mama wants in the bargin. Lay the old Heavy Artillery to her, Hot Dam.

You have to see, these are civilians all of them; traitors some of them; we just take what we need, maybe a little more; and if we sell off what we can't use, pocket the money, it's all fare in war like love, like they say. Lettin' on like we're some kind of outlaw band ourself don't show where we come from, what we're about. Old Zeb threatenin' to call out the State Militia to drive us out of the state. Where did he think the Old 56th come from any how? Finally, there was boards of inquiry and orders coming down from Division and we have to give back what impressed property we had not already ate up or sold. It's a shame the way poor soljers serving their country are treated.

There's two sides to it. Lamuel Wright in the regiment writes a letter home; in it he tries to explain what it's really like:

> when one of us goes out we boath go, when one of us stan
> gard we both stand thare is aheap of deserters about here ...

the People a bout here are nerely all union people half of them
are deserters some of them get very mad when we go to thare
house 1 nite before last we had to Press our nites loging and
do our own cookin and some treat us well they are a feared of
us thare is so many deserters here that the home guard is a
feard to go without a heape of them or some of us ...

We have to give a lot of it back, but you know how the army is,
we squirrel a lot of it away and are pretty well supplied right up to
the end of '63. What we hadn't got off of the civilians, we got from
commissary and quartermaster, who come through too. We got regular issues of clothing - Companies E, G, and I at the end of the year
got all the clothing they needed, all the way from officer's caps to
shoes for the enlisted men. And any one who says money was traded
under the table is just a dam liar.

On October 28, while all this was a-goin' on, General Matt
Ransom asks that the 56th be reassigned back to the brigade then
sittin' at Weldon. Probably it's a ploy to bust up our little op-pre-a-
tion. Anyway, what with Matt on the wire and Zeb writin' letters to
the President, finally George Pickett agrees and routes the request
on up to the War Department to cut the orders. But you know how
the army is. Takes forever to get those orders cut. But we all admit
it's wrong, we're sorry as we can be. And we won't do them things
never no more. Just one more chance was all we was asking for.
And they give us that one chance. We're so grateful for the one
chance to show we're real soljers and not them thieves and robbers
them suns-of-bitches in Raleigh is a-calling us.

And so just one month after that, we're back in the piedmont on
our best behavior really goin' to town in more ways than you can
shake a stick at. Lord, the caterwauling and screeching of them
women; them damn boys a-cryin' for their mommies and then runnin' home soon as your back was turned; never knowed who your
enemy was, 'cept it was night-about all of them. So we get more of
their brandy and honey and boy and horse - we need it moren they
do and if we make a tidy bundle of cash on the side out of it agin -
well, thats war, ain't it? If you misbelieve it, then jest read Wright's
letter agin. That says it, don't it? And if it'll help for me to say it
agin, then I'm sorry agin that it happened; I was even sorry when I
was takin' my fair share of the loot. But I take it anyway, with tears

jest a-shinin' in my eyes and a big grin on my face. Now explain that un if you can.

Any way, Pickett finally has to make a personal demand and a couple of weeks later we're on our way back to Weldon to rejoin the brigade. And we're fat and lively, I tell you, with money to clink in our pockets.

As the year ends, Private Patterson takes a break from what little work he does and writes by candlelight:

Dear father & mother brother & sisters I seate me self to drop you a few lines to in form you that we are well an hoping when these lines comes to hand that may find you all well ... we have not heard from home yet we want to hear very bad the rest is geting letters but us ... I want to no whether you are don soing wheat or not...and whather jane is working at the factory yet or not Tell her to take good care of her filley and not lend her ... I want you to rite to us we send our best respect to all our friend tell them to rite to us and give us all the news ... rite soon fail not.

There's quite a few of us think back to home with Christmas coming. Lamuel Wright writes a right cheerful letter to his folks as the year ends:

last nite was a cold nite but I was out on a scout and slept in a house tonite is a warm plesant nite and I am in camp Father I want you to take my buggy to Jacob Williss and get it mended and pay him while the confederate money will pass I want it mended A ganst I get home so I can take A mery ride with the girls tel all my friends howdy an tell them I will come & se them when I get home.

So, the second Christmas of the war for us comes and goes. Private Willie Patterson finds it to be a "very dul cristmas hear". So it's a holiday and we have the chance to sit around and look into the campfire and argue about what happened in the past year. On the battlefield, the boys had sure failed, just as I said they would, we all knowed that. And back home, the boys may have broke the law, but it was fun while it lasted.

Of course, one of these very selfsame men, huddled over his far, is sure we had failed, once the taking was over. Rejoicing over the fruits, this old codger with his Bible - The Old Parson, we called him - got to a-preachen' and goes around wild as a buck saying whatever promise we had, was still just that, a promise. And the old

fool, takin' the Good Book too serious, saying that those depredations had to stop, that what was needed was atonement; not giving it
back (of course not!) or "right service", but atonement was needed.
Now I ask you, where does atonement come in? What can it do
now? Did you ever hear the like?

Any saving that could come to this dam outfit now is as hard to
catch, much less hold on to, as any heat from that dam campfire. He
goes around a-shouten' and a-hollern' the life of the spirit must be
paid first in the life of the flesh, rot like that. He says what we had
done has a turrible price in blood. And he says we were the very
ones to pay it. We were the ones, dam hypocrite! Why not take the
fruits and enjoy it; what's past, past. No, he has to talk about refin-
ing, purity takin' place first in the far, a-scaren' the boys to death.
Then, he rants on about the whirlwind and any fool can see the night
is jest as still as still. He's worse than the Prophet over in G
Company; All we need is to get him started, too. Why, nary a man
there can understand what that lunatic preacher's tryin' to say, it's
enuf to drive Jesus hisself crazy.

After a while, I plain just refuse to say nuthin', nuthin' at all.
I'm not going to argue no more. Just smoke the cigar I've carried all
the way from Wilkes County and look into the far. After a while, I
spit, get comfortable like, and grin real big. Them hypocrites ain't
seen nuthin' yet. This war is goin' to go fine. Fine, I tell you what's
truth.

*****

JAMES M. DAVIS, LIEUTENANT, COMPANY G

This fire, burning so grandly forth in this night of the new century, reminds me of one other fire a long way from this Texas
prairie.

And what does it remind you of, Mr. Davis?

It reminds me of a night in the winter of '63. You see, it came to
me.

Came to you?

From out of the night. From out of the fire.

I do not understand.

It was just as the psalmist once sang of other wars, other times.
The night is far spent and most of the men of the company are
asleep when I begin my rounds as duty officer. After completing all

posts (all is quiet and nothing out of order, so I note in the report), I return at last to the fire and taking my gauntlets off, I hold my hands out over the flames.

I have been there some time when young McNeely comes over, like some wandering lost soul. He had been promoted to first lieutenant just a few days before, but I have not congratulated him or anything like that. I can tell he is depressed and disturbed, so I say nothing at all until he is ready. And at last he looks up at me with that bright, quick look of perennial youth and says,

"Well, Jim, the boys say you can prophesy the future; look into cloudy time; soothe the raging storm with a Welsh incantation; lay raging demons to rest."

He pauses, looking hard into the fire, and then whispers

"Yes, lay demons to rest, that's what they say. What about them demons, Jim? What about the regiment?"

"What about it?"

McNeely looks up then and speaks in the words of a dead man.

"Damn it, what we've been doing near-about all fall. Outright robbery, it was, with worse thrown in, all for these people we're supposed to protect. Livestock driven off; boys put in the Army who ought to be at home; and, Jim, that poor girl on that farm, Jim, she had two brothers off with Longstreet. What are we, anyway? What are we becoming?"

I lean forward and move a stick of wood into the fire.

"Parson says he knows. He says we're going to hell faster than a dog can trot."

"Are we, Jim? Is that where we're going to end up, all of us?"

I think a moment on what I can say.

"You've been in the Army long enough to know the regiment is a machine, like the ones the Yanks are so good at making, but this is a Southern machine and it runs on emotion, not steam, and so it is prey to all the passions of human nature and that is where it jumps a gear."

I can tell from his eyes that he thinks I am avoiding the question; I'm not trying to do that at all; maybe trying to disassociate myself and him too from what has happened, but no, not to avoid it, for it cannot be avoided.

He stands up and faces me before the fire.

"It's no good, Jim. The regiment's no good. I don't belong with it. And you don't either."

"McNeely, the Yanks did as bad or worse at Hamilton and Williamston, you know that. Conquistadores would have been better, for at least they came with a Cross. Not the Yanks."

"You can't lie about it no more, Jim. We did it to our own people, our own people, for God's sake. We failed and you know it."

He abruptly turns then and walks off into the night.

We failed.

CHAPTER NINE

ROBERT MCNEELY, SERGEANT, COMPANY K

Family. That's what we are. More than anything else, Family. Just like me and John. I've known him all my life. He looked after me when I was just a boy and he looks after me now in the 56th.

Now, he'll come down in those future years as Lieutenant John F. McNeely, Company F, but he's just John to me, 'cause he's my older brother. He's the lieutenant and I'm the sergeant in Company K; there's a similar situation over in G, where The Prophet's the lieutenant, but now his brother Charles' only a private in commissary. Captain Harrill in I has a brother, Amos, who's a sergeant in his company. The captain and color-sergeant of Company A are brothers. There are lots of other examples - cousins and in-laws, if not brothers - all through the regiment. It's just as I try to tell John - the 56th is more of a family than anything else.

But, John is pretty distressed about the turn the regiment took last year and I try talking to him about it. He's only a couple of years older than me and we can talk, not like some brothers I've seen. I tell him it was just something that happened and that we have all kinds - good, bad, indifferent boys in the Old 56th. Nearly every one of them in Company K can talk easy to me. "Sergeant McNeely", they'll say, "Can we go a-foraging?" And I not only pass them through the picket line, but even point out the most likely places to go to. But now mind, the only ones I send out have to pay for what they get, or at least ask for it polite-like, with hat in hand. I know that's what they do, 'cause I go with them now and then. I try to tell John that, even though he knows it anyway, but he'll just look at me and walk off.

Of course, the boys all had a world of practice at foraging last fall, no doubt about that. Things got a little bit out of hand, I admit, but they're mostly good boys who live for today, if not for tomorrow. We all have families and girl friends at home. And we're in good health, have good shoes, morale is high now. Private F. C. Patterson, writes home the first of the year to say:

you wanted to know whether we had saw any pretty girls sence we left or not we havent saw many I want you to speak a good word to some of them for me I dont no as much war news as you do it is a bad place here to hear news we drill some on a larg cannon we drilled some yesterday tha has ben some cold wether hear we get flower and beaf & some potatoes ...

The whole regiment reunites later in January at High Point. We drill and drill and drill some more. Pvt. L. S. Wright in Company F writes home to say:

... I dont no how long we will stay here we may Stay A long time & we may leave here before you get this letter, we have sent after rashens an amunition some think we was cald to gether to Drill a few days an then go on our old buisness a gane I hope this may be the case ... we are Drilling the recruits drill to thare selves the knight we left Thomasville   we got to Hipoint a bout 83.0 clock in the evening it was very cold and the capt. gave us leaf to hunt a house to stay in and us too and Willis P. Lewis.Daugherty got a good tile room with fier to stay in without any cost it snowed a little that nite, but it is warm and pretty now.

Then late in January, we go on to Goldsboro where we rejoin Ransom's Brigade. We're ready now for whatever spring might bring.

We soon have an opportunity to redeem a little bit of our tarnished military reputation. General Robert E. Lee suggests to General George Pickett that troops in the North Carolina area mount an expedition to seize the main Federal base at New Bern, where all the Yanks are that whipped us at Dover last year. You bet that bit of news perks our interest! Pickett organizes and assumes command of the expedition himself and so on the 28th, Ransom's Brigade is ordered to Kinston to join the big force being assembled there.

We arrive in Kinston on the 30th, where supplies and clothing are requisitioned for those companies of the 56th needing them. We then report to General Montgomery Corse and late that same night join five other infantry brigades, reinforced with artillery, for the march on New Bern. The plan calls for three of Ransom's regiments to circle off to the rear of New Bern, while the 56th and the rest will attack the town from the west.

Our march on New Bern is one long column stretching out of sight on the road, with the 56th detailed as skirmishers in the advance. We are ordered to arrest and hold any civilian that sees us coming up on New Bern; of course, we're good at doing that, 'cause this is what we've been doing all along. So, we march on through the night - 23 miles - down the Dover Road (quiet and deserted now), then through Gum Swamp (dark and spectral in the winter silence), past the railroad track and the breastwork with all its memories, and then on to the east to Sandy Ridge on the road to New Bern. Eight miles beyond Sandy Ridge, we go into camp without encountering a single sign of the Union Army. But we know that just a few miles further, there is a Union outpost at Bachelor's Creek.

We camp there the night of January 31 without fires, so there will be no warning. At 2 A.M. on the first of February, our attack is launched on the outpost at Bachelor's Creek.

Considering the numbers engaged, there can be no doubt to it and surprise is total as we overwhelm their picket line. We're anxious to redeem ourselves after last year's defeats in this same area. Companies B and I are in the main skirmish line and take several prisoners. We occupy the Union blockhouse with no resistance and push right on.

We are on the railroad tracks to the rear of Bachelor's Creek, when a Union train that had been parked there suddenly speeds back down the track with a full head of steam toward New Bern. General Hoke wants to capture and use the train to transport the whole command into New Bern. The 56th is ordered to intercept the train at a railroad bridge, but it makes it through just in time and disappears roaring off to the east with its whistle screaming like the Banshee Herself to spread the warning.

Most of the Yanks at Bachelor's Creek are now in full flight to New Bern, but about a hundred men still hold out in a small fortification. We are busy for a while just looking at what we have got so far. The brigade lost eight killed, fifty wounded, but the prize is worth it. Over 250 prisoners, four pieces of artillery, and all of the commissary and quartermaster supplies at the Union outpost are captured.

Meanwhile, that Union detachment is still holed up in the fortification, surrounded by what must look to them to be an entire Confederate division. However, they stubbornly refuse to surrender and that night, we are posted to cover any attempt of that small garrison to escape. We wait through the night, seeing and hearing at one in the morning a big flash and explosion on the Neuse River as a Union gun boat, captured by another small detail of Confederates on flat boats, is blown up. We all think things could not be going better. We're beginning to show what we can do if given the chance, even if it is only in support. It is wonderful.

At daylight on February 2nd, we are ready to wipe out the Yanks in that fortification. Our assault force is made up of the 30th Virginia infantry on the right of the road, while the 56th and other units constitute the left wing, with all the artillery to the rear. But just as we begin moving to the assault, the Yanks accept a last demand for surrender. The spoils here include a section of artillery with the caisson, 100 small arms, four officers, and 120 men.

We are doing well now and we are jubilant, but we know the heavily fortified city of New Bern itself is in a good situation to defend itself and a harder nut to crack. We wait for hours on end for the second assault column to arrive in the rear of New Bern; however, due to a misunderstanding of orders, that column never does arrive in position. Finally, after thirty-six hours, in sight of the Union main line of defense around New Bern just daring us to come on, we all begin a slow withdrawal back to Kinston. We arrive there on February 5, the 56th Regiment rejoining Ransom's Brigade. We have our prisoners still with us and now look on them with interest.

Some of them look Southern, act Southern, and talk Southern. Yes sir, that drawl stands out from that nasal twang of them New Yorkers and New Englanders like the ears on a mule. They try to hunker down among the rest of the Yanks, but Ransom culls them out with a rake and hauls them up before a court martial. Most of them are middle-age, with grey just starting in their beard, but some of them are just young striplings, like me. Anyway, next thing they know they're being charged with desertion, taking the Oath, and serving in the U.S. Army.

So we're put in formation to witness their punishment - and a mass hanging it is, too, right here in Kinston. Twenty-five of them, no less - off the back of a buck board wagon or horse to speed them on their way. They die by slow strangulation mostly - eyes bulging, faces swelling, bowels soiling their pants, feet kicking. It's awful just to see it, especially the younger ones waiting their turn. After they hang there until they're dead, they're cut down and buried in unmarked graves.

It is all done according to the Law of War and we know that. They're tried and found guilty, which is more than the Yanks are doing for civilians they accuse of bridge-burning and scouting. And King Abe is packing the jails with his suspension of habeas corpus. Still, this is a side of the war we hadn't counted on. These are traitors, true, but they are Southerners too. And though I don't say it, I think some of them may have been inspired to switch sides when they heard what we did last fall. The old war sword seems to be cutting both ways.

The next day, we receive orders to return to Virginia and once more board the trains, arriving in Weldon on February 7. Waiting for us are new orders: Virginia is canceled out and we're to wait at Weldon for further word. That word is a long time coming. At the end of the month, we're still there, occupying the vacant, but comfortable winter quarters erected there in the past.

During our stay at Weldon, we keep ourselves busy with daily exercises in company and battalion drill, with each captain successively acting as regimental commander in order to get the experience. Morale goes up and down. One enlisted man, Private James Elliott, notices that his "officers were kind and treated us well; I had been in the army seven months and had never seen a man bucked and gagged". But, other enlisted men are starting to complain of hardships. By February, a slow drop in morale is becoming evident. A deserter from the 25th Regiment is shot and his body displayed for the march pass, but this sight has little effect on enlisted men such as Private L. S. Wright, who writes home on February 19 that:

I am sory to say that we dont get enough to eat ...I recon we will make out we can live on what we get and the sooner we eat out the Confederacy the sooner the war will Stop. it is a bad place here to get wood and it is powerful cold and both of us ... has to go on

guard to nite we have to guard the horses we will have fier so we
will make out ... you need not rite a bout me coming home I will
come as soon as I can if the war dont stop I dont exspect to get
home soon. if you can you may send us a spoon some times we
draw a few peas then we need a Spoon and thare is none to be got a
bout here it is late and I am so cold I must quit by saying I remain
your sun tel deth.

And then there's something else that happens too. In mid-
February, a detail of twenty-five men from Company F and twenty-
five from Company K are detached from the regiment with orders to
guard Union prisoners of war being taken by rail from Belle Prison
in Richmond on south to Georgia. Our detachment is only responsi-
ble for the prisoners from Raleigh to Branchville, South Carolina
and we're engaged in this duty until March 26. When we report in at
the Raleigh Railyard, first thing we notice is the awfullest smell,
like all the cesspools you can imagine in your worst nightmare. And
it's all coming from a train on the siding, with a long line of box
cars and cattle cars behind it.

The Union prisoners, half starved and half naked, are packed as
many as forty to a box car and fed on nothing but a little corn bread
and meat. In those cattle cars, they live like animals, like wolves, a
raging sea of dark, matted hair and wild eyes. The stink is bad
enough to gag a maggot. Sickness and malnutrition has so weakened
them that most are unable to stand without being supported, just
staggering around and then wilting down without someone holding
them up. Dysentery and smallpox are loose among them and some
of the men in the guard detail from the 56th catch it; Elliott can't
help wondering "why we all did not". Moreover, the prisoners are
desperate; on one occasion, they are screaming, hollering, cussing,
threatening to bust loose. "Shoot me! Kill me!", they yell, daring us,
maybe begging us. We're ordered by some officer to fire into the
seething crowd, but we fire instead over their heads. They all crouch
down then, hands shielding their heads, and back off. But when I
give one boy my own age a rank piece of fatback I have, he wolfs it
down in one swallow and says, with tears in his eyes, "That was so
good. Thank you". He then fades back into the shadows and I never
see him again.

Whenever the train stops to let the prisoners get water from nearby streams, we have to be especially vigilant. They practically tumble out of the cars, holding each other up, and lap the water up like dogs. Every now and then, one of them will make a break for the woods; if they escape our guns, then the bloodhounds usually get them. Some get killed, some get caught, and a few get clean away. But when the prison trains steam out of Branchville, the prisoners who are left on board have little hope then, for the next stop is Camp Sumter, down near Andersonville Station in Georgia.

So here it comes, that old double-edged sword again. We know the Yanks are mistreating our prisoners up north. Southern boys are eating rats and freezing to death without blankets at Fort Delaware. We just hear about it, don't see it, but now these blue bellies on the trains we can see, hear, and smell them. And it seems like neither side really cares any more, not malicious or mean, just don't care. One thing for certain: The side that wins this war will make the loser pay good. I guess what I saw in those cars convinced me that we better win this war. But no matter who wins or survives, it will take a deep Jordan to wash all the filth off from both sides. I felt I'd never be clean again when I got back to Regiment.

On February 26th, the 56th is ordered to return to Franklin, Virginia. We had not been in south side Virginia for over a year and our arrival in Franklin brings many a memory of service on the Blackwater.

Our very first duty on arrival is to march right back across the state line to South Mills on March 2, where we serve as a military guard to a long wagon train filled with commissary stores en route to Franklin. The wagon train and regiment travel day and night, with Captain Graham's Company D serving as the rear guard. There's some fear of a Union interception of such a valuable find and bright fires are lighted all along the river banks so there will be no delay at all at night. But the wagon train arrives safe and sound in Franklin on March 4.

When we get back to South Mills, the brigade and regiment almost immediately receive new orders and we're soon on the road to Suffolk, which is held by a light Union force. We halt for the night of March 5-6 at Sandy Cross, twenty miles from South Mills, with no sign of the enemy.

The next day, we march on to within eight miles of Old South

Quay and on the morning of March 9, pass through the village of
Somerton. At an old church three miles outside Suffolk, we run into
a Union picket post held by dismounted black cavalry troopers. Our
skirmish line advance on them, forcing them to retreat across the
railroad, which we promptly occupy. But, three black troopers, left
behind in the confusion of their withdrawal, can't get to their horses.
They barricade themselves in a house and then open fire on the 56th
as it passes by. This just drives the boys wild. The house is surrounded and fired; when the black troopers, bursting out of the grey
smoke into the light, come off the porch steps, they are shot down in
the door yard. One is killed outright, maybe two. One is wounded,
moaning and rolling scared eyes around, but he don't live long.
Three or four of our men shoot him where he lays and then put a
bullet behind the ear for good measure.

We talk it over that night and most of the men feel it's just necessary to kill every Negro taken in Federal uniform. There's a strong
feeling that the Yanks are using our own Negroes against us in
hopes of inciting a slave insurrection, like Nat Turner and John
Brown tried to do. Most of the boys have just women and children
back on the farm; if they have any slaves at all, the only men on
those isolated farms are Negroes. You see, there is real fear of something like what happened to the French down in Haiti. The Negroes
remain faithful and do not insurrect during the war (they do run
away when they get the chance), but we can't be sure now. I can
understand that part of it. But there is something else.

We take the camp of the black unit, with one piece of artillery
and considerable stores. It had been abandoned in a hurry and everything is there. In the quarters, those Negro soldiers lived just like us.
I'm not talking about their dry canvas tents, their stools and chairs,
their warm blankets, kitchen things - all the things we didn't have.
It's something else. There are two or three letters there, probably
written for them, to families up north, references to more family
down south, but every letter talks of Freedom. And there are personal things, like trinkets and pictures. The Prophet is dreaming
away there with papers in his hand, and I catch him looking at a tin-
type of a beautiful octoroon, well dressed, long black hair, the smile
of an angel. The white trash in the regiment always says Negroes
don't have souls; well, most of us grew up with them and know bet-

ter. And these are not Yankees either, but our own people,
Southerners like us, fighting like we are, for Freedom. It's the old
double-edged sword again, cutting every which way.

We push on in double quick time after the black cavalry and
although we're later complimented on our good order in the pursuit,
the chase is called off after three miles. Suffolk itself falls to
Ransom with still another piece of artillery and a large quantity of
stores. The fleeing Federal garrison is pursued as far as Bernard's
Mills. The Yankees have time to burn a few bridges during their
rapid withdrawal, but otherwise leave everything behind them.
Suffolk itself is abandoned later the same day. So it is, with something of still another victory under our belt, we withdraw safely to
Franklin, arriving there on March 11. One of the boys looks up from
his poker game and says his hand's not as good as the old 56th, but
it will serve to call. We sure seem to be on a winning streak on the
coast in both states.

The next day, the brigade once again boards the trains to return
to Weldon. Arriving back in North Carolina, we go into camp near
Garysburg. Here we spend some days drilling and undergoing
inspection by Colonel Faison. Those company commanders who
hadn't the chance to drill the regiment in February are given the
opportunity now to enhance their leadership skills at Garysburg. On
April 11, Private L. S. Wright of Company F gives his family some
insight into his life with the regiment at this time:

... thare was a man chopt off 3 of his finguers yesterday with a
ax I dont no wether he done it a perpose or not from the way our
officers is fixing it looks like thay that we would Stay here Some
time the company is till building tents an they have maid us fix up
Scaffels to sleap on like bed steds though things may soon change
we are both well an hearty thare we are drawing flower now we get
one pound & one eight a day & we paid 5 dollars for a pound of
Soda So we make out to live -dride apples meal or flower is as good
a thing as you can send Sweat bred wont spoil.

So one month ends and another one begins. And for any man of
the 56th who chooses to look on our record, I guess the record is
more dark than light, like there is some growing stain we can do
nothing about. For any way you look at it, southern civilians have
been robbed and looted out of hand; Yankee prisoners herded

together like cattle; southern deserters killed in mass hangings; Negro cavalry troopers shot down outside a burning house. The Yanks are doing the same to us, but I don't think either side thought it would come to this. It takes a lot of the glory out of the war; I know it does for me.

And our battle record. Well, while it is a little better, it is equally flawed. Since the disasters at Gum Swamp, we have served in only supporting roles; not since Gum Swamp have we really been called on to meet the test all by ourselves. Since that May in 1863, our longest stint was as an army of occupation instead of defending the homes and firesides of our own people. All of this has something to do with falling morale among the rank and file. We all feel it.

I begin to understand John a little better as April passes along. For we didn't enlist for robbery and murder. I know I didn't; we enlisted to win our independence, as our forefathers did in '76. And we are now all in this fight as one, as a family. Family. Yes, that's the word. "We Are A Band Of Brothers, Native To The Soil", just like the song says. And brother beside brother is how it began and how it should end. It may be sentiment, but that's what should matter, isn't it?

A few of us, then more and more of us come to the same way of thinking. We know it, understand it, believe it without speaking. But it is mentioned one time by John, The Prophet, and a few others that month.

They're quietly talking and I just sit down, not too close, and listen to The Prophet and John. And Davis is saying,"Remember how it was when it all began? The thrill of the new uniform on market day, the music and the songs, the soft admiration in the eyes of boys and young women, the new officer's sword with a light all its own? Remember?"

"It's not that way now, Jim. When we aren't thieves, we're outright murderers. It wasn't supposed to end like this. Stay long enough and it'll kill us out of hand."

And Davis said, "Not just you and I, but the regiment's in danger, not from the Yanks, but from itself, in danger of fraying away, losing its tone, dulling its edge, twisting its purpose. You can see it sliding every day into anarchy."

"Is it really worth the saving then? Any of it?"

"The Idea of the Regiment is worth the saving - the Idea that made these men enlist in the first place and kept them here until now. Yes, that is worth the saving."

"Then what in the name of God can save it? For I have looked high and low in heaven and earth and can find no miracle to serve any where."

And The Prophet says, "The only thing that can save it will be what led us all into it. Glory will save the Idea, for both are of the spirit. They have nothing to do with the rest of it - the sweat and grime; the brutal greed and murder."

And John laughs and says, "You sound like The Parson. Do you think for one minute that martinet Faison will understand you? Or Schenck? How about Luke? Or any other field officer you care to name?"

And Davis says, "It will come without them. As the Parson says, a whirlwind will come to separate the wheat from the chaff. It will temper all of us, harden us to do what we must do to win this war. For if it continues like this, we will surely lose it."

John then says quietly, "So it's a little blood-lettin' you want from us. Just as in the old lithographs, with the flag and officer with uplifted sword, the flash and roar of a line of battle coming on, and we shall all die performing our duty to God and Country. Or more like, we'll end it all in the mud or in some thorny thicket in another swamp, with nothing to show for it but glory."

"Wherever it is, whenever it happens, we won't die. We can't. Performing that duty will save the regiment, not kill it." He paused. "It is what we must do if we stay with it."

"Then how do you propose to bring it to pass, Jim?"

"We won't bring it to pass. Without any action at all on our part, it will come. Readiness is all and we will know that moment well enough when it does come. We only have to be ready for it - ready to act as we must, rightly and wisely. Even if it comes to blood sacrifice on the Altar."

"I don't think this second Abraham will stay the knife if it comes to that, Jim."

"No, I suppose he won't. But that will be our service to the cause and the nation, if it comes to that."

So that's it, I think as I walk back to K Company. They're saying that we'll have to enter the fire, be refined and purified, matter turned to light, as it were, or as the Parson would say, all the dross burned clean away. And afterwards, any redemption to come will have to first start with the act that only we can perform.

It will be a hard lesson, Sergeant McNeely, I think, but I am young. I have time to learn it. I can wait for that hour to come. I resolve that, for my part, I will be ready when it does come.

So we're still thinking and feeling, whispering and dreaming of these things when the new order comes to us on April 14 to prepare to move on Plymouth.

CHAPTER TEN

JOHN GRAHAM, MAJOR,
REGIMENTAL STAFF

My name is John Graham, Major, 56th North Carolina Troops, Ransom's Brigade. Confederate States Army. I was commanding officer of one wing or detachment of the 56th in the memorable assault on the Federal base at Plymouth, North Carolina, April 16-21, 1864. For the account that follows, I am indebted to the remainder of the Regimental Field and Staff, as well as various company commanders. I also found helpful comprehensive Union accounts acquired from Federal officers taken prisoner in this engagement.

This action, in which the regiment played such a significant part, should rightfully be described by an officer acquainted with the complex strategical and tactical concepts that led to its successful implementation. The reminiscences and memoirs of junior officers and enlisted men, while providing entertaining and interesting insights into the experiences of the common soldier, cannot possess the detailed knowledge, nor the depth of understanding, nor the correct interpretation of events that a more professional perspective can offer.

I must say at the outset that in this engagement, every officer on the Regimental Field and Staff did their duty superbly. All of the ten companies were ably led as well, but before the action, there was some concern with Company G. Its captain was under arrest and one of its two lieutenants (Davis) was an officer of dubious quality. Command of Company G was therefore ably exercised by First Lieutenant Otis P. Mills.

On April 14, the train carrying Ransom's Brigade arrived at the station yard at Tarboro, North Carolina. As the line of box cars behind the locomotive came to a stop, the 56th N.C. Infantry disembarked from the cars with only a blanket, a rifle, and the inevitable slouch hat. They carried no knapsacks, for these had all been left behind at Weldon. Ransom's Brigade and the 56th had arrived at Tarboro and here they were to join the large force under the command of Brigadier General R.F. Hoke for the assault on the Union base at Plymouth.

The next day, April 15, dawned clear and unseasonably cold, and at ten in the morning, the 56th set out for its objective that lay some sixty-five miles ahead, with Ransom's Brigade in the center of the column. The order of march was as follows: Kemper's Brigade; then, Ransom's, and in the rear was Hoke's own North Carolina Brigade. The 56th was accompanied by a battery of Pelgram's Artillery, but there were other batteries in the column as well - the batteries of Stribling, Graham, Miller, Moseley, and Reade. Dearing's Battalion of horse patrolled the flanks. The column moved north all that day and on into the night, camping at last near Hamilton.

When the column moved out the next day, passing Williamston, Ransom's Brigade marched at the head of the column steadily north all day until finally the column passed close to the tiny mill known as Foster's. There the column halted and dismissed, scattering into the adjoining fields and woods and resting under the stars. The night chill was relieved only by scattered fires that marked the small squads of men gathered around them. Plymouth lay less than a day's march away, the focus and the purpose for this expedition and the coming expenditure of effort and life.

To the Confederate war effort this spring, the capture of Plymouth would be of paramount importance. Plymouth, located on the south bank of the Roanoke River a few miles above Albemarle Sound, formed the keystone of the Union perimeter that held within its grasp the coastal plain of North Carolina. The principal waterways of the state, the most valuable fisheries of the south, and many thousand acres of fertile, productive agricultural lands were in the firm grip of the Union occupation. The loss of this region two years before had serious repercussions, not only for the state, but for the South as a whole. Simply on account of the loss of Roanoke Island on the Sound, most of southeast Virginia, including Norfolk, Portsmouth, and the great naval yard, was abandoned to the Union.

In addition, the loss of this area was harmful to war effort and morale both on the front and at home. The hope and the need for the Confederate recovery of coastal North Carolina were never very far from the official minds in Richmond and Raleigh. The first effort to regain control of the area by the recapture of New Bern in the winter of 1862 had failed, but with recent defeats in the west, the need for at least another effort to redress the balance here was advisable. This expedition was this effort and it faced a challenging prospect.

Before the war, Plymouth had been a sedentary, but important depot for the transportation of the "Black Gold" of the coast - tar, rosin, and pitch - and its importance during the war increased, not only for the manufacture of naval stores, but also as a center for the vital transportation of men and material. Plymouth had fallen into Union hands a year before and since then, the Federal garrison had been increased to impressive proportions. Moreover, the town was well defended with a continuous line of forts and breastworks, protected by moats, palisades, and chevaux-de-frise on three sides of the town. The fourth side, the northern side, was protected by the Roanoke, guarded by a small Union squadron of gun and picket boats.

The garrison itself was large and well supplied, and all three branches of the service were represented. At this time, the Union garrison included detachments of the 16th Connecticut Infantry, the 2nd Massachusetts Heavy Artillery, the 12th New York Cavalry, the 85th New York Infantry, the 24th New York Battery, the 101 and 103rd Pennsylvania Infantry, the 10th U.S. Colored Cavalry, and two companies of the 2nd North Carolina (Union) Infantry, the latter recruited from loyalist elements in the state.

The Union soldiers followed a weekly routine of church, drill, target practice, and sick call. The town had a number of resident families loyal to the Union. Armed and in regulation army blue, the Federal soldiers were complacent and calm, certain that the town could be held. This feeling of complacency was shared by the entire garrison, pervading the inspections of General Wessel, the reports of Lieutenant Bernard Blakeslee, and the casual acceptance of duty of Private Robert Kellogg. Plymouth was a peaceful and secure backwater to the greater war to the north.

At first dawn on Sunday, April 17, the men fell into column on the road to Plymouth, now only twenty-two miles distant. The 56th marched steadily northward on the dirt road. An occasional dimly lit crossing passed their line of march and at last the morning light fell on the fence boards and frame houses of Jamesville.

When only five miles from Plymouth, Kemper's Brigade and a number of twenty-pound Parrotts turned off to the west to attack the small Union fort at Warren's Neck, only a mile or so above the town. Hoke and Ransom, including the 56th, turned to the east, crossing a creek single file on a mill dam, and then they were once again in column on the Washington Road, marching hard to Plymouth. That afternoon, when only two miles from the town, first contact with a Union picket post was made at the crossing of the Washington and the Jamestown Roads. A company of Confederate cavalry quickly overran the post, killing two men and capturing nine others. Two Union soldiers managed to escape in the melee, fleeing into Plymouth to give the alarm.

In Plymouth, the two soldiers reported that their first warning came when they had been fired on by five or six Rebel scouts. Surprise had been total. The post on the Washington Road had been surrounded with no warning by grey clad riders and these two had alone escaped. Their words swept through the garrison. Many of the Union soldiers were in church when the alarm was sounded. Private Kellogg was as surprised as any man. When the alarm was given, he had been enjoying his weekly "sabbatical meditation". Now, he took his gun and joined the thousands of other Union soldiers rushing to their posts.

The 56th marched past the crossroads, past a horse standing there with a bullet wound in its nose, and past a dead Union soldier. The brigade was now advancing in line of battle from a point due south of the town. Over the tramping of the feet, the rattle of accoutrements, the hoarse cries of the officers, the men of the 56th could now hear faintly the distant mutter of the drums beating the Long Roll in Plymouth. Soon, the advancing Confederate line came under shelling from the Union line, but the distance was still too great and the Confederate batteries did not even bother to unlimber.

As evening fell, the regiment and brigade were only a mile from the southern perimeter of the Union base. Far to the northwest, we could hear the attack in progress on Warren's Neck, where Dearing's

Battery was heavily engaged with the fort defended by three guns and two gunboats anchored in the river alongside.

The 56th now sent out a strong skirmish line in front of the advancing line of battle. Firing broke out all along the line as the skirmishers came up to the main Union line. Ransom's Brigade was now coming under converging fire from all of the Union batteries on the south line, including heavy fire from the guns of the Union fleet. As darkness fell, the action died down until only the rifle fire along the skirmish line remained.

The decisive action of the day had already been performed on the left, where Hoke's action, supported by Ransom's demonstration to the south, would permit the C.S.S. ALBEMARLE to pass the river batteries and engage the Union fleet. But, as the night grew quiet again, the more perceptive men in Ransom's Brigade were well aware that the main Union lines were still intact. Union Fort Williams covered any approach from the south and could enfilade any approach from the east or west. The men in the skirmish line could see long lines of breastworks reaching out of sight to the east and west, enclosing the entire town. The few roads leading into Plymouth were blocked by wooden stockades.

All was hectic, "organized confusion" along Ransom's line as the night deepened. At 2:30 A.M., 250 men from the 56th were detailed to work on a redoubt for the thirty-two pound Parrott and this work continued through the night. The remainder of the regiment bedded down on the cold ground to wait for day break.

The night was a hectic one in Plymouth too. Rumors swept the town, stating that it was besieged by ten to twelve thousand men and this rumor was remarkably close to the truth. That same night, the wives and children of the loyal unionist soldiers in the town were embarked on the U.S.S. MASSASOIT which immediately left for Roanoke Island across the Sound. A growing sense of despair and desperation was felt among the Union soldiers. Blakeslee sadly remembered that "it was very evident to us that we must either be killed or go to 'Libby'".

At first light on the morning of Monday, April 18, the 250 men working on the redoubt were relieved by other men in the 56th and work continued under fire by one company at a time until noon when the earthwork was completed.

At noon, our artillery opened fire along the front of Ransom's Brigade and the Union artillery replied vigorously. The artillery duel continued on through the afternoon and one man in the 56th was wounded. At 5 P.M. that afternoon, Ransom's Brigade was ordered to march to the right and then to advance on the Union works to draw Union fire while Hoke's Brigade made an all out assault on a redoubt on the left.

As the 56th moved out of the protecting woods, they came into full view of the Union line a mile away on the far side of a cleared field on which targets had been placed to ensure proper range for the artillery. Just as the sun was setting, Companies B, I, E, and A advanced in skirmish order, followed by the rest of the regiment. As they stepped out into the open, the main Union line opened fire from fifteen guns of every caliber - from a 200-pound Parrott on the extreme right down to field artillery and three Union gun boats. I estimate the Union fire to have been coming from twenty pieces and two gun boats, using everything from the 200 pounder down to twelve sixteen-pound Napoleans firing every grade of shell. Some of the Confederate artillery in support fired over 200 times that afternoon. The 56th advanced steadily in quick time, lying down at intervals. But each time, the Union artillery reacquired the range, hitting the regimental line front, rear, and center. Whenever the ground heaved beneath them, the men would advance out from under what I would call the heaviest dose of lead I ever took. After almost a mile of this advance under fire, the Union picket line was driven over the breastworks, leaving only the main Union defensive line in view.

Ransom's Brigade was now ordered to halt while thirty pieces of artillery were brought up in the rear to shell the town. The Union artillery on their part kept up a heavy fire. The men of the 56th lay flat on the ground in the dark while grape shot and shell "whizzed, hissed, and burst" over them. During the occasional seconds when firing slackened, the gunfire of the two gunboats could be heard in the distance.

The skirmish line of the 56th was within a scant hundred yards of the Union works and the firing was continuous until ten that night. At midnight, as silence once again came over the battlefield, Ransom's Brigade was withdrawn. The demonstration had been successful, the fort upriver had been taken, but we were physically and emotionally exhausted. There was some reason to be thankful - despite the experience they had gone through, only one lieutenant had been wounded and fourteen other men, some badly, but these were the only losses in the regiment. One field officer felt that the only thing that saved the regiment from re-annihilation was the rolling contour of the ground that was covered by the advance.

The Union garrison had been shaken too. The entire town was under fire once the Confederate artillery had been advanced and even Fort Williams, the keystone of the Union line, had been partially silenced. The Union soldiers had stood firmly to their guns when the Confederates had advanced at dusk "with wild yells" and the main Union line had held, but the Federals were physically exhausted and demoralized.

At 1 A.M. on April 19, firing died down along the front of the 56th. Toward dawn, the 56th and the 24th regiments were pulled out of line and sent marching to the rear along the Lees Mill Road. Morale was low in the 56th, since many thought they were being withdrawn to be sent back to Tarboro. Many cynically referred to the previous day's ordeal as "only a demonstration" to the general staff who ordered it. But the 56th was not being sent back to Tarboro. A very different assignment was planned for it.

After several hours, new orders arrived. The regiment once again fell into marching order and soon it was learned that Ransom's Brigade and the 56th had been assigned the monumental task of storming the town from the east, up the Columbia Road. In this frontal assault, Ransom would be supported by the C.S.S. ALBEMARLE in the brigade rear. The position from which the brigade would launch the attack must be occupied by dawn.

The fact that the brigade and regiment would be launched in a single massive assault within hours sobered all ranks in the marching column. The men were "marching at will", but closed up, with elbows rubbing elbows and no straggling. The usual banter died away and there was only grim determination in the column. When they turned to look toward Plymouth, they saw only a dark and silent forest.

On arriving on the east side of Plymouth, the brigade turned and marched due west. Late in the afternoon, when only two miles from the town, the brigade approached Conaby Creek, a narrow stream, but deep enough to render it unfordable. The sudden crack of rifles indicated that the crossing was guarded by a Union picket post. The Federals proved stubborn and four guns of Branch's Battery were brought up to shell them into cover. This proved effective and some sharpshooters managed to cross the creek on felled trees. Once the opposite bank was cleared, a pontoon bridge was laid and the 24th regiment crossed first, driving the remaining Union pickets before them. The 56th followed and then the remainder of the brigade crossed without incident.

On the far side of the creek, a line of battle was again formed, with one company from each regiment deployed as skirmishers to the front. Then the advance slowly continued. As the brigade came under heavier picket fire and the artillery along the Union line began to open up once more, the advance was halted and the brigade formed for the final assault to be launched in the morning. The deposition of the brigade was completed by 9 P.M.

The Union artillery fire was heavy and prolonged, extending into the late hours of the night. Shells exploded above and around the stationary assault line, but we did not return fire. Fortunately, the shelling was more noisy than harmful and there were few casualties. Some time after midnight, the shelling slackened and then ceased. Some men lay awake during the long hours before dawn, but most slept on the bare ground, huddled together for warmth in groups of two or three men. If they turned in the night and looked upward, they saw overhead a night sky perfectly calm and cloudless, with a full moon lending beauty to the scene.

Less that two miles away, the Union soldiers did not sleep, but were hard at work through the night, strengthening their breast-works. A Union lieutenant, tired and distraught, noticed that his men were fatalistic. They were frantically building makeshift shelters and bomb-proofs, as if to prepare for the worse on the morrow.

The full moon was setting over the Plymouth skyline when Ransom's Brigade was aroused and formed into line of battle. This morning of April 20 was cold and the men were stiff as they moved into position in the pre-dawn darkness. As they stepped into line, they tightened their blanket rolls over the left shoulder and under the belt on the right hip. The disposition of the line was as follows from the river southward: the 56th on the river, the 25th, the 35th, the 8th, and the 24th regiment on the far left flank. The long line waited, still and silent, except for the field officers quietly saying to the men,

"North Carolina expects every man to do his duty. Pay close attention to orders, keep closed up, and press forward all the time. The sooner we can get into the town, the better for us".

Thus we all waited still in position, but looking intently now into the west. The Regimental Colors stood uncased and motionless in the center of the line, held by a sergeant flanked by the eight volunteer corporals of the color guard.

At precisely 4:30 A.M., the darkness was cut by a single signal rocket fired from Ransom's main line as a signal to General Hoke on the other side of the town. The rocket climbed to the zenith, visible to Confederates east and west and south of the town, visible also to the soldiers in the Union line 600 yards away.

Then Ransom's orders rang out down the line as the rocket sputtered and faded: "Attention, Brigade! Fix bayonets! Trail arms! Forward - March!" and the line moved forward to the assault, with the setting moon before them.

Far to the west, Hoke's and Kemper's Brigades fired signal guns and advanced their pickets in an effort to confuse the Union garrison on where the blow would fall. But Ransom's line moved forward in silence, a silence broken only as the artillery pushed forward at a full gallop to unlimber and open fire on the breastworks directly ahead flanking the Columbia Road.

The Union pickets fired a parting shot at the advancing main line of Ransom's Brigade and retired quickly. Only a few seconds later, with half of the distance covered to the breastworks, the Union artillery opened up with case shot and shell, followed by the heavier guns from Fort Williams joining in the general duel. Ransom's line, until now marching in good order, now broke into double quick time and began the rebel yell. Far over on the other side of town, their distant cry was heard and answered, first by Hoke's Brigade to the south, and then passed on through the Confederate lines to the west. But only Ransom's Brigade was on the move, not Hoke's or Kemper's Brigades.

The Union artillery fire, from both siege and field guns, at first came over the heads of the men in the 56th, just a little too high, but the Union gunners soon got the range. The guns of the C.S.S.

ALBEMARLE, steaming up the Roanoke just behind the 56th, gave some support, but from here on it was an infantry man's war. Blakeslee, seeing the long shouting line of battle coming into view through the early morning mist, felt that he had never seen a more furious infantry charge. Another Union soldier noted that the Confederate line was coming irresistibly on "with wild cheers and yells".

For the men of the 56th Regiment, the advance quickly became a stumbling ordeal of confusion and chaos. When the rebel yell first lifted from the ranks, Ransom had shouted "Charge, boys, and the place is yours!" The line of battle was first broken, not by the rain of Union artillery, but by a panicky herd of cattle that ran lowing through the ranks that first opened to receive them and then closed again. The line of the 56th then descended the side of a six-foot ditch and without pausing for breath, climbed up the opposite side and into the open again, breaking down a wood fence as they did so. Rapidly reforming their line, the regiment plunged on through a small swamp that crossed their immediate front. The men waded through the waist-deep water as rapidly as they could, holding their guns high.

Breaking out of the swamp, the 56th found that it was the first unit on the edge of a level plain, cleared of obstructions and used by the Federal garrison for parades and target practice. Reforming their line for the second time under cover of a low rise that gave only scant protection, the regiment now began an uphill struggle on the double against the blazing crest that marked Plymouth's eastern defensive line. Men fell dead and wounded from the ranks as Union infantrymen opened fire from the breastworks at point blank range. But with a final cheer, the 56th Regiment rushed forward and then over the Union breastwork on the crest. In our front, the Union infantry, firing steadily, was falling back to the shelter of the houses in the town itself.

Ransom's Brigade had suffered heavily in the advance. Hundreds of men were lying dead and wounded in the fields and the 56th regiment had been in the first line of the advance. Forming their ranks for the third time under a heavy rifle fire on the edge of town, the unit, under my command, now began its advance into the town itself.

The 56th moved forward, first driving a Union regiment from the shelter of the houses and fence palings between Water and Second Streets. Several men of the 56th fell dead or wounded at this point. Following the Columbia Road on toward the center of town, the lines advanced, pushing down fences and palings as bullets seemed to come from every direction - from roofs, windows, holes in the ground. A terrific fire of artillery and musketry was also coming from guns hidden in the smoke rising from the far end of Columbia Road.

The regiment pushed on into the center of the town, crossing the respective intersections of Columbia with Adams, Washington, and Jefferson Streets. The men fired, stumbled, shouted, and plunged forward, driving the Union infantry slowly from street to street, from yard to yard, from cellars and bomb proofs. The Union officer Blakeslee stated that "every position was obstinately maintained ... a squad of men here and a squad of men there...". At the intersection of Columbia and Jefferson Streets, in the center of town, the regiment came under additional severe cross-fire from Fort Williams, a few hundred yards away. By this time, three lieutenants were down and many of the enlisted men had fallen.

At an open space around the county jail, the regiment was rapidly reformed for the fourth and final time. Some fifty prisoners had been taken at this point in the advance. At the far end of the street, I could see one artillery piece, unlimbered and trained on us, with its caisson and six horses in the rear. The regiment on my command rushed forward to silence it. The cannon fired before they reached it, but the elevation was set just a little too high and the shot passed over their heads. A volley was then fired by the regiment at point blank range, bringing down two horses, but a Union sergeant exploded the caisson just as the men reached it, killing horses and wounding some of the onrushing men. The Union sergeant, leading the four surviving horses to the rear, was killed in turn by a shell from his own comrades in Fort Williams. Advancing over the smoking wreckage, the regiment came under more fire from the flanks, but pressed forward.

The bulk of the 56th had swept through the length of the entire town without substantial support and now the far western line of the Union defenses was in sight. A heavy fire now opened from the parapet as the regiment bore down on them from the rear, but in a few moments, the men were over the rampart and among the Union infantry in the breastwork. Then 240 Federal infantrymen of a Pennsylvania Regiment silently raised their muskets overhead in surrender. I seized the regimental flag of the 56th from the surviving color-bearer and waved it enthusiastically on the breastwork to Hoke's waiting infantry as a signal that the way was open for their entry from the west.

Plymouth had fallen and thousands of Confederate soldiers were now sweeping into the town from the east and west, but the Union garrison in Fort Williams, with its guns turned on the town, continued to hold out. After several hours of determined resistance, the Fort surrendered on being informed by Hoke that the Confederates might otherwise take the post with no quarter. At the time of the surrender of the Fort, remnants of the 56th Regiment were located just north of the Fort attached to Hoke's Brigade.

Perhaps the finest tribute to the role of Ransom's Brigade and the 56th Regiment was expressed many years later by Edwin G. Moore who wrote: "It was the fortune of the writer to occupy a place in the line which defended Marye's Hill at Fredericksburg, and to witness the repeated onsets of Burnside's thousands against that strong position ... but not upon the famous field of Fredericksburg did he see anything which surpassed the conduct of Ransom's Brigade at Plymouth." Indeed, the late Colonel Duncan K. McRae of North Carolina declared that it was very similar in many respects, and compared favorably in all respects, to the storming of the Malakoff in the Crimean War.

In the final assault on Plymouth, the 56th Regiment suffered a total of eighty-eight casualties. Four officers were wounded, four enlisted men killed, and eighty enlisted men wounded. Ransom's Brigade had a total of 426 casualties. The banner of the regiment had been rent with bullets during the advance and a third of the color guard had fallen. But the regiment had taken 300 prisoners and some artillery in the battle. The long sought for victory for the regiment had at last been achieved.

Union allegations that Federal Negro and loyalist North Carolinian prisoners were summarily executed following the battle are somewhat questionable. These reports, reviewed by a congressional committee of the United States government, claim that a number of Federal prisoners were shot or hanged on the banks of the Roanoke (to which they had fled) by elements of the 6th and 8th North Carolina regiments. I can neither substantiate, nor deny these assertions, as following the battle, the 56th was most immediately engaged in provisioning themselves from the generous stores in the garrison and were not in the area of the alleged atrocity.

Later in the day, the 56th was engaged in processing several hundred Federal prisoners in the town. Certainly, the evidence, freely confirmed by the Federal prisoners themselves, is conclusive. The captives were treated courteously and their knapsacks were not searched. All were allowed to keep their personal belongings and side-effects.

It is my understanding that all the prisoners thus processed later proceeded by foot and rail to Camp Sumter near Andersonville, Georgia, where they were known to the other inmates as "The Plymouth Pilgrims".

The prize at Plymouth was therefore substantial: 2,500 prisoners, twenty-three pieces of artillery, 500 horses, 5,000 stands of small arms, between 600 and 700 barrels of flour, and large stores of bacon and beef. But of greater worth to the regiment was the psychological force of the victory it had helped to win. The 56th was no longer the regiment that had lost at Gum Swamp, but the one that had won at Plymouth. This battle honor was proudly inscribed on the regimental color. The Army, government, and press were effusive in their praise of this entire operation in which the 56th deserved and gained particular mention.

CHAPTER ELEVEN

JOEL HUDSON, PRIVATE, COMPANY A

Once we had the Yank prisoners rounded up and waved off headin' south, we're able to rest up a few days. Like the Bible says, Victory is sweeter in the mouth of them that has it. Well, we have it now and it don't seem like there's nary a thing that we can't do. But some of us, like me, Joel Hudson, can't help wondering if it will be like this from here on out. Or whether we will go back to the way we was on the Grand Tour of North Carolina.

We don't have much time to wonder, for on April 25, we're on the march again, this time to Washington, N. C. We expect another battle, but when we get there the next day, the Yanks leave town for New Bern. So we get Washington without a fight. Plymouth must've scared the be-Jesus out of them to send them scurryin' back to their holes on the coast like that. But we decide we can't just let them do like that, so we take off after them to New Bern. To tell you the truth, we figure we just might as well add New Bern to our winning streak.

So, on the 29th, the hull brigade marches off to Greenville where we have to wait for the pontoons to be brought up. Then, on May 2, we cross the Neuse below Kinston and then the Trent above New Bern. We capture seventy-five men at a cavalry post as we come up on New Bern. We're only ten miles from the town, when we come under purty heavy fire from their gunboats on the river. We work all night long May 5 crossing the river on the pontoons and get ready to storm New Bern the next day like we did Plymouth. We're confident we will win. But new orders put an end to this promising operation.

On the morning of May 6th, just as we're gettin' ready to take

New Bern, the attack's called off and the brigade's ordered to go right away to Kinston, where we'll board waitin' trains to rush us up to Petersburg, Virginia. Old Grant had kicked off his spring offensive; there's hot fightin' in the Wilderness; and Spoons Butler is moving in fast and hard on Petersburg and is about to take the town. It must be serious somethin' awful to call off our attack on New Bern right then.

So, that morning at 8 A.M., we march to Kinston and board the trains for Petersburg. All through that long day, we ride northward by rail, as fast as those wheezy, cranky, old locomotives will take us, crawling through Goldsboro, creeping through Weldon, and then on to the state line. But in the early afternoon on May 9, the train stops and we all get off among burning bridges and depots. This was all that's left of Jarrett's Station which the Yank cavalry had paid a call on the night before. Then the Yanks left heading north, tearing up the track as they went. So the brigade has no choice but to shoulder arms and foot it for Petersburg.

It's a long march of twenty miles. All along the roadbed are burning piles of crossties and rails and we can hear the old owls a-hootin' in the swamps. "That's a bad sign, boys," the Parson sings out, "hard times in Ole Virginny and worse a-comin'". It's sometime after midnight before we reach Stony Creek Depot. The track is whole from here on and we rest until dawn when the trains come down from Petersburg to take us the rest of the way in.

We board them at eight o'clock on May 10 with loaded guns, for there is no tellin' what we might run into. But, nothin' happens, unless you call Sgt. Amos Harrill losing his hat somethin' happenin'. Three hours later, we roll into Petersburg and you can hear the poppin' of muskets off to the north. We get off the cars and march up Sicklemore Street through wildly cheering crowds of civilians. Lunches of cold bread are pushed on us as we march by; women and children are a-cryin' in relief; a woman sees Sgt. Harrill don't have no hat and gives him one. Beautiful girls with heaving bosoms throw bouquets of flowers on us. And we can hear compliments like this - "We are safe now. These are the brave North Carolinians who have driven the enemy from their own state and have come to defend us. These are the brave boys who took Plymouth."

We're sure heroes to them and they're sure glad to see us. It's mighty fine, I tell you. They must be scared to death of the Yanks comin' in - we're the knights with shining arms, I tell you that.

The old 56th marches down to Poppy Lawn grounds and stacks arms by a rock spring in the park. We aren't any more settled in there when here come the women agin. They can't more get over us than a doe with a young buck or a heifer with a bull. Young ones, old ones, purty ones, ugly ones - here they come, with their colored aunties, all loaded down with picnic baskets and cloth covered trays and pots of steaming food. We have a bountiful feast right there with some of the prettiest company you ever did see.

Well, it can't last. Later that day, the brigade pulls up stakes and with four other brigades marches north across the Appomattox and after going a little way toward Richmond, camps near Swift Creek. We spend the night half asleep, half awake, thinkin' on those purty young faces, on them heavin' bosoms, them laughin' eyes, smilin' lips, those invitin' voices...We knew the next mornin' would bring with it the war and there ain't no going back, but you can sure remember.

Early the next mornin', on May 11, we go on up the Turnpike Road toward Richmond. It's an easy march for the rest of the day, marked only by some brisk cavalry skirmishing somewhere off to the right. Then we come through a part that had been fought over just a few days before: shattered trees, abandoned equipment, pockets of clotted blood. At Half Way House, the 56th halts and we form line of battle facing east; Company I is sent out as a skirmish line. We know the Yanks are out there just a few hundred yards away, but they don't bother us none. We sleep that night in line of battle right on the Turnpike Road.

About two in the morning, we wake up with the rain just a-pourin' in our faces. Dawn's a long time comin' and when it come, it's still rainin'. When it gets light enough to see, we move out on a country road and form a new line on some breastworks in a wheat field a mile east of the turnpike. The rain is just a-comin' down. Some companies from the brigade (G and I from the 56th) are sent out as skirmishers and advance toward the Union lines. They're not yet out of sight when they hit the Yankee pickets and the sharp pop of muskets can be heard through the downpour. We remain fixed in position and the skirmish line does all the fightin' there was that day. The rain keeps on fallin' and fallin', right into the night. We hear there has been a big battle north of Richmond. That was the Bloody Angle fight at Spotsylvania. The rain fell hard there too.

On the morning of May 13, everything is quiet in our front. The 56th, 35th, and 49th cross back to the west side of the turnpike and hold a good position there. We figure we will defend that ground against the frontal attack we hope the Yanks will be dumb enough to oblige us with, when - sure enough - we get word that a Yank column is comin'. But it's not comin' against our front. It's bearin' down on our flank.

Skirmishers out of the 49th are sent runnin' back to cover the rear of our position, while Company H of the 56th is sent out to reinforce our skirmishers in front. Ransom has barely time enough to realign the brigade when a strong Union line - a good six regiments strong - marches out of a dense pine thicket in the rear and fires a volley. At the same time, here comes another heavy skirmish line of two regiments on the front of our position.

Well, more'n one of us thought "It's Gum Swamp all over again - front and rear". Our skirmish line in the rear is over-run and Generals Hoke and Ransom have to run for it to keep from being captured; here they come, a-spurring and a-gallopin' their horses right over the breastwork in among us, with the Yanks hot on their heels. Gunfire is comin' in from all directions. Men all around are getting hit. We're in a serious position and drastic action is necessary.

So Colonel Faison, on Ransom's command, orders three companies to fall back on the railroad, while the other seven companies give them cover fire. The 24th and 25th also advance up to form on the railroad and make a new line.

That leaves seven companies in the breastwork, and they are being attacked front and rear. They have to move fast, a-jumpin' from one side of the breastwork to the other depending on whether they're firin' front or rear. But they fire volley after volley on command into the Yanks and the men fire their rifles from the top of the bank and then reach down for loaded rifles handed up by those down below. But we are veterans now and fight with coolness and dispatch. It's a hot place, but we don't scare. We're takin' casualties

- one lieutenant is wounded and an enlisted man killed. One private in Company D fires sixteen rounds with steady aim and another in Company I calmly smokes his pipe through the whole battle. Cap'n. Harrill feels that but for our stubborn resistance, "a considerable portion of the Brigade would have been captured".

Well, it's not no repeat on Gum Swamp. The Yanks fall back - the 3rd New Hampshire taking over a hundred casualties - and in the lull, the other seven companies withdraw to the railroad in good order, where the brigade is massed in a strong position under cover of our artillery. The Yanks move on up to occupy the breastwork we had just left, but they keep their distance. Night closes in; we're in a good frame of mind; and we welcome General Beauregard's arrival from Petersburg with cheers that are passed all along the line.

Heavy picket firin' continues along the front all next day. At nightfall, Company F is sent out on picket and spends the night huggin' the ground under a heavy fire from Union sharpshooters. We continue to take light casualties 'til the next mornin'.

Next mornin', May 15th, General Ransom, standing in the rear of Company F, is wounded and taken off the field. He's hit so bad that we won't see him again for a while. Other field officers in the brigade are wounded and every man jack of us has to be extra careful under the heavy fire that continues all day and into the night. Before we turn in, rumors are sweeping the 56th that Cap'n. Graham had seen Jeff Davis visiting the battlefield and that he had ordered Beauregard to attack the enemy lines and drive them back, come first light.

Well, first light on May 16 is cold and foggy. Sure enough, we're ordered into column and though some of the boys think we might pull back for a rest, most of us know they wouldn't be issuing us extra cartridges for a rest. Those rumors of an attack are right.

The brigade forms a line of battle on the turnpike, with the 35th and 56th in the reserve line along with the Washington Artillery. The assault column in front of us moves promptly off into the mist and at ten o'clock breaks through the strongly fortified Union line. By the time the 56th crosses the breastworks behind them, the Yanks are in full retreat. Casualties are heavy on both sides, but the 56th only has a few men wounded by the over-shots. After the battle, we see Old Jeff Davis and Bory ridin' together over a field literally soakin' in blood in places. But the battle has been won: Spoons Butler is caught now behind his fortified lines from the James to the Appomattox. He won't be takin' the Richmond Turnpike this day. We even got new requisitions of clothing right after the battle.

The next day, May 17, the brigade probed away at the Yankee line and then we dig in a few hundred yards from them. The day passes quiet enough except for the picket firing and a stray shell from the gunboats on the James. The 19th of May also passes without nothin' happenin'. But on the 20th of May, there comes the Battle of Ware Bottom Church.

This is the way it happens. This morning, Companies B and H relieve Company D, which had been put on outpost. A number of our boys go down to a small creek to wash clothes and that's what they're doin' when orders come for every one to fall in line. They come runnin' up from the creek with their clothes just a-drippin'.

Once we're assembled, the 56th and 35th forms in line of battle in front of Brigade and we're told to take the Yankee picket post in our front. The 35th will lead the assault, with the 56th following behind in close support. At two o'clock, the attack is launched in good order, but the 35th, after going a half mile, halts under a strong fire from the Union main line and begins fallin' back. The 56th, advancing on through the ranks of the retreating 35th, pushes on out into a small field covered over with small jack pine and oak trees. The main Union line that had thrown back the 35th is out there in a thick grove of woods only forty or fifty yards away.

As the 56th comes out in the open, they hit us too with a murderous volley. The men are cut down by the score by a witherin' fire given at point blank range. We hit the ground and return fire lyin' down. There's no panic; we load and fire on command, but the fire is murder and our casualties keep climbin'. It is nip-and-tuck, with death and destruction round about. After five rounds, our company commanders are beggin' their field officers to withdraw and the enlisted men, confused by all the cross fire, begin yellin' "They're flankin' us! They're flankin' us!" So, Major Graham orders a retreat and we fall back over a field covered with the dead and dying and only rally when we reach Brigade. When the Yankees advance to follow up on us, the 56th and two other regiments repulse them in turn. The heavy musketry fire keeps up 'til near every man in the regiment has used up all his ammunition. That night, the picket lines are strengthened under a heavy fire that doesn't stop 'til dawn.

Ware Bottom Church. We lost a heap of men there. Oh, we could and did rebuild some in the months ahead, but Ware Bottom Church ... it warn't nothin' but a bloody tragedy for the 56th and a measure of what was to come. The regiment lost in killed and wounded ninety-six men - just about half our force. Lieutenant-Colonel Luke and two lieutenants were wounded. But, it's the enlisted men who carry the brunt and that's the way it was here too. Company D has eleven wounded; Company F, four killed, over nine wounded; Company I, five killed, twelve wounded; Company H has the highest loss, but I don't know the number. Sergeant McNeely over in Company K was hit; he's out of the war for good. We also lost some men who were captured as we fell back toward the Turnpike. Most of the dead are left out there in the pine field where they fell and they're buried in unknown graves by the Yanks. One who is brought back is Sergeant Amos Harrill, who is carried by his brother, Cap'n. Harrill, to the field hospital. When the Cap'n. goes back to the hospital to see after his brother later, he finds Sergeant Harrill slowly dyin'. He still had that hat that woman had given him in Petersburg. The Cap'n. finds a private graveyard for his brother's last rest.

After Ware Bottom, we engaged in fixin' up fortifications all along the line. On May 21, the brigade is switched over to Bushrod Johnson's Division. Next day, a lieutenant and a few enlisted men who had been wounded rejoin the regiment and a truce is held so that the dead lying out between the two lines can be buried.

During the last week of May, a skirmish line from the Brigade charges across that pine field and takes the Union position that cost us such a turrible price. We just rest and try to recover from what happened there. There's some sugar and tobacco tradin' between the lines in our front, but generally we just lie here, restin' in the charred woods within a few hundred yards of the enemy with firin' and shellin' goin' on every day. Seem like the hull war is just becoming one shock and horror.

On June 13, our baggage arrives for the first time since we crossed the state line and it shore is a welcome sight to us. Many of us hadn't even changed our clothes, and our shirts are so stiff with caked dirt and sweat that they will just about stand up right. Worse than that, we have had nothin' to boil water in to cook or warsh with for weeks. Since we're so dirty and lousy, no wonder so many get sick, officers and enlisted both. Colonel Faison is sent to the Moore Hospital in Richmond with the quickstep, but company officers are hurtin' too. Cap'n. Noah Hughes dies in a Richmond hospital and Cap'n A.P. White is sent to the hospital with quickstep. Then on June 7, several more company officers and men are admitted to the North Carolina Hospital in Petersburg. It really looks like what Ware Bottom left, the hospitals will finish off.

And that warn't all either. On May 22, Cap'n. Lane of Company G, resigns for reasons of health and family problems. And his isn't the last of the resignations that soon become a regular flood.

On the 1st of June, we finally march away from those smokin' woods in our front and head north toward Richmond, crossin' the James on a pontoon bridge. We go through Seven Pines and then to the Chickahominey, where we take up positions on the banks of the river. Next day, we make a demonstration in force and drive back a Union skirmish line. For the rest of the day, the two sides lay 800 yards apart and keep up a casual fire. Then about dark, it looks like the woods in front of us are explodin' with muzzle flashes of hundreds of muskets. Our pickets sound the alarm and we do some rapid firin' back until we notice there are no sound of muskets and no minnie balls wingin' pass. Them ain't no Yankees; they're fireflies! We got a good laugh at our own expense until a stiff order comes down for us not to waste no more ammunition like that. No tellin' what the Yankees thought, not to mention them pore fireflies.

On June 3, the brigade's ordered to march north to Bottom's Bridge. The next day, we're on our way, the old depleted 56th down to about half its numbers or less, jest draggin' along too. Bory's protests to Richmond that he's being robbed of a third of his infantry south of the James was to no avail; no one in the War Department ever paid the hero of Bull Run much mind.

We arrive at Bottom's Bridge (that's still the Chickahominey flowing under it; these rivers in Virginia run ever which-a-way) and report to General Robert Ransom, our first brigade commander. Colonel Faison becomes acting brigade commander because Matt

Ransom is still out with his wound. Lieutenant-Colonel Luke becomes acting colonel of the 56th until Faison can come back. We soon make ourselves comfortable and even reach some agreement with Pennsylvanian cavalry across the river for both sides to hold off on the long range sharpshootin' for a while.

On June 9th, Ransom's Brigade marches over to Chaffin's Bluff, where we occupy vacant winter quarters that were set up last year at Fort Harrison. We get some rest here and some of us visit the James River Fleet of the Confederate Navy. The regiment stays here about a week, nursin' our wounds and blisters, of which we have a lot; countin' our losses, of which there are too, too many; and numberin' up our blessings, which are too few. That blood bath at Ware Bottom is still with us, still fresh in our spirit.

Peaceful as it is at Chaffin's Bluff, it gives us plenty of time to think and it makes us jest a mite nervous to think that the force for the protection of Richmond was just too small, so we won't be allowed to stay here for long. We was right.

The rumor begins circlin' around the camp that the brigade will soon be sent south to Petersburg to stop Butler. Well, we stopped him before and he stopped us, but we figure with one good push more, we can handle him at least one more time. He is a foe worthy of our contempt.

At nine o'clock on the night of May 15, the rumor becomes fact. Just as we are a-lyin' down to go to sleep, we receive new orders. The orders are highly urgent and must be carried out at once. We are ordered to join Beauregard, who only has 3,000 men down there, has his hands full, and needs help, for he is under attack. So, we all get our supplies together, pull out in the dark, cross the Old James at Drewry's Bluff, and start out with everything on an all night forced march back south. There had been rain all that afternoon and the first few miles are muddy and slippery but our spirits light up considerable, although we still don't know where we're goin', and by first day dawn we are jest about ready to meet any foe.

CHAPTER TWELVE

FRANK ROBERTS, CAPTAIN, COMPANY B

It's a long all night march down to Petersburg - a good twenty miles in fact - and as the hours pass, the men perhaps think a little of home, wives, families, those small dirt-poor farms most of them come from. But I think of Middletown, Connecticut. One time, in that other time before the War, that was my home.

Middletown was a wonderful place for a boy to grow up. We lived in a nice white frame house, a big family, a good dog, and in the fall, the trees turned with a blaze of color unknown down here. And in winter, you had ice skating on the pond and afterwards hot tea before a roaring fire. And at the Academy, there were Classical Studies and Literature and Oratory, while the older students talked of the Transcendentalists - Emerson, Thoreau. And Hawthorne, and who was that new novelist - Melville? And then going back to the classes on an iron-cold winter morning... They know nothing of all that down here. They lift their eyes to gauge the weather, never to see the stars.

I tried to talk a little to my men in Company B about Henry V and "We Happy Few" and I could see they didn't have the faintest idea who Henry V was or what he did. They had heard the name Shakespeare (some of them), but didn't have a glimmer of what happened at Agincourt. And I know they all must still wonder what brought me here to this place. They all do.

I got a lot of it, too, back home. Now, Frank Roberts, do you actually mean to tell me that you are going down south to live, the land of chattel slavery and rampant ignorance? The land of tobacco chewing and lantern jawed vacuity? You will exchange New England for a peasant civilization? Or are you really going as an apostle to the gentiles, a beacon light to guide the lost sheep to salvation? Oh, they had a royal time with me when I left, I tell you that.

But I did well in Fayetteville. Married well, became a prosperous merchant, grew to love the mild winters and the quiet nights. But, I always missed New England in the fall and winter, and some of the faces in Middletown. (Their churches are different here too - and they have no town meetings, which I think would strengthen these little communities against the state government with its planters in control. Ah, but then I forgot, I am one of that class. Still -)

Then the War came and I enlisted, fought at First Bethel, and then came to Magnum as captain of Company B. Since then, I went through it all - The Blackwater, Gum Swamp, Plymouth, now this. I think the men like me well enough and the other officers have been universally kind and polite. Still, they must wonder. I do myself. Still have family back in Connecticut. I keep expecting to run up against a Federal company out of Middletown, with those same faces I grew up with. What then? Perhaps its fortunate we have muskets, rifles, artillery - then you don't see who it is you strike down, or what strikes you. It's better if it's impersonal like that.

So here I am on the 16th of June, in this sadly depleted regiment of Johnny Rebs of which I am the only officer in Company B left, heading for what we do not know. Prince Hamlet, I always thought, would have made a better soldier than the critics gave him credit for. He had that stoic resignation and philosophical acceptance, that ability to survive the present moment without fretting too very much over killing the king at last, when his moment came, in Act V - Oh, well.

We arrive on the north bank of the Appomattox at daybreak and we are detached from the brigade to guard a cotton factory while the other four regiments rush on to the Petersburg lines. We guard the factory from possible raiders all that night, but before dawn we are on the road again, this time searching for the Union army north of the Appomattox.

Useless, useless marching, as they're south of the river by this time. We are on our feet all night on reconnaissance, aimless marching, with nothing to show in the end for it but bone deep weariness.

Next morning, a distant ray of light enters the consciousness of High Command and this infinitesimal ray of light reveals to them that Grant might really be south of the river after all. So, back we rush to the railroad, spend hours waiting for the trains, at last board the flat cars and hurry across the Appomattox and then out to the defense lines just east of Petersburg. By then, it's June 17. There's only a guard detail, a skirmish line, a few sentries here and there. When we ask where the Army is, we're told this is it. There's not enough of us to stop a determined butterfly and Grant is out there, coming in with a vengeance.

The 56th forms in line of battle in newly constructed breast-works on the Jerusalem Road only a mile from the city. The Yankees are out there and coming all right, and their musketry and artillery fire gradually increases during the day as we continue working on the breastworks at record speed. Lieutenant Joseph Coggins in Company D, only twenty-two years old, is mortally wounded; one man is badly burned when stray bullets explode the percussion caps in his belt; Company F has one man killed and two others wounded. It is this steady, relentless hemorrhaging of the unit that wears us down faster than anything.

That afternoon, about two o'clock, Grant's Army begins prob-ing off to our left and then launches a full scale assault on the line near the river. Apparently they think they might break through here and then be in the city to our rear before we know it. We're able to provide some converging fire and are heartened to see the Union forces pull back without making a really determined push, but it is evident they are saving their main effort for later. I think we all understand the situation. Word passes up and down the line from this or that quarter: The enemy has been repulsed with great loss; hold your position at all hazards; Lee's Army will be here at ten tonight. As darkness falls, I and other officers pass among the men saying Hold our own until ten o'clock, all will be well. But it's evi-dent that the men are in deep despair. Without sleep or food, they know we are vastly outnumbered and facing Grant himself. Many have no hope at all that we will survive the morrow.

Finally, full darkness comes and we wait for the arrival of Lee's Legions, but there is no sign at all of them. A full moon rises over the Union lines and we all begin to prepare for the worst. Shortly before ten, Ransom's Brigade and the 56th are pulled out of line and rapidly march down the rear of the line and form a line of battle in some pine woods near the Baxter Road. Then, in the light of the moon, we are ordered out of the lines and to the front to support Wises' Brigade. Since it's just another change of position, we're not on full alert.

What we do not know is that Wises' Brigade isn't there. They had abandoned this part of the line after dark in another one of those changes in position that will be the death of us one day. At any rate, there is a gaping hole in the Confederate outer line that has just now been occupied by three lines of battle of the Army of the Potomac. They are still getting themselves organized for a further advance, waiting for further orders probably, when we walk right into them.

Captain Frank Alexander and Company K are out front as we meet them and the volley that hits them from out of the dark kills the captain and several others in his command. Frank was only twenty-four years old and was as well educated a young man as you could find, north or south. He was a student at Davidson College before the war, a boy you could talk books with, not like most of these "Southrons". However, all that's all over with now. A good man. He is replaced by young Lieutenant McNeely, who will likely be promoted on up to captain, if he does well in what we are all about to undergo.

With the initial shock, the brigade halts for a moment and then, as the night in front blazes again with the flash of innumerable rifles, we begin madly charging to the front. We swarm over the captured parapets and in we go among the Federals. Not only guns are used in the hand to hand fighting in the bright moonlight, but also bayonets, knives, clubbed muskets, even fisticuffs and strangle holds. It's pretty grim there for a lot longer than such things go, but they are as surprised by our sudden charge as we are at finding them there and toward midnight, the Feds at last pull back.

We had always found at such moments that the better part of valour is not a hasty retreat (that only can get you killed), but instead a sudden charge to the front. And the dark and confusion helped a lot, too. Our casualties in the 56th are somewhat lighter than that of some other regiments in the brigade. Company F had one killed and two captured, and four more are wounded in Company D. Captain Harrill's surviving brother John, in Company D, is seriously wounded. So it goes.

We take a number of prisoners and these are sent up the line to the right. We have a rare look at their arms. Nearly every one of these Feds had an extra gun and many of them are the new Springfield rifles, some with hand carved stocks, with Indians, and crescent moons, and such as that. These were Westerners, Minnesota, I believe we found out.

Then we lay down, right where we are in the breastwork, utterly exhausted, and try to get some sleep for we know what daylight will bring. But instead of sleeping, we find ourselves listening all through the predawn hours with growing horror to the black night, for it is filled with the unending screams and moans and crying of countless wounded and dying men left between the lines. They calm down a little as the worst die toward dawn, but long before that time we are on the move again (But I think I shall remember the horror of that screaming for as long as I shall live).

Sometime between two and three A.M. on June 18, we are ordered to fall back to a final position. Company I remains behind in skirmish order to hold the enemy in the morning as long as possible. All the rest of us withdraw across a small rippling stream, and then up a slight rise to the last ridge where we halt. There is a full moon high overhead and everything is as light as day. Looking over our shoulders, we can see Petersburg in its hollow less than a mile away, its church spires and courthouse bell tower beautiful in the moonlight. This will be the last stand; driven from this ridge, it will be Plymouth all over again, but in reverse and with the war lost, to boot. We all know Richmond cannot be held without Petersburg.

At least, there is one small section of artillery sitting here, waiting to support our part of the line in defense of the Sacred City. But now we have a good look at what that line is going to be.

The line is already staked off for digging by the engineers. The men are tired and even fatalistic by now, knowing that this will literally be "The Last Ditch", but they turn to work at the hard ground with no complaining, too tired to, probably. There are only seven or eight spades and shovels to a company and most of the men dig away feverishly with bayonets, pocket knives, coffee cups and pots, even with their bare hands. We have to wait until daylight to get more shovels and a few pick-axes from Petersburg; by then it's too late. The rising sun reveals only a shallow trench with the men still working frantically to make cover.

With the slow dawn, we can see what is before us. Our final ridge overlooks what I have come to love so much in this land - broad fields, covered by patches of woods, and small creeks shaded by willows at the edge of pasture land. Not many of us stop to admire the view; we are still toiling on the trench when the first Union skirmish lines begins pushing out toward us. We promptly set aside shovel and pocket knife and pick up our muskets. We are as ready as we will ever be now.

Faison is away commanding the brigade and Lt. Colonel Luke, his second, is sent to the rear with a severe carbuncle (of all things), so command of the 56th falls on Major Graham. There really isn't that much of the regiment left - as I have said before. We are formed in that trench in a line so thin that there is no second line behind us to reinforce any break.

A dark ravine is just in front of our center and Graham decides that would be a good marker for the two wings of the regiment. He takes command of the left wing and places me in command of the right. Company I is still out there on picket. We know he will get the avalanche first and Major Graham goes out to join I Company in their baptism from the Army of the Potomac.

It's not long in coming. With sunrise, we come under artillery fire that increases by the hour. By nine or ten o'clock, we can hear by the din of musketry before us that Company I is having a hard time of it. They finally fall back to a fringe of woods, repel a Union skirmish line high-balling after them, and then head for the regiment just as the main Union battle lines begin tramping up over the ridge.

Company I comes over our ditch and we have nothing to do now but watch Grant's Army emerge in all its full power and glory. I find myself wondering for just a moment about Connecticut and Middletown, but it is only for just a moment and it passes. Oh, but it is a sight to see them coming on out there. By ten o'clock, the fields to our front and to the horizon itself are filled by the long blue lines that march silently forward, the rising sun gleaming on rank after rank of bayonets. You can see an occasional Union officer galloping across the fields, and their couriers passing back and forth, while Union batteries continue to come up, swing around, deploy, and add to the universal roar.

We continue to wait in silence and do not fire, for due to the contour of the ground, the Feds are able to bring their lines of battle below the crest of the ridge 300 yards away and mass them there while being out of range of rifle fire. This long silent march of rank after rank of Union infantry that disappear just below the crest of the ridge continues for some time. At noon, it is all still going on, but we do receive a little bit of encouragement - far to the North, we can hear a distant roar of artillery in the background. It is Lee at last, on his way south on the turnpike, fighting off Butler's Army of the James as he comes.

In the early afternoon, the main Union assault finally gets underway. A line of battle five ranks deep first marches up toward Elliott's South Carolina Brigade, holding its position just off to our right. We see the South Carolinians break the Union line with a well concentrated and delivered volley. The Union column, after a brief rally only to meet a second volley, falls back in confusion. Some of our marksmen at my command fire a few long range shots at Union officers in that assault, but most of the right wing hold fire and wait. We know our turn will come soon enough. I see one boy in my company, Private P. T. Sossamon, trembling and with the eyes of a trapped rabbit. I touch him on the shoulder and say "It'll be all right, son". He gives me a sick smile in return.

As the smoke rolls off from the South Carolinians' front, leaving the fields before them vacant, a heavy Union artillery barrage opens on us, preparing for the next assault. We can sense their massed infantry still waiting silently below the crest and know it will now be our turn. We are ready for them. One shell with a smoking, sputtering fuse falls among the men of Company D and an enlisted man tosses it outside the trench with the exclamation, "Get out of there!" We all have to laugh at that. The shells are now striking all up and down the line and I *******

****

PAUL T. SOSSAMAN, PRIVATE, COMPANY B

I see Captain Frank Roberts, hit by the shell, and a scalding hot spray of blood and bone hit me hard on the cheek. Thomas grabs me by the sleeve and yells Look, Paul!, but I see it. The Captain just stands there a moment longer, tall and erect, like Forever, but there is no head, just the bright fountain thrusting seemingly as high as heaven. Then, ever so slowly, the body sways once and then just folds in on itself, on the ground, down to the earth. Then the men of the right wing, after a moment of stunned silence, open fire, our marksmen picking off the Union gunners. After a few minutes, the Union shelling lifts. When the smoke clears, the open field in front of us is still vacant, but everyone knows what's waiting just below the crest. I can't take my eyes off Capt'n Roberts - the blood has just about stopped now where he is and I keep wiping at my face with my blanket roll. I am a-shakin' and Thomas says, "Paul, are you sure you're all right?" I nod my head, but I ain't.

It's now mid-afternoon and during this brief lull, Fields' Division of the Army of Northern Virginia at last comes across the brow of Blantford Hill and files into the trenches. They can't believe it when they see us and how we hold on with what little we got - half dug trenches manned by a single rank of starving, sleepless men; we are as much worn down by the threat facing us as by hunger and fatigue. Some of the men try to raise a feeble cheer of welcome, but most of us just cry a few tears in relief.

The left wing of the 56th is getting ready to retire as the division files on into the trench when at last the main Yankee assault begins. However, there are now two and three lines of men in our ditch and we easily beat this one off. Then the men in Field's Division strip their blankets from their shoulders and pile cartridges on the ground before them as they occupy the position of the left wing of the regiment. That left wing now withdraws in a run across the open field to the rear under heavy artillery fire.

But a handful of men stays behind on the left to continue the battle. Separated from their company, me, Private Elliott, and several others meet Lieutenant Davis and six or seven men of Company G. The Prophet says that part of the regiment had withdrawn, but other parts had remained; and he asks the squad to remain in the trenches with him. We are soon joined by a sergeant and another enlisted man of Company F and we make a line in the ranks of a South Carolina Regiment about 100 yards west of the right wing of the regiment.

A Yank attack soon breaks on the right wing of the regiment, delaying their pullout. The Yanks come on three ranks deep, raise a cheer, and then charge our line on a run. But one good volley sends it fallin' back in disorder. Those of us under Lieutenant Davis, the left wing of the regiment, see line after line of Yankee infantry still tramping down to the branch under the crest of the hill; they are massing down there for another attack.

When the attack comes, it is led by Warren's old V Corps and it comes booming. Their fire is heavy; I see two men shot down beside me, but I don't dare look at the blood. We wait until the Yankee ranks are halfway across the field and about 100 yards away before we fire and drive them back again in confusion. By sunset, they have massed seven regimental flags just under the crest of the hill, but don't make another try.

The right wing of the regiment, still in line, throws back a last Yankee attack that marches up to their front at sunset. The men wait until they are within speaking distance and their belt buckles can be clearly seen before pouring a murderous volley that knocks them into confusion. Then, the rest of the 56th on the right marches out to the rear under a brisk musketry fire as the Army of Northern Virginia occupies its position.

But Lieutenant Davis and his squad stay with the South Carolinians under heavy musketry and artillery fire until midnight before being able to rejoin the regiment in a rear area. We are the last unit of the 56th to withdraw.

The battle of the 18th of June is over, but it ain't over. It ain't ever going to be over. I know that now. We will never know how many we lost since returning to Petersburg, but for certain there are many among the officers alone. Cap'n Roberts, the last officer of Company B is killed; Major Graham is again wounded; Captain Lawson Harrill is shaken by a shell concussion and is unfit for duty for several days. These men are not alone. There are others. This Blood Run, begun at Ware Bottom Church, is hurtin' us bad continuing on June 18th and after.

The next day, June 19, the brigade rests in reserve, with the 56th camped on the Jerusalem Plank Road within musket range of the Yankee lines. The sun (like a burnished bronze disk nailed overhead) is oppressively hot, we are exhausted, and there is simply not enough strength to hold the lines any longer against the Army of the Potomac without Lee. After a rest of 24 hours, we're in somewhat better condition (if there was only water to wash the blood) and we are put on the right of the line to work on fortifications.

On June 22, we report for duty to Lt. General A. P. Hill at the extreme right of the Confederate line and are held in reserve during the Battle of Jones House on that date, in which Hill brought in 1600 prisoners. But the next day finds us back in the trenches, working again on the breastworks.

On the night of June 23, we are on the march again, this time up the line to a point just east of the city. At midnight, we advance slowly beyond the trenches toward an advanced Confederate outpost. When the sun (red as blood) rises again, we are still on outpost and the double line of troops holds position until nightfall while the 56th holds the outlying line. We are under only slight fire, but with no sleep, no rest, with all this blood, it is hard to stay as ready as we have to be in the trenches. But, if we can only hold this line until dawn, we will be fine. We will be fine. But what does it all mean?

From the 25th to the 27th of June, we move back again to the main line, where we work on the breastworks again under the fire of Yankee pickets. We are doing all the heavy labor you can imagine on these breastworks, but it's no more than a shallow ditch brim-top with blood with one thin line holding against Grant's advancing thousands; although I know Lee's whole army is here at last, we are still alone. By the first day of July (another hot day), the front becomes fairly quiet and though we have no shovels or tools that have still not arrived from Petersburg, the Confederate trenches along the front of the 56th are in desperate but excellent condition by July 3. All apart now, all confusion, but on that day, June 18, we knew what we had to do. Yes, the answer is there somewhere - what we have to do, what it all means, what it's all for.

That same night of the 18th, Yankee picket corps fire grows brisker, but within only forty-eight hours, the front is once again quietly flaming scarlet. And so after the deep darkness of cancer, after the sudden touch to the heart and the long and lasting pain, after the final silence at last has come, I know I will return again to that memorable day to find truth in the unceasing roar of cannon, in the crowds of milling troops in the trenches and the gun smoke resting like fog under a dust filled sky. I know that I will be lost and confused once again, but it will be unnoticed there where there are so many others lost and confused on that raging battlefield of

Petersburg, on June 18 in that confused, forgotten year, that lost year of 1864.

I know that I will again push my way through the crowds of shouting men until I find him, the Prophet among the one small squad of men standing about him, with their eyes still on him after all this time.

Then I too will stand among them in all that confusion, yet near enough to hear his last quiet words to them - There is going to be an interesting time here and I want to see it out. If you will stay with me, I'll take care of you.

Then I will step between the men as they turn away, and reaching out, all in an unbelievably unforgettable moment of time, touch him again on the sleeve and say in a barely audible whisper, Lieutenant. And as he turns and looks deep into my own eyes for the second time, I will say, "It's the only way, Lieutenant. The only way we can bring it all back together again. For us to come back here to the Crater, again and again, until we find what it all means. It's the only way, Sir. The Crater's going to be here and we have to come back again. You're a prophet - you know that." A look of surprise, confusion, understanding, and recognition will cross his face and as suddenly be suppressed. "The Crater? No time for that now", he will say, "You know what to do? You keep your head down. You stay where you're told. You know how to - Sergeant Loundon!"

"Yes, Sir!"

"Keep an eye on this boy."

Then he will turn away and the sergeant will force a discarded rifle into my hands and at the same time I will hear the Prophet's voice, measured and calm, say somewhere behind me,

"Step up to the firing line."

Then suddenly, again without quite knowing how it will happen, I will find myself resting the musket over the red clay and looking out over an empty field, at the far end of which will rest a great, vast, still cloud of smoke and dust, and I will then know this is what I will relive all my life long, this is what it was all lived for, all this—just for this one moment.

We are only two men to a yard and I am just wondering if this is all of us that there is going to be when I again hear the Prophet say, "You will wait for the order." I don't quite understand what he means by this and I turn my head and see him standing about ten feet away. He is looking at me when I see him, but then he looks away in an instant just as soon as my eyes meet his - and he stands there, like some abandoned statue, in his worn frock coat, with his legs slightly apart and braced, with his hands clasped behind him; with the leather cover now unbuttoned from the holster holding the Navy Colt revolver at his side.

But suddenly at that same instant, I find myself rudely grasped by the shoulder and thrown back hard to face the field, and the sergeant is saying in a low voice in my ear, "You git yore eyes back to the front, Boy. You ain't going nary place but right cheer".

Among the snickering of the men on each side of me, I say hotly, "You don't have to worry about me none. You worry 'bout some one else, but not me." But the sergeant only glares down at me and says, "Lieutenant told me to keep an eye on you."

And then, at that moment, the great silence ends. On the far side of that field over which stands a sun burnished like bronze, a distant sound of drums begins to rise. For what seems forever, there is nothing else but that faint, unending rumble, but that slowly increasing roar of the drums slowly fills all the sky until at last their first flags slowly begin to rise above all that smoke and dust - the old, bright scarlet, white, and blue flags of their nation, with gold tassels and a tiny golden eagle on the top of each staff; and other flags - and I can recognize the white silk and gold shield of the State of Massachusetts. And then there begin to appear underneath them the first long, straight lines of uplifted rifles, each with its own bayonet glinting in the sun. And then there slowly appear underneath them in turn the long, unending, densely packed lines of marching men of the old Army of the Potomac - not running as we like deer, leaping as deer as we go down to death, but with a slow, measured, seemingly relentless tread, with knees lifting high all at once in cadence, all with rifles carried at Right Shoulder Arms, with faces turned to us all with no expression, and all moving in a silence, a total and complete silence filled only by the encompassing roar of the drums.

As their brigade line crosses a small rise, I can see their field and staff officers appearing behind the on-coming line, each one on horseback, with one hand casually resting on the hip and the reins wrapped twice around the riding hand; then, behind them in turn, even the whirl and flourish of the drum sticks as they are lifted high after each long roll on the drums, but the drummers themselves I cannot see, and wonder why until I remember that they are only small boys.

"You will await the order", the Prophet says, breaking the silence. Then, after a long moment, "All ready on the firing line."

Then, each man brings back the hammer on his musket. I try and find to my horror that my hand keeps slipping off the hammer. Finally, I take both hands and pull it all the way back.

The two men on each side of me begin to laugh.

"Took him two hands to git ready fer the elephant."

"Gits hot enuf, he'll do her with his fanger."

"Gits hot enuf, he`ll do her with his pecker."

The tears burn into my eyes and I try to think of something, anything to say, but before I can respond, that heavy blue mass of men, now halfway across the field, halts, and then in a single slow movement, the rifles come down from their shoulders and all in one instant there is a crashing volley, white smoke suddenly covering their line, through which stab out angry, red, flickering lights, and the dirt all around me leaps and jumps, and the air around my head is filled with buzzing hornets, and I find myself crying out in pure terror, in spite of all I can do. I hear other men crying out and in pain, and for one instant, I see one beside me slowly sliding down to the bottom of the trench. There is no blood visible, only the dark stain of urine and the packet of letters that so many of them hold at the last, pulling them from his shirt as he dies.

The wall of white smoke lies motionless on the field. Then, ever so slowly, it begins to turn darker, and then still darker, and then yet darker still, and then all at once that terrible blue machine once more bursts forth from out of that cloud into the blinding sunlight, once more in motion, but running hard now, yet in unbelievably slow motion too, like in a dream, with rifles now leveled toward us, and no longer silent now, but giving their deep Northern cheer, so different from our own wild cry, a cheer as steady now as their movement was mechanical before - Huz-Za! Huz-Za! Huz-Za! Huz-Za! Huz-Za!

I feel a growing heaving in my stomach, and seem to hear the Prophet's voice only as if from a great distance: "Stead-d-y. You will await the order."

Then he says those few words, quietly and calmly as all the rest: "Take aim." I sweep the sight of the musket first from one face to another in that oncoming line that is now so near, that is too near - Not that officer, he'll be taken care of by someone else - Not him, he has a moustache just like mine - Not him, too young - and then suddenly I find him! I find him! I find him - a bearded file sergeant with yellow chevrons, and I settle my cheek ever so softly against the stock of the rifle, as softly as against the cheek of any loving woman, and half close one eye, and take one last look at that face over the sights. All Hail, My Fellow Seeker For The Truth. And then I slowly lower the sights on down to the brass belt buckle and wait.

The silence on our line is now all pervasive, only broken once by his voice, You will await the order. And then only once more by the single word: "Stead-d-y..."

That brass belt buckle on that Yankee soldier - it's now filling the whole god-damn sight of the rifle - And it is as gold and bronze, as blinding bright and burnished as that sun itself high overhead, but it seems to me to burn with its own special light too, growing slowly larger and larger even as I watch, until finally at long last the two single massive bronze letters on the buckle - U. S. - slowly emerge out of all that blinding fire and great silence.

CHAPTER THIRTEEN

H. A. L. SWEEZY, LIEUTENANT, COMPANY I

Victory is an illusion; survival, doubtful; atonement, impossible. Yes, any kind of atonement for last year is surely impossible. And it would haunt me continually, as it does the others, were it not for one singular event that occurred over a year ago.

For when I lose all faith, whenever I find all this too aimless, too terrifying, then I think back upon the Blackwater, when we were young and anything was possible. Some of us remember that winter with horror, but I remember the iridescent sparkle of the snow, the jeweled icicles on the trees, the first Christmas in camp, and the river, flowing unceasingly through the dark and silent forest. But there was one moment I value above all, the one moment that for a while at least, gave this regiment and me immortality. The boys in Company I still talk about it, even now, in these trenches: "Say now, do you remember how Lieutenant Hal Sweezy took on that gunboat and run it back down the river? Remember? You should have been there that day!" Yes, a man can live on that for a while.

Of course, we have done well in action since the Swamp. Plymouth came first and then with Beauregard, holding Grant's whole army at bay. Any unit in this army can well be proud of that. But the incident on the Blackwater was my own moment - all mine, with the few men who were with me.

Now here, it has all fallen into an indeterminable round of sun and earth. Not much glory here for Lieutenant Hal and the boys. Not even much water here like on the Blackwater; just the blazing sun, the everlasting earth, dirt, dust - whatever you want to call it.

Of course, the Yanks never leave us alone. They fire those damn mortars more and more day by day on the works, reaching a peak on the night of July 17. The next two days, during the occasional lulls in the firing, we engage in mundane, but necessary work details, collecting Union shells and solid shot for the Confederate Ordinance Department; the brigade alone collects fifteen Hotchkiss shells and a quantity of lead.

Any way, most of the work on the trenches has to be done at night to avoid sharpshooter and artillery fire from the densely manned Union lines only 100 to 300 yards away. We deepen the trenches; then build revetments of timber on the inside walls. "Streets" and latrines are thoroughly policed. When the sun is too hot, we set up brush and blanket shelters over the trench. Then, "bomb-proofs" or bunkers are excavated behind the main line. These are dug out in a square or oblong excavation, with stout logs brought in from a mile away to make a heavy roof, which is then covered with a bed of leaves, and over that a mound of earth is placed. We use these for sleeping quarters when the opportunity rises, preferring them to the brush or blanket shelters in the trenches. But by July, most of this work on the breastworks along our front is completed, at least as far as we can make it.

Sharpshooting and artillery occasionally halts by tacit consent, but more frequently the fire is continuous. This is especially the case when the Yanks have a victory to celebrate. Then, they spend a half day or more shelling away at our lines. Our men in Ransom's Brigade, short on ammunition, rarely reply in kind.

During the early part of the siege, the mortar fire is incessant and the men dread these weapons more than any other. We have no mortars on our part of the line and we just have to endure the fire, all the while seeing in the distance the Yanks lounging securely about out in the open behind their main line. In mid-July, Brigadier General Johnson, commanding the division, advocates the construction of wooden mortars using twelve-pound shot as a means of relieving the pressure, but these last only a few rounds before splitting from the powder charge. And even at the best, they never have much range.

There are heavy casualties early in the summer in the brigade, but by midsummer, the casualties from mortars fall as we learn to take precautions. We even become philosophical about it all, one captain of the 56th observing to his men one night that "it is a poor philosophy that fears what it cannot avoid", but the real reason is that we begin to learn how to cope with fear. Yes, that's it. Not the trenches we dig; not the wooden artillery we make; not even good ole grit and pluck; but how to face fear, without flinching.

By midsummer, we watch each minuscule black spot set against a white cloud or overcast sky and learn to take cover. In a sky filled with the blazing sun in a blue sky, as many of these days during the summer of 1864 are, often the only warning is the slow, sudden hissing of the fuse as the mortar shell comes down on us out of nowhere.

As the summer wears on, provisions and supplies for the men steadily deteriorate and this causes us increasing concern. While tobacco and coffee are sometimes traded with Yank pickets (whose uniforms are always so clean and new), most of the men find the food to be miserable by midsummer. Musty meal and rancid Nassau bacon that is nearly all grease is what we eat, along with a uniformly poor quality of bread and cornmeal obtained from Petersburg. It takes a few days to get used to the worms and weevils and then you eat them right along with the rest - an extra meat ration, as it were. All water has to be carried up to the trenches from the rear areas until wells can be dug and so all water is severely rationed at the front. It is as I said, sun and earth - these are the only realities here.

The weather is intensely hot and dust covers everything -equipment, horses, men, all in the same impenetrable powder, so fine that we walk in a cloud of our own making. The trenches lie still and motionless under the sun with not a breath of wind. The shelling continues all day, for each blazing hour until nightfall and even then there is light in the dark, in the sky - wonderful light.

The bright strings of musketry fire flickering, in two parallel lines marking the outposts, make a delicate necklace across the landscape; behind them, the brighter, diamond flashes of the heavier artillery; overhead, in opposite directions, the burning shells in almost horizontal flight, in lines of six or eight at a time, chasing, passing, re-passing one another, momentarily coming together as star clusters in the sky, only to silently separate and then go their ways to different destinations. It would be beautiful, were it not for the terror.

Smoke provides a lurid backdrop to the drama, sometimes hiding the flash of the guns, but more often lighting up beautifully from within. And over all, the sounds: the crackle of the musketry, from the clear, sharp crack close at hand to the distant sustained chatter; the thundering roar of the cannon, followed by the screaming and bursting of the shells, sometimes drowning every other sound, sometimes dying to a sullen silence. And in that silence can be heard the cries, the prayers and curses, the shouts and calls of men, scarcely more human than the weapons and the purpose they serve.

Picket lines in front of the main trenches are manned each night and vacated each dawn. Life in the trenches is described by one man as a "veritable hell", with most of the officers and men on duty for sixteen long hours a day. The five regiments of the brigade exchange positions every week or so, but the duty is the same no matter where they are placed. Men are sent out on picket and fatigue duty every night. From two in the morning until dawn, the entire division, brigade, and regiment is awake and standing at arms in the trenches, peering toward the Union lines. But with first light, the guard is relaxed and then the day-long struggle resumes against the mortars, the sharpshooters, and the sun.

And you learn soon enough that while the sun and sky overhead are to be feared, at last, the earth, in which you sweated so long and hard, becomes a friend, your best friend. It is the one tangible thing you can count on. This sun, this heat that brings the sap bubbling from the split pine facings (too hot to touch) inside the trenches; this slow weakening and ending of the flesh without glory; even this high blue vault spotted from time to time with small white clouds of exploding shell - these all pass and fade, but the earth is yours to the end. You can see it in the crevices between the pales, heaped on top of the parapet, firm and stubborn under your boot sole. To break off one clod and to rub it between your fingers is to become convinced of its reality. And what it can do for that precious life of yours! It shields and protects from nature as well as from man. It is cool and dark, the thick sand-clay soil loose between the fingers. It can be moved to provide protecting space. It is the mother and the one solitary thing in these trenches that man can trust and cling to and bury their faces into and at the end consign themselves to.

Occasionally, the men cheer General Lee as he rides along the lines wearing a white straw hat, but more often the day is simply something to be endured. And of course, casualties continue. As one man describes it:

Soon the word would come down the line that Tom was killed and Dick wounded and from another part of our line it would be Jim and Sam were killed and soon the word would be two killed in Co. - and six wounded in Co. - and so it went on

Our losses continue to climb under these harsh conditions and they are beginning to take more than one form. Colonel Faison is commanding the brigade again on General Bushrod Johnson's recommendation, but by mid-July Johnson is beginning to regret his choice. So we hear, in whispered undertone from the adjutant, that division orders to Faison on July 12 to personally supervise work on the brigade line are ignored and Johnson is demanding explanations in writing.

But I think Colonel Faison's problem in fulfilling his duties is perhaps not so much insubordination as it is acute diarrhea; by July 25, he is in a Raleigh hospital where he will remain for the rest of the summer. Lieutenant Colonel G. Graitiott Luke leaves the front with a severe carbuncle on the 18th of June and by the end of the month is still confined in a hospital. On July 3, he is also sent to a Richmond hospital, where he is admitted for anthrax and at the end of July, he is sent home on sick furlough, suffering from chronic diarrhea, debility, and feruncles. Major John W. Graham, the only remaining field officer present with the regiment, has been wounded in the June 18 engagement, sent to the hospital three days later, and then he too heads home for a month on sick furlough. The duty of commanding the regiment until Graham's return at the end of July falls on the only senior officer present for duty, Captain Lawson Harrill. And of course, company officers and the boys hang on as long as they can.

Casualties from enemy fire during the first three weeks of July are comparatively light. In the entire brigade, only four men are killed and twenty-one wounded during the first week of July. Two weeks later, the casualty rate per week of the brigade is still only eight killed and twenty-two wounded. But, the depleted 56th Regiment is taking its own share of the killing. By July 21, four men have been killed and twenty-two wounded in the regiment since arriving on the line and these include a heavy proportion of company officers.

Some companies of the regiment are commanded only by lieutenants, and soon sergeants are beginning to write the casualty reports to hometown newspapers in North Carolina, a duty that in 1863 would have been the responsibility of an officer attached to regimental staff. But now the non-commissioned officers are taking their own casualties as well and the enlisted men in the 56th are not faring any better. Many men are breaking under the stress and poor fare. Typhoid fever is rampant; nearly all have dysentery. Each day, a train load of sick and wounded steams from Petersburg to Richmond, but the hospitals there offer little hope. Private John Elliott, slightly wounded in the trenches at Petersburg, catches measles in the hospital. Other men of the 56th are dying in the hospitals of typhoid that summer and there are instances where wounded are neglected and do not receive adequate hospital care at all.

And here too, in the hospitals, under the canvas, disturbed only by the persistent flies, those who go there cannot escape the sun - it follows you everywhere in brilliant patches on the wall; there in the silver reflection on the basin, in the silent golden orb printed on the roof of the tent (crossed and recrossed in intersecting lines by one blue bottle fly, circling aimlessly, without purpose or direction for hours). The sun, the heat, the labored breath in the cot or in the trenches; the baked and parched air - these are the enemy and so one turns to the cool earth as to a lover.

Then, late in July, there is a change in all this, a change we do not at first understand. We begin to feel a vague uneasiness that seeps through every rank of the command, through every section of the line. A soldier in the brigade describes it as an intangible, indefinable dread that began to creep over us, something that we could not shake off, that followed us all day; something that haunted us at night, that we could not get away from; something we could not even imagine what it could be, but that kept us restless and uneasy all the time.

Rumors sweep through the trenches; we no longer know what to believe. We only know that it is real and that many things are in our dreams, but there is always one thing in them above all and that is Death. Yes, we know that it is Death, for death is what we think of here, in this place. And so we lift up our eyes to it, in terror, as one does to such an eternal mother, who will bring us such eternal things.

CHAPTER FOURTEEN

WILLIAM CALLAHAN, LIEUTENANT, COMPANY C

Closed spaces in my dreams, the waking ones, the sleeping ones, the whisperer in the dark ... I have a horror of it all and now it seems that we live, breathe, sleep in closed spaces - bomb-proofs, trenches, rifle pits, covered ways, transverses. Closed spaces. I do not tell anyone else of them, but they live in my dreams, both the sleeping and the waking ones.

It begins all one long summer's day in 1845 in Camden County, North Carolina. Of course I'm probably never in as much danger as I think, but it is terrifying. There are only four steps leading up to the porch of the Big House, but where the bricks have fallen out on one side, a small boy can crawl under the steps, under the porch for a hiding place. It is cool under the porch, spacious enough for a boy and his dog, with the bright sunlight and all the great world dazzling outside. It is enclosed there, but safe and comfortable and you hear parents, brothers, and sisters tramping overhead, calling Will Callahan! Now where's that Will?

But today, I find a broken place in the foundation, where, by digging and scraping, a way can be made into still another world - the closed space beneath the great old house itself.

I push my way through the hole I made with only a single candle in my hand. The roof (the floor of that other world of the house) is so low I have to crawl on my stomach and the candle soon goes out; it is dark as night here, the dirt, fine and powdery. There's nothing much here really, but old bricks, the mummified carcass of what seems to be a house rat, the dusky carcasses of dead beetles and centipedes, old dirty spider webs that you have to push aside with one hand, one empty bottle probably left there when the house was built.

And the darkness, the space beneath that house seems to extend without limit on and on into a darker night than I have ever known until now.

I know now, this long night, that it was foolish to do what I attempted, namely to crawl to the farthest limit of the base of the house. Perhaps I thought I was an explorer in a totally unknown, forgotten world (which I was); perhaps it was in the hope of finding lost artifacts, lost treasures, unknown things; perhaps it is just boredom with the long summer day outside. But I venture deep into the dark underworld there, feeling the hard wood pressing ever closer against my back, the air becoming ever more dusty and close; going farther and farther on into that closed night until with a single mighty effort, I turn a quarter turn around and see, an immeasurable distance away, that faint, tiny bar of light that marks where the steps are.

At last, I reach the very rear of the house. There are not even spider webs here, just dust, and dirt, and musty air, and the hard wood pressing me face down to the ground. A closed space, you see. I rest there for a few minutes, listening to the heavy footfalls of the house servants, of the family upstairs (now that must be the back serving area above me), secure once again in the knowledge that no one knows where I am. And then I start to turn to make the long crawl back to the light.

And it is now I discover that I have a problem. I can only make a one-quarter turn and then I am held fast by the wooden frame on my back. Try as I will, I can go neither forward nor back. It is dark and silent here - dark as the nethermost Hell that the Parson talks about, with the air so thick I find myself panting to get my breath. Not to see or breathe is surely the worse of all possible deaths and it is facing me now, in this dark. After a moment of wild panic, I reason that I can be rescued if the very worst comes to worst, but then how can that be, when the entire house will have to be moved to reach me? I call for help until my voice is hoarse - any kind of help - but no one can hear me.

Then I see a dark figure crawling, stealthily, close to the earth, toward me. Does it live here? For a moment, I catch my breath, but it is Cal.

"Good Lord-A-Mercy", he whispers, "What you doin' in here,

White Boy? Yore Ma will whup you sho'."

"She won't never know, 'lessen you tell."

"And what wuz I suppose to say when she see you covered with dirt and bugs? You tell me that now. If you ain't a sight. Yore own Ma wouldn't know you like you is."

Then Cal reaches out his hand to me. What a beautiful hand it is! Warm as earth on the outside, white as mine in the palm, I will always remember when, reaching, it finally touches mine.

Then, by backing a little and making first a quarter turn, then a half turn, we slowly begin to pull ourselves together toward that distant bar of light. It is a long journey back, fighting panic every inch of the way. Oh, we're a sight to see when we finally get to the steps and then scamper out into the wonderful sunlight. Covered from head to foot with dust, scratches all over our hands and backs, shirts torn in three and four places, dripping wet with perspiration, we are really, really terrified. I am able to make up some story to account for all the damage, for I know I will be severely punished if I tell the truth. But there is no keeping secrets from old Jamie -one of our folks who did the yard work for us and he is also Cal's grand-pappy. He looks at that hole under the steps, scratches his white head, and says "Well, now, you see, young marster. Them closed spaces will get you sho." And that night he tells Cal and me down at the cabin the worse stories you ever heard, of what lives under those houses, in those closed spaces - spiders hairer than your head, snakes as long as the Cunnel, rats bigger than dogs, worse of all, The Cumberbund and he never does tell us what that is, it's so awful. Pure horror -that's the only word for that afternoon. I never went under there again, I can tell you that.

And now all this at Petersburg. Twenty years later and more and we are all in closed spaces now. We live in the ground, under the ground, and the Yankee fire is the floor pressing us into the earth. It all comes back too fast, too soon. Closed spaces.

That is why I have so much respect for those other men over there who were able to do what they did. And as one of the men said to me afterwards, "Well, Lieutenant Callahan, you kain't say they didn't hit us with no warning."

On July 21, the first digging sounds can be heard in the front of Gracie's Brigade, but we are ordered to take precautions in our own front, as well. We are pretty certain that the Yanks are driving a tunnel somewhere underneath our works, that they will fill it with gunpowder, and then blow us to Kingdom Come, although of course we have no idea just when and where the Big Moment will come. Soon all the men are aware of the haunting possibility under their feet. Many enlisted men in the brigade notice Confederate batteries to our rear being trained on the salient and, according to one soldier, many feel their "only concern after that (is) we might be placed there". Whether or not all of the men in the regiment share this remarkable instance of clairvoyance (and I think we all do in some measure), we are busily engaged by late July in probing for the mine with augers down to a depth of twenty-five feet and we are cautioned to listen for any sounds of digging beneath our feet. Special squads from the 56th are ordered to begin counter-mines in an attempt to intercept the Union mine.

That is when I again have to take my heart in hand, to venture once again down into those closed spaces. We really don't have much idea of what we will do if we actually intercept the Union tunnel, or what we will find there. A tunnel pretty much like our own, most like, although some of the men jokingly talk of railroad tracks, with a flag bedecked locomotive and freight cars of high explosives, with the smoke from the engine already wisping up from between the cobblestones in Petersburg. But it will probably be a tunnel like ours and in it, men like ours, and then there will come a nightmarish struggle in the dark, in the closed space, with pick axes, shovels, and bare hands before it is over. But we never do intercept them, though afterwards, it is found that one of our tunnels missed the mine by only fifty feet.

The entire brigade stands to arms from two in the morning until daybreak every day. Work on the covered ways leading up to the front line trenches is being pushed by the 22nd of the month, although working parties on this detail are scattered the next day by a rain of Federal artillery. On the 25th of July, men in the brigade note an enemy heavy work near Taylor's House which possibly is earth excavated from the Union mine. On the 29th, we are still working hard on the breastworks and covered ways under the continuous fire of three Union field pieces. When we look up the line with our picks in our hands, we can see Elliott's Brigade on our immediate right occupying the salient on the crest of the other ridge.

Then comes the slow dawn of July 30, 1864. We have been standing at arms in the trenches, as always, since two that morning. Just as the line of battle is about to be relieved, the Union mine explodes at last. To some of the men of the 56th Regiment, only a few hundred yards north of the explosion, it comes as a dull thud sounding somewhere off to the right. But to Captain Lawson Harrill, commanding the regiment, it comes as a terrible explosion and as he springs from the oil cloth on which he has been resting, he feels a rocking trembling motion of the earth. To me, it comes as a sullen, heavy roar, and the ground moves and trembles beneath my boots. When we turn to look toward the salient, all we see is a heavy cloud of dust and smoke, rising and rolling away, fraught with dull red flashes of light, hiding the horizon; a second sunrise as it were, but one dark and red like those in the infernal regions, if there be any such there.

Some of the men are only half dressed, but all of us spring to our posts and the regiment is ready for action within two minutes. A two hundred-gun artillery barrage opens from the Union lines - a barrage so heavy that we wonder if the coming assault will be a general one all along the front. But, no - this is reserved for just where the mine exploded - or The Crater, as it shall be known forevermore.

Against the dawn, a cloud of dust and smoke is still slowly rolling away over what had been Elliott's Salient when Colonel L. M. McAfee, commanding the brigade, orders the 25th and 49th regiments to withdraw and occupy the last ridge overlooking the city to our rear. The 56th Regiment is ordered to move to the right up the trenches toward the crater to occupy the vacated lines. This movement puts us beside the 17th South Carolina, but it is soon withdrawn to participate in the coming assault and so we move still farther to the south to fill its space. Now we are the only unit on the northern lip of the crater, although we can see little in all that confused medley of smoke, dust, and half-filled trenches and traverses. But we do see hundreds of Union soldiers pouring over the edge to disappear into the crater itself - both blacks and whites. By this time, the Union advance is filling the crater and partially occupying some of the traverses and covered ways to each side of it.

The 56th forms in the abandoned trenches immediately to the

north of the crater and prepares to hold them against a frontal assault. The trenches are in good condition, with rifle pits and pointed stakes on the side facing the Union lines. The Federal assault comes a little later that morning and it comes down the opposite hill toward the creek at the base of the hill in our immediate front. It is a full brigade, with a regiment deployed in line of battle, part of the X Corps, but the Union formation loses its alignment in negotiating its way down the steep hill. Most of their troops take shelter under the hill in irregular order and, like their comrades in the crater itself, fail to advance. We engage their skirmishers, but their main line won't push, and so we are able to turn our greater attention to the crater on our right, where our men begin to open a devastating fire on Black Union soldiers at the crater itself trying to enter or withdraw from the growing carnage there.

A number of the men become ecstatic when they see so many targets so near at hand. "Niggers! Get the God-damn Niggers!" they cry out and pour a simply murderous fire into them, volley after volley, or more often, just firing at will until the ground is covered with their bodies. They fire again and again, until the barrels of the muskets are too hot to touch and there seems no end to the killing. "The Niggers! Get the Niggers!"

But many of the men are appalled by what we behold. At the moment, there is little time for reflection (that will come later), for it is one of those life-and-death situations so common in combat, when there is only one primal red haze of tooth-and-claw against the enemy. But then I think again of Cal.

Cal (Father had named him after John Calhoun, the great Southern statesman, I believe) has been my faithful companion ever since I can remember. We eat from the same plate and sleep in the same bed. We exchange Christmas gifts - all while the adults aren't watching. He is near-about my own age, maybe a couple of years older, bigger and taller than I, certainly. He watches over me and takes care of me, even fights the Ames brothers one school day at recess when they're tormenting me. But one soft summer afternoon, we engage in a rough-and-tumble wrestling match and, as usual, I have the worst of it, I must admit. There I lay, pinned to the grass, and he beams down on me, and then there comes into those blood-shot eyes a rage and a pain I have never seen before. He lowers his head slowly down to whisper in my ear, "Bottom rail on top now, Massa Will." And then with a laugh releasing me, "I'se gwine grow up to be a Man! A Man! Remember that when the time come!"

It takes a moment for me to get my breath and all I can say is, "Me, too!" We both laugh then and spend the rest of the long afternoon playing soldiers down in the creekbed in the lower pasture.

Cal grows up just as he said he would and we are very close, now riding together to market, now hunting together, he standing watch one night while I go to Beth Simpson's House of Ill Repute; the next night, I signing Father's name to his pass so he can visit the quarters at Captain Bartlett's place five miles down the turnpike. But he never goes into the Army with me as my faithful body servant, as many another does. One dark night, just before the war, Cal runs away, without even telling me, but he is followed by my own silent prayer that he will make it safe to the banks of the Potomac and New England.

I think that is why I suddenly scream out to the men in my company "Cease Fire! God Damn it!" And then other officers and enlisted men in our line do the same. Although scattered firing at the Negro troops still continues, most of us just stand and watch those distant figures stumbling back to their own lines. Each one of them is Cal to me and I want no part of their death. In any case, we have repelled them on our part of the line and Mahone will take care of those in the crater itself. Our work here is finished, as they are. But if Cal's time has come this morning, then he is indeed a man.

At 2 P.M., the charge of Mahone, a charge in which the 25th and 49th regiments participate, proves successful in occupying the crater and the battle is over. During the truce that is called to bury the dead, hundreds of bodies are thrown into the crater and covered with earth. One officer who visits the site at this time said "The dead lay thicker on this field than any before seen". The 56th Regiment has suffered no casualties.

I, too, go there after the battle, stand on the edge of the crater, see all that carnage and find I cannot sleep of nights, even if the Union Artillery were to permit it. It is not just the massive cavity in the brown earth; the dismembered heads, legs, and arms scattered here and there, the entrails (although a shovel of dirt would do for the entrails); the half-buried bodies of the dead, sitting erect and gaping up foolishly at destruction still. Rather, it is the bodies of the dead - hundreds and hundreds of them, black and white, piled indiscriminately into that gaping maw. And it is the bodies of the Blacks that disturb me most - for these are not Yankees, but our own southern people, willing to fight and die bravely for this dream called Emancipation. And I cannot help wondering what Old Jamie or Cal would think of all this, or whether they would have anything at all to say about it, other than a deep silence. A good number of these dead must have been runaways most likely, like Cal. I look into a few faces, but they are so bloated and caked by sun and earth, I do not think their own mothers would know them. Perhaps he is one of these here and now we meet again like this. Or if he is one of those who survived, perhaps those few lives we saved numbered his own. I will never know and neither will he.

Perhaps some day, if only in some other life than this, there will be another meeting, not like this, but just another meeting between the two of us. But only on the other side of Jordan, which knows no time or death, can we now meet as free men, beyond color or age, life or death, or what we have done to each other here. It would be good to see Jamie and Cal one last time there, not as slave or free, black or white, but simply as the first human beings who ever really took care of me. Cal will always be a good friend. And he will always be more than that.

Afterward, I make some remark about the high casualties they had taken and one of the men says in an aside, "What's one more Nigger, more or less?" I stare him down into silence. For Cal is more than a childhood companion, or an accomplice to my youthful transgressions, or a slave. Father knows it, Mother fears it, I hope for it.

You see, the talk down in the quarter is that he is really Father's son, so that would make him my half brother. He whispers it to me, laughing quietly to himself, "How can I be yore brother, Marse Will? But I am." I say nothing, feeling only the warm glow of pride, not shame. As a boy, I had hoped it might be so, and so it is.

Then we go back to the trenches where we are now, once again in bomb-proofs and shelters, once again burrowing into the dark, against mortar shell and sharpshooter, once again in closed spaces. But then I think of all those dead down the line in the crater - thrown in and buried all mix-matched together, black and white, and then with the heavy earth to hold them all down tight and good 'till Judgement Day. So it is horror enough, without what follows. To my last hour, I wish that I did not hear it, for then it would not come with the dreams.

You see, we hear that some of the most seriously wounded are buried while still alive, there, in the crater. Now the thought that Cal, with my vanishing youth, could be there, one of them, and die like that now, brings all the old horror rushing back. At night, I see him there, in these dreams, see what it is like for him there. Just like under the Big House, but now my hand can't quite reach him here. Almost, but not quite. And if he is there, it is I and this war who put him there. Don't you see? I put him there. My own brother. I did it.

Late at night, as the Union artillery dies down toward dawn, in the deep dead of night, I suddenly rise again from my blanket in terror. It is Cal, I am sure of it, I can hear him, whispering to me, but his voice is coming not out of the dark, but from under my feet, from the earth. I light the remnant of the candle we have and then sit on my blanket, utterly alone among all these vast armies, in this great war, under this deep night. I am trembling, shaking, holding the candle in my hand against the dark, barely breathing at all now, listening to that soft whisper in the earth until the slow dawn comes at last.

Oh, we were all together, every one of us, put in a closed space forever on that terrible day.

CHAPTER FIFTEEN

FESS SMITH, SERGEANT, COMPANY F

Now, Lieutenant Callahan never had no call to order us to cease firin'. Whats a nigger, more or less? Them god-dam officers, with chicken-guts on their sleeve, they are a-goin' to lose this war for us yet. What do they know, tellin' us to cease fire? They was the enemy with their bum blowin' up our trench, then tryin' to bust thru to the city. Well, we stopped 'em cold. And it warn't the officers done it any old way, but we 'uns, with the old enfield laid across the dirt. It was me that done it 'til the sun-of-a-bitch told me to stop.

Well, after that Battle of The Crater, there's several days of brisk sharpshooting and heavy artillery fire all along the line from the yanks, but the men are able to take this in stride. On August 1, we vote under fire in the North Carolina election for governor and give Vance a big majority against the peace candidate, William W. Holden. That shows the folks back home what our real spirit is.

For about a week after the battle, the lines between us and the IX Corps stay purty quiet. On August 6, we explode our own bum in front of the yank trenches, but it's a little 'un and just sends the blue-bellys scamperin' back to their main line. On August 7, we make experiments all along our line to see if we can find another rumored mine, but nothing is found. Next day, as yank batteries are being strengthened out in our front, there's a little scare among the men of Ransom's Brigade when a borer hits an obstacle underground. Thinking that it might be the timbers of another mine, we dig with a will, with a detail armed and ready to go in when we break through. But the only thing we find is a big rock that has been there since Creation. How we laugh!

On August 9, wells are at last dug along Johnson's lines and water is reached about twenty-five foot down. Two days later, with the front still quiet, listening tubes are sunk into the ground here and there along the line and faithfully manned. On August 12, we can see the yanks a-rollin' obstacles out into the front of their main line and by dawn of the next day, their line is well-nigh hidden by a line of stakes and palisades.

During August, Captain Lawson Harrill commands the 56th Regiment, helped out by Captain Robert D. Graham of Company D. But we go right on working at reinforcing the parapets with sand bags and gabions. Special blocks of wood with iron facings are used for the marksmen of the regiment, but in spite of all the cautions, there is still an occasional casualty from a enemy sharpshooter.

Although Cap'n Graves of Company H is knocked out for a while by a shell wound, casualties among the enlisted men from enemy fire is overall light. From August 10 to 16, the hull brigade loses only twenty men in wounded, though some of them later die. But the real killers are sickness, disease, and exposure; these get a lot more than the guns. Company officers are still going down sick and since June, Company F has twenty-five deaths alone from sickness.

And then it starts to a-raining. It rains all day and every night in August and that shore don't help none. The hull brigade suffers, havin' only three field officers present for duty by the 21st, but it is the enlisted men who hurt most. On August 18, my buddy private L. S. Wright writes to his parents and he purty well says what's happenin' to us, especially the pore enlisted men:

I am hur in they beStworkS and they Sound of they guneS and cannoneS ar never Still day nor night and I cant rite my mind is confuSed that I cant rite to do aney good - they men iS - mity pore and pale and look very bad and no wonder a laying hur in they hot Sun day after day let it rain or Shine we have it to take our far is verry bad hur they men is all giting verry tierd a Saying hur and Sum ov they men is a runing a way every now and then and I would bed gead tey would all run away then I think I could git to come home for it lookS like every boddy elce can git home - we have but 35 men abl for duty and they looke bad - I cant giv you no Satisfaction a bout my brother Canady Said he was a bleading verry bad but he cant tell whether he is ded or not Sum Says they think he iS ded and Sum thinkS he iS not ded -

Of course sometimes we laugh and joke, hard though it is gettin' to do like we used. We have what one officer calls a Certain
Grim Humor and you can see it come out from time to time. One
day in August, when a civilian in a silk top hat cum struttin' cross
the earthworks from Petersburg-way, a bunch of us scarecrows come
up to him and sadly offer our respects on his cow dyin'. When he
says he never had no cow, then we ask solemn like, "Then what are
you doing with that thar churn on your head in mourning?" And as
he storms off in a big huff, another soldier hollers after him if he can
borrow the "stove pipe" he is wearin' to finish his shelter with. Such
anticks as that, I reackon, make all the rest of it a bit more tolerable.

On August 15, this bed of roses along the lines begins to pick
up. We work on through the day in a drivin' rain on fortifications
under a light mortar fire. During the day, we're busy lookin' for
more yank mines and trying to draw water up from them new wells.
Another small mine of our'n is exploded close to the yankee works,
but there is no damage we can ever see.

Mortar and picket fire the next day is normal and on August 20,
as the rain keeps on fallin' and a-fallin', picket fire dies off even
more under the soppin' skies, as all that water soaks up the air and
the powder. It seems as if the war will go on forever in this same old
senseless round of mud and rain.

But it is not to be. Early on the morning of August 20, the hull
brigade and regiment marches out of the trenches, through the
streets of Petersburg, and way on out to the far right end of our line
on the Weldon Railroad. Out of those dam trenches at last! And here
we are in the open again, after three months, rain fallin', but on the
move again, in motion. Anything's better than that slow dyin' in
them closed up trenches, with nary a space enuf to breathe.

There are fields of green pasture, and farms, and sparklin'
brooks, and more trees than we ever remembered. The boys are
worse than a pack of young uns' - Look - Thar's a bird nest! or
Look at the grass; Hit's so green! We don't even notice the rain
none, we're so happy and relieved to be out of them dam trenches.

When we arrive on the far right, we're attached to Major
General Henry Heth who is gettin' ready to drive the V Corps from
Globe Tavern. They had taken the place just a day or two before and

cut the railroad, so they have to be driven off. Cap'n. Harrill is sick and the 56th is under the command of Cap'n W. G. Graves, just back from recoverin' from a wound. While we wait for orders, Private Wright sits down and writes home of what is bothering him:

I got they letter and SockS - bred and beef you Sent to me - ans was glad to gitthem and to hur you was all well I Set down and did eat ov my bred an meat and was glad to gitit we are in they breSt work yet not noing when we may be kild - I can tel one thin that i do no we are in a mity mudy plase - I never can tel what to rite when I go to rite I want you to still rite - you Spoke about Sending me Sumthin to eat you cant while we are in Such a confuSio I will have to quit for I Cant rite while my mind iS So confuSed you muSt do they beSt with they Stock you can Sel any thing that you think beSt I will be Satisfide I cant tell you what iS BeSt -

At first dawn on the 21st of August, 1864, the heavy yank line out at Globe Tavern pulls on back to its masked batteries. They have near about twenty-six guns on open ground coverin' the railroad. We later learn they were given orders just to use solid shot firin' into the woods and to lower the elevation so that the shot will hit at the edge of the woods and come in at us on the bounce. That's what we are going to have to face.

Well, the attack comes later in the day. We have coverin' fire from our own artillery, but that turns out to be a curse in a disguise. Ahead of us is a forest and on the other side of it the massed yankee infantry and artillery jest a-waitin' for us up on open elevated ground. At the edge of the forest, we deploy into line of battle and begin the advance, the old 56th right in the center of Ransom's line. The yank skirmishers fall on back through the woods as we struggle over their abatis and push forward. And then all that yankee artillery speaks like with one voice.

As shell and case shot lop off limbs and come in on us at waist level, men topple and fall over all along the line. And no wonder. The ground explodes in front and then that shreddin' hum of shot and shell comes up out of the ground like that dam crater, and into our bellies and faces. Just one vast explodin' roar right in front of our footsteps and then heads, blanket rolls, arms, legs, hats, a big spray of blood flying upward twenty foot or more.

I've been jawin' back and forth with that Wright, right into the attack itself, and suddenly I am slapped lopper-jaw in the face. I grab Wright and yell, Look hyar, God-damn yuh, yuh do that agin and I'll knock the poop outa yuh! And he gasps out, T'Warn't me! It was him! Glory-To-God, if there ain't a hand lying at my foot.

There's jest one long drawed out moan all along the line and then that line first begins to sag, then it starts to bend, and then it begins to break under that terrible fire. Men in whole squads begin droppin' their muskets and then, with one arm over their head for protection, take off skee-daddle for the rear. The color sergeant falls dead, leaving the colors out on the field.

But then, a young boy from the 56th, not even old enough to shave, jumps out in front of the line, runs forward, lifts and waves the flag, and hollers - On with the yell, boys; On with the yell! That holds us, and the Confederate barrage right in our rear is powerful convincin' too. We stumble forward screamin' the old rebel yell like a pack of indians. There just ain't any other place to go, ain't any other thing to do.

Lieutenant Fatherly of Co. C is the first to jump into the now empty yank rifle pits. We quickly dress our line and then we run through perfect hell to occupy a second line of rifle pits at the south edge of the woods. But they're jest rifle-pits. Beyond them, we see through all the smoke an open field, rising ground, and the massed guns and infantry of the main line of the V Corps, a big blue and white band stretchin' all across the high ground up ahead.

We're badly bloodied - worse than we were at Ware Bottom - and we're under artillery fire from both sides. Private Wright says it right when he says we are in "a cloSt plaSe", where "our ShelS was cuming behind us and they yankS be fore uS and we did not no how to dodge". Cap'n Graves, so dum he can't see all that blood right in front of his face, sends back to ask if the regiment is wanted to storm the yank main line entrenchments farther on, but instead we're told to withdraw right away, as it's all no use now, and so we stumble back through the woods covered with them broken trees and torn bodies. That night Cap'n Robert Graham commands a brigade skirmish line to cover our painful withdrawal back to Petersburg. And a painful withdrawal it is too, with the night rain a-runnin' from our hatbrims, a-pourin' down the sloping rifle barrels, a-drippin' from ever hang-dog beard as we jest slosh along in the mud and wet. For once, the crazy prophet and parson stop their rantin' and ravin', they have nuthing to say now, that's for shore.

No complete casualty list ever is made for Globe Tavern, but we lose heavy. We're hurt bad, real bad - losing most half or over what we had left. Lieutenant Sweezy (who had took on the gunboats back in the days we was on the Blackwater) and some enlisted men are killed in Co. I and several more wounded. Co. F loses a number of killed and wounded. In Co. B, there are more wounded and missing. The color sergeant has been shot down with the colors, but I said that.Private Wright writes home:

- I have bin in a mity hard fite yeSterday but was not hurt I thank my god for it - I cant tell you what I no for I cant rite it we av but 22 men with us and Sum of them iS Sick we had 71 men kild yesterday - they Say they yankeS will Soon hav they little confederacy if they hold on and I dont chur how Soon then mebby they SoldierS will git home.

We know we have failed. Globe Tavern and the Weldon Railroad is firm in old Grant's hands this time. We know what it means. Like Private Wright says in an after-thought to his letter, "they iS but they danville road for us to cum out". No more trips back to Tarboro in the Old North State now.

So, in the rain, we're back now in them trenches. Our one moment of freedom from the old life is all over. But we come back to them holes in the ground like they was our homes. Yes sir, we're glad to burrow on down in them this time, to grovel in the old mud again, and glad to see it again too, jest like a tired old fox going to earth befo' the killin'.

I guess there's really not much hope for us after Globe Tavern. Huddled over our little fires of pine shavings that night, we know it without sayin'. Even the fool sentry, standin' out there in the mud in all that drivin' rain, he knows it now.

CHAPTER SIXTEEN

JAMES M. DAVIS, LIEUTENANT, COMPANY G

But tell me now. Why was that one month more unique than the rest? Was September of 1864 truly so special?

Yes, for we had lasted so long. And do you remember, from the Future, what September is like? Do you remember what it is like in the mountains back east, so different from these Texas plains? Surely, it cannot have changed so much. Late September 1864 is still like that in some places of this falling world. I used to think of it as the month of parting, of ending. After all, it is in this month that small children (the hope of all the world) leave their farms to attend whatever school there is; when the fields are harvested; when the low-country planters leave their mountain retreats to return to Charleston or Savannah. And in those mountains now, the cool mountain mist rises in the mornings from every cove and hollow to announce the end of summer, the coming of autumn. Is it still like that for you, now in 1900? In 1964? In 2064?

So too, for this decrepit wood-burning train from Petersburg bound for Danville. It crawls slowly across the south Virginia landscape, its solitary black plume of smoke tending ever east as the train moves ever west, and for it September is surely an ending, a parting. It certainly has too many cars for the capacity of any single locomotive, and it pulls forward tortuously, almost painfully, making no more than ten miles an hour even on the down grade. There are now so many trains on this last remaining railway to the west that this one excites no special notice from farm boy or field hand. But it is special for it carries a shadow as a passenger, the shadow of a man who, as with any man, I suppose, is a universe of possibilities. This one man, so much a stranger even to myself, so haunted by these last two years, may yet be a catalyst for change, but it will have to be in the future, not now.

An important shadow?

In that he lives and is not dead after all that has happened, that is what amazes me, and for what end, for what purpose? Unbelievably, he is still breathing, moving, seeing, feeling, when so many others are bone, with the powder of bone softly sifting even over their memory now. In Petersburg, he first thought of this journey only as an ending, but now I see it too as the beginning that may bring this story of the regiment one day to a somehow fitting, final conclusion. So, far from merely being one more additional actor exiting from the stage, perhaps he will bring the final curtain sweeping down on it all.

Memories have their own scope and life. Like windows and dreams, they are open doors to the past. Now, take this man sitting there on that crowded passenger car in late September, 1864. His memories are real enough to him, real as any nightmare. The trenches, the mud, the smoke, the blood ... oh, it was and is real enough. Sometimes it was the only thing that was real. After the hell of Globe Tavern, we moved back to the trenches east of Petersburg. On the 25th of August, Major John W. Graham returned, having recovered from his wound and replaced the ailing Captain Lawson Harrill as acting commanding officer of the regiment. Graham confirmed to us that the Weldon Railroad was effectively cut beyond any doubt. He had to return to Petersburg by way of Danville. Now, a month later, it remains the only way to escape, the only way to end it.

I remember after Globe Tavern we can see the Union troops and wagons slowly and silently moving on south and west behind their lines; we can distinctly hear the distant roar of guns at Reams Station where yet another unsuccessful attempt to dislodge the Federals from the Weldon Railroad is being made. Our own front remains quiet for several days. But at dusk on the 29th, a heavy Union artillery and mortar barrage opens up along the entire Confederate line for no apparent reason. This is real. But, it is all for no apparent reason.

And now seemingly for no apparent reason, this train leaves Petersburg this particular morning with a full load of convalescent soldiers, soldiers on leave, civilians rich off the black market or poor from the plummeting economy, crates of chickens, pens of pigs, and as always the forlorn, aged couple returning from a visit to, or embarking on a search for an only son. But this train is leaving the war behind it, that is certain, for it is going first to Danville and then to points west and south. The men and women it carries are destined not for further death, but for further life. You can see it for yourself - they ride with a sense of complacency, even calm complacency, sensing that this life will be better or more lasting than the continual death, back there, in the east.

So they sit silently enough all about him now, huddled in their seats, disturbed only by the excitement of the few children (the hope of all the world) running up and down the narrow aisle or by the raucous snores of a soldier asleep against the window. There are unkempt beards, worn and faded clothes, cigar smoke, soot and oily smoke drifting past the window on the outside curve, tobacco stains scuffed into the floor boards of the passenger car - all those things you could expect to find in such a place, such a time as this. And yet there is beauty here too, in the quiet, demure air of the young girl seated one aisle across from my own self, looking back now to the silent, withdrawn infantry lieutenant on his way home at last, so changed from the man he once knew, but maybe still remembering a little, hoping a little. Oh, it is right that they should be so silent and withdrawn, the girl and that one solitary figure in the worn field uniform; it is right that he should look out on this passing world, this swaying aisle, that demure loveliness blossoming there, with those deep, cadaverous eyes of his that have seen too much. And as with her, he too, may have a special role, undreamed of even by him, to play in the whole sad travesty before it is over.

This is why this one train is special, for to this man seated there, the fighting war, certainly that war in the trenches at Petersburg is really over at last. Oh, there may be further conflict back home - barn burnings, night renegades, even a skirmish or two - these may or may not involve this man - but for him, his time with the 56th and the war it knows is over at last. His carefully penned letter of resignation to the adjutant-general for reasons of health on September 21 said as much between the lines. Whatever good-byes needed to be said, whatever memories needed to be taken with him, whatever hopes needed to be however fleetingly cherished - these were all taken care of in the closing days of September. That ended it, did it not? Surely it is ended with that. And now he is here, in Beginnings and Endings, in spite of himself.

Whatever good-byes needed to be said . . . He was there that last night in the lines before Petersburg. John McNeely, captain of K Company now, comes at the last to say good-bye and we talk there over a last fire in the trenches, while the Union artillery ceases and gives us a moment of peace for parting.

McNeely doesn't know what to say at first, so at last he says the safest thing and congratulates me on my promotion. I laugh, saying that "the only reason they did it, John, was my resignation. They want me to be a first lieutenant anywhere but with the 56th. I guess they figure we don't need dreamers or visionaries in the trenches."

And John says that was "maybe because the vision is gone, gone clean-away, Jim, and so there ain't no dream no more. Just look at the flag there. I used to think it so beautiful - so beautiful. All that white silk, the red canton, the blue Saint Andrew, the thirteen stars, just like those in the flag of the old Revolution. It's just as much an American flag as the old one, just as much a statement for independence as the first one. But now it's going down, ain't it? No wonder - rent and torn like it is. Needs a good washing down in the creek-bed, before it will ever fly free and clean as it once did."

He looks at it in silence, furled and still in the night air.

"Well, it's still here, John. Like you and the regiment, it will go on a while yet."

"But to what end? For what purpose now? You said early on that future ages would remember us. But, they won't, will they, Jim?"

There is only the night silence about us, so still that you can hear it as one voice.

"No songs. No odes. No legends like in the olden time. No stories or books. No one will ever know of us, will they, Jim."

"I guess not. Future's about all we have left now. I would like to know what's up ahead for us, but I don't. It's all a closed book. The boys call me a prophet of sorts. They had one all right - maybe a misguided one, maybe even a false one. There isn't any hope, any redemption I can see for all this, not now."

"Not ever?"

"Oh, maybe one day. Long after all the blood has dried and the smoke has drifted away; after all the pain is just a bad dream. And then it will be just one small act, one small deed which probably no one will even notice. But at least it will be a start toward a new life and a new America, another chance."

"Another chance?"

"Captain Harrill showed me a captured Yankee newspaper months ago. King Abe gave a speech up at Gettysburg where he talked about a new birth of something or other. Much as I hate to admit it, the words have remained with me. A new birth, another chance. Only that."

"It won't be given to the likes of us, Jim."

"And for us, here, now?"

"Maybe we have served our turn. Maybe we have done enough, whatever it was all for."

McNeely says nothing more and we just sit there, side by side, long into the night. Toward midnight, the Union artillery starts up again, but they are working Gracie's Brigade. In time, they will come around to us. We live on in their memory yet, at least that is for certain.

At last he stands and stretches, gazing despairingly, bleakly deep into the night. Then he speaks, almost whispering, "I wish I was going out of it too, Jim. For it just isn't any use. There isn't anything any of us can do with the regiment, but bury it. And it will be lucky to get a decent one at that."

And I say "You'll stay, because you must; and I'll go, because I must; and the regiment will hold fast in its own place and time, because it must."

McNeely sighs, hesitates for only a brief moment, then holds out his hand. We shake hands quietly, and then salute, the old casual salute of the 56th, and he walks off into the night. I watch him go until I can see him no more, for I know I never will see him on the morrow, or ever again on this side of Jordan. It is only one among many endings.

But this shadow figure, this shade?

You gaze at me and still do not recognize him? But then I forget, you were not in the war. And it is of that, of the war, you wish to hear, not of ghosts within ghosts.

The future's all we have left now, so I think on that long journey south. I remember a letter written during the closing days of August by Private L.S. Wright, to his family. I saw him, just a boy, torturously spelling it out by firelight. And although I did not see the letter itself, I could have written it, any of us could have written it, for its words were seared in all our hearts...

Dear SiSterS you Said you would be glad if I could bee thare to eat roSenearS & beans & Sweate po tatoes I no it would do mee aS mutch good to cum home and eat them aS it could do you O my god that I could cum home and Stay with you all one more time I am hur in they breSt workes they Sound of they cannon and gunS iS never Stopt it iS a turable time hur I dont want any thin that any are you can do for me I Still put my truSt in god and I think he will bring mee home yet Sumday tho it lookS like a bad chance - i have a bad chance to rite hur to you I never git mutch Sleep hur and I cant rite much.

For how can one rite, how can he or anyone write, how can one put into the printed word all the horror, all the terror this or any man back there has undergone? He, sitting there on this train, certainly does not think so, this man now (who is he?) -First Lieutenant James M. Davis, (was it not?), formerly of Company G of the 56th Regiment (was he not?), now newly promoted and discharged and on his way back to the mountains of Henderson County in Western North Carolina after two long years in the war. No - no living soul, and perhaps not even the all knowing dead, can put into simple words all that this man or any man back there has endured in the trenches. In the words of his discharge, he is now very much emaciated and afflicted with a severe kidney infection. He has been in and out of army hospitals during the entire summer campaign; time and deteriorating health have caught up with him at last. But deeper than the wasted flesh and the hollow eyes is the damage to the spirit. Oh even from here, I can see it in him. There is lasting damage there, no doubt of it - damage caused by fear, uncertainty, doubt of what might just be called the creature comforts - enough to eat, enough to sleep, enough to rest, enough to survive, enough to love. It is the wanting that destroys more than the shells - the simple desire to be left alone, long enough to pull it all back together somehow, at least for a little while. Yes, I can understand it. That is why the war finally had to come to an end for him; that is why he is going home now.

At the least, he will have survived. He tells himself that now with every breath. No final victory - no, not one that was final, lasting, or decisive, so no victory at all that can be a final triumphant closure to what has been endured. Survival - yes. He has done that, has he not? Atonement - well, what atonement can there be for the Horseshoe, for the work house or the auction block, child labor and slavery, the division of the nation, the privation of families, the death of men? There is guilt enough to be shared all around before any thought of atonement can take place. Atonement - had he thought of it (oh, he dare not think so far now), it would be now with a vague, perhaps even humorous dismissal. How can there ever be atonement against the hard impersonal metallic clamor of massed artillery? It is the artillery that is the worst.

On September 2, even more Federal artillery is placed in Ransom's front. On the following night, we can hear loud cheering echoing along the Union lines. On September 4, again loud cheering is heard passing up and down the Union entrenchments, back and forth, back and forth, like some rolling wave of the sea I once saw, and a brisk shelling of our positions comes after dark. We are at a loss to understand all this until we too receive the news from Federal pickets shouting across the lines, "Atlanta has gone up"!

On September 6, we continue a brisk musketry fire on their lines despite a desire of their pickets to reach some kind of agreement for a lessening of fire. The war will go on in spite of the fall of Atlanta. You see, we have no choice. We have to show them we are still there. Life, speaking back to Life, as it were, if what we have become can still be called living men.

Of course, the war will go on without him, but after all, he has memories enough, does he not? Enough to last, surely? Hamilton (or was it Williamston?) in the snow; and Gum Swamp in the midst of its primeval spring; Plymouth in its hour of glory; but then Ware Bottom, Petersburg, Globe Tavern - it began in snow and spring and now ends in the dust and mud of the trenches. And, yet, there have been moments of beauty, of unforgettable beauty. It can be found even here in this war, even here on this train. There, just across the aisle, there - that vision of soft loveliness, no doubt just a week ago in one of the factories of Richmond or (more like) staying with an invalid aunt on Broad Street in Richmond, and church of course at St. Paul's on Sundays, and the rest of the time still protected in her so fantastical feminist world of silk and lace and crinoline. Yet in her own eyes there is something that was not there before - a haunting sadness, a silent fear. Even she knows her world is falling apart about her now, as she watches and waits. He knows that; he understands that. Why, any man who has almost forgotten what it is to be with a woman due to the simple expediency of living for one moment more knows that. And that one moment more not to copulate, but to simply take that one extra breath. He knows that; any man knows that.

And yet, now that the war is perhaps over at last for him, maybe he can take the time now to gaze upon this loveliness and think of that other loveliness at home - yes, Mary, the ever dutiful wife, and more than that - the soft yielding, the hard nipples, the relentless pushing, the warm sleep afterwards - oh, he can think of that now, not knowing that Fate will perhaps give him something else to continue life, the hope of all his world.

Of course, this separation of man from regiment, real enough as it is to him, is not the only one. There are many partings this September; the train itself is testimony enough of partings. For that matter, on September 1, Captain W. G. Graves of Company H was detailed from the 56th for court martial duty and the regiment lost the services of yet another company commander. But Lieutenant Colonel Luke had returned to the regiment and the front remained relatively quiet. In early September, Colonel Faison, on the recommendation of General Bushrod Johnson as "a competent officer", was temporarily appointed acting commander of Ransom's Brigade. Johnson felt that Faison was "the best appointment that could be made from the brigade" and every indication was that Faison would soon get his General's Star.

There will be no General's Wreath and Star for the rest of us. Our reward, if reward is granted, will be simply surcease from the crashing down, the explosion outside the trench, the implosion from within. And the front indeed remains quiet through the 17th, with only occasional distant cheering from the Union lines still celebrating the fall of Atlanta. Details of men from the regiment are constantly working on the fortifications and there is no surcease from this labor. There is always another chevaux to build; another redoubt to exhume; another bombproof to cover; more abatis to place. It is never ending.

Casualties from enemy fire remains light in the brigade, with only three killed and one wounded in one week in mid-September. But steadily deteriorating health continues to be a serious problem and it is taking a heavy toll of officers now. Scurvy is rampant among the men, forcing the brigade commander by September 21 to request a ration of vinegar for the men.   Ironically, the men in the 56th eat well for a change on the same day, for the cattle taken by Wade Hampton in his recent "Beefsteak Raid" are slaughtered and the meat distributed to the men.

Perhaps in reaction to this raid of the cavalry, the Federals become more active beginning on the 21st, with a heavy artillery barrage all along the entire Confederate line. The increased gunfire continues without pause, day and night, hour by hour, to the end of the month.

So, at the end of the month, it is of his wife Mary that he now thinks, but it is the Future, the unknown and mysterious Future, that he is really going to meet on this final journey south. Even he does not really comprehend that. I can see it. You - even you from the Future - you. Yes, you. Pass down this dark tunnel of time; go and walk down the gently swaying aisle; go ahead - touch him on his sleeve and meet those hard eyes; say the name to him; see the blank, questioning look, the vacant, noncomprehending stare; he will not know of what you are speaking. The Future means nothing to him. But it is the Future he is going to now; it is the Future that will most represent to him, what peace is, and restored life, and finally home. The Future is perhaps the only child to be conceived out of all this pain; but it will be a child who, after all the death, will be the center, or almost center of his life, destiny, and fate. And yet that child, the hope of all his world, will be cursed with his curse, stained with his stain. This darkness will surely be passed on to other generations.

And if that is so, then perhaps it would have been better for this man to have died with all the rest in the trenches or on the field at Globe Tavern than to return to such a fate, to such a future as this; perhaps it would have been better for this child, carried in his loins, to have died without ever being, on the streets of Plymouth, in the lush overgrowth of Gum Swamp, than to come to life, to such a father as this. For It is there, in his loins and in his blood. It could have died in him, as perhaps it should have, rather than being born in the closing days of the war, the dark fruit of all this bitter legacy, casting more seed to flower forth in yet darker petals throughout the land. It will carry the sin of the nation to untold generations unless there is some small, even minute particle of atonement. And what hope of atonement can ever now come to pass for all this? And if God did not want him to die, then a slight wound would have sufficed - a wound so slight that it would have hardly inconvenienced this man at all, but it would have certainly preserved unborn generations of man from the residue of hate and pain, of darkness, of what he and the war was to bequeath to them.

But would not his child atone for all this? Was not the hope of all the world for this man worth all the rest?

Captain R. D. Graham, the last effective officer of Company D of the 56th, is slightly wounded on the 22th and signs the roll of officers present the next morning as "1 Captain, if it is a fight, but not for a march". One enlisted man of the 56th was killed on the 24th; another wounded on the 26th. By the 29th, musketry volleys are rolling along the front of Ransom's line at night once again and this continues to the very end of the month.

But you were speaking of the war, of the train, and of a child.

The train steams farther, ever farther into the west, carrying both father and unborn future, forever locked in each other's self, neither one knowing that he and his seed together will be the last casualties, the final doomed survivors of the 56th Regiment in this war.

CHAPTER SEVENTEEN

THE PARSON

The Angel come to me agin in my sleep last night. She's got fiery red coals for eyes and a drop of blood's hangin' off her neather lip. Her hair is just a-streamin' out behind her like in a big wind, but there is nary a breath of air. When she raises up her scabby claw fangers agin me, I run away fast as ever I can go and in a dream, it's a mighty slow run. But this is the dark Angel of Revelation, the Angel of Death and Desolation that follows this doomed regiment of lost men.

But I believe in the other Angel too, the Angel of Light and Salvation. I do believe in Him and tell the boys He yet will come, though they hoot and laugh in their wickedness. They're just boys, most of them, and don't know no better. They have took to calling me The Old Parson, just as if I was some preacher holding forth in the pulpit preachin' Hell Fire and Damnation, but I'm not. Then I'd be one of them Scribes and Pharisees, when I'd rather be more like one of them simple fishermen. But which one of them did the Good Lord prefer, now I ask you that? And on that snowy night in Bethlehem-Town, who did the Angel In Glory invite to the stable? Not the temple priests or King Herod or Caesar, or them that has the land and the slaves, but them poor lowly shepherds, dirty, ignorant, couldn't read nor write. They're the only ones who got the Special Invitation, the likes of me, the likes of these boys in the 56th. If the Angel come to them so long ago, why shouldn't He come now, when we stand in as much need? But I believe on Him. I know he's made Himself scarce, but that's the way of the Other Life. I know it don't make no sense, no sense at all, but that is what I believe and why I believe it.

Or Plymouth Town, where one man was killed on my right

hand and Globe Tavern, where another one was killed on my left hand. And that didn't make no sense either, but it explains why I believe in simple trust and hope that the Angel will serve to protect and guard me through all this fiery ordeal.

So in the words of Private Wright, who could sure pass as one of them poor shepherds, in October of 1864, "I Seat mySelf thiS eavening to let you no that I am well at thiS time truely hoping theSe few lineS may cum Safe to yore distent hand and finde you all well," but the steady blood-letting by gunfire from the II Corps in our front goes right on with two men wounded on the first day of the month. The brigade is now down to "one good line about elbow to elbow", with a few pieces of artillery scattered here and there along the front line.

On October 9, we're on the extreme left of the Confederate line, with our left flank restin' on the Appomattox River. The Yank deserters coming into the lines report that Grant is receivin' lots of raw recruits, conscripts, bounty-jumpers. When we hear that, we know what we are up against and so we begin sending circulars into the Union lines offerin' their draftees protection and assignment in the Confederate rear if they will desert. And, much to our surprise, a miracle comes! On October 11, sixteen deserters from the 5th New Hampshire come into our lines and they continue to come during the next few nights. Some of our observers place the count as high as twenty-five coming in just to the 56th on a single night. Late one night, when a Yank picket hollers across askin' what regiment is in their front, our picket line hollers back, "The 5th New Hampshire!", much to the amusement of the enlisted men of both sides who pass the joke down and across the lines until the laughin' is lost in the distance. The officers on both sides don't find it so amusin' and stop for a while the friendly traffic in tobacco, crackers, and newspapers between the lines.

But we are startin' to lose a steady number of deserters also. Three men desert from the regiment on October 13 and freely give accurate information to the Yanks on the exact location of our brigade between the Appomattox and the City Point Railroad.

Any one can see that life is becoming harder and harder in the trenches. Food is gettin' worse all the time and as cold weather sets in, the first frost whitenin' the ramparts in the cold dawn, we are rationed only eight to ten sticks of green pine wood a day for fire. Rain and mud make livin' conditions miserable and the sand and gravel walkways in the trenches become water-courses themselves. Our trenches are strengthened further, and sand bags and iron plates are used to build up sharpshooter positions. After a while, we just lose track of time itself, these cold months just mergin' one into the other and leadin' to no one knows what.

Those casualties continue to climb at a slow, but steady rate under the fire that is constant day and night. As Private Wright wrote, "they hav bin fighting three days cloSt by verry hard but they hant took uS yet to day they ant fighting hur I cant tell how long it will bee So they yankeS is too hard for us." Although we can keep no complete count during the fall, our casualties in the 56th are said to be by one officer as "considerable - among officers and men". A lieutenant is wounded, a sergeant and private killed in Company F during this time. Captain Joseph G. Lockhart of Company E resigns in October due to nightly attacks of asthma that leave him wheezin' and gaspin' for that next to last breath and Company B has only one officer on duty for the rest of the year. In spite of the constant fire, however, casualties are not as high as they could have been. During one week in mid-October, the brigade loses only two killed and five wounded. Private Elliott says that"I cannot see how we escaped so well, but we learned to lay low, dig holes, and contrive bomb-proofs". But we have no protection against the slow wearin' of bad weather and worsenin' health. "Our paperS seS they yankeS is a going to dig up to Richmond to take it," said Private Wright.

October brings slow fire of fall color to the few trees left off in the distance and we see, one gold afternoon, the gilt and braid of a Confederate general officer and his staff ridin' toward us, still with victory in the air and promise for the spring. As always, we are proud to be a part of this, if only to be just silent spectators of it, only to find that it is just Matt Ransom and Paul Faison returnin' to the brigade at last, to be lost to their own special fate and doom. General Ransom returns to command the brigade and Faison to his old command of the 56th, still in its old position just south of the Appomattox. The lines once again quiet down and now the Union trenches present one unbroken line of strong stockades and earthen ramparts, meandering entrenchments wanderin', criss-crossin', and weavin' in and out, back and forth, with their sharpshooters in rifle pits out front, all under a cold, grey autumn sky, with them dark clouds silently driftin' over from our lines to their's. And while a brisk artillery fire opens up from the Union lines on October 26, it too, like the rest of us, soon falters and dies with the closin' of the month.

And it just seems natural that everything will falter and die along with the rest of the year, along with the rest of the world. It won't be long before winter will be here; whatever will we do then, with supplies goin' down and the men wearin' out even faster from one day to the next? And don't it all come from what we've done? That's what I keep tryin' to tell the boys. Now we went into this War for Independence and States Rights and all that, but now cotton and niggers were mixed up in it, too. I come right out and tell the boys that if this is a rich man's war and a poor man's fight like we hear tell, then we're fightin' for the big planters, too. "Aw, go north and fight for the big factory owners then", they'll laugh. Or they'll say, "Yore a parson. Read your Bible. It says right there about the sons of ham orter be slaves". And I'll come back that the children of Israel were slaves, too, and we oughten be mixed up in all this. And I tell them about what the regiment had done here and yon, about robbin' white civilians and shootin' black soldiers tryin' to escape, about packin' prisoners off to Camp Sumter worsen hogs to a killin'.

And they'll rile up with, "Parson, you don't know what yore talkin' about. This is a war, fer God's sake." And I'll come back, "Thou shall not use the Lord's Name in vain. He will send the Angel to destroy ye, jest as shore as He could send one to save your miserable, God-forsaken souls." And they'll just laugh and say "Angel, shit," but them are the two angels - one good and one bad - that I was a-talkin' about earlier.

On November 1, the whole division under General Bushrod Johnson is inspected by General Lee, who rides down the lines wearin' a simple uniform and a soft felt black hat. The 56th Regiment is complimented on its fine military appearance and the good condition of its arms and equipment. But our requisitions hadn't been honored for some time and the clothes the men wear are in a bad state for a winter in the field. A few recruits (most of them conscripts) help to fill up some of the vacancies in the regiment, but this November we are seriously under manned.

Morale rises and falls day to day, but generally we can look into one another's eyes and see written there that the army has robbed the cradle and the grave and is now in the last ditch. The election of Lincoln is just one more disappointment, added to many. "Now truly there is no hope and god only nose what will becum of uS all har I cant," wrote Private Wright.

On the misty night of November 7, there is a return of heavy picket firing along Ransom's front near the Appomattox, but it is later on found that this ruckus is caused by new and nervous Yank recruits. By the night of the 17th, the front has again quieted down so much that we once again can hear the trains runnin' in the Union rear.

The lines remain quiet for the rest of the month, the brigade takin' in casualties, only three wounded from November 20 to 27. "And I got my Shurt it felt mity good to pull of a lowSey Shurt and put on a clean Shurt but it will bee aS bad in a few dayS hur in theS ditchS - when i get my box i opend it and Set down by it and did eat one good bate and waS So thankful that i had Such a good father mother & SisSterS to Send me Sumthing to eat," Private Wright said. Faison is agin with the regiment and the paymaster is even able to pay off some of the men at the end of the month. The desertion rate for the brigade goes steady on at two or three men slippin' away every night, but even this low rate over a period of several weeks cuts steady into the strength of the unit. It is not what happens day to day, but what happens week to week that is deadly.

Course, it is bad enough, day to day. Weather gettin' colder, winter a-comin' in with a vengeance (soon it would be snowin'), never enough to eat. Salt pork, corn, old musty bread. What I dreamed of sinkin' my teeth into was fresh meat, no more of that old pork, but fresh meat - big juicy beefsteaks, cooked rare, and roast beef done just right. Oh Lord, that's what I dream on. Fresh meat! Like what we had back in September. "Oh, come on, Parson", they laugh, "You ain't goin' to get fresh meat unless you sneak across to the other side." "Well", I say, "you can get beef up in Richmond." "You shore can", they come back like they do, "if you want to pay a hundred thousand Confederit or 500 Gold."

"Or maybe yore waitin' for the cavalry to go back and get some more? Or maybe that Angel's goin' to bring it to you?" And I just say, "Laugh on. You will see first the Angel of Desolation and then (if you deserve it, which I think not), the Angel of Salvation. And that Angel will come in blindin' white robes, and there will be a crown on his head, and his eyes will blaze forth love and peace. And when he comes, he will be wrapped in a Mystery, I tell ye, a Mystery, like in the olden time. But you ain't never goin' to see it and I won't neither, cause it don't look like we're goin' to get no victory, and survivin' all this don't look possible, but maybe we'll have another chance at the redemption." "Parson", they laugh, "Yore as crazy as you look. Ain't no Angel and ain't no salvation for the likes of you". And that son of darkness, Fess Smith, snickers and says, "Oh, he'll get his Angel, he'll get his fresh meat, you don't know the Parson like we uns' do". And they just laugh and go on and purty soon I leave them to their foulness and to their wickedness.

Now I just never had no use for thiefs and liars, liars especially. They'll make this accusation and that accusation and you don't hardly know what to believe, so finally you end up believin' what you want to believe. I have no use for lies or false accusations, for they crawl from ear to ear with their poison, from generation to generation with their old suspicion and hate, cuttin' down people innocent of any wrong-doing, but to the listenin' of them. It always takes two to lie - one to think it up, plan it, do it, and then the trusting one, innocent, wanting to believe and disbelieve at the same time. Two of them - one evil, the other, a fool. Ah, now then! Let the lie work its work.

On December 2, our pickets along the front are ordered to conserve their ammunition and not to fire on the Union lines without due cause. As a result, soon five Yank bullets are fired to every one by the Confederates; enemy soldiers soon begin exposin' themselves carelessly as return fire decreases all along our line. A steady, punishing fire continues from the Union pickets of the IX Corps, who faithfully follow their orders to fire all the time, being constantly resupplied with cartridges at need. "i do hope that god will bleSS you all and keep you all a live till I git home if i ever git home," wrote Private Wright. But the front bye-and-bye becomes quiet toward nightfall, so quiet after the ice-storm on the 7th, we can once agin hear the supply and troop trains passing south in the Union rear far into the night. By mid-December, the situation is still unchanged.

Casualties in the brigade increase due to the heavier Union picket fire during the day. During a one week period in mid-month, six are killed and eighteen wounded in the brigade. In the 56th Regiment, the poor men continue to suffer. Firewood has to be brought in by hand from a mile away. Makeshift wind shelters are put together out of old barrels and boxes held in place by dried mud. "i am hur in they old ditches yet - it does look like all they pore men will be kild up yet," said Private Wright.

Well, it's gettin' colder and colder and snow's in the air. You hardly see the sun from one day to the next and it is cold - Lord, it's cold! And what I wouldn't give for one great big juicy beefsteak, cooked any old how, with potatoes on the side! But now Christmas is comin' and I take to thinkin' of the first one at Bethelem, where the Angel come and gave a special invitation to the shepherds to come to the stable. And it does seem to me that some of them shepherds must have been sinners, just like some of our boys, but the angel come anyway, it didn't make that much difference. And you've seen the old prints of Bethlehem, how them shepherds looked - wearin' just rags, and long lanky hair, and beards, and hardly no shoes at all? Well, that's what we're like, and here its about Christmas-Time, and we're in sore pain, and now where's the Angel? Where's the Angel?

Beginnin' on December 17, the paymaster agin visits the line held by the 56th and pays off more of the men. I took my 11 Dollars and put it up with the rest. That gave me near on 35 Dollars Confederit, for I don't squander my money like pore sojers do, but save it agin Hard Times. Colonel Faison and five of the ten company commanders get brief furloughs and some of the rest of us get even briefer ones. The officers went home if they lived near the coast, but for the enlisted men, there is just Petersburg or Richmond for a one or two day leave. And that was when they come to me about the fresh meat I had such a hankerin' for.

It is just before Christmas and I am a- wonderin' if it is a-goin' to snow when some of the boys come up and say, "Hey, Parson, we got a one day leave, and it's near about Christmas-Time, and we're going up Richmond-way and we want you to come with us". And I say, "I shall not haunt the foul den of iniquity that you seek, for t'is a Holy Season", and start to walk off, but they come up behind me and whisper, "Oh, we ain't going to do that. We got a chance at some fresh meat. We'd bring some back, but lord knows, we just might eat it all up before we get back."

And I look into their foul and perfidious eyes and say, "Now don't lie me none now. Fresh meat, you say." And they say, "Fresh meat, Parson. All right out of the herd. We ain't lyin' you none." And I say, "Wait till I get my money."

Next thing I know, we're on the train on the Richmond-Petersburg Railroad. That retribute Smith brings out a jug of bust-head and begins passin' it around. "H'yar, Parson. Take a dram with us for old Christmas sake". And I say, "I'm not about to, for the likker kilt my pappy and burns away at my innards." But then they all lean in real close, with their rank breath all in my face, and whisper, "No likker, no fresh meat, Parson. And you can bet yore bottom dollar, we'll see to that." So I drink the foul brew to the damnation of us all.

After that, I don't remember much, for they keep plying that filthy cup to my lips all the way to Richmond. Well, I can hardly confess to the shame of it. Purty soon, I'm drunker than the Divil, Sicker than a dog. When we git off the train at the depot, they have to hold me up, although they're staggering drunk themselves. "Wer's the fresh meat?" "Oh, just wait Parson, we'll have to get there first, won't we now? We're on our way, good sojers all, to the Tenderloin now". So I figur we're about to get the fresh meat after all and tenderloin at that.

But when we get to the Tenderloin part of town, just east and down the hill from the Confederit Capitol, you never saw the like of pick-pockets, gamblers, thieves, and robbers crowding them dark and narrow streets. Then them boys get some more likker and say, "Don't go down that way, Parson. That there's Locust Alley, where them sun-of-bitches chicken gut officers go. We're goin' to Ram Cat."

And down Ram Cat Alley we go, where the whores troop the boardwalk under the flickerin' gas lights like to a herd of cattle goin' to the trough. They wear old dirty calico and checkered bon-

nets and have the look of the Evil One in their eye for these gawkin'
country boys. Others are a-leanin' out of winders or standin' in
doors of hussy houses, showin' their nekkid bosoms. Then them
fallen women latch on to us like ducks on june bugs. Tittering and
giggling, them hussies drag us into their foul dens. Children's dolls
are a-sittin' in the corner, pin-ups from Godey of women in rose-
garland dresses, a dirty old kerosene lamp a-sittin' on a table, beside
it an old comb and brush, with hair a-stickin' in it. "H'yar's an
Angel fer ye, Parson. H'yar's yore Fresh Meat" and they push a
Jezebel down on my lap, a-stinkin' with her cheap perfume and with
a missing tooth out front. Near fifty year old she must be, with her
flabby arms around my neck, her oily mouth on mine, big old musty
black hairs a-curlin' out of her arm-pits, her swellin' bosom mashin'
my cheek, her vulture fangers scratchin' at my beard. "Sing us a
song". And the Harlot from Hell croaks out a song about My
Southern Soldier Boy with her old blond wig slippin' over her ear,
and then she mashes her bosom agin on my face. "Yawl frum
Carolina?" She sez, "I've never been so far". And they all laugh like
to a pack of jackals. "Now, you sing us a song, Parson, but no hymn
now". "Sang it to me!", she hollers out, a-stickin' her old slimy
tongue way down in my ear. And I sing a song from my sinful
youth, for all is lost to the Dark Angel now, and it don't matter no
more, Wish I was in London Town A-Lyin' with my Honey And
every time She moans and groans I kiss her on the Tummy. They all
laugh and holler like to a pack of hyenas and before you can say
scat, the shameless hussy packs me off into a back room and while
I'm committing the Act of Darkness with that foul and nasty
woman, I can hear the boys a-singin' away in the front room So
Stand to your glasses steady, 'tis all we have left to prize, H'yars a
health to the dead alreaddy, Hooray fer the next man who dies. And
damme, I wake up in the middle of the night, if I'm not a-lyin'
betwixt two of them, nekkid as they were born, and the other one
about twelve-year-old, with bosoms on her no biggerun acurns, the
old Jezebel's daughter to the shame of it. I don't know if I done it to
the both of them or no, but my back hurt, my head hurt, I'm sick to
my innards with the guilt and all the foul likker I drunk. I feel it a-
heavin' and a-comin' on up and so I stagger on out into the dark
street and vomick all that old likker up in the nasty gutter and know

no more 'til the provost marshal stirs me with his boot with the grey dawn comin' on. And I don't have nary penny to my name.

Well, it just ruints me with the regiment, just ruints me, for it's told all up and down. The boys just grin and grin and some of them don't call me Parson no more, but holler "Fresh Meat" everywhere I go. But what's worse, it ruints me with me. Death is here, at the front, in the trenches, but Death is now in me. I don't care what happens now, I don't care what I might do. War, Regiment, Me - there's nothing to do but wait for the spring and the end. But before it come, I'll pay that god-damn Smith and his cronies back if it's the last thing I ever do.

The next day is December 18 and all the front booms with cannon as the Yanks fire a salute to celebrate the fall of Savannah, and that sure don't do my achin' head no good. The next day is a little quieter, and one more deserter from the 56th Regiment silently slips across into the Union lines. Christmas Day dawns still and quiet on the front and the guns cease as if by mutual consent. The men of the regiment are distributed a ration of small irish potatoes, courtesy of the Governor of North Carolina, along with somethin' a little more, but not much more by the good ladies of Petersburg. But to me and the rest of the Damned, it's just another day with no hope now for any one of us. The snow didn't come, Bethlehem warn't there, the Angel was done gone clean-away, ain't no shepherds.

The day after Christmas, the Yank guns royally fire another handsome salute into the dawn. Food for the 56th becomes more and more scarce. A little coffee and canned beef, when we can get it, is a rare thang and no meat's been issued to the troops by the government for several days. Letters from home are heart-breakin' to read, for it's clear as day that many of our families in North Carolina are starvin'. The men gather about their small fires to speak of the future and here the regiment talks long into the night.

They still try to keep a good face on the ordeal. Captain Graham, when asked in confidence if all hope is not truly lost, just quietly says that the only choice of the regiment is to trust in General Lee to the end. But the men are starvin' and will eat anything. Over in the 25th regiment, they're even eatin' rats and that's one thought I can't tolerate, no way I can, at least not yet.

But it gives me the idea. Eatin' rats, are they. It's New Year's

Eve and it starts snowin' that afternoon, slow heavy flakes driftin' down, but it melts as soon as it falls. But I knowed how them boys in Smith's bunch will be celebratin' the night. So I go down the brigade line to the 25th and talk to a feller I know. And it's the truth, for he shows me the mangy skins they had took off them rats to cook the flesh. And when I ask where they got them rats, he says them was wharf rats offen the banks of the Appomattox. So I trade some good 'baccy for some of the foul meat and take it back to the 56th in a poke. I stew it up good in a pot and then carry it through the camp to the hut where Fess Smith and his gang are all holed up like rats themselves.

They're likkered up purty good and long into a good hand of poker, but they kind of rouse themselves up when they see me standin' in the door with a lantern in one hand and a pot in the other.

"Whut you got there, Parson?"

"Squirrel meat. And I got these left-overs to show there ain't no hard feelings, 'cause we're sojers and comrades all."

"Where you get squirrel?"

"Might be I got it outta a tree. Might be I got it often the earth. Might be I never did say. But here 'tis."

And I lift up the lid to that pot, and you can smell that meat
in the white smoke just risin' up.

"Don't eat it, I'll take it some'er's else."

And then that old Smith ris up and says, "Hold on, Parson. Let's take a gander at whut you got."

So they all sit around that hut and smell that steam, and then they get their knives and spoons out and take to eatin' it, and I just stand there, quiet like, in the corner, with my arms folded, watchin' them, rats eatin' rat. And yes, there's a smile hid in my beard, for I have done to them just like that Greek God Edipus did to his pore mother. I ease over to the door, for there's just one thing more to do, the finishin' touch, as it is.

After they all have a good mouthful and are swallerin' it down, I says to them, "Behold, there is justice. For you have eat of the Abomination. Unclean food have you touched and may it shrivel those miserable souls up inside your bodies, you god-damn sunsofbitches."

And Smith up and says, "Just whut is this, Parson?"

"It's rat meat, you Sun-Of-Bitch. You have eat of the Abomination and be damned to hell, for I'll have no further part of ye."

But Smith looks up at me with a big grin, sticks his knife into the pot and fishes out a long sliver of greasy white meat, slips it into his mouth, winks, and just says, quiet like, "Fresh Meat, Parson. Fresh Meat."

I turn my back on them and their infernal laughter. Never no more, never no more, I say. Outside, the snow is fallin' heavier now and it's turnin' cold. My old rusty lantern won't give much light, but I know my way back to my cold bed. Poor sinners no more, they are fit for Hell-Fire, and nary a one of them deserves the saving. Retributes all, they will never be no different than the dirt they come from. There just ain't no hope for them, for us, for nobody. It's all just one big stink-hole and I had just as leave go home like the smarter ones are doin'. No victory, no survivin', no salvation.

The snow is comin' down really heavy now, just like a white blanket, it is. I stop for a spell and watch it fallin' past the lantern. It's so quiet, you can hear it comin' down. The trench is empty with nary a soul in sight. It must be near on to Mid-Night now; soon it will be 1865. 1865.

The way things are goin', 1865 will probably mark the end to all this. It's just as well. Just as well.

Then I hear a slow shufflin' sound and I don't know what it is at first. But it's just a figure comin' up the trench from the right of the camp, just a boy without his rifle. He don't have no shoes, just bare feet all wrapped up in old rags. He has a tattered old blanket pulled tight around him and over his head like a kind of hood, with part over his face. He's nigh about covered with the snow, so he must have come a way. He does take out one hand long enough to pull that old blanket closer to his face; he's a sight to see stumblin' and staggerin' along there, just like the rest of us, I guess.

He comes up towards me, almost as if he wants to ask a question. I figure he's after some 'baccy or maybe he just wants anything I got to eat. And I'm on guard, you bet you, in case it's one of Smith's gang out for another prank. But he don't say nothing as we pass in the trench, just keeps his head on down, for the wind's a-blowin' hard. I walk on a few steps more, but then somethin' makes me stop and turn around.

He's stopped too, just a few feet away, and turns around too, and is a-facin' me, just as I'm a-facin' him. I can't see his face good in the dark with that old blanket pulled over it, but a strange feeling come over me. It's just a boy, like all the rest of 'em, tousled hair all uncombed and a long, long way from his Mama. But I have to be sure.

So I step up to him, hold my lantern up, and look right into his face. You can't see much for the blanket pulled over it agin the cold (there's a whole row of tiny icicles along the edge of that blanket, I do see that), but I can see his eyes, under his brows all white with snow, a steady blue gaze that looks straight into my own with no fear, and in those eyes there's such a strange and distant peace, as if he's thinkin' on another time than this, another place than here.

I drop the lantern (it goes out with a hissin' sound, leavin' us in almost total darkness) and I fall down on my knees right there in the mud and hold up my hands in adoration. "I just knew you would come", I say. And after a long moment of gazing still into that peace, I slowly bow my head, clasp my hands, and weep in thanksgiving for us all.

I guess this is the one thing I will remember from this war. The late night darkness closin' in, that long and deserted trench, the two of us alone there together, one quietly standin', the other kneelin', and all that old snow just a-comin' down in Glory.

CHAPTER EIGHTEEN

JAMES F. ELLIOTT, PRIVATE, COMPANY F

"You goin' sparkin' agin tonight, Elliott?"

I smile quickly and nod, for I find it best to humor Sergeant Smith. He's one man I don't want to tangle with. He's usually into spirits and it brings out the worse in him. My mother always said a gentle answer turns away wrath. Sometimes it works with Smith, sometimes not, but he will leave me alone for the moment. He is once again staring at the Negro, as he has for three nights now.

It is January and powerful cold. Rain, sleet, and snow come on one day or the other, and then one or the other would stay on for days at a time. We rarely see the sun now. The men look like animals, especially when they crouch over their small fires. Most are starving, for rations are almost non-existent. And since there are so few of us to hold the lines now, all furloughs are terminated and it is all one unending round. There is only one way out of here - either General Lee will pull another miracle out of his hat or else the only alternative is to skip away in the middle of the night. As the boys lose hope more and more, that second choice seems the best and many a man takes it.

One night, twelve men from Company F simply walk out of the entrenchments. We're goin' home, boys, home to the Old North State and ain't nobody a-goin' to stop us, they say. And off into the dark they go, with full rations and carrying their guns. This growing desertion of the enlisted men is bad enough, but then it begins among our officers, too. Our own officers! At the start, it was lieutenants, but then captains, and finally even the regimental staff officers are absent without leave for days at a time. Some of them come back after a week or two, stay a few days, and then they are gone again. Probably half of them are holed up in those dives in Richmond; God knows where the other half go. This deadly trend goes on up through the ranks until even Colonel Faison disappears without leave. Our own regimental commander, who led us through so many hard fought battles, skee-daddled! The adjutant says General Bushrod Johnson, the division commander, is in a fine dander about it. Lieutenant-Colonel Luke takes over, but it is a devastating blow to our morale, this growing desertion of our own officers. When they lose faith, what hope is there? Surely, they know better than we what is happening and this is what frightens us more than anything. More and more, you see groups of men only under the command of non-commissioned officers; more and more, you see companies only led by lieutenants; and all in ever dwindling numbers. It can end in only one way, we know this.

It is terrible in the trenches with the cold and the hunger and watching them go like that. But on the 15th of January, a small squad of us gets a lucky break. Six of us are detailed to transport wood from Petersburg up to the front. There are not enough officers left to spare one for us, so we are pretty much on our own. It would be hard work for a couple of weeks, loading wood on the barge and then seeing that it got on the wagons. But it was worth it just to get out of the mud for a while - to see the town and escape for a little while from the slow dying back there. But now there are two new problems: the Negro and Jennie Dean.

The Negro is the first. We needed a place to stay the nights in Petersburg and we see a likely looking wood shed near the brigade wagon yard. The problem is that it is owned by a free black man of advanced years. We walk in without so much as a bye-your-leave and look around. It is a single large room with a fireplace in the middle. Everything is very neat and clean; against one wall is the old man's bedding, thick soft blankets and coverlets neatly made. There is a shelf of books against the wall. The Negro is sitting at a small table, reading with his wire-frame spectacles perched on his nose when we all crowd in. He is dressed in a brushed frock coat, a faded vest, brogans that had seen better days, but nevertheless all very neat and well cared for. And we tell him this is his place and he is welcome to it, but we are moving in too for the next few nights for we need shelter from the cold night wind that comes off the Appomattox like a glacier.

He quietly puts the book down, carefully marking his place, and says that we are welcome to what space he has. We can see he doesn't like it a bit, but he has no choice. "You gentlemen may take one wall; I will remain at the other" is all he says and places his book back on the sheaf. So, we put all our equipment against one wall - the rolled blanket, the canteen, the cartridge box, all of it. A common fire will burn between the two races.

The night comes on fierce and cold and the wind is up. We ask him finally what his name is. But there is no way we can call him Thomas. He is Uncle, or Tom, or Uncle Tom to us, but not Thomas.

As the hour grows late, the cold begins to eat into us. The fire is small, the shed as full of drafts as a sieve. We are shivering in our thread-bare blankets. And finally Sergeant Smith says "Give us some of them blankets, Uncle". And he looks up at us and says "No, I shall not". And very softly and somewhat sadly, he says again "No, I shall not."

I think Smith will hit him now, but know at the same time he will not, for the sergeant is that kind of man who likes to hurt slow, to kill by easy stages, to toy with pain as a cat does with a mouse. And so Smith just shifts his position a little, grins, and says "And why in the god-damn hell not".

The Negro takes his spectacles off, folds them neatly, and puts them carefully into his coat pocket. Then he quite calmly looks at Smith and the rest of us and says, "Your odor, a pestilence; your lice, a multitude; your dirt, deep as earth; your manner, an abomination. So scowl me no scowls, beetle me no brows, Mr. White Man. For I am free as you, free as the bird on the wing, free as the living wind in the spring."

"Lincoln soldiers set you free and now you come crawlin' back? You one of them yankee niggers?"

"I was granted my freedom, ten years ago, by my master, Dr. Jamison of this fair city. His death and his will gave me freedom, God bless and rest him for that. I am not one of those you speak of in your derogatory fashion. Yes - your derogatory fashion."

"You sure he ain't insultin' us? Callin' our uniforms rags?"

"It ain't nuthin' good, comin' from his fat lip."

"You right sure you're not one of them Lincoln darkies? How we know you ain't?"

"Because I am a Southron, as you profess to be; because I have paid my ten per cent tax in kind to the Government of the Confederate States of America; because I have two nephews who are teamsters with General Lee; all that, my dear sir, makes me a loyal Confederate Negro by any criteria. Do you not agree?"

"Never thought I'd see a confederit darky."

"My dear sir, we are all that. Put us in uniform. See for yourself. There is talk of it even now in the Congress. Certainly, some will go over in the night, as yours do, but others will stay, as I will, and hold the last ditch with you. This is the South and it is our country as it is yours. Can't you see that? You trust us with your women and children, and your possessions, while you go forth to fight the invader. What greater trust is there? Then trust us with the South, trust us with America."

"It ain't part of yore America."

"Of course it is. Haven't you seen a one hundred dollar Confederate note? What is the illustration primarily represented upon its face? Not the orators, or the planters, or even the brave soldiers such as yourself, no - none of these. It represents hard-working black laborers of the South, does it not? And what does it say? Confederate States of the South? Confederate States of the Planters? Confederate States of the Slave Empire? Of course not. It quite clearly says Confederate States of America - Of America. America and the South is our home, as surely as it is yours."

"Africa is yore home."

"No more than the England of the Restoration is yours."

"Why don't we jest take them blankets and to hell with him? Six of us, one of him."

"We can't do that. He's a confederit negro, didn't you hear him say it his very own self?"

"A confederit negro - Shit."

"He's a southerner who says he's loyal. Now deny that if you can. Look at it any way you want, he's with us and there just ain't no way we can get around that."

Sergeant Smith says nothing at all for a full minute or more, just glares hell-fire and brimstone at the Negro, who calmly undresses, gets under his blankets, and turns his back on us. Finally Smith says, "Elliott, go get some more firewood". So out I go into that howling storm and bring in a good armload covered with ice. But soon we get warm and then warmer, until heads began to nod and eyelids begin to close. All but old Smith. His eyes alone remain fixed on that slumbering form. Every now and then, his fists open and clench, tighten and relax, but he says nothing, only stares with those burning eyes at the Negro, until his eyelids too begin to close, slowly at first, but still awake, with the flaming hatred still blazing forth. Yet further still they settle until only half, then only a quarter, then only one thin line of that hate is left, flaming like one thin sliver of fire before dying, like dying coals, into the blessed sleep that knows neither love nor hate.

And then there is Miss Jeannie Dean.

I think I will always remember her as I see her first one cold afternoon a day or two later. Sycamore Street is crowded as always with army wagons, soldiers on leave, civilians in old tattered overcoats. At the Courthouse, there is the usual ragged cluster of the poor begging for charity. I first see her coming up the hill from Old Town, with a market basket filled with potatoes. She is having a hard time with the weight of the basket and the crowds, not to mention the mud. So I step over to ask if I can be of assistance and she raises her eyes to me and after that, all my life changes forever.

The house is a simple two-story building badly in need of paint and general repair. Here she lives with her mother. Mrs. Dean was perhaps in her late forties; staid, conservative, and clearly over-burdened with being the head of a family. There is another sister, seldom seen, and a ten-year-old boy. They are all still in mourning for an older son killed at Globe Tavern. Lonely, lonely people, trying their best to survive as best they can.

I offer to cut the firewood and go to the market, do the simple necessary repairs to the house and grounds; they give me hot meals in return. They are nice people, needing a lot of support and attention, but my eyes return again and again to Jennie Dean.

She is only nineteen. She has blue eyes, dark hair, and a most lovely form and figure, but what I love most is her expression when she looks at me. An honest and sincere expression, that when it meets mine, speaks of trust and simple affection and enduring respect. It speaks of her heart.

One grey afternoon, we walk out into the small garden behind the house. She tells me it had once been a flower garden with roses and marigolds and sunflowers, but since the war only vegetables have been planted there. Now it is a rank wilderness of dead tomato vines and cornstalks rattling in the wind. It is then, without any forethought or hesitation, that I take her hand. She does not resist or try to pull away, but leaves her hand to rest in mine. Despite the cold, it is some time before we go in, for it seems that I could walk that enclosed waste with her forever, her hand quietly resting in mine. We are very young, but we find then that love has its own language and need never be spoken to be real.

I don't actually ask her to marry me, but the understanding is surely there. For we talk of all those things that married people know - of what kind of house we would live in after the war, of my family's farm in North Carolina, of home and children, of all those things we thought the good life must include. But unspoken are the more important things - the sense of mutual trust and understanding we have that goes deeper than words.

One late afternoon, we are in the garden, for that is the only place we can be alone. She is sitting in the faded garden chair, hands folded in her lap, and she has absolutely no hope at all. I tell her, "You are important to me, I will never forget you and if I ever lost you, I would return to find you again."

She lowers her eyes and whispers, "But how can you be so sure. No one knows what may happen now. This war. I am afraid. So afraid for you, for us."

"The two of us together are the only sure thing either of us can hold onto during these last uncertain months. It is the only thing that can defy time."

"But this war, this war", she says, looking at me through her tears. "It has you, and me, and all the rest. It won't let us go."

She lifts one hand quickly to wipe away a tear on her cheek, only to quietly lay that hand once again in her lap. I reach into my cartridge box and take out a minie cartridge. "This is your war. This is your death." I fling it against the garden wall, where it falls in the dead grass. "I tell you it doesn't exist. And it won't ever come back. To you. To me. To anyone. It doesn't matter to us. It isn't real. We are. We are the only reality. My dear Jennie, can't you see that?"

Can't you see that? I hold her close to me now, smelling the sweet fragrance of her hair, whispering can't you see that?

She becomes thoughtful now, quietly and slowly withdrawing into her own world, and I let her go, for I know that she, as women must, has gone within to contemplate Life on her own terms. For women can see nothing unless it is fringed with lace, laid in silk, incensed with perfume, and young as I am, I already know that it is a world no man can ever enter or understand.

"After the war", I tell her, "it will be different, it surely will be different from all this. After the war, we will rebuild our own lives as they should be and can be. We are young, we can control our lives, we can start now. And yet I know of one act that will begin it now, that will seal us together and it can be done now - a simple photograph, a tin-type or daguerreotype perhaps, to be taken in Petersburg of the two of us together, now in the dying winter of 1864. Finding peace only with you, in you, I will not wear this uniform of this dead war, but a dark frock coat of the finest make. And you will wear your mother's lace shawl and perhaps the cameo brooch at the throat. And this memorial will be an assurance to both of us that we have not only survived, but surmounted the worse that this war can give us. It will mark not an ending, but the new beginning for us all."

She lifts her eyes to me then and in them there is all the love that any man can hope for, but there, too, is the lasting   sorrow of women, for they feel deeper and longer, know more and understand better the life that is the curse, the blessing of all living things.

The photograph is never made, for the very next day we receive orders to return to the trenches and rejoin the 56th Regiment. Jennie sadly makes some sorghum molasses cakes to take with me. I tell her it will be but a few days, that I will return as quickly as I can, and then I kiss her on the cheek and leave her standing there. She remains there, alone, in all her soft beauty, as beautiful as I found her, lovely as I will remember her. It is the first time I have kissed her.

The boys at the hut are all packed up and ready to go. It takes only a moment to get my blanket roll and put the molasses cakes in my cartridge box. Uncle Tom is standing in the doorway, his hands in his coat pockets, and not a word does he say. Sergeant Smith shoots a last fiery look at him and just murmurs, "Condferit nigger -

Shit", and walks away. I look back one last time at what has been home for two weeks, for it too is important. It has brought me to Jennie Dean. Uncle Tom is still standing there.

I adjust my blanket roll over my left shoulder, pick up the rifled musket, hesitate for a moment, and then turn to him.

Perhaps I have in mind a simple word of thanks for his patience with us, but somehow they don't sound right, any words I can say, so I just wish him well. He politely inclines his head, but says nothing. I will remember you, I think to myself, for you have fought and won as hard a battle as any of us these past few days, and with greater courage. But in his eyes there is no sign of any message given or received. He only continues to look at me through the wire framed spectacles with the old wise look of age toward any youth: compassionate, understanding, with pity.

A cold rain begins to fall and mist from the Appomattox is drifting in. There are just the two of us now. I know Uncle Tom deserves something for taking us all in, but I have no money, nothing of really any value to give him. But there is one thing I can give him. I slowly come to attention and raising my right hand to the brim of my hat, I salute him.

I hold the salute for a long moment, for I think it might mean something to him and perhaps it does, but he only looks at me. Then he turns and walks back into the shed and slowly closes the door.

I am alone now on that lonely and deserted street with the low clouds coming over and the wind in the rain stirring a stray wisp of straw across the wagon ruts, now rapidly dissolving into mud. This old black man, this young white girl, this War and me - what is it all for? Why are we all here? Who can fathom it, who can ever fathom it?

So we return, as in a dream, to the old 56th, which is still holding the trenches on the City Point Railroad. Regimental headquarters are excavated right in the face of the railroad cut itself, with bracings and supports of heavy timber for protection from artillery fire. The lines run down each side of headquarters from there. We have been away only two weeks, but even in that short time, you can see that the men are in even poorer condition. Most are weak and ill from malnutrition. It did not seem possible, but the hell we returned to is worse than the hell from which we had escaped a few short weeks before.

Despite the freezing weather, the sleet and the snow, there is some comfort in the bomb-proofs, over the small fires, but one has to be careful of too much smoke, for then it makes a good target for the excellent Union artillery observers. Means of transportation to any point is limited. The 56th - indeed the whole army for that matter - is cut off from the rest of the world. All that is real or that matters is the regiment.

Now there is just one man to every yard of line in our front, with absolutely no reserve. It would be laughable to fight a war this way, were it not so tragic.

We spend the next few weeks there. The same old cold and mud, the same old hacking and coughing, the same old dying, the same old round of missing faces in the morning. We are falling apart, even as we watch. There is no hope. We no longer dare to look into the faces of those who are left, for we see written there our own despair, our own bleak future. We lift our eyes to the smoke-filled sky, and then turn back to the mud and sleep.

On the 15th of March, the brigade and regiment leave the trenches and move out to the extreme right on Hatcher's Run. The few days spent there are occupied in standing guard and drill, but it is only the quiet before the storm. On March 24, a courier rides up with a message for our commanding officer. Lieutenant-Colonel Luke is absent on convalescent leave and so Major John Graham receives our new orders. The regiment immediately begins to prepare for a night march.

Before daybreak on the 25th, we move back through the silent streets of Petersburg and as in a dream, I find myself in that long column silently passing under the dark windows of the Dean house. I know which window is her room and I can fancy her sleeping there, the eyelashes closed on that lovely blue, her soft breast softly rising and falling in her sleep. And I think that this too is not a parting, but simply still another meeting, her in her sleep, I on the road below, forever passing and repassing in the night. Shortly before dawn, the regiment is once again in the entrenchments. Here a line of battle is formed and for the first time we are told that we are to join in the great assault on Fort Stedman.

It is to be a desperate attack, the one great gamble Lee would take to shorten Grant's line, so that a detachment from our army can break free to join Johnson and defeat Sherman in North Carolina. Fort Stedman is selected for the assault point, for it is located close to our lines, a stone's throw from our forward trenches. Fifty men with axes will cut a path through the Union frasies; three redoubts will be taken by three detachments of a hundred men each; and the main force will take Stedman and the trenches on each side. Over four divisions, over a half of our total force in front of Petersburg, will be devoted to this massive onslaught. If we are successful, Grant will weaken his left to strengthen his right and we will be able to side-step him to Johnson; if very fortunate, our assault column might even drive all the way to the Union supply base at City Point, conceivably even capture Grant himself.

The 56th, under the command of Major Graham, follows the attack during the pre-dawn darkness with no opposition and we leap down into the now empty Union trenches just to the north of the fort. It is dark, but we can tell that these trenches are well made, with wooden facings smoothed all along the interior walls. They had been hastily abandoned and there are a few haversacks, cartridge cases, and even rifles thrown hither-and-yon. I rummage through one haversack and find a jar of apple jelly and hardtack and eat it as I stand there. The rest of the boys are doing the same. The fort and three of their batteries (10, 11, and 12) fall with little resistance to our comrades on the right. We are on the extreme left of the Confederate force occupying the Union works and we are preparing to move on out to our left to take adjoining portions of the Union line when the counter-attack comes roaring in.

We rapidly form our line in the trenches. We can see large Union assault columns appearing in the early morning light on the rising ground to our front and right. Moments later, when the attack comes, it is thrown back by steady volleys from the 56th; the Federals then regroup around their colors, raise their cheer, and again advance for a second, and then a third time, only to be repulsed. There is a moment of silence on the front. But although our brigade has overrun the 57th Massachusetts, the Yanks fight on from their holding positions at right angles to their trenches. We use our bayonets to dig in about 500 yards short of Battery 9. There is much confusion in the faint light of morning and the trenches are a bewildering maze of intersecting lines and angles. And then we look to our right and see our doom. Fort Stedman and all the positions we had captured earlier are being abandoned by our men; we can see large numbers of them running back toward our own lines.

The attack has miserably failed. The three Confederate detachments never found the redoubts. Many starving soldiers, once they were inside Stedman, began ransacking the Federal rations stored there. At eight o'clock, four hours after the attack began, General Lee orders a withdrawal as the Federals converge from all directions on the captured works.

As the withdrawal begins under increasing Union fire and amid growing confusion, Ransom orders Major Graham to hold our position and provide covering fire for the retreat. We are to withdraw only after all other Confederate units have been evacuated. The main Federal attack now falls upon our remaining units occupying Stedman and a few hundred yards of adjoining trench. As these positions fall, one after the other, the enemy turns his full attention on the 56th, for we are the only ones left in the trenches now.

We hold on until all hope is lost. And then as we try to make a run for it, we are hit by devastating concentrated fire from artillery and massed musketry fire on our left flank. There is no order, just every man running, stumbling, falling, shying away even as we try to escape that constant blazing fire on our left. Major Graham is wounded, shot through both legs, and has to be carried off the field. The color bearer falls, hands the colors to another retreating soldier, and the last time I see the wounded man, he is painfully trying to drag himself back to our lines. Company I, on the extreme left, is ordered by Ransom to hold the transverse to the last. A few moments later, the 2nd Michigan storms over the position, capturing Captain Harrill and twenty of his men; twenty others escape somehow in the confusion. Company F lost its captain and thirty-six of its forty-four men. The 56th Regiment lost in all 250 men, one half of our total enrollment reporting for duty that morning. Brigade losses were as grievous: 1,364 lost out of an original 2,300 men.

I am among those in Company F captured on that terrible morning. A crowd of cheering Union soldiers swarm over us and we just quickly put our guns on the ground and then stand there waiting. Much to my surprise, the Yankees are just boys, as young as I, and they crowd around us with flashing eyes, and the loveliest smiles on their countenances, and shaking hands with us in the most enthusiastic manner. But this cordial reunion of the states doesn't last long. Soon a detail arrives to take us to the rear. A bayonet pricks my back end and a gruff voice says, Get along, Johnny.

We are herded to the rear through the Union camps and see soldiers playing baseball like nothing has happened. In fact, we soon learn from our guards that our massive onslaught has been repulsed by only a single corps of the Union Army. That afternoon, we are put in a large stockade and President Lincoln and General Grant ride by to look us over. Naturally, we get to our feet and give them a looking-over in return. Grant is a very ordinary looking general with a cigar and we think he would be more at home as a colonel. King Abe rides a horse as bad as you could imagine, with his spider legs and arms trying to keep some degree of coordinated dignity. But there is something about his face that catches one. I don't know what it is until I realize it looks like ours do, but why his should be saddened is beyond us.

This man is fighting the war to free the Negro and enslave the South. So they say. And now General Lee is saying that Negro soldiers in our army should not only be given their freedom, but welcomed to all the advantages of southern life. So it occurs to me that if Thomas is ever to become a fellow American, whether as the Confederate soldier he professes to be, or as the liberated Freeman in the restored Union the Yanks want him to be, then his equality is dependent not on the South's defeat or the North's victory, but on his own effort in a country, North or South, that allows him to make that effort. Neither side has done so, the one forcing him to remain in what the Abolitionists call Bondage, yet the other still refusing him the right to vote. Therefore, this President can only liberate the North by first defeating the South. The Yanks are fighting to free themselves by freeing the slaves and they don't even know it.

And our President in Richmond fights to keep America as it has been in all its greatness; theirs, to change it into perhaps something more. One defies the Past, to keep it from the maw of time; one defies the Future, to mold it into a new form. But both follow the spirit of America in their defiance, as it once was, as it may yet become.

Both Presidents are dreamers of the American dream; both necessary to America's promise; both, brothers-in-arms, even after all this.

The defiance that marked this nation's birth is the same defiance that will mark its end, that will mark our end here. And, yes, there is something to be said for defiance against the odds, the old defiance of Uncle Thomas, of our two Presidents, of every man-jack of us, the old Defiance that first lifted Man from the first wilderness and that will stand him in good stead to the end of time.

The President is followed by a long line of carriages filled with officers and beautiful women. The women wear outlandish hats with feathers, ribbons, and tassels; they lean forward at the windows, smiling; they are beautiful. But we are obviously a spectacle for their entertainment, as if we are part of some theatrical troupe, and most of us turn away as they pass. I can feel their smiles and light laughter burning a hole through my back. I never feel so lost as I do now.

The officers are carefully separated from us and sent elsewhere. Then the enlisted men are loaded on flat and freight cars and shipped to City Point. There, we are put in a large barracks and given some boiled fat pork and a handful of hard tack. More prisoners constantly come in until soon there are over 4,000 of us. There are prisoners from the infantry, artillery, cavalry, all crowded together. A few of us from the 56th remain in a small group amid all that milling confusion.

The next day, a Union general, a white-headed old man with his sash and sword, gets up on a barrel and makes a speech. He says that President Lincoln offers an amnesty to all who will lay down their arms or join the Union Army and that if we come over to the Union side, we would be allowed to go North and work. All we have to do is take the Oath of Allegiance to the United States Government. But if we refuse this gracious opportunity, we will be sent to a prisoner-of-war camp indefinitely. There will be no exchange and no reprieve.

I think of Uncle Thomas that night in the shed and how he stood up to Smith when not one of us dared to do it. I know now what I have to do. The issue is not that we, as citizens, are no longer in a free union, but rather a forcible one. It is not that this general, this government, this nation, these guards so complacently and so assuredly look upon us as the Lost and the Damned. No, It is simpler than that. For so long, you see, we have been the chaff before the wind, and now we are even less than that. But we are not cattle, not rebels, not prisoners. We are Americans and the fact that we are Americans transcends any race or nationality, party or government. And first and foremost, we are men. There comes a time to be men, and we will be no less than men.

I whisper the words first, but then they come forth strong and free, and I raise my fist and shout, "No, I shall not!" and only then realize that these are the words, too, of the old Pilgrims and the brave Regulators, of the Revolutionary Fathers - - and of Thomas. The other boys in the 56th, after a moment of surprise, begin shouting, "No! No!" as well. Then, from all that vast crowd of prisoners, there comes a rising chorus of "Hell, nos", "Tell it to the Marines!" and "Go to hell". Out of the 4,000 there, about thirty finally step out, with furtive and hang-dog looks, but they are followed by further shouts and taunts of "Yore welcome to that'un; he's as cowardly as any of yore hirlings". The general bows his head and steps down off the barrel and then we immediately march to a wharf and board steamboats to Point Lookout, the great prisoner-of-war camp on the Maryland East Shore.

So, we arrive at Point Lookout that evening. The old sun is going down, marking the end of another day. It is a big camp, with dirt roads winding among the dirty tents and hovels. There are armed guards on all the streets and on the palisades. But, there is no smoke from any fires; these are not permitted. And prisoners are not allowed any mail or newspapers. Just outside the camp stockade, there is a cemetery, with burial details even now at work. There is a rising miasma of corruption and decay everywhere.

I wonder for a moment how the regiment is faring now. Where is it? What is it? Are any of the boys left? Probably by now Old Mother Earth has claimed them, every one.

The prison is a teeming, seething cauldron of all that is left of the Southern Confederacy. Not only soldiers are here, but English sailors, blockade runners, civilians, political dissidents, even Negroes who had been captured with their masters and refused to take the oath right along with everyone else.

But now I can see where we are. Yes, now I see what is here. Death is here. You can smell it, see it, touch it and feel it in your inmost self. The old sun eternally going down to night; these faces without hope; this rising odor of human waste, of dysentery, of typhoid, of the giving-up, the letting-go; not one blade of living grass anywhere to be seen; the blue sentries silently pacing their rounds; the waiting cemetery out there, as big as the camp itself; and over all, the great vault of the sky that covers us all, the living and the dead.

Oh, my fairest Jennie, I will see you yet one more time.

CHAPTER NINETEEN

Captain John McNeely, Company K

A t nine that morning we tumble back into our trenches, those of us who are left. We fall to the earth in those trenches, lying where we fall, back against the wall of the ditch, panting, sweating, disheveled, our flesh crawling with that which only imminent violent death can convey, trembling.

There are less than two hundred of us left. Companies are down to fewer than twenty men. The men lie flat on the ground, sit in small disconsolate groups, some kneeling in exhaustion, heads down, all the fight gone out of them at last. We have put the greater part of our army in against Grant and have made no more than a dint in Stedman and not a lasting one at that. Now truly there is no hope. It is all over. We manage a roll call later that morning, but that is it for the day. We just sit there, not daring to look at each other, staring bleakly at the trench wall in front of us.

The Union fire is now unceasing.

The next morning, Lieutenant-Colonel Luke returns from convalescent leave and resumes command. The man is dazed, in shock by what he finds. He walks down the trench with a cane to steady him, but I can see his hands are shaking. "Captain McNeely, where is the rest of your company?" "This is all, Colonel, all that are fit for duty. Fourteen here, eleven others in hospital". He looks at me vacantly, then drifts on to Company H, which is in even worse shape than mine. He stops once or twice to catch his breath; we watch him go, expecting to see him fall and add one more to the list. This outfit is finished and he knows it. Maybe now they'll put us all in commissary or maybe just let us go home and make it all official in accordance with the God-Damn Regulations. The old 56th is gone and all it needs is a helping hand with the shovel to lay it to rest.

But they won't. They won't in all their stupidity. They only see the shadow and think it real. The officers and enlisted men, under arms, no matter how few, and still with the flag, no matter how tattered, is all that matters to Division, but the 56th is gone. The word resounds like a knell, a dirge. We still have the organization, the arms, we are still listed as active, we still have the flag, but the 56th is gone. The only thing left is the will to go on just one more day and the enduring wonder of why that should even be necessary now at the end.

On the 27th and 28th, what is left of us are moved out to the right. The heavy musketry fire all along the lines day and night is constant now, a never-ending roar to bring the curtain grandly sweeping down on us all. But the men respond, however grudgingly, and we return fire, however sporadically, against the heavy skirmish lines of the enemy edging in ever closer. The rest of the day is spent in reinforcing the earthworks. Several Union attacks probing along our front are repulsed, but we know these are only the first heralds of the approaching storm.

Night falls long and slow at the end of March 28. It has been just three days since Stedman, and the men have recovered enough to begin to break out of the terrible silence. I occasionally come upon them quietly talking to one another; when they see me, they go back to their work, but I know their thoughts. Who can blame them for it? The war is lost, the regiment is lost, there is really no need for them to stay on through this. Frank Roberts used to talk about "We Happy Few"; he should see us now.

It is impossible to sleep under the infernal shelling that goes on all night long. Beautiful, though, in its own way. You can trace the high flight of almost every shell, the bright point of light so grandly rising from over there, so slowly crossing the smoke filled vault, paths criss-crossing, a fire in the night, the whole trench line sometimes lighting up, showing every splintered wall facing, every chevaux-de-frise, every clod of earth. And then everything plunges back again into darkness deeper than Pluto's Realm, the only constant being the unending roar of the heavy artillery.

I am duty officer that night and while making my rounds, I enter one of the innumerable bomb-proofs the men use for shelter. It is about ten o'clock, maybe later, and the Union artillery has paused,

as even it must from time to time. I pull the blanket aside serving as
a curtain, finding a few men from different companies there, huddled in their blankets against the wall. It is dark in there, so dark I
cannot see anything clearly, but I can hear the dry cough, the hard
respiration, the heavy breathing all around me. I ask if they are all
right, if they need any thing. And then a voice, with some command
still in it, says "Beg yore pardon, Sir, but there's something the boys
been meaning to ask you."

And I know what it is before the words are even said, but sometimes the speaking of it, the hearing of it puts a kind of finality or
seal on it, and even that helps a little.

"Beg pardon, Sir, but it's about over for us, ain't it?"

And I say, "I expect so, unless General Lee can find some way
to break free, but then Richmond goes, so I reckon we'll hold on a
bit longer."

"A bit longer. How much longer, Sir?"

"Not long. Not long now. But we fought a good fight."

And the voice says, "That's the dam truth, ain't it, boys?"

They murmur quietly, and even seem to brighten just a little at
the thought.

"We showed them what we can do. But what for, Sir? Why, is
what we need to know, Cap'n. That's what we were talkin' about
when you come in. What's it all for?"

And another voice in the dark says, "Orter ask the Prophet that.
But he's done gone clean away to North Carolina, dodging bush-
whackers instead of these shells".

"He's got a brother still over in commissary."

"But he ain't no prophet though."

"Parson's gone too, though he never was of much count. Back
in the Old North State before now, cause he ain't been seen since
that big snow on New Years."

"And that's the problem, Sir. Now this is the way I see it, beg
yore pardon. Here we are, all mix-match together, from different
companies. Some of us are from Company A, some from Company
F, and so on. Some from the east of the state, some from the west.
And then there's the ones who give us orders, ones who tell us to dig
and fire, ones to say come and go, but there ain't nary a one to tell
us what it's all for. 'Lessen it's you, Cap'n."

"It's not me."

"It shore ain't them field officers, that's for shore. Colonel in arrest, Luke sick as a dog, half the men without officers."

"Then, way we see it, half of the men are better off."

They chuckle at that, quietly laughing among themselves, and I feel their eyes on me in the dark. I wait, breathing slowly in the close air. Outside, the Union artillery has opened anew, but now it seems distant, withdrawn, muted.

"Oh, present company aside, Cap'n. But serious now, who is it, Cap'n? Who is it can tell us what it's all for?"

"It's not me, God knows."

"God knows, boys, but now He ain't sayin' nothin' neither. He's done gone and left us too for good. He's done forgot about us."

"Maybe there ain't no God, or if there's one, He's wearing blue. Just look - they got all the men and guns, they got all the ships and money. They're so all fired righteous on this slavery thing. So, maybe they got God on their side along with everything else. But where does that put us?"

"Old God just a-settin' on his cloud, just tips the scales one way, then the other, never no never mind. Right now, He's tipped North and now we're the Lost Sheep, if ever were."

"That ain't true. He's a-savin' us, every man jack, for somethin', else we'd gone the way the rest of them did."

"Savin', horse-shit. You call this bein' saved?"

"No, maybe saved for somethin' else. Lieutenant Callahan thinks so."

"Another crazy 'un."

"Be it so, he put in to officer one of them black regiments being raised in Richmond. His papers didn't come through, though, with all this goin' on. But I heard he was bothered over all them niggers we killed at The Crater last year."

"Killed a sight of them, we did. Just kept a-comin' on into that hole we buried them in, even when the Yanks run."

"They was niggers, but they died hard."

I say nothing, but listen to them talk, thinking I do not belong here, for this is dying slow and hard too, and if I am saved, it will be for something far from this place, this night.

"So maybe Callahan all his own self thinks he can somehow

make it alright now, bringin' all that spilt blood back new. But Callahan's got his own personal devil to quiet down, don't he, all the boys know that, and it ain't goin' to work no how. I mean, if God's on the side of the Yanks, lettin' them win like they are, then there ain't nothin' will put him on our side now, will it Cap'n? I mean, it's too late for anythin' like that now, ain't it?"

"I don't know."

And then a young boy's voice, heavy with the fierce sharp tears of adolescence, says, "He ain't forgot us. He's bigger than all this war and fightin', He's just got to be. And there's got to be a purpose in it all. I don't understand it, I don't understand it at all, but I know He ain't forgot us. But, Cap'n, I wish I could go home now, I wish I could just go home."

"Hell, boy, yore from Pastantonk County. You probably ain't got no home no more."

"It won't be the same for none of us, goin' back."

"Dam lucky if we ever get back. Sherman is already there, wherever we're goin'."

"None of us got no home no more."

And then I say, my voice softer and quieter than theirs, but growing harder with anger and defiance at our fate even as I speak, for the darkness protects me as it has them, "Maybe you're right. Maybe that's why we're still here. Maybe none of us have any home left now, unless it's here, right here in what's left of the 56th. And we're still here, aren't we? We're still alive, aren't we? And what for, if not for each other?"

I angrily throw the words out into the invisible dark, against the doom facing us all.

"Why are you still here, if not for him? And you - if not for him? And you too - if not for him? If we are saved for anything, it's for that. We'll stand by each other, because that's the only prayer I know."

I pause, listening to the silence in the bomb-proof, feeling self-conscious and embarrassed. What must they think of me? Faison, Luke, Graham - these are the officers to make speeches to these men, not me.

"It's all we have left now", I say softly. "It ought to be enough to go on, for at least a little while longer."

They are still silent, but I can't tell if they are now watching me or not. I pull the blanket aside, and step on out into the cold night. I take a deep breath then and look up into a cloudy and fiery sky, the smoke and clouds flaring with each bursting shell. Even with all that celestial fire above, there is a threat of impending rain, but not yet. It will not rain tonight and perhaps not even by morning. But by tomorrow evening, as the night falls, it will surely come.

And so morning comes, but slow and halting, with heavy clouds sweeping in from the west, and rain not so far distant now. About nine o'clock, couriers begin arriving on the front and we know a change is imminent. In any Army, there is a vital electricity in the air between men. One can read much in the impetuosity of a courier or the condition of a horse, the look in the eye, even the quick snap as the dispatch is handed to a field officer. In a matter of minutes, quick confirmation comes from our own field officers; men are shouting; everywhere there is a sudden stir; and then we know. The brigade, in fact a good part of the whole Army, is moving out of the trenches. Word passes through the ranks that large Union columns in motion to the south and west indicate a major movement of infantry against our right flank. The force apparently is advancing toward the South-Eastern Railroad, the last rail supply line left to Richmond and Petersburg.

The 56th is reduced (I think I have said) to less than 200 men. We form column in the midst of Ransom's Brigade, somewhere in Bushrod Johnson's Division, lost somewhere in Anderson's Corps. I assure the men in my company that probably we will not see any action at all, as our numbers are too depleted for that honor. Perhaps we'll be detailed in the rear somewhere, guarding supplies, road or provost duty perhaps, perhaps guarding the thousands of Yanks to be taken in some climatic Confederate victory now at the end. The men keep in line in fairly good order, muskets careening off of shoulders at odd angles, canteens and cups clanking, feet slowly shuffling, all one long column toiling again into the west. Toward dark, the rain begins to fall, first in small cold drops like sprinkles of iced blood, then harder, faster, steadier until it is one gray deluge on that long column. We march on into the black night and sleep in the mud at the side of the road.

The next morning dawns in a continuing deluge of pounding

rain. A gray mist rises from the encampments on the roadside; the fields, the banks, and the road itself are running seas of mud. But it is the falling rain we try not to notice, that we try to shut out, the rain pounding and drumming hard on hat brims and wagons, running into our eyes when we look up for some surcease, holding us fast in sinking water halfway to our knees. We pull ourselves together and once more enter the road, facing ever west.

It is a long, never ending ordeal, just pulling one foot from the mud to merely set it in even deeper with the next step. The fatigue is not only in the legs, but in the shoulders, the neck, and the back. The rain continues to come down in a pounding deluge, never stopping, never slowing. We are now told that we are attached to George Pickett's command and are to follow the railroad to the far right, to Sutherland's Tavern, ten miles from Petersburg. From there, we are to march on to Dinwiddie Court House to determine the identity and gauge the strength of this unknown Union force.

And with every passing mile, that force, somewhere to the west, assumes a lasting reality all its own in our mind... huge, colossal, fringed with bayonets, elusive in all this mud and wet. Yet, once met and defeated, we sense an ending of a kind, a summation of all that has gone before, and so we look forward to that final meeting with anticipation as well as apprehension, for we have met it so many times before.

But as we move on, mile after weary mile through the rain, it changes, we change. As fatigue builds and spirits fall, more and more of us begin to feel that there is no hope in this, no sense at all in it. What after all is the purpose in it, in this useless prolongation of the inevitable? What is the purpose? What possible intent can there be in pretending to continue? Surely, any man can see it, for all men are conscious of what is happening now, and yet we go on and on and so I, like that unknown boy's voice in the dark bomb-proof, I now do not understand it at all. I guess we're just dull, inanimate beings with no choice but to march on into the ether in the everlasting rain, still with no purpose, no intent to it at all.

During the afternoon, we begin to hear the first faint popping of skirmishers, and we know we have found the enemy force we have been hunting down at last. But there is no way to tell whether they are infantry or cavalry, probably cavalry, for only cavalry can move quickly in all this flood. Our own cavalry leads the way, followed by our infantry on to the northwest now. Toward evening, we cross through a drenching country crossroads, where five roads from nowhere, leading nowhere, come to a brief meeting. I ask a passing staff officer on horseback the name of this place. Five Forks, he shouts, his horse pounding on in the rain.

Five Forks. We move on and pass it. As darkness comes, the rain settles off just a little and when we are told to file off the roads and camp in the adjoining fields, we have our first chance to look at the lay of the land. There is nothing of very much consequence here, very much like Eastern North Carolina where we once served in another life. Here are the same monotonous pine forests, the same broom sage grass, the same flat and level land stretching off into the dark - it is all here, as it was there. It could pass for any part of that land around Kinston, New Bern, and what was the name of that other crossing -Dover, was it not, at Gum Swamp.

March 31 comes in gray mist and thick fog, with the rain still falling. Once again, we move out toward the unknown Union force. As I suspect, the 56th - indeed a good part of Ransom's Brigade - remains in support as we begin our drive. Soon word comes back that the Yanks are indeed retiring and they are only cavalry, as I thought, Sheridan's, and they cannot hold against our infantry. Our drive moves forward fairly well, but the roads are terrible and at last the Yanks finally begin to hold. We assist in repelling a Union column apparently feeling out our positions, but the 56th sees no other action. In the afternoon, the Yanks, using dismounted troopers as infantry, begin making progress in restoring the line they had held in the morning. So the see-saw battle ends as it began and with darkness, both sides remain in place. But these are only cavalry and they will surely drive before us come daylight. There is only one slight concern -so slight that it goes unmentioned - and it is that Pickett's brave force is now separated from the Army of Northern Virginia at Petersburg. Whatever happens, we will have to handle it ourselves.

During the long night, the rain slowly fades away and we awake the next morning in the first silence we have known in days. Before first light, we withdraw back to Five Forks, our way on the road lighted by pine torches, flaring and hissing in the night. By now, the slight concern has become an ominous reality and we tighten our position accordingly. Around the crossing, we prepare our line, cutting down the pines at the edge of the forest and then dragging the logs, ten men to each one, to form a rough barricade facing south. The log barricade is built as high as our chest, but it is a makeshift affair for all that - a 150-yard-long barricade on the front in the form of an angle. It is the only angle we see in either direction; there is no other angle anywhere on the line; forevermore at Five Forks, it is The Angle.

We remain confident as we take our positions in The Angle. Moving from the left side of the inverted V, there is first the 24th N. C. Infantry, and then the 56th almost to the apex; in the apex itself, there is the 25th N. C. Infantry; then on the right side, the 49th, with the 35th Regiment completing the transverse. All in all, there are less than 500 men on the Brigade front. I count only about 175 men in the 56th. Where we are, we can see over the slashed logs of the barricade dismal clearings and thick pine woods, all under a clearing, lowering sky. "This is some commissary detail, ain't it, Cap'n. Us takin' a stand here, air we the Hunters or the Hunted now?" I shake my head, but say nothing. I am trying to remember. Somewhere, sometime in the war, something like this happened before, but where?

The men, only two lines deep, lean against the logs, huddled in their coats and blankets. All of us are ravenously hungry, but there are no rations. Some of the men are shivering, either from fever or cold. It is very cold. I pull my collar tighter to my throat and wait, still trying to remember.

The afternoon passes quiet and still as we wait for we know not what. Then, shortly after four o'clock, a sudden scattering of fire from our skirmishers flickers all along the front. No brief argument among skirmishers this, but something else is coming. We rise and peer over the log barricade. And the pine forests out there, even as we watch, are filling with blue and there they are at last. An advancing horde, a moving continent of blue, stretching off in either direction as far as eye can see, as far to the distant horizon as eye can see. This is what we have come to find, I find myself thinking. We have finally run the fox down. But it is no fox; it is no longer just Sheridan and cavalry. It is the infantry of Ayre's Division of Warren's V Corps.

I immediately call the men of my company to arms, but they are already there, ready, resting their rifles across the topmost log of the barricade.

So this is it. I watch them coming on, a dense blue crowd to the horizon, a raging incoming sea of them, but they are magnificent in their coming, beautiful in their alignment, flags and mounted officers to the front, and the setting sun gilding the forest of bayonets that keep rising from the earth. I look at the men at the barricade, crouching behind the logs, hats pulled low over their brows, clasping the rifled muskets close to them like children. General Ransom rides up just behind us and I hear him shouting to Luke, "You must hold them, Colonel, you must hold them, Sir." Luke lifts his cane in salutation.

I have one quick glimpse of our regimental flag, fixed in the center of our line before the storm falls. It has gone through so much - Dover, Plymouth, Ware Bottom, Petersburg, Globe Tavern, Stedman - now here. But there is no time to see more than the torn blue and red bunting clinging to a staff off to my right.

The Union line is now only a hundred yards away, closing fast, and still not a shot has been fired. And then the order comes down the line and I shout, "Fire! First rank, reload! Second rank, fire!" and the flame and smoke erupts from our line. Looking quickly around the side of a log, I see under the smoke the ground writhing with dead and wounded men, and the Union force falling back. Our men cheer, but it is lost in the rising roar of gunfire all up and down the front.

We only have a few moments before the man next to me shouts Here they come again! And they come in at a hard run this time, leaping over their casualties and this time we wait until they are close indeed, fifty yards or less, and then again, "Fire! First rank, reload! Second rank, fire!" Again there is the same searing blaze of fire from our front. I can hear their wounded screaming and see a mounted officer go down, horse and all, the hooves flailing and kicking. This time, I really think they might break through, but no, they are falling back again. Somehow we have held.

There is bedlam all around us now - in the sky, on the earth, in our breasts. We see everything indistinctly in the smoke. It takes them only a few minutes to align and then they come on for the third time.

I only have a brief chance to gauge their distance when a hand suddenly grabs me by the shoulder and the bearded face of a man I don't recognize, but who must have served with me for these three long years, screams, " Cap'n, my God, for God's sake, Cap'n!" and he points trembling. And I look to the left and the 24th is overrun, crowds of Union soldiers even now clambering over the barricade or pulling the logs down. On our side of the barricade are a brief flurry of short range gunfire, swinging muskets, men in a torturous embrace falling, other men beginning to break and run. Looking to the rear to see if there are any supports to close the break, I see only additional Union forces streaming past the 24th into our rear.

"Here they come again!" The cry echoes down our front. And at the same moment, I hear that vast subterranean roar of many feet, see over the log parapet the advancing flag, hear the shouts of that irresistible tide advancing. At my own order, the men turn from what is happening behind them and again level their muskets across the log to face the foe in front. Again, I hear myself screaming from a great distance, "First rank, fire! Reload! Fire at will"!

They come now up to the barricade itself this time, falling against it, sliding down against it, blood and splattered brain tissue across the topmost log. Through the smoke, I see scattered blue figures standing in shock in random groups, others falling back, still others painfully crawling away. Somehow we have held again.

Suddenly a running man knocks me all the way to my knees and as I start to rise, another one steps on my wrist. I look up in anger, but these are not our men. These are men from the 24th who have fought as long and as hard as they can, but who can fight no more now. Almost immediately, our position is filled with jostling, shoving men of the 24th screaming, " Run! Get out! All lost!" And it is at that moment that the 25th, in the point of the angle on our right, is overrun as well.

I do not see much on the right, other than an indistinct blue sea pouring over the barricade held by the 25th. There is a confused eddy in The Angle as it fills with Union infantry, seemingly as many coming in from the flanks as over the breastwork. Only seconds later, men from the 25th begin darting and weaving among us, shouting, "God-damn! Get out!"

Behind the 25th, I see General Ransom's horse going down, but an aide brings up a second one within moments. The general is screaming orders, but now there is nothing we can do.

The 56th is trapped, trapped in The Angle, with the enemy now on each flank and breaking into the rear. Luke shouts for us to fall back, but the enemy is everywhere now, exultant, cheering. We form a small square, with guns pointing to the rear as well as to the front and flanks, just as we learned it long ago at Camp Magnum. I cast a quick look at the parapet and see scores of Union soldiers climbing over it, dropping down on our side to kneel and then fire.

I step over the body of one of our men, then over another one. A single rank of men in front looks quickly at me for some direction, but do not cease firing. But now we are truly alone, our ranks thinning fast, men toppling forward and back, hitting me as they fall even as I stand there.

It is impossible to hold any longer, for men from the 24th and 25th are still crowding through, desperate in their own attempt to escape. We have time to fire one final volley; it staggers them for a moment, but in the next, our square collapses. Blue and butternut uniforms are all mixed together in a weltering maelstrom of revolver shots, bayonet thrusts, clubbed rifles. I see our flag toppling back and forth, grasped by invisible desperate hands, and then it slowly tilts to one side and falls. One man lurches hard against me; I turn and look into the face of a Union soldier, his startled eyes bloodshot (I can see it) and saliva flecking his lips. I strike hard with my right fist, but only hit him a glancing blow, and then bowing my head, I rush through the seething crowd toward the base of The Angle. Four or five of my men are with me; as in a dream, I see General Ransom lying under his writhing horse, some of his staff officers pulling him from beneath the kicking hooves and dragging him off into the smoke.

Loud cheers are breaking forth all around me from the Yanks as the entire line gives way; a few hundred yards to the right, Pegram's Battery is overrun, the gunners fighting to the last. Like lost waifs, orphans, I and four of my men follow after the staff officers carrying Ransom to the rear. We suddenly find ourselves among crowds of our soldiers madly running into the setting sun, a sun soon blocked by dense pine forests. Few of these men belong to the same unit; it is simply a crowd of fleeing soldiers, without unit or designation, almost without rank. I stop by a large pine tree to catch my breath; the four men who escaped with me lie where they fall. Where is the rest of the regiment? Were any others saved? I look back on the battlefield, but see now only drifting smoke, floating, dissipating into air. And there is only a great light and silence to mark whatever ending there might have been. At last there is silence, there is peace,

We stay beside the tree only for a minute and then, avoiding the road, we make our way slowly through the scrub pine thickets on to the west. Once we see a large squadron of Union cavalry cutting across our front and we crouch down, hiding until they pass. We take longer and longer rests in the thickets as the sun sets and darkness begins to settle; the old instinct telling us that darkness will be our best chance to escape. With the first stars in the sky, we make better time and soon come upon the wreck of the army crossing Hatcher's Run - wagons, teamsters, infantry, cavalry, field artillery, all crowded together in one indiscriminate mass. We fall in with them, the walking wounded, the tarnished gallants, gentlemen and rogues all, the old army we had served in so long, wounded fatally now, crawling back to its den, with a long trail of blood behind it. We walk until we can walk no further and then leaving the road for an open field, we collapse among many sleeping men, and sweet sleep falls on us even before we touch the ground.

The next day, the retreat continues and slowly, painfully, unbelievably the rest of the 56th slowly comes together again. Most of the survivors are men who had been in the rear area of The Angle - teamsters, hospital orderlies, couriers, commissary and supply personnel, cooks, clerks, men sick or disabled, not soldiers at all. Of course, a few men in The Angle had escaped as we had, but not many. Even with everyone counted, the 56th now numbers less than a hundred men, most of them non-combatants.

All through the long day of April 2, we toil on our way toward Petersburg. But when we arrive there, we are told to cross the Pocahontas Bridge over the Appomattox, that the city and Richmond, too, are being abandoned and we will try to regroup at Amelia Courthouse. Among the less than one hundred men of the 56th, there is no direction, no guidance. Luke is nowhere to be seen, perhaps in some ambulance, perhaps dead or a prisoner. We no longer know, no longer care.

We head northeast into the dead of night. In the far distance, we hear the faint roar of exploding Confederate gunboats on the James. All the night sky to the northeast is flaming red and we are told that it is Richmond burning. Now it is truly final, truly the end. The only mystery is why I survived when so many did not, why I am still here when so many others are not. But nothing really matters but to somehow stay with the column on the way to Amelia.

The next two days and nights pass in a haze of absolute despair. The march is a forced one, and the pain of merely putting one foot in front of the other at least sometimes prevents thought. Many men are sleeping even as they walk and I do myself, drifting, drifting until lurching suddenly awake in the moving darkness. At least, we are promised rations at Amelia. This is the only thing that keeps us going. However, when we finally arrive there on April 5, there is nothing there for us, nothing at all. But the deep despair is still there.

Gradually the extent of our losses at Five Forks becomes evident. Our casualties in killed and wounded remain forever unknown, but the Yanks count over 5,000 prisoners, thirteen regimental flags (whether one of those was the banner of the 56th we never learn) and six guns from Pelgram's Battery.

At Amelia, the hundred men of the 56th are directed off to the left of the road where a staff officer from Brigade waits on horseback. We sit or stand at ease as he looks down at us, his face drawn and haggard.

"You men of the 56th and the rest of Brigade will fall in with Anderson's Division until further notice. Provisions are being gathered from the area - it won't be much - but we will march as soon as they are distributed."

We stare at him vacantly, uncaring.

"Who is the commanding officer of this regiment?"

"We ain't got one, don't want one."

"You, the Captain there. Yes, you! What's your name? Step forward, Sir!"

"John F. McNeely, Company K."

"You are now the commanding officer of the 56th Regiment until you have been formally relieved of that duty. Your men will have a fifteen minute rest here while provisions are distributed and then you will immediately rejoin the column. I'll inform Brigade and they'll be getting you orders."

"Sir."

I walk among the men. Most are lost in stupor, a very few turning to look at me as I pass, but saying nothing. One man is plucking at my sleeve. "What do you want us to do now, Cap'n?" I say nothing to him, but pass on until I can breathe, yes, now I can breathe easier now, yes, now that is better, now I can face what I must face, do what I must do.

So. So - this is what I was saved for. Not for Victory or Survival, or Redemption, no, not for those things (illusions, dreams, fantasies), but only saved for this, to bury these men, to bury this regiment, yes, this is it, this is it, it was for this I was saved.

CHAPTER TWENTY

CHARLES F. DAVIS, PRIVATE,
REGIMENTAL COMMISSARY

"Well, boys, it looks like we got a new commander and he's about the youngest one we've had yet." But they didn't pay that much attention to me. We were all just tuckered out, completely exhausted. Since I had been in commissary for most of the war, they used to be nice to me when requisitions were handy. But now that we don't have any, well, they kind of begin to let their true feelings show. "Here, Boy, take this", and one of them shoves a discarded musket into my hands, "No more of that commissary life for you, Boy, yore infantry now."

But I wasn't in commissary through any fault of my own. That was where they put me, early on, back in the fall of '62, when we first organized. I think part of it was Brother Jim. He was a lieutenant in Company G and that's where I would be too if Jim hadn't stepped in. "Listen, Charles", he would say, "we'll be in some strong action someday and we'll need the ammunition sent right up to the line; I'm counting on you to do that." Whether the real reason was Mother or ammunition, next thing you know, orders from Regiment come down: Private Charles Davis is assigned to Commissary, 56th N. C. Troops and it had Faison's signature on it.

Commissary wasn't bad, although sometimes it was boring, mostly paperwork and arranging transport. And we were always with the regiment on its campaigns: the Blackwater, Gum Swamp, then Plymouth, the Virginia Campaigns, now this, but always in the rear areas. We were always in the background, so to speak.

Even there, I heard that some of the boys got the crazy idea that Jim was a mystic and they took to calling him a prophet. But Jim was always a dreamer and a thinker. Now, most of the rank and file in the regiment weren't and so they didn't quite know how to take him. Anyway, he left the 56th more than six months ago and no one mentions him no more now.

So now at last, here at (what is it?) Amelia Court House on April 5, 1865, I am no longer commissary, but simply infantry like the rest of them. There are only about a hundred of us left now and I move into and among them like Dante in the Inferno. You see, in commissary, you always had first pickings, shaved every day, associated with the better class of soldier, had time to boil the lice out of your clothes. But here in the ranks, well, there never is much chance for any of that. It's a different world entirely. I am a graduate of Mossy Creek College in Tennessee, Class of '59. These men are mostly uneducated. They are unwashed, unfed, dirty, stink to high heaven, and look like they're bound for hospital or worse. I'd seen it all before, but never had to become it. After Five Forks, there wasn't no commissary no more - we didn't even have a wagon - and so I became infantry in no time. But everywhere I go, I still get the sly look and sometimes the word commissary, like as if it were a dirty word.

While we're resting up at Amelia, a wagon does come out and we're given roasting ears gathered from farms round-about, but we are told we'll just have to cook it at night or eat it raw on the way, that it is time to fall in and resume marching. So off we go in column, leaving Amelia behind and heading ever west and then, after a while, north by west.

What's left of the Army of Northern Virginia is pretty well reunited at Amelia and our line of march is simple enough. Rooney Lee's cavalry leads the vanguard (they also patrol our flanks). Then, there is Longstreet's Corps up at the head of the column, followed by Anderson's Corps (that's where we are, the wreck of the 56th in the wreck of the Brigade in the wreck of Bushrod Johnson's Division in the wreck of Anderson's Corps); then, behind us, is Dick Ewell's Corps, followed by the wagon train, with Gordan bringing up the rear guard.

It's supposed to be a forced march and we force it as hard as we can go. But we are so exhausted and disoriented by now that we can advance only at a crawl. On a forced march, you see, you match time and distance, time to the lowest numeral, distance to the greater. On a forced march, you are always aware of time, just as you are in a race against the clock. Well, we are surely doing that, but it doesn't work because in our heads there is nothing to regulate it. Or maybe I can put it better this way: Our mind is in it, but our spirit and body are not.

After Amelia, a lot of the men simply lose all hope. The only thing keeping us going to Amelia is the promise of plenty of rations waiting for us there. When that hope is crushed, a lot of the boys just give up. Oh, they keep their weapons, they keep their place in column, they obey orders, but deep inside, where no one can see, they just give up.

Many of them lose all track of time after Amelia, don't remember exactly where they were or what day or hour it is. Hunger is a raging demon and many men just step out of the ranks to look for something to eat. Some of them catch back up with us; some never return at all. Other men just fall by the roadside, totally exhausted or famished; we look down on them as we pass, and then ignore them.

A courier on horseback pounds on by, the hooves throwing clots of mud over us and I shy away. Once when I was a boy, I was kicked by a horse and have had a fear of them ever since. Back early in the war, the boys would stand around a particularly fine horse. "Come on, Davis, touch him one time, he won't bite yuh none". But I would just smile and watch from a distance. Now Jim always liked horses, he liked cavalry, but then Jim was never kicked by a horse. I have the fear of them, I tell you. I'd rather be infantry like I am, I guess.

It's just better to keep your eyes on the road ahead anyway, for that way you don't have to say nothing to nobody and you can just focus on that next step you're going to have to take. But you also have to keep a wary eye on the roadbed, for you can easily trip and fall down over the obstacles there, and I'm not talking of sleeping soldiers or wagon ruts either.

First, there are single ones; and then they begin to appear in threes and fours; and then finally the whole roadbed is littered with them: discarded muskets, blankets, pots and pans, haversacks, canteens, keepsakes and personal things, and finally even catty-cornered wagons and abandoned artillery pieces. This is equipment just thrown away by Longstreet's Corps up ahead and most of the boys feel if Longstreet can do it, then Anderson can too.

So, many of the men in the 56th begin dropping their gear too, although the infantry veterans are experienced enough to keep the blanket and canteen for last. But more than one musket is quietly dropped and the man just shuffles on. Captain McNeely tries to keep some order, but the men are just oblivious to anyone or anything now. He's always so soft spoken that the boys either ignore him or don't hear him. I saw him carrying four muskets at one time, but whether he had offered to or whether he just retrieved them from the road, I don't know.

It clouds up toward evening and as we go into the fields to camp the night, it starts to raining again. And it's a heavy rain, as heavy as the one that came just before Five Forks. Naturally, the more superstitious men begin getting edgy, wondering whether this downpour in the dark means another big battle. Personally, I don't see how it can. We're just trying to get away now and when we're run to earth, we'll just give up. Anyway, it's really raining now.

Well, like I said, a lot of the men, especially those who have been clerks and teamsters, have even thrown away their blankets and they are just miserable. I kept mine and try to rig it up on sticks for a few of the boys, but the rain is coming down so hard now, it soon becomes water-logged and just sinks down of its own heavy weight. We crouch beneath a pine tree, huddle up, and try to keep warm. A few of the men take out their roasting ears and try to eat them raw, since it's hopeless to build a fire in all this wet. Now, trying to chew those hard kernels off the cob is an ordeal in itself. You have to use those back molars and that rough cob can cut your gum or inside cheek like a knife. At best, it's like eating rock, but it's better than nothing and all we have.

There is no order or discipline. McNeely and a sergeant come by about nine, but they just look at us and pass on. The men are too tired to even look up, but I peer at him from under the brim of my hat. He looks tired and haggard; maybe what he is doing is just out of force of habit. But if he can still make that gesture of making his rounds, well, I guess that is something to hold on to. I don't see no purpose in it, but it's something tangible, you see. This dead drifting of the spirit is the only alternative and there is no hope in that, no possible way. Of course, there is no hope anyway.

At two in the morning, I get up to relieve myself. The rain has stopped now, just a few drops still drip dropping here and there from the pines. The 56th is pretty well all together in these pines, all sleeping the sleep of utter exhaustion. It is still and quiet, so different from all those nights of bombardment back at Petersburg. Anyway, on my way back to my drenched blanket, I see a red glow through the trees. I softly step forward to where I can see what it is. Somehow, someone has gotten a small fire of pine shavings started for the sentry. And sure enough, there is the sentry at the edge of the forest, sitting at the fire, staring into it like a lost soul. I start to turn away, but there is something about him that makes me look again. It is McNeely.

I think about it as I go back to my blanket. I figure if he can stand it one more day, then maybe I can too. When he gives up, I will, too. Now, that's fair, as fair a deal as I can make, Jim. Jim would like that. Jim and McNeely had buddied up early in the war. In fact, that's what made me look again back there at the fire. I thought it was Jim for a moment there. So I figure I can go on as long as McNeely does. After all, that pride is all we have left now and that makes us men, don't it? Either that or we are the three biggest fools that ever lived.

The next morning, we are on the march again, ever west toward Farmville. It is April 6 and the old sun is trying to peek through the low clouds left over after last night's rain. It's another long day of just plain trudging along, without much order in our going. Longstreet and Ewell are in the lead today, followed by Anderson. There is constant skirmishing going on all the time with the Yankee Cavalry and since we are bringing up the rear, Anderson becomes more and more separated from Ewell, because our skirmishers have to hold the Yanks off. We are still that way, following Ewell on the Rice's Station Road, when we come down into the hollow. There is a sloping hill and a little valley there. The sun is warmer now and there's a slight haze over everything. And at the bottom of the little valley, there's a little creek purring along among the reeds - Saylor's Creek.

It is shortly after four that afternoon when Ewell runs into heavy resistance. In fact, firing is breaking out all over that little valley. But we think it is only the cavalry that had been dogging us all day long and infantry can always push on through cavalry, everyone knows that. But then Ewell is suddenly attacked by infantry - Wright's VI Corps. Ewell tries to hold, but now he has the fight of his life on his hands.

We can hear that heavy roar off to the north, see that rising smoke, feel that electric tremor in the air that precedes every disaster. We form a line of battle facing the only enemy we see, that persistent cavalry off to the south, who are now massing there in heavy numbers.

We know a big fight is on with Ewell, but we have no way of knowing how it is going. All we know is that we have formed a line on the north side of the road and just have time to throw up some brush, saplings, and logs when we see them coming. It is cavalry all right and not just skirmishers. It is Wesley Merritt's three divisions - 8,000 men strong against the 6,000 of Anderson. As they wheel into line, squadron after squadron across our front, we receive word that we must hold, for Ewell is hard pressed. Anderson and Ewell are now fighting back to back, protecting each others' rear area.

We stand there in a moment of silence and watch their force massing all across our front. It is a wide expanse of horses and men, guidons flying all along their line, and although we cannot hear the order, we see all their sabers draw and flash in the sun at one time. Ransom's Brigade is on the far right of our line and the unit in front of us is a Pennsylvania Brigade commanded by one Colonel J. Irvin Gregg. There are 1,300 of them in that veteran brigade; only three or four hundred in ours. We have only two ranks and our men are spaced seven or eight feet apart. But my eyes are drawn back again and again to that host out in front of us. I don't think I've ever seen so many horses in one place before and every one of them looks as mean as all get-out.

They don't attack at first, only sit on their horses in all their multitude. Then the blue division comes forward, first at a walk, then a canter, then a gallop. McNeely stands behind us with his Navy Colt revolver drawn and says, " Hold your fire and wait for my command."

I had of course seen Cap'n. McNeely during the past three years and had heard him speak before. But this time, there is a musical lilt, like a bell ringing, in his voice that I have never heard before. There is a clear ringing call in it that so startles me that I turn to see if it is really him. Some of the men also turn and look at him and some in angry disbelief. But I see there only a shining radiance in his face. He is only a few years older than I, but he catches my eye and then smiles, a boyish smile that I never would have expected in that time or place. But now there is no time for anything else but to try and hold.

We fire the first volley into them when they are only a hundred yards away and it is my first real battle with a gun in my hands. A loud, high pitch crackle of the muskets goes off; McNeely calls out, "First rank, reload! Second rank, fire!" You can't see anything in front for the smoke, but there is a prolonged screaming and thrashing out there, a screaming like women in labor. I know it is the horses and as much as I fear them, I feel for them, for here they scream as people do. I know it now, through my own terrible fear of them, I know it. A couple of them, the saddles empty, come leaping across our line and as the smoke lifts, I can see the ground covered with men and horses, the rest of their line reforming three hundred yards away for another assault.

That is when we hear a tremendous crescendo off to our left and it is there where the battle reaches its peak. Seven Union brigades are hitting the rest of our line and it simply can no longer hold. We know the end by the gunfire sweeping down past our left flank and on into the rear. Looking to the left, I can see a rising cloud of smoke and scores of our men fleeing into the woods. They have broken our line and all is lost. And at that same moment, we can hear the rising thunder of hooves as Gregg's Brigade begins its second assault.

Most of our men turn to face McNeely now, with quick, frightened eyes on him, on the field in front of us, to the rear, at one another. "Five Forks, Cap", they say angrily, "Five Forks!" Some begin to step away from the line; others defiantly throw their guns to the ground. But McNeely steps forward, his eyes flashing, and says, again in that clear ringing voice, "You men won't die like this, like dogs. Who are the men who will stand with me?"

There is only a second in which we stand there, watching him watching us, and then Fess Smith leans down, picks up his musket, and says, " Don't you fret none, Cap, we'll stay with you."

And we all turn back to our crude breastwork of branches and await their coming.

We fire two volleys into them and cheer as we do and that is the cheer Gregg's men hear as they hit our line. But the cheer is not for victory or even for survival, but for McNeely and Smith and all of us who are to die. For all of us, for the Regiment.

There is a crashing of wood and timber that can be heard even above the gunfire. Where I am, the slashed limbs and branches piled there simply explode into earth and flying splinters, and then not men (I see no men), but horses, a raging tornado of horses burst through, horses with flaring nostrils, bulging eyes, foam down the withers, slashing hooves.

I run wildly to the right to avoid them as they come through, but suddenly a terrible blow strikes me on the back of the head and I fall. Everything is black for a few seconds, but I finally stand up, reeling, holding my head, feeling warm blood trickling between my fingers. The first line has gone on past me and I am now alone in a small, small space amid the storm.

Then, I hear a slow, but growing thunder, the ground trembling under my feet, the thunder coming louder as it comes in, and I turn in time to see a new Union squadron taking the barricade less than fifty feet away, horse after horse coursing over like the wind, slowly soaring like birds over the line beside me. But this time the horses have men on them, some with the reins in their teeth, hands clutching saber and revolver, and one man sitting aloof and proud, face forward, with a red and white guidon snapping back and forth in the wind.

A horse's hindquarters, suddenly wheeling around, knocks me sprawling. I rise just in time to avoid a slashing saber from a bearded cavalryman and dart away, dropping to crawl on all fours under another horse's lifting, stamping hooves. I rise again in all that milling confusion in time to see McNeely fall under a descending saber and disappear under the hooves. And then I run, I can run now, just as fast as I could when only a boy. There is nothing, nothing at all to keep me here any longer. I can run, run as I have never run before, even as a boy. And for the first time in that war, as I run, I weep, the deep racking sobs sounding even as I run.

I crash against a good many trees in that forest, bruising my shoulder terribly, but never stop running. All around me, other men from the Brigade thrash through the thickets, but not one of the 56th is there. I run, run like the wind now, wiping the tears from my cheeks, even as I run. At last I slow my pace, my breath slowly comes back, I no longer run now, but walk, walk really fast. The Yanks are still back on the road rounding up prisoners and since they have taken 6,000 of them, that takes some time, so we who have escaped aren't being pressed so hard now. And all around me, I can see other men no longer running, but walking, even pausing from time to time now to rest with one hand on a tree, even sitting, even lying prone on the ground. But I walk on into the night for only there, in the darkness, is there safety and peace, only there will it all be over at last. Surely it is over now. But all of them are gone, all of them, and I will never hear that voice again as I heard it back there at the barricade. They are all gone; Silence has them.

It is deep night now and black as pitch, but you can tell direction by the stealthy movement in the brush on every side and all that movement is going but one way. We travel to safety alone and yet together, without a word said in all that dark silence.

I pause under a tall pine to rest and looking up, there is no rain or cloud in the sky, only an immense sea of stars. Even as I watch, one faint meteor drifts slowly to the south and I make a wish, remembering home. After all, so I was told, shooting stars come and go, but when we make a wish, it makes their coming special and then it becomes more than just stone. So Mother told me long ago. And so my silent wish now is for all the living and the dead, that what we have endured will yet serve some lasting purpose for this land and nation, that even our defeat will serve that end, if it must. It is a childish act, but I do it, standing alone under the tree in that moving forest, under that multitude of stars.

After stumbling for an eternity through one dark thicket after another, I come upon our first cavalry pickets, who look down at me with neither pity nor sympathy, but silently wave me on.

At last, I see scattered fires ahead dotting the blackness here and there and small crowds of men standing around each fire. I go up to one and warm my hands, but no one says anything at all to me. Finally, after I have stopped trembling, I look around and ask, " Any of you fellers know where Ransom's Brigade is at?" "Up the road a piece". And at the next fire, "Down the road a piece." And then toward ten o'clock, I find what's left of the 25th in a pine thicket, all gathered close around a single fire. And I ask "Do any of you fellers know where the 56th is at?" And they point to a single small fire some distance off and it seems like a star in the night to me.

I walk up to it. Not a sentry is posted.

There are only twenty men there or so. I stand in the fire's warm light, swaying, feeling faint for the first time, feeling saved and lost all at the same time.

"Hyar's another one of them, Cap. It's Private Davis."

A figure stands up from the fire and comes toward me. It is Captain McNeely. He can't smile very well, for there is a dark crust of dried blood down his cheek. But his eyes smile and now I know he will speak, breaking the silence at last.

When you see him... Tell the Prophet.....Tell your brother....

He pauses and I can see it is painful for him to speak, but he will speak.

"Tell your brother.... We have had our little blood-letting...."

And then he puts his hand on my shoulder before turning back to the fire.

****

The next morning dawns fair and quiet. More men have come back to the 56th during the night and there are now about thirty-five of us. We stiffly rise up from the cold ground and soon we are again in that toiling column, that wreck of the army, moving ever west.

"Where in the hell are we goin' now?"

"Well, if not to Hell ..."

"We done bin there."

"Well, there's Farmville up ahead. We've been tryin' to git there the last little while. There's Appomattox Courthouse. And on the other side of that, there's God's Own Country - the Blue Ridge Mountains - where we can maybe pull back together agin."

"Pull back together?"

"Yes, Sir. We're a-goin' to pull back together agin. That's what the Cap'n says. Cap'n says if we don't git to Joe Johnson, we can get to those mountains and then we'll just pull back together agin. We ain't licked yet."

I listen to them talk with growing excitement, for the Blue Ridge in North Carolina is where I and Jim and all the boys in

Company G come from. Pull back together.... For the first time, I look around at the spring sky and the sun and the trees, the new grass growing, the light coming through the clouds. A spring sparrow is singing away somewhere. Yes, we're going to pull back together.

But it refuses to be over. It seems it will never be over, it will never end. For with each passing mile now the hunger, the exhaustion, the pressed marching, the long hours merge into one red haze. The agony and the defeat, the agony of that defeat, day and night merge into one constant pain, for we are less than a company, only a part of a company now. Those that remain are mostly men like me, accustomed to cooking or rolling bandages or compiling lists, but not combat, not this, drifting along in the wreck of a disintegrating army, through dense columns of smoke covering the horizon, men and horses falling with exhaustion, and everywhere dead mules, dead horses, dead men.

It's all over now. There are no drums. We quietly march into the field with all the rest, our muskets carried at Right Shoulder Arms. We return Chamberlain's salute. We halt, make a right face, we dress our lines. Then we fix bayonets, stack our muskets, and carefully hang our cartridge boxes on the musket. The flags are then folded and laid on the ground; since we have none, we simply stand at attention until it is all over. And now it is all over at last.

At Appomattox, there are sixty of us on the list, for many stragglers continue to come in to get their paroles. I am not one of those who see General Lee or who touch Traveler, for I just want to go away to myself and work it out alone. And when I have worked it out, I realize that this is indeed the end, that it is over.

When I return to the camp late that afternoon, many of the men have already left for their distant homes. There are seven of us in Company G and because we have the longest distance to go, we decide to travel together. We are the last of the old 56th and we know that as long as we are together, it will be too. And when we part, it will vanish as if it never was.

But we know, too, that we have shared something important, that we were there at a turning point in America's history, and so one more night here will do no harm. We will have an early start in the morning. Besides, the Yanks are generous and they treat us now as one of their own.

I see John McNeely for the last time that night. He is sitting on a broken wagon looking out over the empty fields. The warm April wind is blowing and it is very quiet. McNeely looks at me.

"When you see your brother, tell him ..."

I wait for him to continue, but he does not. He makes no other motion or sign, only looks into the soft night. The first stars are coming out and it is absolutely silent. He says nothing more, so I just quietly say Sir and withdraw. The next morning he is gone and I never see him again.

Then the seven of us, all that's left of Company G, shoulder the Yankee rations and, leaving these empty fields to history, first head due east, leisurely walking and catching rides on farm wagons, laboriously retracing our route to burnt Richmond. Then we travel by train south to burnt Columbia, South Carolina, and then there's still more walking and borrowed rides to Spartanburg. But, we have not far to go now.

We walk long into the night on the old turnpike north to Saluda before leaving the road to camp in an abandoned corn field. We build a small fire, one last insignificant spark under still another sea of stars. The next day will bring us home. And that is when the realization hits us, sudden and hard, that it will all be different now, that we will be different, those whom we love will be different.

I say nothing as they talk among themselves.

"Well, come tomorrow, we'll be home. Wonder what we'll find there."

"And what in the hell do you expect to find there? The same old house, the same old woman, the same old farm? One thing for sure, there'll be changes, big changes. And if it's even all the same, there'll be change, 'cause we've changed and our old eyes have seen too much blood. Never will they see things the way they're supposed to be now."

"That's the truth. Like the old Parson said, we've been baptized in blood alright, but not the Blood of the Lamb."

"It was blood alright, blood of our own. Seems like there can't be no better sacrifice than that. But that warn't the atonin' the Prophet talked about, now was it, Charlie? Or was it?"

I say nothing, listening to them speak our elegy, without even knowing they are speaking it.

"I reckon all that time before the war and all the people back then is gone clean away. I bet you'll look into your woman's eyes, she won't know you. Your Mama won't know you, 'cause you've changed, they've changed."

"After all that's happened, I bet my own brothers and sister won't know me."

"Hell, Boy, they never did know you."

"But even when it was at the best, I bet none of them will know us now, I mean really know us. So we can only look at each other like way across some big gorge and that gorge is the war."

"It's their gorge too, remember. It's infected and changed them, same as us."

"Nothing ain't going to be the same now."

"So what's there to do, but go on? Start life all over agin, 'cause the world we knowed is swept clean away. This Peace is goin' to be our next war and we're goin' to have to fight it out, each one on his own, 'cause it's all goin' to be different now, ain't it?"

"Not everythin' in it will be gone."

"But everythin' we knowed in it, that's gone clean away."

The next morning at daybreak we can see what we could not in the night. The sun is burning the low mist off all over, and rising out of the rising mist, we can see the roof of a barn, then a farmhouse, trees, the deserted road. And then I see them coming out of the mist and I point and say, "Look, boys, here they are. They've come to meet us." Then the boys all rise and stand with me.

There, off on the far northern horizon, are the mountains, still distant, misty, gray and blue ramparts, all stretching out from east to west, but still the same as when we left them three long years ago.

"Look, there's Hickory Nut over there."

"And look, there's Sugarloaf, same as ever was."

But my eyes are only on Tryon Peak, for on the other side of that is home. And I say, "Well, boys, it hasn't all gone. Those old hills, they're still there, waiting for us to come back, all this time."

I feel a hand on my shoulder then and we all kneel down, right by the road, with hands on each other's shoulder, and the tears are in our eyes and the youngest one of us begins to cry, his quiet sobbing breaking the stillness, not for what the unknown future may yet hold for us, but for what the past has bequeathed to us.

As we walk on into the mountains all that long day, they keep on rising higher and higher until they cover all the northern sky and then the first trees stand out, green on all the lower elevations, where invisible creeks and streams extend green fingers reaching up the lower slopes, but everything still gray and bare on the high tops. Soon we are surrounded by trees - hundreds of trees on all sides of the rising road, with water falling from every ledge, the ground thick with Jack-In-The-Pulpits, Solomon's Seal, and Trout Lilies. Still higher up, we see the dark glossy leaves of Mountain Laurel and Moccasin Flower all over the higher ridges, and then the sky begins to open up blue and clear just ahead, and we reach the top at last. And looking behind us, all that past world we have left behind lies far below, blue and gold in the late afternoon sunlight.

I am the first to leave them, for the Davis place is at the top of the range, just across the state line. The other boys silently lift their hands and then disappear on down the road toward Hendersonville and I know I will see them again, in front of the Courthouse and on the street on Market Day, but never again like this.

Then I walk up the drive, seeing Oakland still there, the brick still warm and red in the afternoon sunlight, the great old oaks still standing around the house. I see Mother and Hattie working together in the garden and start to call out. But when they turn to face me, slowly, as if in a dream, they see the face of a stranger and I, the faces of strangers. I sharply turn and look back at the road. But the regiment has already left and try as hard as I can, I will never find it again in this world. I must fight this new war alone and now it is time to come home.

He rides over the next evening from his home in Horseshoe. Jim and I go together into the small sitting room where a fire is burning in the grate. He is still much the same, the same dark beard, the same thoughtful eyes, but he's wearing a worn cavalry jacket. He is quiet and I can smell the whisky on him. And I tell him about what has happened to me, but never will he speak of the war in the mountains.

So I tell him of all that has happened since he left - the winter in the trenches, Fort Stedman, Five Forks, Saylor's Creek, Appomattox. He says nothing, but listens, his dark eyes gauging mine.

"And you", I say, "How has it been with you?"

"Mary has had a child, a little girl. I shall name her Ella."

"Ella?"

"She is the new beginning I have waited for, for so long. We will bring all this back together again in the mountains... What's the matter?"

"That's what Captain McNeely said, sometime during that terrible retreat. Something about bringing it all back together in the mountains. But no - I remember, he was talking about the war, not this. It was very confusing then, as it is now... as it is now."

"And McNeely?"

"He did as well as he could with what was left. There really were not that many at the end. But there was something he wanted to say to you after it was all over, at Appomattox."

"What was it?"

"I don't know. He never told me. I don't know what it was."

Jim looks at me with that deep look of his.

"If you ever see John McNeely, tell him that I will see him and all the rest again. Tell him to bring the command to Petersburg, to The Crater, and I will meet them there."

"Jim, the war is over. The 56th is gone. It's all over now."

"I said if you see him again. One day. Remember that."

I shake my head and lapse into silence. I suppose he's just talking in riddles again, perhaps thinking all of us and the war are inseparably united forevermore or something like that. Or maybe it's just the whisky, for he had been drinking hard and heavy before he ever got here. He says nothing more and we sit there, long into the night together, staring into the fire.

A few years later, Hattie and I move on to Tennessee and Jim and his new wife move to Texas. Ella, all grown up now, remains behind, having just married a businessman in Hendersonville. So I guess it all has a happy ending after all. Certainly Hattie and I are content, having put the war behind us at last.

We live a quiet happy life today in Morristown, Tennessee. We have a small farm with a milk cow and an apple orchard and good corn land down on the Lower Bottom. Our home is a small cottage with roses and grapes climbing all over the porch and the walkway bordered by huge sunflowers. We have a little girl of our own - Cora Lee - and her generation has absolutely no interest in the war at all. Perhaps they are right. It was long ago; it's far away now.

And Jim and Captain McNeely, and Petersburg? I never saw any of them ever again. We are too young, and life too new, for us to be haunted by ghosts. And I am now reminded of those ghosts only by the simple things, the inconsequential things of Life: the stars at night, the clear voice of Cora Lee calling, the smell of pine, the threat of rain at dusk, and horses.

EPILOGUE

They called me a Prophet when I was only a man, seeking some meaning, some answer to what we underwent, not finding that answer in pain or death, or even in the innumerable fires that burned across that South, but only in the vague, ethereal hope that the future gives to new life, the hope of all the world.

But speaking to you now, or rather from the future beyond these memories, I think you never found it, for still you gaze continually into this fire, still you listen to this wind at the door. And what of those others? Did they find it?

They found what they sought for.

Which was?

Charles went to Tennessee. Colonel Faison became an Indian Agent in the United States Interior Department; he died later in Oklahoma Territory. Major Graham became a prominent lawyer in his hometown of Hillsboro; Major Schenck, a wealthy Cleveland County cotton mill and railroad manager. Doc Harrill became a member of the State Board of Health and later a state legislator; Captain Grigg, a successful merchant and postmaster in Lincolnton. General Ransom served twenty-four years in the Senate and four years as Minister to Mexico. Captain Mills ...

But there were others.

Captain Roberts, somewhere adrift in the fall foliage of a Connecticut autumn. Sergeant Harrill, still searching the moonlit tracks for the hat lost on the train to Petersburg. Lieutenant Sweezy

But what of the others. What of John McNeely? The Parson? Sergeant Smith? Callahan?

The night has them. It has them all now.

And you alone are left?

I alone am left.

Meaning?

You, a Prophet should know that. A Prophet should know everything. And the Atonement - the one minuscule act that will be the necessary first step in redemption for you, the one insignificant act that will begin in its own small way the compensation for what you and this nation have done to one another, the one gesture that will begin to put a quietus on the pain and suffering you and all of us underwent. Was that ever done? Was it ever even initiated? Or was it too lost, with so much else? And your wife, Mary? And Ella, the (what was it?) hope of all the world? Atonement? The hope of all the world?

The questions fade now into silence, leaving only the bedroom and the fire in the grate burning slowly, but inevitably leading into the glowing coals that will mark its end. All things must end, even as these flames, and this will too. It will soon end now, as it does for Mary in 1865.

She dies only a few months after giving birth to Ella. But even at her grave, I can see a new beginning, a new world brought to birth in this one small infant. I take Ella to Oakland and leave her with Mother. Mary is dead, but Life, Everlasting Life must go on and although in time I bring her back to Horseshoe, Ella returns again and again to Oakland, for that is now her first memory, there her first home, there, the grave of her mother, now thick with grass. It is a good place, a safe place for a little girl to be - close to nature, a stern but loving grandmother, the small school in Green River, clamorous with barefoot children in the spring of the year. She loves it there, but when I come for her, she still runs down the drive in her one simple white frock, crying "Papa! Papa!" and then throws two frail arms around my neck and she is indeed then the hope of all the world. No war burns on in those loving eyes. And from that hope, new hope at last comes into my life.

In 1870, I meet a young schoolteacher in Greenville, South Carolina. She is lovely, quiet, demure, with the touch of the eternal mystery of woman that I find, as a mystery, that I still love so well. We meet, we talk, and although I am older, she moves to me, loving my stories of the war, marveling how we survived, those of us who did survive, living, like Ella, in the glow of that imaginary man she sees in me. She is young and so beautiful, and we are married in Greenville that same year.

But she knows and feels the iron heel of Reconstruction grinding ever deeper into our life. Taxes rise each year; crops for each coming year, if they do not fail, they do not suffice to allay hunger. The long hours poring over account books by candlelight, the constant worry of living from one meager crop to the next, the bleak realization that it will not ever get any better- this long defeat is more damaging than the war, for then we had some hope, if only for cessation, if not for victory or survival. Ella, only a small child, is the one bright star, always loving, faithful, and true. She sees in me that which all other men cannot. But hope fades into uselessness, it is useless, it is all useless. Without hope, with only the lees left in the cup, even a prophet must come to the end at last.

The spring of 1873, another ending to too many endings. I spend most of that last night alone at the table, over the ledger and account books. If you use this figure instead of that figure - if tobacco and cattle bring more this year - if we can decrease cost, if drought does not cut income, if - if you move the pen this way in the light, the shadow goes that way - if you turn the pen over, the shadow will turn over. If I take the inkwell and hold it against the light, I can see the red reflection of firelight in her hair; if I now slowly turn it, see the black stream slowly forth; see the black flood rising to devour number after number, a dark spreading lake covering all the world. It is the end.

That morning, I walk through the bright sunlight to the sheriff's office in Hendersonville, sign the necessary papers, and file for bankruptcy. Stepping out into the crowded streets, a hand shyly touches me on the arm. "Cap, have you a dollar for me, sir? Have you a dollar for an old veteran?" "I have no time for you now", I say, walking away. "I have no time for any of you now."

I go down a side street to a small tavern. The whisky here is cheap and in the right frame of mind, it will go a long way. In time, the warm numbness comes stealing in, the room reels slightly, everything turning, but I keep drinking and drinking, for reeling, turning, only in this way can I escape. Late that night. Everything reeling. I stumble out into the dark street, clumsy hands catching, holding me, "It's the old prophet, drunker un skunk. Here, Cap, the boys'll take care of you." I drift wonderingly slowly awake in the early morning light. The buildings across the street are dark enclosing walls; the ground beneath my hand, wet and cold. Overhead, a few vague stars - Antares in the Scorpion, heralding summer drought yet to come - and one lone meteor slowly drifting into the east. I feel a stirring, see two vagabonds, two tramps, huddled against me, who were once men, as I once was.

So the basic instinct is all that matters now, the old, old instinct for survival and self-preservation. And it matters not to what baseness it descends, for it is all alike down here, the damned having the only true democracy. And it is all right, as long as there is life at the bottom. One can live on without redemption; do not most men? Procreation, Gluttony, Self Indulgence, the ancient reptilian urge, the eternal slime - descend so far, still life is there, as it is here. That is the true meaning of it all - Slime. And what is elemental Slime, but that from which Old Primeval Earth and Life itself arose? And what are men but the lost, blind creatures that crawl, at random, over its surface?

In 1884, Ella, a young woman now, is engaged to be married to a young businessman from South Carolina. I now do what I have to do, for there is only a slow dying here, but before I do the tearing down, the ripping apart, first, first and foremost, I shall give a parting gift to Ella. She does not expect it, any more than she fears the other. It is a beautiful dress for her, all silk and satin, sequins like stars running all over it for her, white and pure as that worn by the little girl running to meet me, ordered all the way from New York. It has all the ruffles and flounces in vogue now; it sweeps the floor like a silent cloud. Ella does not expect it, any more than she fears what must now follow, at first looking on it in wonder, shyly reaching out to touch it and then as quickly withdrawing her hand, and suddenly embracing me. "Thank you Papa" Thank you. Thank you.

She wears it again and again; the last time I see her, she is still enveloped in all its white aura, looking at me through her tears.

You see, I have to do it, to make that final break, even as I must, to rip that hope of all the world from my heart. It must be done to create that newer world from the ashes of this dead one. Human life is so fragile - no war needed to teach me how much so - but women will weep, when men must act. Act, I must, for to drift on downward to my own destruction is not my way, but rather to seize Fate by the forelock and compel it to follow me, rather than let it lead me further to where I will not go. Ella will understand in time, for love feels no limit, finds no boundary, knows no ending. There will be time for her to come to understand. There will be some kind of resolution to hatred and she will understand in the end. So say every philosopher of the olden time; so say every sage who ever thought, every poet who ever felt. So say the prophets. So say they all.

I leave these mountains forever and I and my new family and my new life venture forth into a new land on this continent. We come to Texas, with a name from the states, and we start anew, first in Salado, then in Dulaney's Mill. I teach school, operate a small hotel, and invest in railroad stocks and bonds. Texas, New Life... And what is New Life, but new men, new goals, new lands? But my heart is never at peace because of The Others - spirits, ghosts, memories, for Memory alone survives everything. Memory lives on and on in a mystery as deep as Life, and Death, and Woman. But no man deserves to live Life under a curse; not I; not any man.

In 1902, I move on to Mertens with four of my children of this second marriage, at last to this house, finally to this room, at the end to this fire. But there was something else in the war yet to be done, something about The Crater. But now I forget.

It has now been almost twenty years since I have seen my daughter. She never answers my letters; she never sends me a photograph; she never sends me a single word that all is well, that she is happy and content, that her love and memory of me still endure. But she still has time to do that. There is still plenty of time. Fate, Man's Fate may set limits and say - Here, no farther must you go. But Love - the love of any daughter for any father (there is no more powerful love than that) - it will find ways. It will find ways.

******

Papa could be a hard man, everyone knew that back then, everyone but me. Oh, I could see it, but I never felt it. He was half Welsh and sometimes came on with all those stars and dragons and sorcerers in his eye, but never was he like that with me. They all said he was never the same when he came back from that war, that it was the war that destroyed him and keeps on destroying him, always drinking and brooding and dreaming. But to me then, his was the one hand to which I could cling, the one star by which I set my course. My mother died, you know, shortly after I was born, so I never had a mother, really. But when I remember Papa, which isn't often, I think of him as I knew him growing up over in Henderson County.

I still have this photograph of me as a young girl. It was taken in the last part of the last century, long ago. This is really my wedding dress I'm wearing in the picture. But look at me ... these eyes, young and brave and confident as they are, now these are the eyes of a young girl, aren't they, confident and joyful and excited and full of life, all at the same time. But look now, look close, you can see something else there as well, if you look close, can't you, the pain, the sorrow, a looking back, a looking in, for something or someone lost forever. It was my Papa, you see. The only parent I ever had, he called me the hope of the world. And it was he who took the light out of these young eyes.

For this young girl you see, looking into your own eyes from this yellowed photograph, is haunted by the silent ghost of her still living father. I guess he still lived, if you could call it life, breathing, speaking, walking the earth like other men do. Yet there was something in him inhuman, locked behind that graying beard and dark eyes, a raging demon, cold, without heart, without pity. This is the dark secret I have so carefully hidden from all the world these many long years. But I knew. I knew - poor lost me in the white dress - I knew how much I loved and hated him, so much that the very word Father to me turns blood to ice, love to hate, speaking to silence.

You see, can't you now, without a mother, as a little girl, I only had him as the center of my world, the one firm rock I could cling to in those hard years. I only had him and Grandmother to teach me what I needed to know, all I ever could know of having a home and family, of father and daughter. For I had no mother to comb my hair a hundred times at bedtime, to dress me up on Sunday morning, and to buy me the little things that little girls depend on so much. There was only him, but because he was my father, he was the all, he was enough.

I remember how on Sunday mornings we would slowly ride together in the carry-all to the little Baptist church on Green River, bowing to the neighbors as we enter the door; or go together to Hendersonville on Market Day, with its streets an absolute quagmire, and shop together (I, at least, able to help him in that); we could talk then. And now that white satin dress, like a white star, he bought that for me, ordered all the way from New York, most like. I wore it on my wedding day, but I then folded it, oh so neatly, oh so tenderly, and put it away and never wore it again. That's what you do with shrouds, don't you? For it became the shroud that covered him, that covered my dead love for him. It's a shroud, you see, and he placed the accursed thing on my heart with his own hands. And what man could commit such an act as that and still be called human, like other men?

Sally Tompkin, at school, told me that her brothers said that in the Army, he was a magician or seer of some sort, foretelling the future, prophesying by the stars, and all that. As his daughter, I'll tell you now he was most likely reeling drunk when the Devil spoke to him, so there wasn't anything to him, not anything to him at all. And if he could foresee all that is in the heart of a daughter, of all that is to come, then why could he not foresee my hate? And if he did foresee it, then my hate meant nothing to him; I, his own daughter, nothing to him.

Once, he had been a man among men, hard to understand, as all men are, but easy to love, assured, confident, proud, and seeming to know and understand things as other men do not. But what I think disappointed me most of all was that he failed in spite of all. He failed. He lost the war, he lost mother, he lost his own children, he lost me. He failed in everything because he was impractical and greedy, cold and unfeeling, willing to forget the dead and abandon the living. Any daughter who can say this of her own father must either despise him or forget him. For many years now, I have succeeded in doing both. He once spoke of atoning for something in the war, but he most needed redemption from me. So far as woman and daughter can ensure it, he will never have that redemption now, here or in the hereafter.

All of us - all of Mama's children - we absolutely cannot understand why he did what he finally did. The War and Reconstruction destroyed him, first one, then the other. But then it was also the simple allure of any perfumed younger woman with money to spare, of course, for that wreck of a man facing destitution, facing vacuity, old age, death. I am certain that was part of it. I remember her perfume, the slow side-long glance under the long lashes, her hair so neatly coiled - that was it too, a woman almost twenty years younger than he, something a little softer to him, a little different from that first wife asleep in glory, and the daughter, the abandoned daughter.

My family died when he left, died as surely as if he had killed it himself. And it was he who finally did it, he who made the choice, not us. He sold off all the property my poor dead mother owned, leaving us nothing; there were whispers whether that was all the money he took. And he, a man of age and experience, left for Texas and a New Life (so he called it) with this woman. I was left with that satin dress, my grandmother, and the most helpless young man for a husband I ever saw. Yes, Papa made the choice, he decided on a new life, a new world for himself, but at the cost of those who loved him most dear, at the cost of me.

Had he died then, as he should have, it would have been better - that would have put a proper ending to it all - but he lived on and on and on, like the ogre in the Welsh fairy tale who could not die. Oh, the fool man, you could not call it love, what he felt for that schoolteacher; you could not call it love, when what he did led to so much greed and hate, to so many bitter tears.

Yes, that was the beginning of it. And the end? First the dress, which I loved, for it was from him. But then he told me why, what it was really for, what it really meant. There, in the parlor at Oakland, he facing the two of us, the daughter and the other, not wife or mother, for there should be only one of those, but the woman, look-ing at me with barely suppressed triumph, I'm sure. And he said, "Ella, Josephine and I are leaving the state. We can no longer live here, like this. We are leaving for Texas soon; we will never return."

I could not have been more astounded if he had said he was going to Mars or Jupiter. "But what about me, Papa? What about me?" He looked at me and in his eyes I read my fate. "You will stay here, Ella. You will be married soon, with your own life to live."

"But, Papa, how will you live? There's no money. No one has anything. I don't have anything."

Then the woman smiled, walked over, stood by Papa. "My fam-ily will help, Ella. There is money, my dear."

I told her then to "Shut up"! and Papa rose and said, "You will never again speak like that to Mother - not ever again, Ella." And I whispered, "Papa, Mama is buried, remember?"

I turned away then and tried to leave, but he tried to hold me. "Ella!" And again he tried to hold me. I turned and slapped him, hard, and then ran to my room, screaming, "I hate you! I hate you!" leaving him standing there in the parlor, the words finally subsiding into sobbing, whispers, whispering sibilantly over and over into my pillow I hate you.

I never saw or ever spoke of him again. There are no bitter tears now, only the iron silence that has lasted for forty years. It is over now, for in the grave there is only silence, and hate and love sleep quietly there in the dark. I shall take my love and hate there, carefully cherishing them every step of the way, for they will still be with me in my last hour. But once he did love me, the hope of all the world.

Oh, he tried to reach me over the years, he tried many times, the poor lost man. He wrote to me "My Dearest Ella...", but those letters went unanswered. Down in Texas, amid a new generation of children spawned from that marriage, he carefully inscribed in the family Bible there, "Ella, My Beloved Daughter..." Once he sent me a photograph of himself all the way across the nation and there he was, our eyes once again meeting, for the first time in decades, affluent, debonair, obviously of good reputation, but black as night with his thirty pieces of silver. I placed the picture in the bottom of a trunk and never took it out again. I will carry that sorrow with me to the grave and only there, in the starless dark, can it at last be laid down and put to sleep. Papa died in his great old age in 1905 and he's long gone now, really just a fading, silent shadow to me now, and nothing more than that now.

The dress was thrown out years ago, dry rot and mildew both having had a turn with it until it was nothing much. But I remember when it was new and I was young, its silkiness reflecting starlight to the eye, its satin smooth and cool, as my hands smooth it over and over again to already absolute perfection. It is the sort of thing a young girl will treasure forever, at least for a little while.We mustn't live in the Past, must we? It's the Future that matters after all. It is only in the Future now that there is any hope for the world. After the first few children, I was too busy to worry very much, or even to remember very much. Rolling bandages in the Great War for our boys Over There was the closest I ever came to enduring what Papa did, but losing one of my own in that war gave me more pain than Papa ever knew. And after that, through the twenties, thirties, I was busy raising all those children to adulthood. The last boy was sick and frail, nigh about died of Tuberculosis, so sick he was. We had to take him out of school when he was only in the sixth grade.

An old mountain doctor told us, "Fresh air. Fresh air is what that young'un needs", and raised the window with a slam. It was the dead of winter and we looked at each other in disbelief, for how could a sick child survive what a grown man could not in that arctic cold? But he spent all that long winter all propped up in bed on an open porch, many the time opening his eyes to new fallen snow on his blanket in the mornings.

The long months pass and still he is there, pale and thin, but now looking through the open window for the first time,watching the birds gather around the feeders we build for him, later listening to opera on the wind-up phonograph by the hour. We don't much expect him to reach twenty, but I do for life is just too good to ever let go.

******

Papa is Town Mayor. We live in a large house up on the hill overlooking the town. Off on the south side of the house, there is a porch with windows on every side and that's where I spend two years while I am sick, with the windows at least partially open year round. But I think that is what makes me love nature so much: watching the cold light of morning come, the warm spring rain coursing over the lawn, the still moonlight making shadows on the windows, silent shifting shadows that lull me to sleep. And I think it is opera that keeps me close to people in my loneliness, the men and women singing against their fate through it all, proclaiming with every note that life and love are more important than death and oblivion. And of course, Papa is always there with his pipe or cigar, asking how I feel today. And Mama, with the shadow in her eyes.

I guess I stay over home a bit too long before getting out on my own. But it is a safe haven and my other brothers are doing the same. It is more fun to ride around town with the boys on a Saturday night and work in Papa's general store on Main Street, to live the life of any other young man around town in the Twenties. When I finally leave, I am twenty-five or so and it is to Chicago that I go, for there are times when the mountains and the past must be put behind. America is out there, Life is there. I work in a factory to pay the rent on a small apartment and make every adjustment I can to the great America beyond the mountains. But I had known a sheltered, protected life and always feel a little threatened by the strong masculine drive of the city, with the cold wind coming off the black water like ice. I am able to engage a little in management at the Chicago Opera Company and even have a torrid affair with an aspiring New York soprano who is sure that one day she will be the star of the Chicago Met.

Her smile and easy laughter belies her. There is something else here and in time I see what it is. It is the North, in all its power and pride, its strength and will. Never having known defeat or privation, it has the moral righteousness that the rest of the world sees as America. But it is not the America I remember - rural, small town, the South.

I try to fit in, drinking prohibition and playing cards for high stakes long into the night ("O.K., Johnny Reb, call or pass"). I read the Tribune and believe most of it, dress to perfection, attend the parties and concerts, hiding my southern accent as best I can ("Please, Dear, say something to Robert"), slowly finding myself an attractive eccentricity from the distant South, perhaps a coffee table curiosity, to be displayed and observed behind the appraising eyes and quiet smiles. But even a young soprano from New York has a thing or two to learn about men from the southern mountains. One rainy night I board the train without a word and return south, for a man must do what he has to do and I will not be led where I will not go.

Like most mountain people, I left to follow the guiding star to a newer world, only to return in the end to the one I know best.

I borrow the money and open a quiet antique and florist business in the town in which I was raised. Here I live and move among fine old furniture, through the clear ringing call of past china, the silent sheen of old silver on velvet, and then enter the blaze and color of all green growing things. I am once again on familiar ground, among the old houses and trees and people I have always known. It will serve for a new start, a new life.

It is a few years later, on a hot July day in 1934, when I rent a house in town to a family from Georgia: three small boys, a man with a haunted face, and the greatest mystery in a woman that I ever saw. Three years later, it is all official and I hold her hands in the shifting moonlight on the porch of the rented house and ask her to marry me, my face wet with tears. And that is all I will say of those years, for every man has those memories he must keep in the silence of the heart. But she had the dark hair, the smiling mouth, and the eyes in which any man can lose himself, only to find the old, interminable round of life relentlessly forging ever on to the known ending, the unknown ending.

In the spring of 1937, Mama passes away. The months move on in their seasons and we have a son; a few years later, a daughter. So here I am in middle age, raising one generation and getting ready to start on another, with a family that would drive Jesus crazy.

Mama has been dead now these many years. She never spoke of the war. Those were hard times for everyone and I always felt it was the biggest mistake the South ever made. But it's over now. Those years are long gone and no one I know ever talks about it anymore. My son once did ask me if anyone in the family fought in the Civil War. I just said, I guess they all did, and let the matter drop with that.

For I am a peace-loving man and lived through all the wars, but never served in any, being too young or too old or too married or just too disinterested. War movies, novels, stories, music - all that killing and it doesn't settle anything at all in the end. Life goes on - you get up, work all day, go to a few parties and concerts, talk the usual town gossip with cousins, sit in a rocker next to your invalid wife's bed for a few minutes, go to bed, get up, the whole daily round beginning once again, over and over.

If anything is the center of my life now, it is families. Not family, but families. This one in this old Victorian house, then the one over home, this one on this hill, that one on the other hill - that's what makes life the marvelous thing it is. And looking back - Papa's family in Henderson County, coming there from South Carolina in the 1880's. And Mama speaking on and on of this aunt, and then of that aunt, but never did she speak of her father. That was a closed book to us.

The most we ever understood was that he had done something

wrong, something terribly wrong when she was just a girl and it was a big scandal. He ran off to Texas and never came back; all the rest was left to our imagination. It's hard to tell the truth in families - I learned that from having twelve brothers and sisters. You love them, but you have to fight for your place and space, even in the affections of your father and mother. And it is hard to tell the truth in almost anything, especially when several of them combine against one, as they do.

I wonder sometimes if that is what happened back then. Maybe it was just all one big, gigantic lie that led to the war and then, wrecking vengeance, passed on to his disappearance in Texas. Since then, one deep silence in the family, both on the war and on the man. Yet there was a war and there was a disappearance, sudden and permanent, almost as if he was just whisked away, vanished just like the old moon does at daybreak. You can't deny that it happened, but why? And if there was loss from that, who's going to pay the piper, who's going to atone for all that pain and grief? Who's going to do it now, I ask you. We can't. They're all dead and gone now, turned to dust. We can't. Then, who can now? It's not worth worrying about. No one can do anything about it anyway.

There's nothing anyone can do after all this time, but turn the dead dust over and over and that's useless. Still, they are there too - the memories, the epitaphs, the monuments, the stone wall enclosing the cemetery on the hill. You can't escape memories, maybe most of the way, but not all the way. Sometimes they come back to haunt you, as they did on that autumn day in 1967.

On that day, my boy and I visited Oakland together. He and I pushed our way through an unbelievable labyrinth of tangled weeds and climbing honeysuckle to the old house site. The trees overgrowing the place were just beginning to turn all one blaze of red and gold and even purple, and the air was crisp and fine, the westering sun setting to its own glory. We fought our way through all that underbrush to the house. Under foot the bricks were still there in wild abandon, half buried and covered with lush, green moss; the drive, a shallow depression sunk deep under thick blackberry and Virginia Creepers; but yet the same sky overhead, the same old earth underneath.

Then we walked on up the steep hill and found the family

cemetery of the Davis Family - the broken stone wall enclosure filled with trees and shrubs and choked with weeds, one lichen-covered stone obelisk rising over all. It was getting on toward evening now, darkness steadily creeping up the hill and a harvest moon sitting on top of the ridge, and there, among those over-grown graves, I told him the little of the story that I knew. I told him that my mother's father had left family in Texas, but I didn't know just where.

"But are any of them still alive?"

****

Daddy said, "Probably not", it was a long time ago, and we never mentioned it again. Time and the world passed on in turn, just as they have been doing for forty-seven hundred million years. But to me, all that is an open invitation. While everyone else is cursed with living in the present, I am cursed with living in the past. It is a curse, as everyone keeps telling me, but a beautiful one.

To me, the present is never as enthralling as the past or distant future, so all through adolescence, I endure family and school, but breathe the clear, refined air of books. For reading is the one strength I have; I go to that strength and it saves me. And it is all there, in the old books - Achilles returning the body of Hector to Priam, the Spartan hoplites at Thermopylae, Francis Marion fighting the British in the South Carolina swamps, Pickett at far distant Gettysburg, the rising flag at Iwo Jima, the One, Small Step on another world and into a new age - all of it bathed in the clear gold and bronze light of the living day. It all seems more real to me than what I see all around me. A little more interesting, you see, than our own mundane, work-a-day world. Here, people go the daily and nightly round of attending social teas, eating, fornicating, wandering the Town Mall on a Saturday afternoon, living lives of incredible and miserable dullness. I live in that world of the past, to the detriment of this one. What have you (so I imagine God speaking to them on the Final Day), What have you done with the inestimable gift of the Human Mind that I gave you? And they will say - Well, I washed the car, I ironed the clothes, I made a garden. But what have you done (God will say) with the Power of Thought, with the Flight of Imagination? What can you give me now in return for what I gave you on the day of your birth? And they will not answer, for they will not even understand.

No, Nature is what lasts; like us, He made it what it is - sunrise, sunset, the cold dew under the bare feet, wild flowers. Of course, I love nature - sunrise and sunset, the cold dew between my toes, wild flowers. Once, as a boy, I am on my father's farm and wander alone down toward the river. I look around in the moving sunlight, at the burning fields, the cool forest close by. There is perfume in the air. Now I wonder what that is? Violets. I find a cluster of blue violets and a cluster of grey violets facing each other by the side of a peaceful meadow brook. Now there are the Yanks and these are the Reb Violets, now let's see who will win this time and I sit back for the next few lifetimes, for a boy has many of those, and watch the Civil War grow again in miniature. During the next year or so, the spring campaign begins anew, with first one side and then the other having the advantage. Then I lose interest in that particular project and go on to others, but years later, I come back to that field. And the meadow is covered all over with the Union and Confederate violets, but they are now all mixed up among one another and spreading everywhere together.

Then at the end of one hot afternoon in the fall of the year, my father and I visit the site of Oakland and then climb the steep hill to the ruins of the old family cemetery. There I learn for the first time that I might have family members - cousins - in Texas, separated from my father's family for over a hundred years.

I think that it was then the thought first came to mind that perhaps one of my many purposes in life will be to restore peace to that family, for in the grave there can be no hatred or sorrow or remembrance of what is divisive, but perhaps there is still a thought or two among all those ghosts of love and parenthood. And although I will be dealing with intangibles of love and sorrow and time, such an act, in itself, will atone for it, will it not? Certainly it will mean something in redressing whatever wrong, in bringing a fitting end to whatever conflict that has lasted four generations. It is not an imperative need I feel to do this, just an interesting exercise. Or perhaps it is only a practical application of genealogy, a case study, as it were. There, that would make it professional.

I cannot bring these dead back to life, but I can work with life and not with death, with light, and not darkness. There are living people to work with. There are the descendants of James Davis still alive somewhere in Texas. Yes, I will find them and after a hundred years, reunite the family once again. I can, at least, point to that as something Man can do.

My father dies in 1976, so he is not there when the time comes. And when it comes, it comes with almost predestined swiftness, so swift that one wonders if it was worth all that pain for all those years. It does take some preliminary work, several months of searching by mail and telephone, all through the flat Hill County of Texas in which he was buried, for even his children from that second marriage had long since followed those of the first in going their separate ways. But finally I reach someone who knows someone who knows someone else who knows of a woman in Grand Prairie who is a granddaughter of James Davis and then I know that I have found them at last. I found them. I found them.

Well, the usual letters are exchanged; the few long-distance telephone calls are made; and finally two of his grandchildren drive all the way from Texas to see me. There is a certain tension as I wait for them at the Henderson County Courthouse that day, for once again it comes to mind that I am really dealing with primeval things here, things elemental, beyond our own present time and space. Perhaps the dead, as well as the living, will come to some kind of understanding at last....

So we meet on a Thursday afternoon on a busy Main Street in Hendersonville. I shake hands as everyone introduces themselves. I find my eyes returning again and again to one cousin who has my father's eyes, but with a Texas accent. Strange - now how can that be? Then I take them to the site of Oakland and afterwards to the old Davis Cemetery high on the top of the hill.

So there, after a hundred years, the two branches of this family are once again united. It is raining that day, for once again it is April.

Standing there in the rain and mist, in the overgrown family cemetery on the hill, watching them take photographs, I feel a growing chill in the air passing over me. Perhaps it is only the rain and the damp, for it is falling heavier now, but it seems to me that we are not alone, that there are more than three people here ...that my Father is here, his eyes on them and on me, but whether with commiseration or condemnation, I can not tell; and that James Davis is here, the grey uniform already beginning to darken in the rain, standing there in a silence mysterious and foreboding; and over there, in a corner of the stone enclosure, there is a young girl in a white dress, weeping bitterly in the rain.

Ella was right. For her, the past is irrevocable.

You failed.

Some years later, when the night is once again on my soul, I visit the battlefield at Petersburg, Virginia. I have the disquieting feeling that perhaps something is waiting for me there too, that perhaps even something else is fated to happen there. But when I arrive, it is like most Civil War battlefields today, with paved roads, signs, and mostly pine forest. But there is something else here and it is a long moment before I recognize it for what it is. It is the Silence - an almost watchful silence, as if the end of the war is not yet, that something remains to be done. But what could it be after all this time? And why? Whatever answer there might be was lost long ago, here in these fields.

But there is something here, I am certain of it now. I can feel it. I turn around, seeing nothing but the trees, the wide sky, the blazing sun high overhead.

No - there is no one here, but I. Imagination is playing tricks with a fool, on a fool's errand, as before. No time for that now. The history will be interesting enough without all that. But no guided tour. I know what happened here.

So then, this is where it all started - the darkness and night that engulfed that family as well as the nation. And for such a catastrophic event, surely there must be left here some residue, some lingering remnant of the Awful Hand of God, or Fate, or maybe even just blind, impartial chance? Surely, the earth has scars, as families do.

I know the section of the line where he was stationed and when he was present for duty. Using topographical maps and regimental histories, and even Union records of what they saw from the other side, I can pin-point his exact location at any time during that summer of 1864.

So that will be it then - the moment when I stand in his place, see what he saw, perhaps even see the lingering shadow come looming up out of the Union lines - perhaps I will know then what it is that drives any life so furiously toward the dark. And if there is any vision of what America is all about, if there is any vision of what it was all for, it will come then, will it not?

I go alone on up the hill to where The Crater lies. There is no one here and I find where the left of the regiment had rested; I find the ravine and the soft mounds of Confederate trenches marked with the "Do Not Disturb" signs of the National Park Service; I find the place where he stood, here, in this place.

Oh, with imagination, you can bring it all back, that summer of 1864 ... the smoke rising, the dust in the air, the shouts of men, the rattle of muskets, the low roar of artillery - and then, out of all that fury and pain, the wraith spirit, the demon slowly and certainly emerging, still speaking no word to us or to the yet unborn daughter, but only to those here who he knew better, who understood him best.

But no, there has simply been too much hate, too much evil, on both sides - both in the war and in the peace that followed it. What kind of recompense is possible here for national unity and self deter-mination? For industrial child labor and agrarian slavery? For Irish ghettos and slave quarters? For Hamilton and for Plymouth? For father and daughter? For the dead? The dead. Now over a century later, what inconceivable final act can now bring peace at last to those men on both sides, to these families on all sides, to any war in any place, at any time? What one event can ever compensate, even if only in some small way, for what they and the war had done to their seed and the nation? It is indeed too late, is it not, for any kind of fit-ting closure to all this? Ella might have told me that.

Go, see for yourself. There is now nothing here, nothing, but the eternal trees, standing silent and tall in full summer foliage, the grass all rich and green, perhaps one kite standing high against the sky. And over all, the sweet wind that perhaps God thought, casually perhaps, of adding at the Dawn of Creation.

There is nothing else. And their history, dark now as night. Their death, long as eternity. Their burial, deep as sleep. Their mem-ory, lost in silence.

There is no vision, there is no message - no victory here, no sur-vival, not even that one small act of atonement, the first necessary step on any long road to redemption. There is only the present moment after all, and what is that worth beyond the actual breathing of it? So it was all meaningless, never any purpose to any of it, was there? So it was all useless, after all, was it not? All come apart in the end after all. It ends, as it began, in chaos. Chaos.

Like James Elliott in this same place eighty odd years before, you can go there yourself to stir the soft pine needles underfoot for some answer. See here - see - there is no answer here, no answer at all, only the earth is here, the lasting earth that shall enclose us all.

I look around, standing silent, expectant, waiting. Yes, I am alone here, truly alone among all these honored dead of this regiment, who have died in vain, who were sacrificed for no reason. For no end. To no purpose.

Nothing moves, absolutely nothing moves at all, except the wind and the sunlight in the trees. Yes, now you know. You can breathe easier now. Now you know.

But now what is that sudden smell, that stealthily rising odor of rotting meat and decaying flesh so relentlessly drifting near and now hovering close to me in the air?

(oh, it is only fragrance, sweet fragrance of the nodding daisies and buttercups there, in the crater there, all the flowers blooming in the field over there).

But now what is that sound just now, that sound of quiet whispering and barely suppressed laughter, hoarse from so much abuse, from so much disuse, which I can hear very near?

(oh, that is only the wind, the wind shadowing all, shadowing all through the pines over there, the tall pines standing right there).

But what now are those gray shadows that I so clearly see over there, so silently standing there beneath the pines, all of them leaning forward, so intently watching me here?

(those are only monuments by men to these other men, to men long dead and gone and long since buried, still sleeping in the earth here, all about here).

As I slowly walk back to the parking lot just down the hill from The Crater, with my maps and clipboard under my arm, I see two cars pull in and park. One is a white family from Alabama and the other a black family with Massachusetts plates on the car.

They all get out, nod politely to one another, and then stand for a moment indecisively together. They are middle-age or so and there are children with both families.

It is the black man's face that catches my attention, for it is radiant. He comes straight toward me, smiling even as he looks around.

"Excuse me, sir. My name is Callahan – Bob Callahan. My great-grandfather was at The Crater - 43rd United States Colored Infantry - July 30, 1864 - I tell you, Man, I've dreamed of coming here since my Granny told me the story. It's around here some-where, I know, we saw the sign".

Then he looks at me, seeing me as it were for the first time.

"What was yours?", he hesitantly asks.

"56th North Carolina Infantry, Ransom's Brigade".

He looks at me for a long moment.

"Then you're on the right of The Crater".

"No," I softly say, "We're on the left".

He starts to say something then, but doesn't, only looks out over the tall pines, the flowing grass, the bright sunlight everywhere. Then, after a long pause, he whispers, "It was hard. You can still feel it, can't you"?

"Yes, but we came back, didn't we? And we're here now, aren't we"?

He still says nothing and so we just stand there together in silence, the late afternoon sun all around us now. And then he qui-etly says, "And it's still America, isn't it"? I look to the distant hori-zon and simply reply, "Yes, it's still America".

There is no sound and the sun is blinding.

"I know where it is. Come and I'll show you".

He glances back at his family. They are having a good time throwing a catch ball with the family from Alabama.

"The kids will be fine for a few minutes", I say. "It's right up there".

He holds out his hand and we shake hands without a word spo-ken.

He begins to laugh and then starts to climb the hill in great, reaching strides.

"No", I smile, "Let's go together".

Acknowledgments

The author is particularly grateful to Mrs. Patty Wheeler whose suggestions and editing were most helpful. Deep appreciation goes as well to Mrs. Jenny Owen and Delos and Karen Monteith, who were always encouraging and who believed.

All of the major events and most of the characters in *Across the Dark River* are historical.

Many primary and secondary sources are consulted over a quarter of a century. Regimental histories on both sides were reviewed. Most helpful of all was the regimental history in Walter Clark's *Histories of the Several Regiments and Battalions of North Carolina* (5 volumes) (Goldsboro, NC: Nash, 1901). This source has an original collection of photographs taken in 1862 which provided an accurate physical description of many of the characters. James C. Elliott's *The Southern Soldier Boy* (Raleigh: Edwards and Broughton, 1907) gave a good enlisted man's view of the regiment's operations. Clifford Dowdey's *Experiment in Rebellion* gives an excellent war-time portrait of Richmond. E. B. Long's *The Civil War: Day by Day* was helpful in keeping track of the war in other theaters. And, of course, *The Official Records of the Union and Confederate Armies* was always invaluable in giving both sides of the same conflict. The Wright/Patterson/McDougald Letters are all to be found in the University of North Carolina Library in Chapel Hill. The Time/Life Series on the Civil War has invaluable maps for locating the regiment's exact location at the Battle of the Crater, Five Forks, and Saylor's Creek. Among the State's press, *The Fayetteville Observer* was especially helpful since one of it's columnists from 1862 to 1863, "Long Shanks," was, in reality, the regimental adjutant!